HOT SEAT

A YEAR INSIDE COLLEGE FOOTBALL'S PRESSURE COOKER

JAY PATERNO

Hot Seat
Jay Paterno

This is a work of fiction. Names, characters, schools, places and events are used fictitiously.

Published by Blue Line 409 LLC

ISBN: 9798644060863

Printed in the United States of America

For Brooklyn's own "Gold Dust Twins" Joe and George Paterno my father and my uncle. They played and coached this game for over 90 years from Brooklyn Prep to Brown University to Penn State, Michigan State and The United States Merchant Marine Academy—They taught me to love and respect this game....For all the people who coached me....For all who played football with me....For all the men I coached and coached with....For all who coached against us or played against us and the great competition...

And for the memories that linger every time I pass a field....

TABLE OF CONTENTS

INTRODUCTION

What you are about to read is an unflinching behind the scenes look at what it is like behind the curtain of college football. While this book is a work of fiction set in the modern era of big-time college football, many of the stories in this book are based on true stories. Many of them were personally witnessed on the recruiting trail, in meeting rooms, on practice fields and in some of the great cathedrals of college football. For over 20 years I was a college football coach and lived some of the same pressures, the same conflicts that you will read in this story.

The decision to base this story at Ohio State was grounded in nothing other than the familiarity I had with the program and the state after seventeen years recruiting in the Buckeye state. The names of other schools were chosen at random. Let me repeat that they were chosen at random so that no one gets upset with a story they may not like being linked to their school.

The idea of using actual school names was made simply because it reads better and helps the college football fan read along without having to understand where fictional schools play and what conferences they are in.

"All-Access" shows may show some of the things that go on, but they do not take you into coaches' meeting rooms when a star player is accused of a sexual assault. They do not show you the dilemma a coach faces when a big-time recruit comes looking for an under the table payoff. It is all here; concussions, gambling, agents, arrests, race and the sex, power and big money. There is also triumph and setback. You'll find that and more in this book from a man who has walked this road.

While social media seems to be giving fans greater access than they've ever had there's a lot more behind the protective wall that coaches and administrations have built up. They've used social media as a diversion to distract the prying eyes of a media that covers the sport with less resources and less critically than ever before.

So as we set out on this journey you'll find right after the prologue a depth chart and list of the coaching staff just like you would get from a media guide or game day program. It will help you get excited for the season that's been written here.

Like the football year, the book is divided into three separate parts. The first begins in January, carrying you to the start of spring practice. The second part covers spring practice, summer workouts and preseason camp, while the third covers the season. In this era there is no offseason. Drama-filled days of potential conflict lurk even when the season seems far away.

Hope you enjoy this in-depth look, this telling of college football's story as never before.

PROLOGUE

Standing in my exposed brick-walled den on a bitterly cold winter day, I am warmed by a crackling fire and smooth sips of Knob Creek Bourbon. Through window panes frosted at the white wood-trimmed edges, outside I see snow softly falling. It settles atop the several inches already accumulated on the elevated plot of ground that in the warmer months serves as a vibrant vegetable garden for Candace, my wife of twelve years. She is gone visiting her ill mother in Arizona leaving me alone in our house.

This is a rare moment of solitude, a chance to reflect. Only now do I have all the pieces in place to begin to tell this story.

I've learned all the facts, everything that happened over the past fifteen months. With the story completed by the school's investigation, now I fully understand what it was we went through. In a few weeks I will know the NCAA's verdict on that investigation. They could accept the conclusions and move along, or they could conduct their own probe. We could hang in limbo for another year or two before we know what happens to all of us.

The past year on one of the hottest seats in college football left me bruised mentally; constantly weighing my integrity versus results in a world where "What have you done for me lately?" is measured in weeks not years. It is a high-profile, high-pressure, high-wire balancing act played out day after day and week after week.

Physically I added gray hairs, creases on my forehead and dropped twenty pounds because of erratic and sometimes non-existent eating patterns. Almost every day of the past year sleep escaped me for hours at a time, often all night. Even after big wins, I found no rest at night anticipating what could go wrong the next week. Every night my darkest demons emerged to pull at the threads of my sanity.

As the Head Coach at The Ohio State University I'm expected to pursue and attain the loftiest goals *every year*. There hasn't been a coach in the modern era at this great school that ever walked away from this job unscathed. Columbus, Ohio and the entire state is tough on their Buckeye coaches.

This is a major city, but one devoid of pro sports in the NFL, NBA or MLB. Columbus does have an NHL team. But The Ohio State University is the flagship college football program playing in the state capital of a football-mad state. There are actually 5 NFL teams in markets smaller than Columbus, and the Ohio-based NFL teams in Cincinnati and Cleveland have had little success.

A big-city media mentality, here in Columbus as well as Cincinnati and Cleveland, competes to cover every move of this team. No other team commands the same interest from the sports-media consuming public in Ohio like Ohio State Football.

On sports talk radio and on internet blogs Ohio State Football is always in season. At any moment of any day I could get blindsided by a comment, or a tweet by a player, or a media member or a misstep by a student-athlete with the law. It never ends, I am always on the clock and the pressure is always cranked up.

But this past year was the toughest of all. If tough times teach us the greatest lessons then I've had the best teaching moments in all of college football. The decisions I faced were so much bigger than a game, they challenged the bearings on my moral compass almost daily.

I know this; I have learned. I failed to trust some people I should have trusted, trusted others I shouldn't have. But I now know who is on my side and who never really was. Under that type of pressure you must rapidly and constantly evaluate and re-evaluate the loyalty of everyone around you; *even family members.*

Last month I walked out of my inquisition during the investigation, the last person questioned by the committee. I could finally put the whole year together in my mind, seeing that while I've survived as a man, it did not come without cost.

Even after a quarter century coaching college football, this past year challenged me in ways I'd never been tested. I gained perspective and I was forged in ways only the highest pressures can provide. But big time college football did exact Shylock's pound of flesh from me. The last year left me a changed man; better in some respects but also certainly worse in others.

It all started thirteen months ago right after that bowl loss to Tennessee.....

OHIO STATE COACHING STAFF

Head Coach: Ed Hart 8th season at Ohio State (79-27) Overall (136-59) (57-32 in 7 Seasons at Kansas)

Ohio State Seasons: **Big Ten Champions

10-3	Won Peach Bowl over Georgia 24-13	Final Ranking #9
7-6	Lost Insight.com Bowl to Baylor 14-38	
9-4	Won Outback Bowl over South Carolina 17-12	Final Ranking #18
10-3	Lost Gator Bowl to Ole Miss 14-20	Final Ranking #15
13-1**	Won Orange Bowl over Clemson 23-21	Final Ranking #3
11-3**	Lost Rose Bowl to Oregon 20-45	Final Ranking #10
10-3	Won Outback Bowl over Auburn 28-6	Final Ranking #12
9-4	Lost Citrus Bowl to Tennessee 41-52	Final Ranking #23

Coaching Staff (Seasons at Ohio State)

Position / Name	Seasons	School	Age
Offensive Coordinator/ Quarterbacks:			
Quinn Banks	2 seasons	Houston '07	Age: 35
O-Line Coach			
Otis Lewis	8 seasons	S Carolina '90	Age: 52
Running Backs Coach			
Roger Barstow	5 seasons	Ohio State '98	Age: 43
Tight Ends Coach			
Terry Ellis	6 seasons	UCLA '95	Age: 47
WR Coach/ Recruiting Coordinator			
Wayne Robinson	8 seasons	Kent State '07	Age: 35
Defensive Coordinator/Linebackers			
Dave Cafiero	8 seasons	YSU '83	Age: 58
Defensive Line Coach			
Doug Leonard	4 seasons	Texas '80	Age: 61
Defensive Backs Coach			
Dwayne Baxter	6 seasons	FSU '05	Age: 36
Safeties Coach			
Freddie Smith	3 seasons	LSU '14	Age: 27
Special Teams Coach			
Saul Tessio	3 seasons	Montana '10	Age: 31
Offensive Graduate Assistant			
Greg Owens		OSU '18	Age: 24
Defensive Graduate Assistant			
George Denson		Michigan '18	Age: 24
Strength Coach			
Sal Cafiero	8 seasons	Kansas '98	Age: 44
Conditioning/Speed Coach			
Chris Sanders	8 seasons	Kansas '98	Age: 44
Recruiting Coordinator			
Rick Carter	5 seasons	Princeton '13	Age: 29
Special Assistant to the Head Coach			
Sally Anderson	8 seasons	Kansas '02	Age: 40

Administration	President: Gerry Gorton	6th year
	Athletic Director: Art Simpson	4th year
	Sports Information: Sid Inge	8th year

DEPTH CHART—OFFENSE

Pos.	Player	Class	Ht/Wt	High School
QB	#12 Marshall Remington	JR	6-2 210	Mater Dei HS Santa Ana, CA
	#17 *Carter Jones*	*FR*	*6-3 215*	*W.G Harding HS*--Warren, OH
FB	#33 Alex Daniels	SR	6-0 242	Benedictine HS--Cleveland, OH
TB	#20 Pokey Wallace	SR	6-1 230	Brookhaven HS-Columbus, OH
	#3 Roger Carson	JR	5-10 190	Saginaw HS --Saginaw, MI
	#22 Malcom Jackson	*FR*	*6-3 225*	*Palm Bay HS--Melbourne, FL*
WR	#1 Anthony Daniels	JR	6-2 205	Mt Carmel HS--Chicago, IL
	#88 Martin Wallace	SR	5-11 185	St Xavier HS--Cincinnati, OH
WR	#2 Malcolm Jennings	SOPH	5-11 190	Glenville HS---Cleveland, OH
	#13 Ted Stanton	SR	6-0 175	Dr Phillips HS--Orlando, FL
TE	#81 Parker Watson	SR	6-4 260	St Thomas Aquinas HS- Ft Lauderdale, FL
	#89 Manny Rodriguez	FR	6-4 250	Mooney HS—Youngstown, OH
OT	#68 Mark O'Reilly	SR	6-5 308	Chaminade-Julienne HS Dayton, OH
OG	#64 Dan Hanson	JR	6-4 302	Piqua HS--Piqua, OH
C	#70 Andy Dawson	SR	6-5 320	Steubenville HS Steubenville, OH
OG	#62 Bobby Thompson	SOPH	6-5 317	Jesuit HS-Dallas, TX
OT	#61 Gene Banks	JR	6-6 312	Parkland HS Winston-Salem, NC

DEPTH CHART–DEFENSE

DE	#99 Floyd Simmons	JR	6-5 260	Gateway HS Monroeville, PA
DT	#5 Marcus Dawson	SOPH	6-5 300	Male HS Louisville, KY
DT	#90 Antonio Patterson	SR	6-5 320	Chadsey HS Detroit, MI
DE	#7 Pierre Carter	JR	6-5 245	West Jefferson HS Harvey, LA
$	#35 Alvin Wallace	SR	6-3 227	Buchtel HS Akron, OH
	#31 Carson Grady	*FR*	*6-3 217*	*Central Catholic HS* *Allentown, PA*
B	#45 Karl Metzger	SR	6-3 245	St Ignatius HS Cleveland, OH
W	#9 Darryl Shabazz	SOPH	6-1 217	Wayne HS Huber Heights, OH
LCB	#4 Ronnie Liggins	SR	5-11 180	Washington HS Massillon, OH
SS	#25 Lance Baxter	SOPH	6-3 210	The University School Memphis, TN
	#27 D'Antonio Wilson	*FR*	*6-2 205*	*Chaminade-Julienne HS* *Dayton, OH*
FS	#18 Carson Miller	JR	6-2 205	Holy Spirit HS Absecon, NJ
RCB	#6 Donte Carter	JR	6-0 190	McKinley HS Canton, OH
	#5 Roger Hill	*FR*	*6-1 195*	*Hoboken HS* *Hoboken, NJ*

Specialists

P	#10 Rick Miller	SOPH	6-0 180	Cathedral Prep Erie, PA
PK	#44 David Lance	JR	6-3 208	St Francis DeSales HS Columbus, OH

SCHEDULES AND RESULTS

The Season Ahead

YOUNGSTOWN STATE
TOLEDO
TEXAS
At Purdue
At Rutgers
at Maryland
IOWA
MICHIGAN STATE
at Wisconsin
INDIANA
at Penn State
MICHIGAN

Last Year's Results (9-4/ 3rd in Big Ten East)

OSU RANK			
12	@LSU (6) (in Houston)	L	31-35
15	AKRON	W	63-0
15	SAN DIEGO STATE	W	49-6
14	RUTGERS	W	52-10
14	at Northwestern	W	44-21
15	at Michigan State (17)	L	34-38
21	NEBRASKA	W	35-27
20	at Indiana	W	63-20
18	PENN STATE (21)	W	42-24
14	ILLINOIS	W	56-17
13	MARYLAND	W	48-14
10	at Michigan (12)	L	39-49
CITRUS BOWL			
15	Tennessee (16)	L	41-52

Final Ranking #23 (1-4 against Ranked Teams)

1. AFTERMATH OF A BOWL LOSS

Waking before dawn, a restless night of fitful sleep hadn't made the pit in my stomach go away. When the last seconds of yesterday's bowl game ticked off the clock we finished with a second-straight lackluster loss. As the Head Coach at Ohio State I knew season-ending collapses to Michigan and to Tennessee in the Citrus bowl would haunt me all offseason.

At 10:00 a.m. I was hustling to pack up the last of my stuff. Everyone else traveling home with us from the bowl was on the busses idling outside over twenty floors below; all waiting for me. I was running late because I'd battled through an 8 a.m. season-ending press conference filled with repetitive questions about the direction of the program.

The questions were tough, but I understand why they asked them. Our win totals the last four seasons were 13, 11, 10 and now 9 games. It certainly fits the pattern of a downward trend. The most offensive question came right away.

"Coach did the Ed Hart era at Ohio State peak four years ago?" It was asked by a young college newspaper reporter who probably spent all night thinking up his "gotcha" question.

Did he really refer to me like we were talking about someone else? I'm Ed Hart and I was sitting right there. Both the question and the young punk questioner pissed me off.

I was seated in front of them for an hour in the generic hotel conference room spewing answers that were as evasive as I could make them. Even when asked if I would fire my defensive staff because we'd given up so many points the past few games, I kept my temper in check.

I characterize losses two ways. There are games where we did all we could and the other team simply had a better day. I can sleep after those games. Then, and this included the previous day's game, there are ones where I know it got away. A decision here or there will haunt me. All night I toss and turn. When I do fall asleep I dream about key game moments and am jolted awake.

In the regular season I jump back into my routine refueling with the hope of the next week's game. Not so after a bowl game, I woke this morning in a posh but strange hotel suite atop the luxurious Hyatt Regency Hotel in Orlando. As morning sun came through the curtains it dawned on a day when the potential redemption of the next game was still nine months away.

After yesterday's loss I wasn't even 100% certain that I had a future at Ohio State.

As I hustled into the bathroom to get my toothbrush and razor to pack I caught a quick glimpse of myself in the mirror. The reflection of a man, seemingly many years older than I was even a month ago scared me. Under my eyes were the dark bags, the Scarlet Letter of the sleep deprived. The Ohio State stress looked like it aged me twenty years.

I am just over fifty years old which is suddenly old in this profession. Younger coaches seemed to be lapping me, living a 24/7 Red Bull-fueled lifestyle of recruiting and self-promotion on social media and mainstream media. When do these fucking guys ever sleep?

After my self-pity I put the last of my toiletries in the suitcase and a folder in a briefcase. As I zipped up the briefcase I heard a knock at the door. My wife, no doubt, had sent someone up to get me. She was impatient at times, and this morning I certainly deserved it.

"I'm coming, I'm coming" I uttered as I walked, bags in hand, quickly across the white and gray marble floor.

Opening the door without looking, I was startled to see University President Gerry Gorton standing in the doorway. A chill ran up my spine. This was an unplanned visit, and every coach knows that Presidents don't just "drop in" the morning after a season-ending loss to say hello.

"Coach, may I come in?" Gerry asked.

Normally he called me Ed, so his formal use of "Coach" made me a little uneasy.

"Sure, sure come on in."

I put down my bags and gestured for Gerry to walk ahead of me to the living room area of the suite. He strode deliberately towards one couch while I followed. The spontaneous nature of this meeting weighed on me. Historically, he always followed a formal protocol of meetings scheduled well in advance with written agendas. This was different and not in a good way.

"What's on your mind Gerry?" I asked.

"Ed I will get straight to the point."

I'd been in football long enough to know he wasn't here to congratulate me on a job well done. Gerry stared directly at me and spoke.

"I had a number of the school's trustees and major donors at my suite after the game. They wanted to discuss the football program's direction. Before I go any further let me get this on the table, I am not here to replace you. I don't want to, but I was in the minority opinion last night."

I felt the relief of a man avoiding a death sentence, but still knew there was to be some sort of sanction, *something* was coming. Would I have to fire some of the assistant coaches? In a pre-emptive strike I decided to defend our performance.

"Gerry, we'll finish in the top twenty. What is wrong with the direction of this program?"

"Three years ago you had thirteen wins, followed by eleven wins, ten wins and now nine wins. They see a trend. You were supposed to be a top 5 team this year."

"You know we had some tough losses on the road."

Gerry sighed and leaned closer across the glass coffee table that separated us.

"You know we aren't paying you $6.5 million a year to get close losses on the road. Your staff is well paid, the highest paid in Ohio State history. The last two games you couldn't stop two teams that you should've beaten by two touchdowns. To the Trustees and to me it looks like you lost this team."

Like a kid in the chair across from the principal's desk, I shifted my weight and squirmed at the reference to my salary being thrown back in my face. The next words I spoke were more carefully considered.

"Before we react we need to sit down and get a handle on what happened. On top of all that we have to be on the road recruiting in two days. Did Art talk to you about this?"

Art Simpson, the school's Athletic Director, and I shared a mild mutual disdain for each other. He'd been a star quarterback at Ohio State and had been an NFL General Manager. Because I'd been hired at Ohio State four years before Art, I wasn't his guy. He made no secret that he wanted to hire his own guy, a coach with NFL experience to coach this team.

Perhaps Gerry sensed my unease and wanted to at least settle things down, if only temporarily. He raised a hand, his palm facing me to signal for me to stay calm.

"Just sit tight," Gerry said. "I know we're late for the bus, but the busses will wait for us. I only need another minute or two."

"Okay."

"The school has committed big money to this program. In addition to your coaching salaries, we budgeted $52 million to upgrade facilities that were already the best in the conference. You hired a chef from New York City to run the training table meals for the team. You have more than everything you need to be a National Championship contender."

Gerry paused looking directly into my eyes to let the big fiscal commitment to our success settle in. It settled in all right. He'd nearly even convinced me that I'd underachieved. He wanted a response from me.

"We're close. I mean that. We just need to round out this recruiting class the right way."

"I will be watching carefully what happens in recruiting and next fall. Three years ago you recruited a top 5 class nationally. The last two have barely cracked the top twenty. We both know recruiting is the lifeblood of any program. You can help yourself with these boosters by signing a Top 5 class. From what I've read you have a chance, but you've got to finish. I'd like a written report every couple of days on how it is going. Okay?"

I was about to ask the President if he was kidding but I could tell from the tone of the request that he was dead serious.

"Okay." Resigned to my fate, it was all I could feebly muster in response.

"I also want a written weekly update on the team's progress so I have a record of what you're doing to file in my office."

My stomach turned, this was beyond insulting. I'd been a head coach for eight years here and seven seasons before that at Kansas. At Ohio State we'd won roughly 75% of our games. But the sore subject was we had just two Big Ten titles. This program expected nearly annual conference championships.

Like it or not, I had no choice but to report to Gerry. Having lost the last two games, I didn't have public sentiment to stand on and play this dispute out in the media.

It seemed I was cornered, but I would talk to my agent to see if we could use any of the other high profile coaching vacancies as leverage. It looked like UCLA was going to come open, while Georgia, LSU and Florida were already open. Getting my name in play through the media could create pressure on Gerry to back off or even extend my contract. That was something to consider when we landed back in Columbus.

Gerry stood up and extended his hand to me so I shook hands while forcing a smile.

"Ed, let's get down to the busses. They're probably waiting for us."

As we left the room and took the elevators down, neither of us said much. Walking across the lobby we were spotted almost instantly by Matty Buck the writer for the website Go-OState.com. Matty walked directly to us. As we kept our pace he backpedaled in front of us and began asking questions.

"Why are you guys late for the busses?" Matty asked.

"No reason." I said.

Matty persisted as he skillfully walked backwards across the lobby "Were you meeting? Were you discussing Ed's future?"

Neither of us answered the question.

"Come on Gerry, you can answer me." Matty insisted.

Gerry looked straight ahead and didn't say a word.

"Are you sure you don't want to tell me anything?" Matty asked again. "Would I be wrong if I said you met to discuss Ed's future? Will Ed Hart be the head coach here next year?"

I glared at Matty before holding my composure and walking silently with Gerry out the front door and to the busses. Matty was a veteran. He knew that a no-answer spoke volumes. He'd videoed the entire exchange so he had that to post on his web site. Unfortunately my last glare would make a great video image to post with his story.

As I got on the bus and sat down next to my wife Candace, she whispered in my ear.

"What was that all about?"

"Nothing." I said.

She knew I was lying, and I would talk to her about it when we got home. As the busses started to pull away, she took my right hand in hers on her lap. Framed by her long brown hair and light eyes her soft smile warmed my heart. Although I was ten years older, she had the wisdom and patience of a woman many years older. She put up with the long hours, the time away from home and mood swings based on game results. My first wife made it through two football seasons before she walked away and into rehab for alcohol and prescription drugs.

Two seats behind me, Offensive Coordinator Quinn Banks saw Gerry and I walking out together. He'd been through this before at Texas; he knew the deal. In his mind I was either getting axed or was on a very short leash. With a reputation as an offensive genius and a million-dollar smile, Quinn was on the fast track to a Head Coaching job. If I got fired, that threatened his rapid rise up the ranks, not to mention his $1.4 million annual salary.

Quinn pulled out his phone and texted his agent. "Something is going on here. Test the waters for me for Head Coach/or Coordinator positions"

His agent Warren Thompson got the text and replied "Will Do".

If I'd known at the time what he was up to behind my back, I would've wanted to demote him on the spot. Truth was the outstanding performance of the offense would've made that move impossible. But the string of a juicy coaching rumor had begun with a single text.

Warren Thompson knew his first call had to be to Jason Harvey from the search firm Korn Ferry. They had a large sports practice overseeing the hiring of big-time coaches and athletic directors. Jason would know what jobs were open and who would be looking.

Jason was already conducting searches for coaching vacancies at Florida, LSU and was put on retainer by UCLA in case they did fire their Head Coach. Jason told Warren that those jobs would probably be long shots for Quinn but the Syracuse job had been open for two weeks. They were having a hard time with the top names on their list.

Jason asked Warren if he should put in a call to Art Simpson to get Ohio State's job search business if they were firing me. Warren guessed that I was either getting fired, or was going to shake up the defensive staff. Just one phone call can quickly crank up the coaching rumor mill. It was true with me as it is with every coach, if you are the subject of a coaching rumor you are most often the last to hear about it.

Jason and Warren decided to look around and see what they could do for Quinn.

Warren Thompson hung up the phone with Jason Harvey and sent a text back to Quinn telling him that he was working a few angles. He would call Florida State, Oregon, Stanford and Auburn as they were looking for new Offensive Coordinators. I know all this now because, while Quinn may be a smart football coach, he didn't realize using his Ohio State cell phone gave me access to his records.

Now that Jason Harvey knew something was going on he immediately called my agent Nathan Weinrich in Cleveland.

"Nathan? Jason Harvey calling. How you doing?"

"I'm doing great. What you got going on?" Nathan asked.

"We got a couple of searches going."

"Yeah I know. You got almost all the big ones that are open now. Your Syracuse search moving along at all? Word on the street is that it is dragging."

"Yeah, a little bit. But there's a new name we're putting on that list that could get some people talking."

"Oh yeah? Who is that?" Nathan asked.

"He's one of your clients......Ed Hart."

"Ed Hart?" Nathan asked revealing surprise in his voice. "Ed Hart wouldn't leave Ohio State for Syracuse. That wouldn't be a good move for him."

"Of course not, but I'm hearing things."

"What are you hearing?"

"Have you talked to Ed today?"

"No."

"Word is he had a meeting with Gerry Gorton. I'm hearing that he may get axed or be asked to do a major staff shake-up. If your guy wants to beat it out of town one step ahead of the posse, I could make the Syracuse thing happen very quickly."

"He's on a plane now so there's not a whole lot I can do just yet. When he lands I will talk with him."

"You ought to get in the loop." Jason delivered the sentence in a tone that was half-playful and half-chastisement. "Don't discount what I am saying about Syracuse. They'd give him a six-year deal. How many years does he have on his contract at Ohio State? Two or three?"

"Two."

"That means after next season if they want to dump him, it costs them virtually nothing. I'm talking six years. He wins here they'll give him an extension."

"Look it's a bit premature to be talking about this."

"Okay, but talk to Ed and don't be a stranger."

Two hours later our plane was taxiing on the tarmac at Port Columbus Airport. As I turned on my phone I saw a text from Nathan Weinrich asking me about a "reported" meeting with Gerry Gorton. How had he heard?

Sports Information Director Sid Inge powered his cell phone back on. The day after a bowl game is usually a slow day, but he saw that he had twenty text messages and eleven voicemails. Before the plane even came to a stop on the tarmac, he listened to the first voicemail, one from Roger Santos from the Columbus Dispatch.

"Sid this is Roger. When you get this can you call me back? We're seeing reports that Ed met with the President this morning followed by reports from internet sites covering Syracuse that he is talking to them about their head coaching vacancy. Get back to me as soon as you can."

The next four messages were all the same from writers who covered the team and even one from Kirk Herbstreit at ESPN. The text messages were the same thing from other media members. Sid Inge did a quick check of Twitter and there were a lot of mentions of a Go-OState.com article and an article from the Syracuse newspaper's site.

As we got off the plane, Sid hustled up to grab me before I got on the bus. We had a twenty minute ride back to campus and Sid figured he'd better talk to me before someone else did.

"Ed..." Sid said.

I turned around and saw Sid.

"What's up Sid?"

Sid looked around to see if anyone else was within earshot before he asked "Did you meet with the President this morning?"

"Yeah I did. That asshole Matty Buck probably wrote something about it. He saw Gerry and I walking out of the hotel together."

"He posted a story all right. Read this." Sid said as he handed me his iPhone.

Sources Say Gorton and Hart Met To Discuss The Future of OSU Football

Multiple sources confirmed a meeting this morning between University President Gerry Gorton and Head Football Coach Ed Hart before heading home a day after a lackluster Citrus Bowl loss. Sources tell Go-OState.com that University Trustees are concerned with the continuing downward trend in the direction and results of the football program.

Despite dramatic investments in higher coaching salaries and facility upgrades the team's win totals have dropped every year for the past four seasons. It remains to be seen whether Ed Hart will remain as the head coach, and if he does whether or not he will be forced to make changes on his coaching staff.

When approached this morning, neither man would confirm or deny whether a meeting took place, nor would they comment on what may have been discussed if such a meeting did take place.

Go-OState.com will stay on top of this story as it develops. There is more on this story on the members' exclusive section of our website.

As I read each word my blood heated ever closer to the boiling point. How I hated that asshole. My first thought was his statement about "multiple sources". Who were they or did he just make that crap up to look connected?

"Is there anything I need to know or should be preparing for?" Sid asked.

"No. Why?" I snapped back at him causing Sid to flinch in surprise at my anger.

"It's being reported as something bigger than just a friendly chat."

"No it was mostly friendly but there's nothing to write about."

Sid hesitated. I'd never lied to him, in fact Sid had been and remains a confidant in many matters. As he stood I realized there was more to discuss.

"What else you got?" I asked.

"There are reports out of Syracuse that you're considering their Head Coaching job."

It took a moment for that to sink in. I just stood there trying to imagine who or what might have triggered that rumor. An icy breeze blew across the tarmac reminding me that we weren't in Florida any more. Around us was the bustle of people deplaning to waiting busses and the airport workers scurrying to unload the bags onto a truck. In the distance a roar arose as a 757 jet revved up and began its sprint down the runway into takeoff.

"Where is that coming from? I've never even talked to anyone from there." I yelled so he could hear me over the jet's roar.

"Some sites that cover them are reporting that you're a candidate."

"That's news to me." I laughed.

"Maybe you should call Nathan Weinrich and have him try to squash this. It could seep into the news cycle and then you'll have to answer questions from recruits and their families."

I nodded and turned to get on the bus. This time of year was the worst; a daily parade of bullshit coaching rumors. Some guys in this profession spent half of their days on internet sites or calling coaching buddies to discuss every rumor. Most were completely false. Guys on our staff made up rumors about coaches on rival staffs getting fired so players we recruit would see them.

I'd have to get our social media interns on the message boards as well as the social media sites to start planting positive rumors and stories about the "productive" meeting this morning and how we even discussed a contract extension.

I knew one thing; we needed to spin our own internet rumors or risk getting burned by someone else's.

When I got on the bus I told staff Assistant Sally Anderson to tell the coaches and staff that we needed to meet for an hour or two when they got back. It gave them time to get home, get changed and back to the office. The coaches would be on the road recruiting tomorrow so I wanted to be sure they were all on the same page before they left.

The busses pulled out and headed towards campus. One season was now in the books and the year's second season, recruiting, was about to heat up. This was the dirtiest part of the entire year. Here you had no friends.

Increasingly it seemed I was becoming a dead man walking. Friends would be in short supply no matter where I looked.

2. ON THE ROAD AGAIN

Just two hours after returning from the bowl loss I assembled our coaches in the football staff meeting room. By hastily calling this meeting I'd fueled the paranoia common to all assistant coaches that they can and will be fired at any time. As a head coach, maintaining that leverage can be useful.

"Yesterday's game was simply unacceptable. We're a better team than Tennessee, and dammit we're better than Michigan too. We're either underperforming or getting outcoached. Either way it falls on us, the people in this room and that includes me."

I hesitated to look around the room. This was a staff of very good coaches but something was missing. Maybe it was chemistry, maybe I hadn't provided enough leadership. Maybe some staff changes were needed.

I spoke again.

"We're all anxious to get out recruiting but first we must evaluate yesterday's game to make an honest assessment of our team and of ourselves. We can't simply resort to blaming the players. Remember what I've always told you about what you see on tape; you're either coaching it or you are allowing it to happen. Either way we got our asses kicked by an inferior team. It will be another offseason listening to SEC fans talk about how they dominate us. I'm tired of that shit. We should've beaten LSU this year and Tennessee yesterday. Any questions?"

Rick Carter, the obsessive recruiting coordinator waded in with both feet. He was a smart young guy, just seven years out of Princeton where he'd played football. The guys on the staff called him Biff behind his back because he looked like a typical East Coast Prep School Ivy League white boy.

"Ed, just so I can start planning, what do you want to do recruiting this week?"

I smiled sarcastically at Rick but kept my voice calm.

"Look Rick, don't worry about arrangements. Art Simpson has planes ready to go tomorrow. By 11 a.m. everyone should have reviewed the bowl video. Also by then I want written evaluations on the guys who are still on our recruiting board. We signed good players in December but there are really big fish still out there. We have six scholarships left but if we go over we can make some adjustments."

"We have written evaluations on them." Rick said.

"I know that. But those evaluations are only from one or two coaches. I want every coach to look at video of the last dozen or so guys we have out there. I want as many eyes on these prospects as possible. We *cannot* miss on any of these kids. We need six or seven or eight game-changers for this class. We need a top five recruiting class if we can get it done."

"Coach, evaluating the game and the recruits will take some time." Rick said.

"Then get everyone in here by 5:30 a.m. Put on extra coffee and I'll give you some cash to pick up donuts. Get it done. I don't want anyone in here tonight. Go home, unpack and put your kids to bed. The next four weeks are going to be tough enough so be at home tonight."

They all headed home. Ahead of them were several hectic weeks of travel, most days waking up in a new town, a new state and talking to another prospect.

On my way home I returned a call to my agent Nathan Weinrich.

"Nathan, it's Ed."

"Let me get right to the point Ed, did you have a meeting with Gerry Gorton without me?"

"Not intentionally; he dropped into my suite before we left. Now suddenly my name is on this Syracuse thing. It doesn't look good and it makes me look like I am trying to get out of here."

"We may have to talk about this Syracuse thing. We may need to respond in the media to make sure that everyone knows there is no truth to this."

"But does that make me look guilty by being defensive?"

"Maybe. If you let it go the perception may also set in among the fan base that you've talked to Syracuse and at Ohio State that would be considered an insult. In the Buckeye fans' minds you either retire, die or get fired from here or leave only for a good NFL job. That doesn't include the Browns by the way."

"I think we just let it go. Where do you think it started?"

"I got a call from the search firm in New York that is handling the hiring for Syracuse. They told me they heard from sources that you had a meeting with Gerry. They smelled smoke. They thought if you were in trouble that there might be an opening."

"When did he call?"

"This morning. You guys were just leaving Orlando."

"How would he have heard about the meeting so quickly?"

"I don't know. I thought maybe it was from media reports but the first story on Go-OState was after he called me. He had to have heard it from someone close to Gerry or someone close to our program."

"See what you can find out."

"Will do. If Syracuse calls what do you want me to do?"

"See what they want but keep me at arm's length. I need rock solid deniability on this one."

"You got it."

Nathan hung up and called Jason Harvey at Korn Ferry. He reiterated that if Jason were to call him in regards to the Syracuse situation that he would listen. He also pressed Jason to find out how he'd heard about my meeting with Gerry Gorton. He cited media sources so Nathan knew Jason was being less than honest. That pointed Nathan in the direction of either the University administration or someone on the team busses who must've put the story out there.

. . . .

The next morning the coaches looked at the video from the bowl game loss two days earlier. We hadn't been able to stop Tennessee. On the plus side the offense scored points despite starting almost every possession deep in their own territory. Our no-huddle high-scoring offense of Offensive Coordinator Quinn Banks had performed as advertised.

Our two kicking game "turnovers" swung the game to Tennessee. One fumbled kickoff return led to a Tennessee touchdown. The second wasn't a traditional turnover but a roughing the kicker penalty after a big defensive stop gave Tennessee the ball back and led to another touchdown.

Tennessee held the ball for thirty-eight of the game's sixty minutes. Tennessee's style of play led to long possessions that chewed up the clock while we played at a frenetic pace.

Defensive Coordinator Dave Cafiero had strong thoughts on our frenetic offensive pace that often gave his defense little time to recover between possessions. He and Quinn argued over and over again. Everyone on the staff felt that tension every time we lost a game.

After reviewing the bowl game, the staff evaluated the remaining players we were recruiting. I wanted them to be absolutely sure that the last six or eight players we signed were difference-makers. We signed very good players in December but I only saw some of them as guys who would play right away.

We needed a fast outside linebacker able to rush the passer on blitzes and able to make plays in the open field against all the spread offenses we played.

Before they looked at the video, Rick Carter handed out the recruiting sheet. On the sheet were several players we felt we could get. In Ohio we always feel we are in the driver's seat with the in-state prospects. But Michigan was always a threat.

Before they looked at the players Rick spoke to the group of coaches seated around the table.

Prospects List-----

	Needed	*Commits*	*To Go*
QBs	*0*	*0*	*(take 1 if possible)*
RBs	*2*	*1*	*1*
FBs	*1*	*1*	*0*
WRs	*2*	*1*	*1*
TEs	*1*	*1*	*0*
OTs	*2*	*1*	*1*
OGs/Cs	*1*	*1*	*0*
Offense	*10*	*7*	*3 (4 if we take a QB)*
DTs	*3*	*3*	*0*
DEs	*2*	*1*	*1*
ILBs	*1*	*1*	*0*
OLBs	*2*	*1*	*1*
CBs	*2*	*1*	*1*
SAFs	*2*	*2*	*0*
Defense	*12*	*9*	*3*
Totals	*22*	*16*	*6 (7 if we take a QB)*

Offers on the Board:---Offense

QB Carter Jones 6-3 215 4.4 Warren Harding HS—Warren, OH
Basketball & Track 10.3 100 M, #2 Athletic QB in the Country
Top 5 Schools--Ohio State, Texas, Alabama, Florida State, USC

RB Malcolm Jackson 6-2 225 4.3 Palm Bay HS—Melbourne, FL
All-State Basketball, Baseball & State 100M Champion 10.1 #3 Recruit in the Country
Top 5 Schools—Florida, Alabama, LSU, USC, Ohio State

RB Aaron Smith 6-2 210 4.5 Rogers HS—Toledo, OH
Big Rep—plays basketball and runs track 100M 10.35
Top Schools—Ohio State, Notre Dame, Penn State, Michigan, Michigan State

RB Carson Walker 5-11 185 4.4 Glenville HS—Cleveland, OH
Plays Basketball and Runs track 110 Hurdles 13.7
Top Schools—Ohio State, Michigan State, Tennessee, Illinois, Maryland

WR Boxer Davis 6-4 208 4.4 Mainland HS—Daytona Beach, FL
Basketball Top 100 prospect, Drafted 8th round outfielder in baseball
Top Schools—Florida, Florida State, Miami, Alabama, Ohio State

WR Lance Marshall 5-10 175 4.3 Pershing HS—Detroit, MI
100 M 10.1 state champ
Top Schools—Michigan, Michigan State, Colorado, Ohio State, Cal

TE Manny Rodriguez 6-5 240 4.5 Cardinal Mooney HS—Youngstown, OH
Basketball top 200 prospect, Baseball, #2 TE in the country
Top Schools—Ohio State, Kentucky, Oklahoma, Nebraska, Michigan

OT Jake O'Reilly 6-6 305 4.9 St Edward HS—Lakewood, OH
#4 OT in the country, plays basketball, throws shot 59+ feet
Top Schools—Stanford, Ohio State, Penn State, Michigan, Notre Dame

OT Brad Jones 6-7 340 5.1 Bishop McDevitt HS—Harrisburg, PA
#3 OT on the country
Top Schools—Ohio State, Penn State, Notre Dame, Maryland, Tennessee

Defensive Prospects

DE Jamar Tucker 6-5 240 4.4 Benedictine HS—Cleveland, OH
#3 DE in the country, Basketball All-State, Track 4x100 State Finals shotput
Top Schools—Ohio State, Texas, Alabama, UCLA, Michigan

DE Alphonso Simmons 6-4 238 4.5 St. Xavier HS—Cincinnati, OH
#2 DE in the country, Basketball top 150 prospect
Top Schools—Notre Dame, Florida, UNC, Ohio State, Nebraska

DE Darwin Tucker 6-6 228 4.6 St Vincent-St Mary HS—Akron, OH
Basketball All-State
Top Schools—Michigan State, Ohio State, West Virginia, Pittsburgh, Georgia Tech

OLB Carson Grady 6-3 215 4.4 Central Catholic HS—Allentown, PA
#2 OLB in the country, state champion wrestler, baseball and track
Top Schools—Penn State, Notre Dame, Boston College, Ohio State, Stanford

OLB Danny Morris 6-2 220 4.6 Piqua HS—Piqua, OH
Top OLB in Ohio, wrestler and track
Top Schools—Michigan State, Ohio State, Michigan, Notre Dame

OLB William Wilkins 6-3 225 4.6 Wayne HS—Huber Heights, OH
Plays basketball and baseball
Top Schools—Kentucky, Florida, Ohio State, Oklahoma, Texas A&M

OLB Derrick Nelson 6-3 230 4.4 DeLaSalle HS—Concord, CA
#1 OLB in the Country, basketball, track 4X100, 100 M 10.2
Top Schools—USC, UCLA, Oregon, Michigan, Ohio State

CB Roger Hill 6-1 185 4.3 Hoboken HS—Hoboken, NJ
#3 CB in the country, track 10.2 100 M, All-NY Metro in Basketball Top 100 US
Top Schools--UNC, Ohio State, Georgia Tech, Michigan, Rutgers

CB Artie Manson 5-11 175 4.3 DeMatha HS—Hyattsville, MD
#15 CB in the country, basketball
Top Schools—Maryland, Virginia, Virginia Tech, Ohio State, Penn State

CB Darryl White 6-0 185 4.5 McKinley HS—Canton, OH
#1 CB in Ohio, Basketball and Track 10.4 100 M
Top Schools—Ohio State, Nebraska, Michigan State, Michigan, Penn State

"Look Guys," Rick started "there are a lot of big names on this list. We have six scholarships to give, maybe an extra two or three if we get that lucky. We have to focus on our glaring needs. Offensively we are good. If we can get a quarterback, that would be great. In fact all of us know that we are close to getting Carter Jones. He can be the future of this program. As for running backs there are two on the board, two great ones. Malcolm Jackson is the best one I've seen in a couple of years. How are we doing with him Dwayne?"

Dwayne Baxter, the defensive backs coach, was the coach recruiting Malcolm. Dwayne played at Robert E Lee High School in Jacksonville before playing at Florida State. At 36 he was in the same peak physical shape as the day he finished playing for the New York Jets six years earlier. His Florida roots gave him a chance with Malcolm and with the wide receiver from Daytona Beach Boxer Davis. Dwayne had also mastered the art of bullshit.

"Rick I think we have a great chance. Turns out his mother may be moving to Cleveland to be closer to Malcolm's grandmother who's lived up here all her life. But Gramma's having health problems so Malcolm's Mom wants to be nearer to her. She is looking for a job up here if anyone has any leads."

"D-Bax are you suggesting we arrange a job for her?" Quinn asked sarcastically.

D-Bax was Dwayne's nickname earned when he played defensive back.

"Yeah is that what you're asking?" Offensive line coach Otis Lewis chimed in. "Maybe that's how it works for the Seminoles but there are NCAA rules we actually follow up here."

Otis was always good for a laugh. He'd been with me for all five of our seasons at Kansas. Otis had played at South Carolina, finishing up in 1989. At fifty-two he was the third oldest of the assistant coaches, and one of the three coaches who'd been here for all eight seasons at Ohio State. Otis had a perpetually sunny personality often referring to himself in the third person as "this juicy brother".

Strength Coach Sal Cafiero, the brother of defensive Coordinator Dave Cafiero, Conditioning and Speed Coach Chris Sanders and Special Assistant to the Head Coach Sally Anderson were the support staff that had been here all eight years.

Otis wasn't done with Dwayne. "You know this juicy brother would be happy to help. Great running backs make our line look good running over or around unblocked defenders. Great receivers also help us avoid sacks, so how are we doing with Boxer Davis?"

"We're in good shape." Dwayne said "It'll come down to us and Alabama. His home situation is messed up and he has no real ties to Florida. He'll go wherever he thinks he can play the soonest."

"He thinks he can play right away at Alabama?" Rick asked.

"They all think they can play right away." Defensive line coach Doug Leonard said in a thick Texas twang.

At age sixty-one, Doug was the staff's elder statesman. He'd played at Texas in the late-seventies and had coached at ten schools in every major conference; Texas, Stanford, LSU, Virginia, North Carolina, Wisconsin and now Ohio State. He was a true Southerner, sprinkling his speech with colorful expressions.

They reviewed the film on the two running back prospects. They really liked Aaron Smith from Toledo and we were in first place with him. The school that worried them the most was Michigan. Toledo is actually closer to Michigan than to Ohio State and over the years the Wolverines had stolen a lot of good players from Northern Ohio.

"Does anyone else have any Running Backs we should be offering or chasing?" Rick Carter asked. "We need a big-time back and there is no guarantee that we get either one. Doug how about the kid from the private school in Dallas we talked about earlier this year? He's getting a lot of attention and supposedly he has Oregon in there now. Is he still out there?"

Doug laughed a little before he spoke.

"Rick," Doug said "you've got to stop reading all that recruiting hype on the internet. I've seen that over-rated boy play in person last spring and on tape this past fall. That boy must have naked pictures of whoever does those recruiting rankings."

"But Doug," Rick started "the kid rushed for 2,200 yards and has a lot of people chasing him."

"Son, I've been recruiting Texas a long, long time. He's playing in a private school tennis shoe league. Check out the tape and tell me how many other brothers are on the field. He's the only one and he's playing in the "White Flight" Conference. If he was at Madison High School in Houston and ran for 2,200 yards I would be sitting in his coach's office now instead of talking to you. Write this down: that kid couldn't play dead in a cowboy movie."

"Okay I hear you." Rick said. "Should we go to Aaron and tell him we need to know now and force the issue?"

Roger Barstow, the running backs coach chimed in. He was a 1998 Ohio State graduate and had been back on the staff for five years. Through this process he'd spent a great deal of time with the two running backs.

"Rick we could ask him to commit but what if he says no? Then he's called our bluff and we stand there with our dicks hanging out? We have to play this out. Aaron knows we're chasing Malcolm and Malcolm knows we're chasing Aaron. They talk all the time. That's the way these things go. We may get them both."

They talked about all the guys on the list. Names were moved around the recruiting board. As they looked at the films they came to the offensive linemen. There were two they had on the board ahead of everyone else. They wanted to take another offensive tackle to strengthen their pass protection. The top two on the board were big strong players. Jake O'Reilly was from Ohio and Brad Jones was from Pennsylvania. They had a great shot at both of them.

Safeties Coach Freddie Smith talked up a lineman he had in California. As they watched video of him Freddie was trying to sell everyone in the room to offer him. He was listed at six feet six inches tall, three hundred ten pounds and looked every bit of it on film.

"He is a great athlete." Freddie said. "He plays basketball for Mater Dei and is on the baseball team. He's always liked the Big Ten because he lived in Cincinnati until he was eight. He is a tall kid and on top of it all he has long, long arms."

Long arms on an offensive tackle are like a long reach in boxing giving the tackle an advantage in reaching the pass rusher before he can reach him.

"He sounds good to me." Rick said "Have you seen this kid in person?"

"I've seen him twice. He looks like Tarzan." Freddie said.

"Shit, that boy may look like Tarzan but he plays like Jane." Doug Leonard interjected with his typical Southern-spun humor.

Despite being weary from the day's early start, everyone in the room could still laugh from Doug's commentary. Most coaching staffs have someone like Doug who pulls no punches but softens the blow delivering them with homespun wit. Even Freddie had to laugh.

"Shit Doug. I've been here three years and by now I thought I'd heard all your lines." Freddie laughed.

"That said," Offensive line coach Otis Lewis began "he's not the worst kid we've seen. That tackle from Indiana we looked at was slower than a herd of turtles."

"You stealing my lines?" Doug asked in mock horror.

"Yep, but remember imitation is the highest form of flattery." Otis responded.

The meeting wore on until I arrived at eleven a.m. and they had a plan of the guys they needed to go see. They handed me all the written evaluations from the video they'd watched.

“Thanks Rick.” I said “I am looking forward to reading Doug’s evaluation to see if he has any new one-liners.”

“He’s already dropped a few on us this morning.”

“Okay tell me where you need us to go and then have Sally make the arrangements for the planes. This weekend we’ll meet to plan where I need to travel. We have our single head coach visit left for all the kids on this list. Is that right?”

“That’s right.” Rick answered.

“Okay. As for the game yesterday....” I changed the meeting’s focus. “I watched the video; offense, defense and special teams. The two plays in the kicking game really hurt us. But we may have to talk about the pace of our offense. In a game like that we have to be able to slow the pace to keep our defense off the field and keep them fresh.”

By his frown I knew that Quinn Banks did not like that statement. Slowing things down would mean fewer plays and less total yardage. Every offense is ranked nationally by total yardage. Quinn was widely seen as a hot head coaching candidate and knew his coaching stock was valued on the big yardage numbers he posted. If those numbers fell back, his stock would fall.

Today wasn’t the day to fight that battle. Quinn held his punch and figured he’d wait to fight another day. In the meantime he had to hop on a private plane for a quick flight up to Youngstown-Warren Airport. He was scheduled to see quarterback Carter Jones that afternoon before a private jet flew him to Florida to see Malcolm Jackson and his mother the next day before driving up I-95 to see Boxer Davis’ basketball game that night in Daytona Beach.

The day after that he was flying to Toledo to see running back Aaron Smith, then to Detroit to see wide receiver Lance Marshall and then to Youngstown to see tight end Manny Rodriguez. In three days he’d cover almost 2,500 miles in private jets and recruit players in Ohio, Florida and Michigan.

The same hectic schedule also awaited the other coaches running around the country to recruit their players. Before they headed on the road I reminded them the stakes were very high for the future of the program. In my head I knew that the stakes for my career and the staff’s career were perhaps even higher.

3. TALES FROM THE ROAD

As the private jet touched down and taxied across the tarmac towards the small terminal at Youngstown-Warren Airport, Quinn looked out to see wind-blown snow flurries falling. Quinn took out his phone to text Jeff Barnes, the head coach at Warren Harding High School, letting him know he'd be at the school in a few minutes.

It was 2:30 and school was letting out. Quinn was to meet Ohio's best quarterback Carter Jones and his mother before basketball practice began at four. They'd be at the school's field house which housed the football team's weight room and coaches' offices. Quinn thought they were close to getting Carter to commit to them, but they had expected him to announce his commitment at the High School All-Star game he'd already played in.

Recruit announcements had become a parody of themselves. Each guy wanted to outdo the last guy. One high school senior announced his commitment to Georgia on signing day with a $3000 pure-bred bulldog puppy. Another landed a private plane to step off and announce for one school only to switch to another school just a few months later.

As Quinn stepped off the plane he turned the collar of his cashmere overcoat up to shield his face from the sting of the deep chill. He'd grown up in Texas and even after two years in Ohio, he still wasn't quite used to the cold.

Quinn drove through what was left of a once-thriving industrial rust-belt city and pulled behind the high school and to the field house. He strode assuredly, his footsteps crunching through the still snow-covered parking lot. Quinn felt confident Carter would come to Ohio State, joining a decades-long line of great Buckeye players from this school from Paul Warfield to Korey Stringer to Maurice Clarett.

In the windowless coach's office, Carter sat in the dim artificial lighting wearing a bright scarlet Ohio State sweatshirt.

"I like that sweatshirt." Quinn joked as he walked into the small coach's office.

"Yeah Coach, I thought you would."

"He wears that almost every day." Coach Jeff Barnes said.

Jeff was the head coach at Warren Harding. An energetic and confident man for his forty years, he was a good fit for this tough job. He wore his hair in a flat top and looked like an Eastern Ohio farm boy but had an easy going manner that helped him relate to his nearly all black football team.

This was Jeff's third year at the school. The job paid well but the fans' expectations were through the roof often leading to the hiring and firing of the head coach just about every three years. On the desk was the State Championship Trophy they'd won just a month earlier. Jeff joked that the title was good enough to keep him from getting fired for at least another year.

Carter sat across the desk from Jeff and next to Quinn.

"If you wear that sweatshirt every day that tells me something." Quinn said to Carter.

"I don't wear this one almost every day. I have three like this one, but I do wear Buckeye stuff most days. That's my school." Carter said.

"Then what are you waiting for?" Quinn asked.

"Well me and my Mom just want to hear how you think I fit in down there." Carter said.

"Is she coming over?" Quinn asked.

"Yeah, she's taking a late lunch before she has to go back to work."

Carter's mom worked for Trumbull County. It was just down the road, an easy five minute drive. Quinn usually stopped in to see her there so all the other Buckeye fans in the office would make a fuss and tell her to send her son to play at Ohio State.

Carter's Mom arrived and Quinn went over and gave her a hug. Quinn had met her within weeks of joining the Ohio State staff two years ago. Carter was high on their priority list even as a sophomore. Gloria was young, having given birth to Carter when she was seventeen.

She managed to get a two-year degree while raising Carter, and had worked for the county for fourteen years. She loved hearing the football recruiting pitch, but she really wanted to hear about the academics. Quinn really liked her no-nonsense approach and her beautiful smile.

On campus before a game she had joked with Quinn "You know Quinn, you're my type, a single good-looking white boy about my age. Carter's dad was white you know. You better watch yourself."

The three of them sat down and caught up on small talk about the holidays and the stuff that the Ohio State players got to do on the bowl trip to Orlando. Carter really enjoyed hearing about the $500 shopping spree the players got at an Orlando Best Buy.

"I'm sure you would've spent your $500 getting something for your mom, right?" Quinn asked.

"I'm sure he would have." Gloria smiled.

Quinn was good. In single-mom homes, he recruited the moms, always playing on the usually strong mother and son connection. There'd been rumors about how close Quinn was willing to get with some mothers, but I never knew any of them to be true.

After the small talk Quinn got down to business. He leaned forward in his chair signaling a shift in the conversation.

"Look Gloria and Carter let's get to it. Right now I know you have some great schools chasing you. Alabama, Florida State, USC and Texas are all great schools with great traditions." He paused to smile at Gloria. "But knowing you and your mom have a great relationship, do you really want to go to school so far from home?"

"I don't want him far away. I want to see him play and I want him nearby so if he gets homesick I can go see him in a couple of hours by car. I don't make the kind of money where I can fly all over the place to see him play." Gloria said.

Quinn nodded.

"Your Mom is smart. Plus all the people of this community want to see you play. They've been watching you since you picked up a football in the second grade."

Carter smiled.

"Heck I've seen the video of you making all those kids miss when you were playing running back as a little kid. Your Mom showed them to me."

"I hear you coach. I understand all that." Carter said.

Quinn leaned back in his chair to a more neutral posture, a move meant to invite them to take the floor and speak their minds.

"Coach I think Carter has something he wants to tell you." She said.

"Coach," Carter said "I am committing to Ohio State."

Quinn smiled, relieved that his confidence had been rewarded. His years in recruiting had taught him that all the confidence in the world didn't mean a thing until you got them to jump in the boat.

“That’s great.” Quinn said.

He stood up, shook Carter’s hand and gave Gloria a big hug. Quinn took out his phone to call me. In my office I paced excitedly as I talked with Carter. This was a big get for us and a quarterback commitment would have a big impact on others we were recruiting.

“So Carter when did you make up your mind?” I asked.

“Over Christmas, but I wanted to tell you in person and wait until after the All-Star game.”

“Why is that?”

“Coach that game ain’t nothin’ but a circus and I didn’t want to be a sideshow.” Carter laughed.

“I hear you.” I said. “All that matters now is that you are a Buckeye and I get to coach you.”

Then Gloria got on the phone “He also felt this was where he should announce. The newspapers here have been covering him all through his career so he felt they should be the ones to get the story first.”

“That’s very perceptive on your part.” I said. “Gloria, you’ve raised a very loyal and considerate young man.”

“Thanks Coach.” She said “Now you’ve got to take care of my baby.”

“You know it.” I said.

After the phone conversation, Carter’s Coach Jeff Barnes got up and said “Let’s get some pictures.”

They took pictures of Carter and Quinn, then Carter with Quinn and Gloria and then finally Carter with Quinn and Coach Barnes. Nearing four o’clock it was time for Carter to go to basketball practice and for Quinn to go. Gloria grabbed Quinn before he left.

“Quinn, do me one favor.” She said.

“What’s that?” Quinn asked.

“Go out and get us a running back and some receivers for my boy to throw the ball to.” Gloria smiled.

“You got it.”

"Then come back and see me again next week. Don't be a stranger."

"You know I'll be back." Quinn said.

Quinn got back in the car and headed back to the airport. The jet was waiting there to take him to Orlando where he would meet Dwayne Baxter. Dwayne was recruiting the two Florida kids and wanted Quinn to pitch the offensive scheme to them. By the time the jet took off for Florida Quinn had fallen asleep.

Back at the office I called Rick into my office to discuss recruiting.

"Rick," I said "you know the recruiting breakdown you gave us yesterday? Can I get a copy of that e-mailed to Sally? I need a copy of it in my files."

"Sure thing." Rick said and left.

I walked out of my office to Sally's office. As my special assistant for the past twelve years, she was able to anticipate things I needed before I even asked. Above all she was a tremendous friend and an even more effective organizer and administrator.

"Sally, Rick is going to e-mail you a recruiting breakdown. Can you please file one and print another for me?"

"Sure thing Ed."

I went back into my office and within seconds Sally walked in with a copy of the recruiting breakdown. Sally left and I took the sheet out. On it I circled Carter's name and wrote "Committed to Ohio State today!" I took out an envelope and put the papers inside before yelling for Sally to come in.

"Sally," I said as she entered the office "please shut the door."

She turned and shut the door before walking back to my desk. At nearly six feet tall, Sally made for an imposing presence. Her long strides covered the length of the over-sized office in just a few steps. I reached out my hand extending the envelope with the recruiting breakdown inside.

"Sally, I need you to take this over to the President's Office and hand this directly to Gerry Gorton."

"Can I just give it to his assistant Barb?"

"No this has got to go right to him. No one else can read it. He knows you're coming. Take a purse or something so Barb doesn't see you delivering documents directly to him. As you know Barb is a bit gossipy."

"Okay."

It pissed me off to have to do this but Gerry was the boss. I was telling Gerry before Carter would make his announcement public, to give Gerry the impression that he was in the innermost loop.

My cellphone rang and it was assistant coaches Wayne Robinson and Otis Lewis. They were visiting with Jake O'Reilly a big time offensive tackle. In the high school they sat in the coach's office. On the walls were photos of at least two dozen former players who'd gone on to play college football. The white walls were trimmed in green the main color of the St Edward Eagles.

Despite Wayne and Otis both exceeding two hundred and fifty pounds they were dwarfed by Jake, a man-child who'd eclipsed the three hundred pound barrier as a high school sophomore.

"Wayne. Tell me some good news." I said.

"I have good news but not great news yet." Wayne said. "In fact I'm sitting here with Jake right now."

"Well put him on."

Wayne handed the phone to Jake.

"Coach." Jake said.

"How you doing Jake?" I asked.

"Good. I'm about to head to basketball practice."

"How you guys doing?"

"Well we have a big game tomorrow night against Toledo St John's."

"Are they coming to you guys or do you guys go out there?"

"We go there so we get out of school early."

"That's a plus. How's St John's look?"

"Good. They're 14 and 1 and they have a big athletic six-nine guy who is going to play at Marquette next year."

"That will be a good test for you."

"Yeah I'm looking forward to the challenge."

I decided to shift the direction of the conversation away from the basketball season.

"So Jake, let me ask you a question. Where are you on your decision process?"

Jake looked up at the ceiling and leaned back in his chair.

"Well Coach, I've taken three visits. I have Stanford and Notre Dame left to visit. I'm not too high on Notre Dame but my Uncle is a priest. He's convinced my mother I should take a visit there."

"The God card is tough to beat, but I am sure that you'll be guided to Ohio State when it is all said and done. I know you want to take those visits, but you've been here so many times and you know us so well I have to ask what's holding you up?"

"Nothing really, I love it there and I've always wanted to be a Buckeye but..."

Jake leaned forward in his chair.

"But?" I asked. I hated to hear "buts".

"I do have a question for you coach. A coach from Michigan was here this morning and he said that you were thinking about leaving for Syracuse because you're in trouble at Ohio State."

I snapped the pencil I was holding in my right hand. Schools dug up every bullshit rumor and used it against one another. One school had twelve interns monitor every site that covered their school and fought all negative posts. They also went on other team's sites to post rumors and negative stuff about certain recruits. It was a shadowy world of recruiting disinformation campaigns.

I inhaled for a moment to be sure my voice did not have an edge when I spoke.

"Jake, first of all what does a guy from Michigan know about what's going on here at Ohio State? As much as these two schools hate each other do you think they have inside information on us?"

Jake laughed, but I knew I still had to deny it directly, not just joke about it.

"There are also lots of internet rumors. Someone from Syracuse started that story to make it look like I want their job. I've never even been contacted by them, and that job is not something I am interested in. I've talked with the President here. We're not in trouble, in fact we're talking about a contract extension. I'm going to be here for a while."

“That’s great coach. That eliminates that worry for me.”

“Tell your Uncle that it was a sign from God.”

We both laughed said goodbye and ended the call. I knew the Syracuse rumor would get around the coaching world and be used against us in recruiting. It was hard enough to deal with negative stuff that had factual basis let alone all the false stuff people just made up.

I got a text from President Gerry Gorton.

“Just got your update and am very pleased”

I texted “Thanks” back to him.

Later that afternoon before I headed home I asked Rick to come in and update me on the day of recruiting so far. I wanted to know who had checked in, and who was where that day. Each night Rick had a conference call at ten p.m. and just about everyone called to give his day’s rundown. It was a way to keep them all connected and on the same page. Then the next morning when I was in town Rick would come into my office and give me the daily recruiting briefing.

That evening, at around 6:45 p.m. the private jet carrying Quinn landed in Orlando and pulled into the private terminal. He no longer needed the overcoat he’d worn in Ohio. The dark evening was warm with clouds and humidity that hinted at rain in the near future.

He was scheduled to visit Dr. Phillips High School to watch a top junior football player play basketball. He put on a light Ohio State jacket with a big logo on the back. It was always important at these games that everyone in the building know that your school was there.

Just inside the gym doors he was met by Ohio State alum Ralph Jones who lived in the area. He was a local attorney with two sons at Dr. Phillips High School. Every time a coach from Ohio State came to town Ralph would make sure they knew the lay of the land.

“Quinn.” Ralph said as he extended his hand to Quinn.

“Hey Ralph, great to see you. Sorry I’m a few minutes behind schedule. I just landed from Ohio.”

“Not a problem. Tipoff is still fifteen minutes away so you can catch the last five minutes of their warm-ups. Let’s get in there. Notre Dame, Miami and Arizona are all here too. This is a popular night to be here.”

"Why are they tipping off so late?"

"This one is on TV. They're playing Tampa Catholic and they have a very good team this year....Hey I know this kid's parents if you want to talk with them."

"I can't do that, he's still a junior."

"I know but you could *accidentally* bump into them."

"Not with all these other schools here."

"Well then you're the exception. All three of the other schools talked to the kid as well as the parents."

"Hey the last thing I need is to get in trouble over a junior in Florida."

They stood at the edge of the court so that the prospect and his teammates would see the Ohio State jacket and Quinn's presence. Midway through the third quarter Tampa Catholic started to pull away behind the leadership of a big-time point guard who would be playing at Duke next year. The player Quinn had come to watch was playing very well and had scored twenty points through the first three quarters.

At the end of the third with Dr. Phillips trailing by fifteen, Quinn excused himself and headed to the Airport Marriott.

Back in Columbus I was seated in my den at my desk watching game tape from the Michigan loss trying to get an angle on why we'd done so poorly. At Ohio State it was *never* too early to talk about the Michigan game. With each defensive lapse on the tape, I pulled out my pad and angrily scrawled another note.

"Missed tackle" or "Bad defensive call" or "Missed assignment" or "Blown coverage" or "lost contain" filled the pad. Each note was written more determinedly than the one before. These were the things that next year would mean the difference between keeping my job or losing it. I am not as psycho about Michigan as some other Ohio State coaches had been, but the countdown clocks to the Ohio State-Michigan kickoff were always running in both team's football buildings.

I knew if I wanted to still be studying tape in this mahogany-paneled den with a nice fire roaring in the fireplace next year at this time, we'd have to beat the hated Wolverines. This town, indeed the entire state, was consumed with beating them.

My phone rang. It was Sports Information Director Sid Inge calling so I answered.

"Evening Sid." I said.

"Good evening Ed. Sorry to call you so late."

"Not a problem, what's up?"

"Are you in negotiations on a contract extension?"

"No, why do you ask?"

"I'm getting calls from media outlets citing a report that you're in contract extension talks."

"Where the hell would that come from?" I asked.

Before Sid could even answer, I remembered my earlier conversation with Jake O'Reilly. I knew right away where it had come from. Jake had probably been interviewed and mentioned it. Damn, I hated the recruiting internet sites.

"Your recruit Jake O'Reilly did an interview with one of these recruiting sites. He says you told him you're close to a contract extension."

"He doesn't have that quite right." I said. "I told him I wasn't going anywhere. But just let it die. The last thing we need is to contradict a recruit publicly. Just don't call any of the media guys back."

"Okay, I got it. But understand this story may not go away on its own."

"We'll deal with it if we have to."

"Okay."

I hung up and started to watch the video again. Ten minutes later my phone rang again. I was surprised to see Gerry Gorton calling this late. Gerry was well known to be a guy who'd have a scotch at 9:00 and then head off to sleep. I knew this was not a call to exchange pleasantries.

"Hello Gerry, How are you doing tonight?" I asked.

"Well I'm doing fine, except I just got an interesting phone call. One of our Trustees was on-line and noticed that you're getting a contract extension."

Even with years of experience with internet recruiting stories, I was surprised this had gotten to Gerry already, and that he even cared about it.

"Gerry, where would he get that idea?"

“Why don’t you tell me?” Gerry roared “Apparently an internet recruiting site has it that you’ve told people you’re really close to an extension.”

“That’s probably Jake O’Reilly. He just misunderstood what I told him and got the story wrong.” I tried to calm Gerry down.

“What exactly did you tell him?” Gerry was starting to yell “I’ve got this Trustee and a few of his associates on the Board who want to know why the hell you got an extension without them approving it.”

“You told them that it wasn’t true?”

“I sure did, but they now think that I may be lying. You know I answer to them. They are my bosses.”

Candace happened to be passing in the hall and Gerry’s voice was coming through loud enough for her to hear in the hall. She looked at me with a worried expression before I raised a hand to calm her. She kept walking upstairs.

“Aren’t they old enough to know that they should trust your word over something on the God damned internet?” I replied.

“Ed, these guys are nuts. These are some of the same guys that wanted you fired. This really pisses them off. Now I’ve gotta issue a statement so they will calm down.”

“You want to do what?” I was incredulous.

Gerry was a bit taken aback by my insolent tone.

“I’m gonna have to issue a statement. They’re telling me to do it.”

“With all respect Gerry, if you issue a statement in response to every internet recruiting web site story that got something wrong that would be the only thing you’d have time to do.”

I made some sense, so Gerry backed off the gas pedal.

“Well Mr. Public Relations Genius, what do you suggest?” He asked.

“I may not have all the answers but I know this; if you issue a statement they will call Jake O’Reilly. He will look like a fool and you can be damned sure he won’t come to Ohio State.”

Gerry remained quiet for a moment to collect his thoughts.

"So Ed, what *exactly* did you say to the kid and what do *you* think we should do?"

"First, the kid asked if I was talking to Syracuse. A coach from Michigan told him I was headed to Syracuse because I was getting fired here. I told him that I hadn't talked to Syracuse and that things were good here and that we may talk about an extension some day in the future."

I was fudging what I'd told Jake, rolling the dice knowing Gerry probably wouldn't check on it.

"In the future? You mean like if you win a boatload of games next year?"

"Be that as it may, the kid took that as a positive sign and we are still in the hunt to get him. So we fended off that rumor."

"Okay so you didn't lie to him, he just got the story wrong."

"Pretty much. Let's figure out what you have to say now."

"Okay, you got any ideas?"

"Yeah, call that Trustee back and tell him what I told the kid. But also tell him that we can't publicly contradict Jake O'Reilly if we hope to land him as a Buckeye. Whether they end up firing me in a year or not they'll be glad to have this guy in this program."

"Okay."

"You can tell them whatever you need, but tell them that there will be a lot of misinformation out there on the recruiting trail; that's the nature of the business. We just can't get all wrapped up in it. If we did issue a statement I can guarantee you one thing..."

"What's that?"

"I can guarantee you that every coach in the country, and particularly Michigan, will be in Ohio waving it around that I'm not even being considered for an extension. That will kill the rest of our class and make it pretty tough to even hold on to the ones we've got."

"You make a convincing argument. I'll call these guys and back them off."

"Heck if you want to tell them about us getting Carter Jones before he announces tomorrow morning you can throw them that bone too."

Now I not only fended off this threat, but I'd given Gerry a bonus. The Trustees would be getting inside information from Gerry ahead of everyone else. I hung up and stared from my chair at the fire in the fireplace. The wood was crackling and the logs that had been in there when I started the fire had already started to break up and glow bright red. The room was getting warmer maybe because of the fire and maybe because of the call I'd just handled. It amazed me that some of these Trustees who were very successful in their own work were spending time reading internet message boards.

Well I'd put out one fire tonight, but the other one I was going to sit back and enjoy while I sipped some bourbon.

In his room in Orlando Quinn got a call from his agent Warren Thompson. The substance of the call was that the search firm hiring the new Syracuse coach wanted to meet with him. They would fly into Detroit to see him between his recruiting visit in Toledo and the one in Detroit. Warren would fly up with the power point presentation and materials Quinn used in interviews.

After he hung up Quinn looked at the clock and saw it was time for the evening conference call with all the coaches. Quinn hated the guys who droned on about every detail of the day all the way down to the type of cookies that a recruit's Mom served when they visited the house.

After dialing in Quinn heard Rick Carter get into the meeting's agenda. Rick started with the defensive side of the ball. The most pressing needs were getting a big-time outside linebacker and a big-time pass rusher.

Dave Cafiero followed up talking about linebackers. He'd been in Piqua and Wayne High Schools today. Those schools were both close to each other so he got to both of their schools and saw their parents before a plane took him from Dayton to Pennsylvania's Lehigh Valley. Tomorrow he'd see Carson Grady lift weights at 6 a.m. in school before having breakfast at the house with his family at 7:30. Then he would fly out to the west coast to see Derrick Nelson and visit him at home before jumping on a red-eye back east that night.

Doug Leonard started to talk about the defensive end he'd seen in Cincinnati. Tomorrow he'd head to Akron to see Darwin Tucker before heading up to see Jamar Tucker in Cleveland. They were cousins but Jamar was the much better prospect. Alphonso Simmons, who Doug had seen in Cincinnati was a great player but Jamar was the guy everyone in the room wanted. He'd racked up sixteen sacks as a sophomore, eighteen as a junior and twenty as a senior on the state championship team.

As Doug was talking he cut short his sentence.

“Rick,” Doug said “I’m getting a call from Ted Ginn at Glenville, I better take this.”

“Okay just drop off and call back.” Rick said.

Ted Ginn was the head coach at Glenville High School in Cleveland. He’d sent a whole slew of players to the NFL; most by way of Ohio State. He was a key connection in Ohio State’s most important recruiting area, so whenever he called Doug answered.

On the conference call, Dwayne Baxter talked about the two cornerbacks he’d visited that day. He started at DeMatha High School near D.C. to see Artie Manson before flying up to see Roger Hill at Hoboken High School near New York City. Dwayne had just gotten back from watching him play basketball.

“How’d he look?” Rick asked.

“Shit, in basketball he’s as good as anyone I’ve ever recruited. He had thirty points, twelve assists and ten rebounds.”

“A triple double as a point guard? That is a hell of a game.” Rick said.

“I wasn’t done. This dude had nine steals as well. The guy he was playing against is going to Saint John’s to play basketball.”

The conversation turned to the offensive side of the ball and the coaches started to re-cap the day’s visits. At that point Otis Lewis talked about his visit with Jake.

“Hey Rick, we had a great visit. It seems that asshole from Michigan told Jake that Ed is in trouble and that he’s talking to Syracuse because he’s being forced out here.”

The tight ends coach Terry Ellis chimed in.

“Hey, I got that same question today. A coach from Notre Dame was telling a kid that today and I denied it.”

“Well,” Otis explained “I called and put Ed on the phone with him. Ed shut that crap down right away. In fact he told him he was getting a contract extension.”

“He is?” Terry asked.

“Hell I don’t know, but it shut that down in a hurry. Is there any truth to that Rick?” Otis asked.

"How should I know? All I know is that Jake told a reporter that story so it is making the rounds. Just go with it. I don't think anyone will contradict him so let that story run as far and wide as it can. It will only help our cause." Rick said.

After a few more guys spoke, Quinn told them all that Carter Jones was committing publicly tomorrow morning. To create some momentum, Rick told them to go out tomorrow and really play up that commitment.

While the staff was talking about recruiting, Doug was getting very bad news. Ted Ginn called to tell him that recruit Jamar Tucker had been shot in an attack that was likely aimed at someone else. Jamar played at Benedictine High School, a private Catholic School. He would've gone to Glenville but a booster at Benedictine got him a scholarship. Ted had stayed close to Jamar and did his best to keep him focused on his future.

Doug quickly decided they should call me. When my phone rang I was expecting to get a routine recruiting update after the staff conference call. The call was anything but routine.

"Coach," Doug said "I've got Ted Ginn on the line and he has some bad news for us about Jamar Tucker. It's pretty damned serious."

"Coach," I heard the familiar bass-heavy voice of Ted Ginn "I wanted you guys to know that Jamar Tucker got shot tonight. What I know now is that he is alive and he is in the hospital and he should make it okay. But with gun shots you never do know for sure."

It took a moment to process what I'd just heard, to consider this young man's life and his future. Obviously his health was paramount right now, but this was a young man who had everything ahead of him, everything that could change his life. It was such a tragedy. We'd known he was in a tough place but there was nothing we or any other team could do for him.

"How did this happen?" I asked Ted.

Ted explained "He was at his cousin's house with his girlfriend and someone blew a couple of holes in the front door with a shotgun. Jamar took a shot in the leg and the abdomen and is in surgery right now. His cousin and girlfriend are dead."

"Ted, is there anything we can do?" I asked.

"Coach his life was already a mess. Most days when Jamar goes to school he's not sure where he's sleeping that night. He keeps his stuff at his cousin's place, but his cousin deals drugs out of that house." Doug said.

"I know we've never met any of his family in the recruiting so far. Where's his Mom in all this?" I asked.

"Jamar can't stay with her. She's got a boyfriend who lives with her and has her strung out. Sometimes she turns tricks at the house for drugs and money. The boyfriend lives off her. Jamar threatened to beat him up and the boyfriend told Jamar that he'd shoot him if he messed with him. I can't blame the kid. Who wants to live in a house where your Mom is turning tricks two and three times a night?"

There was little hesitation in mind about what we needed to do first.

"Ted, here's what I want to do for him. Doug and I will be there early tomorrow morning. Just tell his mother that his scholarship offer is still on the table. I don't care if he can ever play again. His college education is paid for. I will have that in writing for him when I get there tomorrow morning. That should at least help him focus on his recovery without worrying about losing his college opportunity."

As I sat in my million dollar home sipping expensive bourbon I thought about the reality that faced many of the young people we recruited in their home communities. The ones we recruited were the lucky ones, they had a way out. So many others were beyond our reach and the reach of society.

We were lucky, we came into those communities to recruit but we got to leave and go home and sleep in our beds in upscale neighborhoods.

As I sat in my den I thought about the two young people who were now lying dead in a morgue, and another who was fighting to survive. How could this happen?

After he hung up with Ted Ginn, Doug Leonard got back on the conference call and broke the sad news to the other coaches. They too were understandably shocked by the news. The realization was that many of these kids lived in the most dangerous places in this country. Drug dealing and gun violence were commonplace. Stories like this brought that home with a fury.

"I talked to Ed. He's decided that whether or not Jamar can play his scholarship offer to Ohio State is still there." Doug said.

"He won't be out of surgery until well past midnight. Ed is going to fly up in the morning to tell Jamar and his coach in person and in writing that the scholarship offer is still there." Doug said.

The tone of the call had changed and now everyone was anxious to wrap up and get on with their evenings. The upbeat mood at the call's outset was decidedly somber at its conclusion. Jamar was a great kid caught up in messed up circumstances well beyond his control.

Quinn planned to go to bed after the call, but this news had upset him. He needed a beer or two before to help him sleep so he went down to the lobby bar.

He sat alone at a corner table and ordered one beer and then another. Just after ordering his third beer he saw a woman approaching his table. She was an attractive brunette dressed in professional business attire. Before even saying a word, she sat down with Quinn. She had light brown eyes and an easy smile. To Quinn she looked to be in her early thirties. Quinn preferred mid-to early twenties but she was still in his wheelhouse. With her approach the pitch seemed to be over the plate.

"Can I join you?" she asked.

"I think you already have."

"I noticed your Ohio State football shirt. You're a coach there right?"

"Yes."

"Are you Quinn?" she asked.

"That would be me, and you are?"

The woman hesitated, smiled and then revealed her identity.

"I am Cecilia Morgan."

"That's a pretty name."

"Yes apparently my parents enjoyed the musical stylings of Simon and Garfunkel."

"Good thing they weren't Phil Collins fans or your name would be Sussudio."

"Good point. So why are you in Orlando?" she asked.

The waitress came back and asked if she'd like a drink. Cecilia ordered a blueberry mojito.

"Put that on my tab." Quinn said.

"Well thank you." Cecelia said "Already buying a lady a drink."

"Hey I'm originally from Texas. That is how gentlemen are raised to treat a lady."

As they talked Quinn learned Cecelia was an Ohio State graduate living in Cleveland and in Orlando on business. She'd passed the bar in both Florida and Ohio so she did business down here for her firm. She was supposed to fly out that night, but her flight was cancelled. She wouldn't be able to get out until noon the next morning.

Quinn knew he didn't have to pick up Dwayne until 8:30 the next morning, which was a late start for a recruiting day. Tonight he had an attractive lawyer from Cleveland in front of him easily outpacing his drinking. He'd worry about tomorrow in the morning.

4. THE LONG AND WINDING ROAD

By 8:30 the next morning, the wheels of our football program were turning furiously. Already Dave Cafiero had eaten breakfast with the top outside linebacker east of the Rockies and was on his way to the airport to fly to Oakland to go see the best outside linebacker west of the Rockies.

In Columbus Coach Wayne Robinson was in his office talking to two freshmen players who were friends with Jamar Tucker to help them deal with the shooting and with their own emotions. With a master's degree in counseling Wayne was valuable in building great rapport with the guys on the team. The rest of the team was busy with classes and cycling through the weight room to get their workout in for the day.

In Warren, Ohio quarterback Carter Jones was announcing that he would be signing with the home state Buckeyes. His home town newspapers got the story first, just as he'd promised them they would. The story exploded across the recruiting sites. This was a huge pick-up for us.

Rick Carter and I had just landed a private plane at Cleveland's Burke Lakefront Airport where a waiting car took us to the Cleveland Clinic.

Four other assistant coaches were visiting recruits in Ohio, Pennsylvania, Texas, Georgia and Michigan. Back in Columbus, Rick Carter was seated in the recruiting "War Room" tracking the flights, and checking in with each coach as they traveled from place to place.

In Orlando Quinn was meeting Dwayne Baxter who'd flown from Newark to Orlando on a 5:45 a.m. flight. The two of them were likely going 90 mph on their way to Melbourne's Palm Bay High School.

At the Cleveland Clinic we found Jamar awake and doing well. Jamar's mother was there with other people that we didn't know. Doug Leonard was there, he'd gotten there about a half hour before us. Although attached to tubes and wires with machines making electronic noises Jamar smiled when I sat down next to his bed. Some morning sunlight was peeking through the slats of the vertical blinds that were not quite fully closed.

Through the emotions of the room, I promised Jamar that Ohio State's offer of a scholarship was still on the table regardless of whether or not he played football. Jamar was conscious and seemed to be following the conversation, even though he was not really himself.

It was difficult to see such a strong young man laid so low in a senseless shooting. He didn't have a lot of good options. Between Jamar's trick-turning mother, her drug-dealing boyfriend and nephew it was probably just a matter of time until this type of trouble found them. It was clear that Jamar's cousin had many enemies in the tough East Cleveland neighborhood where he'd been dealing. Jamar was just in the wrong place at the wrong time.

By 9:30 the news in Northeast Ohio was the commitment of quarterback Carter Jones and then my hospital room visit with Jamar Tucker and our honoring of the scholarship offer. Back in Florida, Quinn and Dwayne had arrived at Palm Bay High School. The school has a great tradition, but most of the big-time Palm Bay guys had gone to Florida.

In the weight room they sat down with Malcolm Jackson and Quinn showed video of the ways they would use him in their offense. Malcolm asked about our starting running back Pokey Wallace who would be a senior the next year. Quinn assured Malcolm he could come in and play right away. Pokey had some liabilities in the pass game and given Malcolm's great receiving skills, he could be the third down back right away. Quinn liked Malcolm because he carefully studied the video and asked good questions.

Malcolm's mother Wanda came over to visit and talked to them about her move to Cleveland. She was actively looking for a job up there and asked if they could help her in the search. Quinn and Dwayne told her they would do everything they could within NCAA rules.

"I can say this," Dwayne said "given the huge Ohio State alumni network in Northeast Ohio the mother of Malcolm Jackson will probably have a few ins."

"I should probably know this, so forgive me for asking but what kind of work do you do here in Florida?" Quinn asked.

"I'm a legal secretary." Wanda said.

"Really? I happen to know an attorney up there I could put you in touch with. I bet she'd be happy to talk with you."

Quinn was glad he'd spent the night with his new friend Cecelia Morgan. Wanda was someone he could recommend to Cecelia without hesitation. On their way out Wanda pulled Dwayne aside and confided in him out of earshot of Malcom.

"Look Dwayne," she said "he's visiting Alabama and USC, but I can tell you that you guys are right there. It is down to you guys and Florida. If I'm in Cleveland I don't want him in California, or in Alabama where I don't know anyone. If I had my choice he'd be near me, but we'll see what happens. You have to convince him."

"What can we use to hook him?" Quinn asked.

"I think today was great. He enjoyed seeing how you planned to use him, and that you don't plan for him to sit this year." Wanda said.

"I'll tell you what I told him. He is too good to sit on the bench. This fall he will help us immediately." Quinn said.

Quinn and Dwayne got back in the car and started up I-95 towards Daytona Beach. By 3:30 they'd pulled off I-95 and were heading up International Speedway Drive. Suddenly the Winston Towers and the huge grandstands of Daytona International Speedway rose from the landscape.

"We're just about there." Dwayne said. "Mainland High School is just beyond the airport. This may be the easiest in and out from airport to high school in the country."

"Good. No long drive after the basketball game tonight. Right over to the airport and on the plane. Let's go see the coach before we grab something to eat."

NCAA rules did not allow them to talk to Boxer Davis, the recruit they were seeing, before the game. Understandably the high school coaches wanted their players focused on their games and not distracted on game days by visiting coaches. Already that day coaches from Florida, Florida State and Miami had been by to say hello to the coach and all were coming back that night for the game. They were playing cross-town rival Seabreeze High School who had a talented quarterback who also played basketball. All three of those schools were recruiting that quarterback as well as Boxer Davis.

Out west, Dave Cafiero was at DeLaSalle High School in Concord, California. Dave's brother Frank was his "in" with Derrick Nelson, perhaps the best outside linebacker in the country. Frank lived in nearby Walnut Creek and had been Derrick's 10th grade geometry teacher. Frank also was an assistant coach for the football team.

When Dave arrived at the school he went right to Frank's classroom. The period was just changing for the last class of the day. Frank introduced his brother to the class before they got started.

"Class, today I want you to do a quick review of what we talked about yesterday and I'll get right with you." Frank said to his class.

Frank went to the phone and asked the office to have Derrick sent to his classroom to see Dave. While they were waiting Dave heard one of the students groan about the lesson.

"What do we have to do this for? We'll never use this again."

“Really?” Dave said as he stood up from the chair where he was seated. “You’d be surprised.”

The student was surprised but he spoke up again.

“You coach football, how do you use this stuff?”

Dave went to the board and grabbed the dry erase marker and diagrammed a football play. The students were unimpressed.

“Okay now,” Dave started “look here at this wide receiver. He is seventeen yards from the ball standing on the line of scrimmage.”

Dave pointed at the diagram and showed where the receiver was and then showed that he would be running to a spot 15 yards downfield. Then he turned to the class.

“Now he is seventeen yards wide and fifteen yards deep, and the quarterback has dropped straight back and is standing seven yards deep. How far does the throw have to travel to that receiver? Anyone know how I’d figure that out?”

The class was staring back blankly at Dave.

“The Pythagorean Theorem...does that ring a bell?” Dave asked.

The heads in the class started to nod.

“Okay A squared plus B squared equals C squared. So the quarterback is seven yards deep and the receiver is fifteen yards downfield so that is 22 yards, plus the seventeen yards wide. 22 squared is 484 and seventeen squared is 289. 289 plus 484 equals 773 and the square root of 773 is...........”

Dave pulled out his iPhone.

“I’m good at math but I’ll need help on this one. What is the square root of 773?” he asked his phone.

A voice spoke up “The answer is approximately 27.8029”

Then Dave turned to the board and drew a line and said “So we’ll call it 28 yards. So now I know that the ball has to travel twenty-eight yards. Now how far does my outside linebacker have to be from the ball to have a chance to get there?”

He pointed at the linebacker at five yards deep and seven yards from ball. Doing the calculations for the class he found that the width from the receiver was ten yards by ten yards.

"Now my linebacker is ten yards inside the receiver and ten yards shallower from the end point. So 10 squared is 100 and 10 squared is 100 giving us a total of 200. The square root of 200 is around 14 yards. So in the time the receiver runs 15 yards my linebacker has to run 14 yards to intersect that point. Given the receiver knows exactly where he is going and that my guy doesn't know right away whether it is a run or a pass the odds are still slightly in the offense's hands.....unless my linebacker is Derrick Nelson of course."

The class laughed and then applauded the lesson they'd been given. Dave really enjoyed that moment and he could see Derrick in the back of the room smiling.

"Now if I didn't have a great athlete like that I might have to move my linebacker a little wider, but then I give up something in defending the running game. So on obvious passing downs, I can widen my guys a little to give us better leverage and get them closer to the receiver. So I hope my guy in the front row who wondered if he'd ever use geometry again sees how valuable it can be later in life."

After the class Dave spoke with Derrick in the coach's office. For the first time Dave felt like they had a legitimate shot to land Derrick. It would still be a big uphill fight, he was after all a west coast kid and with USC, UCLA and Oregon all in the hunt it would not be an easy get. The good news was that Stanford and Cal were not in the mix so all the other schools were like Ohio State, a plane ride away.

One of the strong selling points was the fact that every Ohio State game was on television. In fact Derrick had watched every game with his linebacker coach and geometry teacher Frank Cafiero last year. Derrick loved the Horseshoe, the Buckeye stickers on the helmets and our great Buckeye tradition.

Dave knew they were a long way from closing on this one but at least he knew we were in the fight.

Back in Florida Dwayne and Quinn were headed into the gym at Mainland High School, appropriately named the Vince Carter Athletic Center after the school's most successful basketball alumnus. It was Quinn's first time inside the beautiful modern gym. Inside they saw the coaches from three of the Florida schools who made comments to them about Ohio State coaches being a little too far from home.

It didn't deter them and both Quinn and Dwayne sat with Boxer's mother Regina for the second half of the game. Quinn was amazed at how intensely she watched the game and how much she knew about sports. Quinn found out that she'd been the state 100 meter champion in her high school days at Mainland High School.

"So Gina," Quinn asked "how old was Boxer when he finally could beat you in a race?"

Gina laughed and then looked dead at Quinn with a straight face.

"What makes you think he's ever beaten me?" she laughed.

Gina explained that tonight's basketball game was personal between Boxer and Darrell Masters, the quarterback at Seabreeze who was being recruited by the three Florida Schools in attendance. She explained that the two of them really disliked each other. Including high school playoffs they'd played seven football games and ten basketball games against each other.

If Boxer disliked this guy that much, Quinn and Dwayne decided that Darrell Masters going to a Florida school would be a positive for Ohio State as it would eliminate at least one of the schools. By the end of the game Mainland had won 72-71 as Boxer hit a three-pointer at the buzzer, a shot he took and made just over the outstretched hands of Darrell Masters.

As the day ended on the east coast all the coaches called in again for the conference call. There were no new commitments to report but the reception they were getting on the road was very good.

The next morning after visiting with running back Aaron Smith in Toledo, Quinn drove up to the Detroit Airport Marriott where his agent told him they would be meeting in a conference room just off the lobby. As Quinn entered the room he saw three men he did not know all seated with his agent Warren Thompson. All of them stood up and came over to shake Quinn's hand.

The men were Jason Harvey from the search firm Korn Ferry along with Syracuse Athletic Director Andrew Davis and one of the school's trustees Steve Tanner. Steve told Quinn he had played football at Syracuse for Dick MacPherson back in the 1980s.

After a few minutes of small talk, Quinn started to talk about his career and the Ohio State offense. This was one of those pressure moments where Quinn thrived. Inside this nondescript hotel conference room he seized the moment to describe his vision for a football program that he could call his own.

His presentation included charts, numbers and statistics that the offense had run up in his high-paced no huddle offense. His charts included all the statistical rankings of the offenses he'd run at Ohio State and at TCU.

The three men from Syracuse seemed impressed. As the statistics and national rankings went up, they all nodded along and made notes. Then they asked him about his recruiting background, his family situation and about his relationship with the media.

"Quinn we are very interested in the media and marketing side of this," said Andrew Davis "because we need to sell tickets. A young guy with great media presence and a flashy offense is what we think we need. Sure defense may win championships but offense puts asses in the seats. My first concern as the Athletic Director is to maximize revenues so I can balance my budgets and keep all my coaches happy."

"Well Andrew," Quinn said "winning is the ultimate salesman when it comes to tickets."

"That's true," Steve Tanner said "but unfortunately what too many new head coaches forget is that when they arrive they haven't won any games yet, so they have to quickly build a relationship that fans can trust enough that they will part with their money."

The interview went on for close to two hours before it was time for Quinn to get back to recruiting. Andrew Davis and Steve Tanner indicated that they would be interviewing a couple of additional candidates before a second round that would take place on campus.

Quinn headed into Detroit to Pershing High School calling Warren on the way. Warren had stayed behind to talk to the Syracuse contingent. He reported that they were very impressed and liked all the gaudy statistics he'd shown them.

"Quinn," Warren said "these people don't know who can coach and who can't. They have no fucking clue at all. But you show these idiots a bunch of statistical rankings and they get hard-ons because they have some kind of empirical data to show their constituents. They think of this like it is a mutual fund prospectus."

"Well Warren I can tell you this; go after this one full force. I don't even want to take a chance that Ed is going to put a stop to our no-huddle offense."

"What?"

"He made a hint in the meeting after the bowl game about ball control and keeping the defense off the field." Quinn was nearly shouting now. "If that happens, the offensive statistics suffer and I am less marketable. Fuck this team stuff. If the defense can't hold them below thirty points we don't deserve to win."

"Calm down Quinn. If we get it then great, if not you and I will have a talk with Ed."

Quinn had made it to the school so he hung up with Warren. Pershing High School had been a much different place years earlier. When the city was booming decades ago this school's enrollment was much bigger. But it remained an oasis of learning in an area still scarred by burned out shells of buildings from race riots decades ago. Other places were torn down and replaced by vacant lots now overgrown with weeds.

Quinn's meeting with Lance Marshall went well. He didn't have much in the way of family and was being raised by his grandmother. His mother had overdosed when Lance was ten years old and his father had never been in his life, until Lance started getting national attention as a big-time football recruit. Lance was smart enough to be suspicious of his father's motives.

Quinn's real hope was that they would get Boxer Davis because Quinn really favored the bigger and taller receivers. While Boxer wasn't as fast as Lance, Boxer's extra height more than made up for that. Quinn compared Boxer to Julio Jones who'd been a big dominant receiver at Alabama before being a first round pick by Atlanta. But Lance had that electric speed. If he got into the open no one would catch him.

By the time Quinn left the school he knew they were in great shape with Lance. It would be tricky to keep Lance from committing before Boxer made his decision. Getting both of them would stretch our scholarship numbers thin, but also give us two game-changing receivers and impact our recruiting ranking.

At the airport Quinn's plane was waiting. Within fifty minutes he'd taxied, taken off and landed in Youngstown for the second time in three days. This time he headed south of downtown to Cardinal Mooney High School. The school had produced a lot of great football players through the years but was also known as a producer of football coaches. Three Stoops brothers had played there eventually becoming head coaches at Arizona, Kentucky and most notably oldest brother Bob at Oklahoma. Former Nebraska Coach Bo Pelini was also a Mooney graduate.

All of those schools were recruiting Manny Rodriguez. We already had a tight end committed, Frank Sanders from Cincinnati, but he was not as good as Manny. I had told Quinn and the offensive staff to get Manny and to let me handle any issues that would arise with too many tight ends. The easiest way was to simply tell Frank Sanders that he could postpone his enrollment at Ohio State until the following January which would essentially push him into the following year's recruiting class.

Most of the time the recruit who is asked to delay enrollment gets the hint and "de-commits" when they see the other higher-profile recruit that commits. I've never wanted to "pull" an offer from a kid. While this approach wasn't technically "pulling" an offer it had the same result. It's a shit move this late in recruiting but this year I couldn't be above bending my normal ethics.

Fair or not, Quinn knew that Manny would make us a better offensive football team when it came to throwing the football. Having a tight end that neither linebackers nor safeties could cover one on one made the entire coverage scheme for a defensive coordinator very difficult to devise.

As Quinn arrived at the school Manny was just finishing up basketball practice for a game the next day. Father Flanagan, the team's chaplain and resident OSU fan, sat next to Quinn. He was there for the end of practice before he set up the weekly bingo in the school cafeteria that raised money for the school. He was always good for a joke.

"You gonna come to bingo tonight?" he asked Quinn.

"Depends on whether or not you can fix a game or two for me." Quinn answered.

"Hell Quinn, I'm Irish. Only the Wops can fix games here." He laughed. "But quick question for you. You know what's got 75 balls and screws old ladies once a week? ....Bingo!"

Father Flanagan got up to leave as they both laughed at his joke. Kentucky head coach Mark Stoops was in the gym, seated on the bleachers and watching the last part when the players' conditioning was defending three on two fast breaks. If they got three stops in a row the practice was over.

Manny and a teammate stepped onto the court on defense. The first possession an errant pass ended the possession. On the second possession the offense settled for a missed mid-range jumper that Manny's teammate rebounded. On the third possession Manny's teammate overplayed a pass and left Manny to face a three on one. The guard drove the lane where Manny confronted him before the pass to the other offensive player. With lightning quickness Manny reacted, flew into the air and swatted the attempted dunk.

Across the gym Quinn could see Mark Stoops and his assistant both smiling at Manny's display of athleticism. When they saw Quinn they came over to say hello. Coaches on the road would discuss in general terms how recruiting was going but never got into specific players. Recruiting allows no permanent alliances, it is a landscape of constantly shifting sands.

They did reveal that they'd met with Manny's parents already that day. Manny's mother and father were both on graveyard shift jobs this week. Manny's father had worked at the Lordstown General Motors assembly plant before it shut down. Now they both worked security at night at the vacant plant. His mother also volunteered in the cafeteria at Cardinal Mooney's weekly bingo to help earn a tuition break at the private Catholic school.

That was where Quinn was going to talk to her tonight.

"What are you doing for dinner?" Mark Stoops asked. "If you don't have any plans come down and grab something at the M.V.R. with us."

Quinn didn't have to be asked twice. First the M.V.R. has a great family-run atmosphere and great inexpensive food. Second this was a chance to sit down and talk football with Mark Stoops and that couldn't hurt his coaching career.

5. ROAD GAMES AND HOME GAMES

Inside the MVR, a Youngstown institution, Quinn and Kentucky Head Coach Mark Stoops sat down at a booth covered by a plastic table cloth. Before he even got to look at the menu Quinn could smell the aromas of the kitchen.

On the wood paneled walls hung black and white photos from the glory days of Youngstown sports. This was a proud town and a tough town. No less than five world boxing Champions had risen from these streets most notably Kelly Pavlik and Ray "Boom Boom" Mancini, a favorite among the Italians in town. Above all this town like so many other Ohio Rust Belt cities loved football and punched well above its weight in turning out players.

Mark Stoops was a Youngstown native who played at Cardinal Mooney High School. His brother Ron was meeting him for dinner before Mark headed to Cleveland to see William Wilkins, another player Kentucky was chasing. Over dinner Ron asked about the Ed Hart to Syracuse rumor and Quinn was quick to deny them. Quinn mentioned that some other schools were using those rumors against them in recruiting.

"I'm not sure who all is on that Syracuse list," Mark Stoops said "but one of our guys did a Skype interview with them yesterday."

That got Quinn's attention. He didn't want to reveal that he had interviewed earlier that day in Detroit.

"It turns out our guy played at Syracuse with one of the school's trustees who is also on the search committee. I talked with him on the phone yesterday because they wanted a reference. I'm not sure my guy would go even if they offered, but I'd tell him to go. It is his alma mater and it is a chance to be a head coach."

The Cassese family who owned the place, knew Mark and Ron Stoops well. They brought out bread and large steaming plates of pasta and sausage. In the summer this place hosted Cardinal Mooney's football fund raiser; an all-day bocce tournament that raised well over $100,000.

Quinn was starving and dug right in. During the meal they traded coaching rumors, recruiting rumors and talked about Ohio High School football. Quinn was a native Texan but admitted how impressed he was with the level of play and the top-notch coaching in Ohio.

After dinner Quinn visited with Manny's mother at the Cardinal Mooney Bingo before rushing to the airport to catch the plane back to Columbus. Recruits were coming in the next afternoon for make or break official visits. It was a weekend where we put our best foot forward. If recruits and their families were comfortable with the coaches and their prospective Ohio State teammates we would be in the driver's seat.

Friday morning Quinn and the other assistant coaches were in the office early. The staff was assembled, but also joined by recruiting interns; the vast majority of which were attractive female students. There were four guys in the group of twenty interns who also helped. Another twenty interns were "off duty" for the weekend which meant they did undercover recon at parties the recruits attended.

Ten recruits were coming in and each had two interns assigned to them. Rick Carter paced the room like a Marine Corps Drill Sargent quizzing the interns. They had to know family member's names, hometowns, vital statistics, other schools recruiting them, favorite music or video games among other things. These interns had also been tracking these guys' social media accounts for over a year or two.

Every bit of information collected by the coaches, on social media or on the internet was catalogued and memorized by the interns who would help host them. It was a well-oiled operation.

Then Rick handed out a cheat sheet for all the coaches, including each family member's names. It was also sent to our phones. When we drew blanks on a name, we'd duck into a corner to check the name of a mother, father or brother of an important recruit. It was vital to be right on these things.

Ohio State Recruiting Weekend---Basic Overview/ Tip Sheet

ALREADY COMMITTED:

QB Carter Jones — *Warren Harding HS, OH* — *Mom: Gloria Carter (single mom)*
Academics: Undecided — *Note: Mom works for the county tax office*

DT Marvin Hancock — *O'Dea HS—Seattle, WA* — *Parents: Clyde & step-mom Bonnie*
Academics: Business — *Note: Dad is a Boeing engineer*

ILB Archie Lewis — *Hamilton HS—Hamilton, OH* — *Mom: Shamika Hall*
Academics: Education — *Note: Mom teaches kindergarten*

NOT COMMITTED:

RB Malcolm Jackson — *Palm Bay HS, FL* — *Mom: Wanda Jackson*
Academics: Undecided or CSI — *Note: Mom moving to CLE & looking for work-Legal Sec*
Schools-Rank: ***Florida****, OSU,* ***LSU, Alabama, USC***

OT Jake O'Reilly — *St. Edward HS, OH* — *Parents: Seamus & Patty*
Academics: Finance — *Note: Dad is executive with BP*
Schools-Rank: ***Stanford****, OSU,* ***Notre Dame, Penn State,*** *Michigan*

OT Brad Jones — *Bishop McDevitt HS, PA* — *Parents: Sean and Cindy*
Academics: Pre-Law — *Note: Dad works for State of PA as an auditor Mom is a nurse*
Schools-Not Ranked: OSU, ***Penn State, Notre Dame, Maryland****, Tennessee*

DE Alphonso Simmons — *St Xavier HS, OH* — *Grandmother: Judy Carter Dad: Rex*
Academics: Administration of Justice — *Note: Grandmother is drug/alcohol counselor*
Dad: Construction
Schools-Not Ranked: OSU, Notre Dame, ***Florida, Nebraska, UNC***

OLB Carson Grady — *Allentown Central Cath. HS, PA* — *Parents: Mike and Kathy*
Academics: Pre-Med — *Note: Father is a OB/GYN mom runs the practice*
Schools-Rank: ***Penn State, Notre Dame, Boston College,*** *OSU, Stanford*

OLB Danny Morris — *Piqua HS, OH* — *Parents: Dad -Rob and Stepmom Laurie*
Mom – Allison and stepdad Frank Barnes
IMPORTANT NOTE: Mom lives in Ann Arbor—parents are like oil and water
Academics: Agriculture/ Pre-Vet — *Dad runs a bank, Stepdad is GM exec*
Schools-Rank: ***Michigan, Michigan State,*** *OSU, Notre Dame*

CB Roger Hill — *Hoboken HS, NJ* — *Parents: Robert and Amelia*
Academics: Undecided — *Note: Dad is a police officer*
Schools-Rank: ***UNC****, OSU,* ***Georgia Tech, Michigan****, Rutgers*

CB Darryl White — *Canton McKinley HS, OH* — *Mom: Hannah*
Academics: Education — *Note: Mom runs a daycare center*
Schools-Not Ranked: OSU, ***Michigan State, Nebraska, Michigan****, Penn State*

As recruits arrived throughout the afternoon they were given tours of campus before dinner. After dinner they returned to the football building for dessert and a highlight video. At each seat in the tiered team meeting room, the recruits found a pair of wireless scarlet and grey headphones. They were told to adjust the volume to whatever level they wanted.

On the large screen in front of them, the video was a hard-hitting, fast-paced compilation of great plays from the season. There was even narration by noted Buckeye fan LeBron James. The chairs were wired like a Disney ride and every time a hard hit or touchdown appeared on the video the chairs rumbled and shook. It was just under three minutes long—which we had found really stretched the attention span of the Instagram-twitter-snapchat-TikTok generation.

At the conclusion of the video I stood in front of the group and introduced Archie Griffin, college football's only 2-time Heisman Trophy winner. Archie spoke about tradition but challenged these players to be a part of Ohio State's future.

Running Backs Coach Roger Barstow introduced Archie to Malcolm Jackson and his mother. Wanda's mother had long been a Buckeye fan and knew all about Archie Griffin. Archie told him that he was ready to let someone join him in the lonely two-time Heisman Trophy winner club, but only if he was a Buckeye.

Before the recruits went off with their Ohio State player hosts Quinn made sure that Malcolm and Carter Jones would hang out together. They knew each other, but Quinn pulled Carter aside and told him to work on Malcolm. Malcolm was being hosted by starting running back Pokey Wallace, a Columbus native who knew his way around town.

Quinn pulled Pokey aside and said "Hey, this is a big recruit for us."

"I got this." Pokey said. "I'm the best host on the team."

"You do have a pretty good track record." Quinn admitted.

"Don't worry I got Scary Mary lined up." Pokey laughed.

"Scary Mary?" Quinn said.

"Don't ask coach. It's better for everyone that way."

That night the recruits and their hosts headed to a house party. The house was owned by starting quarterback Marshall Remington's father as his home base when he came to town from California for games. It was a pretty simple stone house, nothing fancy. Marshall used it as a getaway from campus. On weekends Marshall hosted parties for his teammate for two reasons; to build team unity and keep guys out of trouble at the bars.

Tonight the players and the recruits were invited so that they had a place to hang out. As with all of Marshall's parties there were plenty of beautiful girls and a lot of beer. Marshall's Dad had a canned beer-only rule. That meant no hard liquor or mixed drinks where guys could slip drugs into a girl's drink, and no glass to get cut on. It was a pretty smart policy.

In the basement starting wide receiver Anthony Daniels was the DJ. The bass was pulsing through the whole house. This was more than a hobby for Anthony. In high school he ran parties around Chicago's South Side using the money he made to help pay his school tuition at Mount Carmel and to help his single mother and four siblings.

As Malcolm followed Pokey through the kitchen to the basement guys were greeting him. As they descended the stairs Malcolm could feel humid heat rising from the mass of bodies dancing and sweating. The basement was mostly unfinished with cinder block walls exposed on two of the four sides. In the corner a mass of people were standing at a bar drinking beer.

Pokey introduced Malcolm around but everyone already seemed to know who he was. Malcolm was getting a great vibe from his potential future teammates and their friends.

In the basement people were packed in and dancing. Across the room Malcolm saw a beautiful girl dancing and towering over the others. As she saw Pokey she made her way over to them and said hello.

She was stunning. Her long blonde hair, blue eyes and dazzling smile grabbed Malcolm's attention. While Malcolm stood six feet two inches this girl was looking at him almost eye to eye.

"Malcolm," Pokey yelled to him over the loud music "this is Mary. Mary this is Malcolm."

"Great to meet you." Mary smiled at him. "Welcome to OSU. I hear you're from Florida."

"You heard right." Malcolm said.

"They got any Great Whites in the Sunshine state?" Mary asked.

"Sure we got sharks down there." Malcolm said.

Mary laughed and winked at Pokey.

"Malcolm," Pokey said "she ain't talking 'bout marine life."

"Please educate that young man." Mary said "I'm gonna get a drink. You want anything?"

"Nah I'm good thanks." Malcolm said.

"Seriously?" Mary asked.

"Nah, this boy don't drink nuthin'" Pokey said "He's focused so he doesn't put any poison in his system. Ain't that right?"

Malcolm nodded before Pokey started again.

"Mary, this is the best damn running back in the *NATION* comin' out this year. I need him to take over for me when I jump to the league."

"All right I'll be right back." Mary said.

Mary strutted off towards the bar moving to the beat of the bass pumping through the speakers. Malcolm watched her the whole way across the room inspecting every curve of her body.

"What's a Great White?" Malcolm asked.

"Boy you never heard of a Great White? My old school Dad taught me that term. That's pretty much any six-foot white girl....well not any one they've got to look good too. I mean a six-foot white girl that tips the scales at two-fifty is NOT a great white."

"I learned something new on my visit."

"Boy you need to get out more. Forget it, here comes Marshall Remington, the host of the party." Pokey said and nodded in the direction of Ohio State's quarterback.

As Marshall made his way towards them, the mass of people seemed to part instinctively as he strolled casually in their direction.

"Hey Pokey," Marshall Remington said to Pokey as he gave him a hug. "This must be the famous Malcolm Jackson."

"You got that right." Pokey said and turned to introduce Marshall.

Malcolm already knew who Marshall was. He'd watched plenty of Ohio State games on television. These guys were like stars and now he was at their party and they knew all about *him*.

"Hey man," Pokey said to Marshall "would you tell this boy to make up his mind and commit already."

"Malcolm you need to get on board. We got a good team coming back but this guy," he pointed to Pokey "needs help. He needs you to push him and make us all better. I need you to come take his job because he is kinda sorry."

They laughed but Malcolm got the message. The three of them talked for a few minutes and it was easy and comfortable. Malcolm felt at home with the guys he was meeting on the team and that was important to him. They were joined by Carter Jones and he too was hammering Malcolm about coming to join the Buckeyes.

Before Marshall moved on he turned to Malcolm "Hey man give me your number so I can text you and stay in touch. You're gonna be one of us."

After they traded numbers, the conversation stopped when Mary came back with a drink for Pokey. Then she turned to Malcolm and asked him to dance. Who was he to say no? They danced for a while before Mary grabbed his hand whispered into his ear and led him upstairs and to the front door.

"Wait a sec," Malcolm said. "I gotta tell Pokey where I'm going."

"Don't worry, I'll get you back in time tomorrow. You're with me now."

By early morning Malcolm had been through a night he'd never forget before Mary dropped him off at his hotel to get dressed for a full day of recruiting activity. He hoped that his mother hadn't checked on him and found him missing.

When he got to the room Carter Jones, his suite-mate for the weekend, clapped as he came in the room.

"One night in C-Bus and you're taking down top shelf females." Carter said.

Malcolm said nothing and just shrugged his shoulders.

"You think it was fun now, wait until you start scoring touchdowns." Carter laughed. "You know that Mary is on the Volleyball team. You should see her ass in those tight shorts they wear for games. But hey you better get showered. We get picked up for breakfast in half an hour."

"I'm just gonna get changed. I already took a shower."

. . . .

On that official visit Saturday our football office was a hive of activity. Interns and football operations people swarmed Rick Carter who directed all the traffic. With just forty-eight hours allowed under NCAA rules for a visit we needed to squeeze in everything we could. There were meetings to get the recruits to and everything was tightly scripted down to the minute.

Rick called everyone together and asked for any information the interns might have. Ten of them had been at Marshall's party to keep an eye on the guys. Rick wanted to know who looked like they were having fun, who looked distant. He wanted to get all the bits and pieces of conversations that they overheard or even had with the recruits.

One of the interns, Ashleigh Wallace, had caught up with Carson Grady the linebacker from Pennsylvania. He'd told Ashleigh how his sister, a UCLA track athlete, was unhappy there and wanted to transfer to the school her younger brother chose.

Rick told his assistant to get the Ohio State track coach on the phone to set up a meeting with the family. Ashleigh already knew the track team had a weekend meet at Arkansas, so they decided to send a plane to pick up the track coach after the meet. He'd be here for a breakfast meeting with Carson's family the next morning.

The other interns gave Rick bits of information but nothing as big as what had come back on Carson Grady. Overhearing one of the other female interns comment that it was amazing what Ashleigh could pick up in pillow talk, Rick kept his head down and pretended not to hear anything.

In and out of the building it was a constant stream of interns, coaches, recruits and their families. Every time the recruits and their families walked through the glass lobby they passed an array of dozens of trophies that seemed to catch their attention every time. Even after all my years here, I still always notice the seven Heisman Trophies won by Ohio State players in our lobby.

The logistics involved vans and getting people from place to place. Amid the chaos Rick kept his cool, adjusting the schedule if a meeting went longer than expected or if one recruit got off schedule. Juggling recruits' meetings with the coaches, the team academic advisers as well as the medical staff and professors in their academic interest is no easy feat.

Mostly they ate; a big breakfast, followed by a bigger lunch, followed by a huge buffet dinner. It was a day of meetings wedged between meals. And the meals were a constant parade of lobster, filet and prime rib. Alphonso Simmons' Dad Rex was crushing the meals. At dinner he ordered two lobsters and two filets. As I noticed what looked like 8,000+ calories on his plate he laughed.

"I'm gonna get mine on this trip.....when's dessert?" Rex asked.

Finally after dinner we were headed to watch the Ohio State-Michigan State basketball game.

As they entered the game as a group the recruits looked up and marveled at the vast basketball arena where every seat was filled. The coaches and interns walked the recruits right past the students where they began chanting.

"Play for Us! Play For Us! Play for Us!"

Quinn purposely held Malcolm back a few paces behind the group. "Miraculously" the student section saw him and then began to chant his name.

"Mal-colm-Jack-son....Mal-colm-Jack-son"

The truth was interns strategically placed in the student section started the chants. All during the game people approached the recruits. Media photographers snapped their pictures for their publications. Some people even asked for selfies with them. Most of them relished the attention that wasn't completely spontaneous.

At halftime we took the recruits into a lounge to socialize. Defensive End recruit Alphonso Simmons' father Rex approached and asked to speak with me about something privately. I could sense there was something of importance from Rex's manner, so I pulled him to a quiet out-of-the-way corner of the room.

"Coach, my son really likes it here."

"That's great." I said. "Tell him he can get it over with any time he wants."

Rex laughed and answered "Oh he knows that."

"Then what's the hold-up? What can I do to get him off the fence?"

"I'm glad you asked coach. You see my boss where I work construction the owner in fact, is an Ohio State alum. I think you may know him, Mr. Dailey."

"Yes I do. He's given a lot of money to the school."

"Yeah, he tells me he's a big donor. But what I was wanting to ask was could you call him for me? Maybe get me a promotion or a raise? It would sure help our family and help get this process over for us."

"Rex, I'm pretty sure that the NCAA rules don't allow us to do that. But I will look into it and if I am allowed I'd be happy to call."

Rex's hesitation told me he had more to say.

"One other thing Coach. You know I run the weight room at Alphonso's high school. I'm the one who trained him and developed all that size and speed. I train kids from other schools in the area that I can help you with too."

"I'd heard that."

"I'd like to get a job here as a strength coach next year. Alphonso would really be comfortable if I was here helping him train."

I played it carefully. What Rex was asking was against NCAA rules. I didn't know if Rex spoke for the kid so I said I'd check into the NCAA rules and get back to him. Maybe the kid had no idea what his father was doing and maybe he did. Either way Rex put "the ask" right on the table.

Across the room Malcolm's mother Wanda had Dwayne Baxter and Quinn's full attention talking about her recruiting stories. On an earlier visit to LSU she'd met with the running backs coach. Wanda is very religious and takes Malcolm to services every Sunday and Bible Study every Wednesday night. Wanda started a story about the LSU coach recruiting Malcolm.

"On every call the LSU coach talks about his spirituality. On our visit there on his office desk in front of his chair was his Bible. He told me that it was a Bible he'd had for years, his most trusted guide all his life. I looked at that Bible and there wasn't a single crease on that spine. It was like it had never been opened. What kind of fool does he think I am? So I called him out."

"How'd you do that?" Dwayne asked.

"I said coach you've been readin' from that very bible for years? He said "Yes ma'am" and I laughed. I said coach there ain't so much as a single crease in that book. In fact it looks like you just picked that up off the Sam's Club book rack this morning."

They all laughed at Wanda's story.

"You know I like you guys." She laughed "You may be heathens but you don't try to hide it. That's honesty."

Both Dwayne and Quinn recognized a comfort level she'd reached with both of them. They just hoped that it would hold.

"Are you having a good time here among the heathen?" Dwayne asked.

"I sure am. Ultimately I know you guys will take care of Malcolm and that I will be just a few hours away when I move to Cleveland. To me this is the best set-up."

"That's good," Dwayne said "so where does that put us with regards to his timetable?"

"He told me right after dinner that it is down to you guys and Florida. In fact he called the coaches from LSU and USC to tell them they were out of it." Wanda said. "I don't know what his final timeframe for announcing will be yet."

Dwayne excused himself and told Rick that they should schedule a good chunk of time for me to meet with Malcolm tomorrow before he left. We needed to make a big push.

After the game the recruits went back with their hosts for another night out being treated like royalty on the campus of a big-time football program. After another night with Mary, Malcolm needed to be sure that his mother would not see him being dropped off by a college girl, especially a white girl which would bother his mother. He would be subjected to Mom's lecture about pre-marital sex, a man's responsibility and the reminder that his own father had run from them.

As they pulled up to the hotel Malcolm saw Carson Grady getting out of Ashleigh's car at the same time. They made quick eye contact and smiled but kept their heads down hoping none of the parents were in the lobby for an early coffee.

Later in the morning when they all were coming down for breakfast Malcolm and Carson found themselves alone in line at the breakfast buffet. Malcolm told Carson that he was leaning this way and he wanted Carson to be teammates.

During breakfast the Ohio State track coach met Carson's parents. They were impressed he'd been picked up by a private plane just so he could meet with them. He'd tried to recruit their daughter coming out of high school so he let them know that the door was open for her to transfer.

Down the hall from the breakfast room I was meeting with Alphonso Simmons. At the end of the meeting Alphonso told me that he liked everything about Ohio State. He was considering cancelling his last visit to Georgia Tech and he would let me know. As they stood up Rex paused and turned to me as Alphonso left the room. As he shook my hand Rex looked me right in the eye.

"Coach, he is sincere in what he's saying." Rex said.

"Good. What do we need to do to close this out?"

"I think you know what I mentioned to you last night."

"Okay. We'll talk tonight or tomorrow morning. I'll let you guys get home and watch the NFL playoffs. That should give you guys a chance to talk." I said.

As Rex walked out of the room Malcolm and Wanda Jackson walked in. As the meeting's conversation carried on in the ornate hotel conference room, Wanda's comfort level with me soared. When we talked we spoke directly and honestly, there was no sales pitch bullshit. She liked that.

Then Malcolm threw me an unexpected curve ball when told me that Ohio State was his choice to commit. He planned to make it official Wednesday when he announced for us at his school. His mom looked on with a wide smile. This was a special moment for her too.

I was stunned, but happily stunned. This was a huge pull for our recruiting class, one that would shake things up. We'd gone to Florida and pulled the nation's top running back from SEC country.

"That is *great* news, unexpected and GREAT!" I said. "Welcome to the family!"

I stood up and gave Wanda a big hug and then hugged Malcolm. Dwayne was beaming and he hugged both of them too.

"Dwayne, get some of the other guys." I started to say.

"Coach, can you hold on a minute?" Malcolm asked.

"Okay. What's up?"

"Coach I'd like to keep this quiet until Wednesday for my press conference. I want to call the coaches at Florida before I announce. I want them to hear it directly from me. They've been recruiting me for years and I think it is only fair. I've already told LSU and USC that they are out."

I was impressed at this young man's consideration for the people who'd invested so much time in him. This kid had class written all over him.

"Okay, Dwayne and I will keep it quiet. But I am excited. I will be grinning like an idiot for the next three days until you announce."

On his way out of the meeting Malcolm saw Carson. He pulled him aside quickly and let him know he was announcing for Ohio State on Wednesday. He asked Carson to keep it quiet, but also asked him to join this team. Carson told him that Ohio State had pulled in front of everyone else. The visit had been phenomenal.

The Grady family came in to meet with me. They were impressed with the track coach who'd just talked to them about Carson's sister and her potential future at Ohio State. It demonstrated in their minds that this coaching staff cared for the whole family.

That gesture alone created a huge turnaround for Carson's Mom. She was concerned about the size of Columbus and that her son might get lost out here. Having his older sister with him would be huge. No other school had thought to arrange for the track coach to meet with them. In her mind this was a staff that paid attention to every detail.

By mid-afternoon all the recruits were gone and the staff had met to plot their next week on the road recruiting. It had been a great visit. On his way home Malcolm had called Dwayne to tell him that Carson had Ohio State as his number one and that Carson' parents felt the same way.

The plan was to get me on the road to see Carter Jones at his school and then get to see Simmons, Jackson and Grady. We wanted to close out Simmons on Monday if possible, then see Jackson Tuesday so Wednesday's announcement would look as though the head coach's pitch in the home visit had done the trick. Then I would see Grady to try and get that done and then see Jones.

It was as much recruiting as it was media-driven. The Ohio State trustees and fans would see a huge recruiting week if I went on the road and closed out Jackson, Grady and Simmons. Those three commitments alone would rocket us into the Top 5.

After the meeting the coaches went home to spend a few hours with their families before heading back on the recruiting trail Monday morning.

About five o'clock Dwayne's phone rang. It was a Florida number that he did not recognize. It was a familiar area code, the same one as Melbourne, Florida. Dwayne normally avoided calls from numbers he didn't recognize but it was the stretch run of the recruiting season so he answered it.

"Hello is this Dwayne Baxter?" a voice asked.

"Yes it is."

"Coach, we haven't met but I am calling from Melbourne, Florida. I am Minister Carl Johnson and am the head pastor at Faith and Hope Church."

"What can I do for you?" Dwayne asked.

"Well you see as part of my church I have a large youth ministry. I take a very active role in advising the young people. One of my best protégés is someone you are familiar with—Malcolm Jackson. He is very high on your school and I know you guys are very interested in him. As his spiritual adviser I have a very active role advising him on his future."

"I do know that both he and his mother are very involved in your church." Dwayne said.

"I wanted to call and talk to you. You see the people of this community have put a lot into Malcolm and he represents the hopes of many in his church. We just want a way to see Jesus' will through Malcolm's career where he can achieve stardom and become a vessel for the glorification of Christ."

"Well we hope he comes here and does just that." Dwayne said.

"Yes, but for our church community they will be asking me what kind of guidance I will be giving to Malcolm and his mother. As part of that I want to know if you are a man of the word and a man of your word."

Dwayne did not like the way this conversation was going. Even over the phone he could tell this guy was a grade-A bullshit artist wrapping himself up in the cloth.

"Pastor Johnson, I may not be the model Christian but I can tell you that you have my word that we will do everything here at Ohio State for him to have a great future."

"I hear you, but you see we don't really know each other. If there was some way, some act to open my eyes to see your intentions."

"I can come see you this week when we come to visit Malcolm and we could talk then."

"No, no...in fact it is best that we do not meet. What I had in mind was a donation to our church's needy family ministry."

"A donation?"

"Yes, yes.....perhaps a gift from one of your alumni who live in Florida that would enable us to minister to families in this community who need financial assistance. We do a great deal of good helping households headed by single mothers including Wanda Jackson."

"Can you fucking believe this?" Dwayne thought to himself. I'm getting a shakedown from a minister. He figured he'd better find out how much he was looking for.

"What kind of gift are we talking?" Dwayne asked.

"If you could arrange a gift totaling $200,000, that would do so much good in our community. It would really enable me to counsel young Malcolm to make the right decision in his life." Pastor Johnson said.

Dwayne had seen some things in his days but a Pastor calling up and asking for that kind of money was pretty ballsy. Dwayne promised the Pastor he would look into what could be done and get back to him. The Pastor explained that he would call back the next afternoon on this phone. He told Dwayne not to call him as this was a phone that he would not answer.

Dwayne drove over to my home to speak to me personally. This was not a conversation that he wanted to have over a university-supplied cell phone. As we sat in my den Dwayne laid out what the Pastor had asked for in the phone call.

"That is some shady shit." I said.

"Yes. He flat out told me that $200,000 would help him guide Malcolm's decision."

I was not surprised but the excitement of Malcolm's commitment was now in doubt. Dwayne could see my concerned expression as I stared straight ahead. Feeling the uncomfortable tension, Dwayne looked around the room at photos of teams and players I had coached over the years. We sat quietly for a few moments pondering our next move.

"You think the other schools have already made their gifts?" I asked.

"I'm not sure, but I just wanted you to know where we are at."

"Well are we even sure that Malcolm or his mother are even aware of this ask?"

"I'm not sure. Should I bring it up with them?"

"No, no don't talk about this with anybody else. Whatever path we take has to be kept between us. As far as Malcolm goes, he may not even know and if we bring it up then we have pitted ourselves against their Pastor who from what I understand is a big part of their lives. We can't side against him, because we will most likely lose."

"I did talk with some coaches I know down there and asked about this guy. They said he asks for money and if he gets it he takes a cut. It is a genius scheme. The alums who donate to the church get a tax deductible donation and plausible deniability that any of the money was targeted to a recruiting payoff in any way."

"That is genius." I said.

"Maybe I should call his bluff and tell him we won't get into that."

"No don't tell him that. This player is too big a get for us to not play the game. Let me think about this overnight."

"Okay Coach. He's going to call me around mid-day tomorrow so let me know how we play this one."

When Dwayne left, I returned to sit at my desk facing a critical decision all alone. This week I could visit two recruits and get commitments from both. The recruiting class would catch fire with huge momentum to get the alums and fair-weather fans off of my back. Above all making the payout to the Pastor and getting Alphonso Simmons' father a raise at work would get two game-changing players that would make us a better football team right away.

A great recruiting class was critical to holding onto my job, but I faced ethical decisions I'd never stared down before. It would be easy to give in, but could I live with myself? In the corner of the den the grandfather clock ticked away the seconds before ultimately tolling the change to a new hour.

6. THE FINISHING KICK

All night long I tossed and turned because the best running back in the country wanted to come to Ohio State from SEC-territory. But......

Now we're dealing with an evangelical shakedown to get the kid here. This would be a huge recruiting coup for us, but at what price? Is it a set-up? Is this pastor taping these conversations to catch us cheating? What would I do if I absolutely knew we would get away with it?

At 4:30 a.m. I was still twisting both ways.

"What's bugging you?" Candace asked. "Your tossing is keeping me up too. Anything you want to talk about?"

"Nothing I could share with you."

"You can't tell me?" She sat up and turned on a small lamp on the nightstand.

"No." I said as I rolled to face her.

"Well, every night since we got back from the game, you've been tossing and turning and your sleep patterns have been a mess." There was concern in her voice. "And now you tell me you can't talk about it? Just remember I'm on your side, I'm on your team no matter what."

She was right, but how could I explain that after twenty plus years of coaching I was seriously considering buying a couple of recruits to save my own ass? I couldn't.

"Nah, it's really nothing I can talk about." I repeated.

"Then do me a favor....go battle your demons in the den. That's where you do your best thinking."

When my wife tells me to do something.......I went to the den.

A recruiting payoff was dangerous but this would buy me a lot of political capital. Admittedly I was a little bit surprised because I assumed the going rate for a kid as talented as Malcolm Jackson would be higher. Back in the mid-1990s schools tried to buy a defensive tackle out of Memphis for $250,000. Even Cam Newton's father allegedly asked for $250,000.

This was the way to do it. When people handed bags of cash to recruits or high school coaches, there was always the problem of what to do with the cash and if the plot was revealed there were serious tax consequences. The church scheme was beautiful. On the church's books the "needy family fund" could be distributed to several families when in fact the cash would be given to the recruit's family.

On top of everything, the NCAA was not going anywhere near the politics of church finances.

In the inside of the window pane I caught sight of my own reflection. Could I face myself knowing that I'd broken the rules? Could I bear to lose this job and everything that comes with it. The money, the fame and the roar of the Ohio Stadium crowd when a running back breaks into the open on a Saturday night?

And what about my wife, my family, my friends? What would they think of me if my face was plastered across web sites, newspapers and on ESPN if we got caught? My father never cut a corner or took payouts to help people get union jobs. It killed him young but he went with his integrity intact.

I'd go see Jackson tomorrow and if we got him without paying the minister then, so be it. If we didn't get him we'd go fight like hell to get one of the two tailbacks we were recruiting in Ohio.

I got my cell phone and dialed Dwayne. It took four rings for him to answer.

"Did I wake you up Dwayne?" I asked.

"Yeah Coach, I won't lie. You sure did.What's up?"

I told him that I decided not to pay the minister but we'd still visit Malcolm the next day.

"Look I know you've put a lot of effort into this one and who knows maybe we'll still get him. But we're going to do this the right way." I said.

Deep down, this was not the news Dwayne wanted to hear.

"We won't get him coach. I talked to a couple of guys down there. The minister has his congregation completely drinking his Kool-Aid."

"Well, I'm going to give it a shot, but in the meantime I'm going to tell Roger Bartsow to go after Aaron Smith full speed ahead. We've got to get a running back. I like Malcolm but we just can't do it this way."

The words hit Dwayne. After he hung up with Ed he sat on the edge of the bed and stared at the wall. He'd put two years into Malcolm. Because he was not a defensive coordinator he knew the fastest way to raise his profile was to create a reputation as a national recruiter—particularly in Florida.

He couldn't let it go. Then it hit him; Frank Stetson.

Frank Stetson was a Florida State alum who'd helped Dwayne get a lot of the Northeast Florida talent. With a construction firm that did work from the Georgia line all the way south to Vero Beach, he'd built more beachfront condos than maybe anyone else on the planet. The players who went to FSU from that area referred to him as "Chief Osceola".

Florida State wasn't in it for Malcolm. He'd eliminated them a long time ago but Dwayne knew where Malcolm was going if he didn't pick the Buckeyes. In recruiting, each recruit creates temporary alliances. The enemy of my enemy is my friend.

Dwayne knew Frank Stetson wouldn't want to see Malcolm Jackson become a Florida Gator. Dwayne's and Frank Stetson's mutual enemy was Florida. Maybe Frank would donate money so that Pastor Johnson would not let Malcolm go to Florida where he'd play FSU every year.

"It's worth a shot...." Dwayne told himself. "Hell 200K isn't a lot to pay to keep from having to play Malcolm every year. Stetson wakes up every morning and shits out 200K just to start his day."

Dwayne knew he couldn't call up Frank Stetson himself. He'd leave that to his agent Derrick Anderson in Atlanta. There could be no record of any direct contact between Dwayne and Frank Stetson. Landing the top running back recruit in the country would boost Dwayne's stock and that was what agents are supposed to do.

Later that morning Dwayne got Derrick on the phone to explain the situation. Derrick understood this would have to be handled discreetly. Derrick represented current assistant coaches from Florida State and Georgia so he'd heard rumors that Florida was ready to pay Malcolm.

Derrick agreed to contact Frank Stetson for Dwayne. He sent Stetson a text saying he wanted to talk about a search for Florida State assistant coaches. That way he'd have an electronic cover story for calling Stetson if anyone ever dug into this. This whole business was about plausible deniability and the text created an alternate explanation for the call.

As one veteran coach and a successful cheater for many years once said "As long as you are willing to deal with cash and are willing to lie you'll be okay."

But since 9/11 and the mad drug rush of 1980s Miami, cash had become a lot tougher to move in large amounts. Today's investigations all focus on electronic data; e-mails, phone calls and text messages leave trails. The trick was to make them point people the other way.

I got ready to go on the road feeling that I'd done the right thing. Dwayne felt good because he'd taken the steps needed to win and do it in a way that could never come back on him or on me.

By Monday afternoon Doug Leonard and I were visiting Alphonso Simmons and his father Rex at his high school. Rex asked to speak to me alone. Rex once again asked for a promotion at work until he was hired as a strength coach by Ohio State.

"Rex, you know I can't do either of those things. They would put our program and your son's NCAA eligibility in jeopardy." I said.

"Hey come on coach. I know how this game works. There are plenty of other schools that will do what I asked."

"Well that's something that I'm just going to have to live with." I said.

"Well is that your final position? You're telling me no?" Rex asked.

"Yes I am."

"Okay then coach. Just to be fair and let you know we're going to announce for Georgia Tech tomorrow morning."

I was enraged but held my emotions in check. Alphonso hadn't even taken his official visit to Tech and now he was going to announce for them the morning after I visited his school. It would be a very public and damaging rebuke of our recruiting.

"Did they promise you a job?" I demanded.

Rex laughed the laugh of someone who held the cards and the power.

"Now coach," Rex said "you know that's against NCAA rules."

My emotions burst forth and pointing my index finger at Rex, I spoke directly, but calmly with anger in my voice.

"Look Rex, you better have everything straight and above board because I am going to look under every rock. If I find one shred of evidence I will bury you with it."

Rex was taken aback by being chastised.

"Coach, then you and I got nothing left to say to each other."

I stormed out of the room and back into another room where Doug Leonard was still talking to Alphonso. I shook Alphonso's hand and wished him luck in making his decision. Then Doug and I walked out of the school.

Doug could sense my anger but knew not to ask until we got into the car. Once we'd driven away Doug asked what was wrong.

"He's going to Georgia Tech and he's announcing tomorrow." I said.

"What? He never said a word."

"He doesn't know. His father asked me for a deal on Saturday night and I told him no so he's going there. They must've bought him."

"What did he ask for?"

"He wants me to get his boss to promote him until we hire him as a strength coach."

"We can't do that?"

"I didn't put all these years in to start compromising my values now."

At the airport a private jet waited to take us home. Getting home at night allowed me to catch up on correspondence and sleep in my own bed before flying down to see Malcolm the next day. We were going to take a hit on Simmons' announcement. We hoped to hold onto Jackson and get him to announce on Wednesday morning to blow up the bad news cycle day.

Before we took off, I called Dwayne in New Jersey and on his way back to the airport from Hoboken High School. Dwayne had gotten the message from Derrick Anderson that he'd wanted. Unknown to me, Frank Stetson was coming through to prevent Malcolm from going to Florida.

"Dwayne, how are we doing with the DBs? You're in Jersey visiting Roger Hill right?" I asked.

"Yeah coach and then I am off to see Darryl White in Canton before I go to Florida in the morning."

"How are we with Hill?"

"Our visit really got him excited. It is down to us and UNC."

UNC was the last school that I wanted to hear about right now.

“Shit.” I said.

“What’s up?”

“Is there anyone tougher to recruit against right now than Mack Brown? He’s killing it there.”

“The big draw with UNC is the basketball. He wants to play both football and basketball and they’ve told him he can play both. They’ve convinced him that he can be an NBA point guard.”

“He’s six-one right? A six-one point guard is just a guy in the NBA. In the NFL a six-one corner with cover skills is All-Pro. In the NBA he’s competing for a job with players from all over the world. In the NFL if he’s the best corner in the country coming out of college, he’s the best corner in the world period.”

“He knows he can play both at our school. Hell he just watched our guys beat Michigan State Saturday night. I’ll work on that angle about all the international players in the NBA. I hadn’t thought of that.”

“How are things with Darryl White?”

“Good news Ed, Darryl is really religious too.” Dwayne laughed. “Apparently his Pastor would like some help guiding him to Ohio State.”

“Tell me you’re kidding me.”

“I wish I was.”

“Well let’s get one of the other guys. The last thing we can afford to do is arrange payoffs to ministers in Canton. That’ll get all over the state and the next thing you know we’ll have ministers recruiting high school prospects so they can get payoffs too.”

“Okay we’ll go hard after the other guys.”

“How are we with Malcolm? Are we still solid with him or are we gonna need to aid that process?”

“He’s solid. I think the minister was over-playing his role. As far as I can tell Malcolm didn’t even know that the minister was out making that ask.”

“Okay. We are going to need his announcement on Wednesday to create some big momentum.”

“Well I will see you tomorrow coach.”

They hung up and each headed to their next destination.

No one had talked to Quinn that day. A private plane had picked him up in Columbus and taken him to Syracuse. No one saw him get on or off the plane. But a dispatcher at the Syracuse airport had noticed a private plane owned by university Trustee Steve Tanner had picked up someone in Columbus and brought him to town. The dispatcher had been paid by a Syracuse Sports Fan Web Site to keep an eye on the comings and goings for potential head coaches.

The dispatcher called the web site operator and informed him that someone had flown in from Columbus which renewed speculation. The web site ran with a story that I'd been flown in late afternoon and was meeting with University officials at an undisclosed hotel location somewhere near the airport.

They were able to sneak Quinn out of the airport before anyone else knew. He toured the facilities after five p.m. when all the university athletic department staff had left for the night. He sat down once again with the Athletic Director and University President and Steve Tanner. They were down to three candidates and would be making a decision before the end of the week.

Because the story had gotten out about the plane they arranged to have a car drive Quinn to Rochester where the plane would pick him up and fly him back to Columbus.

Back in Columbus Sid Inge had gotten a call from a newspaper writer about the rumors popping up again on the internet about me going to interview at Syracuse. He called me at home.

"Ed I have to ask you about another story that's popped up. A writer in Syracuse has you on a private plane owned by a Syracuse University Trustee flying from Columbus to Syracuse today. Anything I need to be aware of?"

"Hell no. I was in Cincinnati visiting Alphonso Simmons today. I've got plenty of witnesses."

"Okay, I'll tell them that you were in Cincinnati recruiting. Thanks Ed."

The fact that we were losing Simmons made me think of Jamar Tucker. If Jamar could make a full recovery we wouldn't need Simmons anyway. To get an update I called Rick Carter who was evasive about Jamar's long-range prognosis but only because he did not have a good answer, and neither did the medical staff yet.

Before trying to sleep I said a couple of extra prayers for Jamar's full recovery, mostly for Jamar's future, but also for my own. Then I chugged some Nyquil to knock myself out.

. . . .

Tuesday morning the day was heating up. By ten a.m. Dave Cafiero was on his way to California, Quinn was on his way to Mississippi and Dwayne was headed to the airport to meet me for our flight to Florida to see both Malcolm Jackson and Boxer Davis.

Quinn's job was to go establish a contact at Provine High School in Jackson, Mississippi where the top junior quarterback in the country was playing. There was also a big-time junior defensive tackle at Neshoba Central High School in Philadelphia, Mississippi so he would see both guys on that swing. The coach at Provine had been a senior at Houston when Quinn was a freshman so he had an in with that coach. The defensive tackle had relatives in Dayton, Ohio and had been a Buckeye fan for years.

In Cincinnati Alphonso had his press conference announcing that he was going to Georgia Tech. The message boards, blogosphere, and social media universe blew up. The reaction to Simmons leaving the state to go to an inferior team in the ACC angered almost everyone. Immediately the Ohio State fans started attacking me for losing this kid.

I had to sit quietly knowing that Simmons may have been bought. We could've leaked some things but I knew it'd look like sour grapes. We needed to nail down Jackson's announcement to re-energize everyone. Losing a defensive end is one thing, but picking up the nation's top-rated running back from Florida would make everyone forget Simmons.

Just before I got into the car my phone rang, it was Gerry Gorton.

"Ed what the hell happened with Simmons? I've got a big trustee from Cincinnati who wants your head on a platter for this. He told me you walked out on the kid at his school yesterday. Please tell me that is not true."

"It's true."

"What?" Gerry was in disbelief.

"Simmons' dad asked me to talk to his boss and get him promoted to a high-paying no-show job and then wanted us to hire him as a strength coach; which he is unqualified to do. All of that is against NCAA rules. I told him we couldn't do that, he told me they were going to Georgia Tech so I left."

"Oh shit. How can we handle this with the media?"

“We can’t. What we can do is watch this play out and then turn in Georgia Tech.”

“Okay. I just can’t believe stuff like this goes on.”

“With all due respect you have no idea. There are ministers shaking us down for $200,000 so they will give players spiritual guidance to come to Ohio State.”

Gerry Gorton had been in academia for a long time so this was news to him. He inhaled a deep breath before he spoke.

“Are you serious?” He asked.

“Dead serious. We’ve come a long way from the old MUTT scholarships.”

“MUTT scholarships?”

“Money Under The Table—the acronym being M.U.T.T....hell old coaches used to keep a safe in their office for the cash.”

“I guess it’s gotten more sophisticated. What did you tell them?”

“The only thing I could tell them; N-O.”

“Okay, God this is no fun. I’ll have to call this guy back and set him straight.”

“I do have some great news for you.”

“Oh yeah?”

“Yes sir, tomorrow Malcolm Jackson, the top running back in the country is going to announce that he will be a Buckeye next fall. So the Simmons news cycle won’t last.”

“That is fantastic.”

“As for defensive ends we have Tucker from Benedictine. He’s the better of the two players between Simmons and Tucker.”

“Tucker....you mean the kid who got shot?”

“Yeah. He’s gonna be okay long term.”

Now Gerry was worried about his school admitting a kid who had been involved in a shooting. The streets and what went on there were a million miles from Gerry’s life experience.

“What kind of a kid gets caught up in the kind of things that get him shot?” Gerry asked.

“He’s a great kid. But his family situation is a complete mess. The shooting was in no way his fault.”

“Okay, I just don’t want us recruiting trouble.....unless they can get to the quarterback or run for touchdowns.” He laughed just enough to let me know he was kidding...mostly.

“No, not at all.”

“Hey I know the President at Georgia Tech do you want me to call him on this?”

“No, not yet. If they hire Simmons’ Dad then we’ll make our move.”

“Okay. I am elated about Jackson though. That is tremendous news. I’ll call back that trustee and tell him about it.”

“Please don’t do that. Jackson asked us to keep this quiet until he announces. He wants to tell the Florida coaches before it gets out. He wants to respect the time and effort they put into recruiting him.”

“Wow, that’s a respectful kid.”

“Just wait until you see him play.”

We finished up the conversation because I had pulled up to the airport. Now I really had to deliver on Jackson this afternoon. If we lost him I’d look like an idiot. I’d shown my cards.

Gerry immediately dialed back the trustee from Cincinnati who’d called him earlier about the team losing Simmons. After they exchanged greetings Gerry got to the point of the call.

“I know you’re upset about Simmons, but I just talked to Ed. They’re getting Tucker from Cleveland who they think is the better player.” Gerry said. “He’ll make a full recovery before the fall. But I have even better news that will blow you away. You can’t share this with anyone, in fact I’m not even supposed to know. You didn’t hear this from me......but tomorrow morning Malcolm Jackson is announcing for us.”

. . . .

Down in Mississippi Quinn had landed in Meridian, MS and drove to to Neshoba Central High School to watch a lunch time workout by Andre Carter. He was the top junior defensive tackle in the south and his workout justified the hype. He was all of six-foot four and all of three hundred pounds and unbelievably light on his feet. Quinn just could not believe his quickness.

His Coach Terry Allen spoke in a thick southern drawl.

“Well son,” he said to Quinn “that young man raught they-ah plays centerfield on our baseball team. Now I don’t know what baseball is like for y’all up in Ohio but down here we take it real serious.”

“Coach,” Quinn responded “you don’t have to tell me. I pitched for my high school team in Texas. But I gotta admit, I ain’t never seen a man as big as Andre playin’ centerfield. He mus’ be legit ‘cause y’all got a great baseball team.”

When Quinn recruited in the South, he broke out some drawl and casually dropped in a reference to his Texas roots.

“There was a kid, damn near as big as him that played centerfield up in Amory back in the late nineties but he wasn’t quite as big as Andre.” Terry Allen said.

“Well if you don’t mind can you do me a favor? Jus’ tell him he’s got an offer from Ohio State. I just wanted all y’all to hear it from us. And he’ll be close to his kin up in Dayton.”

“How far is Dayton from y’all’s campus?”

“Less than two hours.”

“Okay, I was just wonderin’, see I was thinkin’ about bringin’ Andre and some of the other boys up to y’all’s camp this summah.”

“That’d be great.”

Quinn wasn’t allowed to talk to Andre, but during his workout Andre walked over to Coach Allen and “bumped” into Quinn. That was how the game worked.

Terry Allen told him another school avoided the non-contact rule in a unique way. Andre sat in the school Athletic Director’s office across from Terry’s office. Andre talked to the coach over the phone from the next office. They could see each other through a window like a prison visit. Technically they didn’t break any rules....technically, and it left no electronic footprint.

Quinn got in his car and drove to Jackson and Provine High School to watch basketball practice. On the court he watched Walker McCoy a six-foot five, two hundred twenty pound quarterback who was the closest thing Quinn had seen to Vince Young...ever. He was a phenomenal athlete. Though still in his junior year he had over eighty offers from Oregon to Miami to USC to Texas to Ohio State to Florida and everyone in between. He had a chance to be ranked the number one recruit in the country for next year.

The visit gave Quinn a chance to catch up with Reggie Thornton who'd been the starting QB at Houston when Quinn got there as a freshman. He helped Quinn adjust to college life and the two had stayed in touch. This was the biggest recruit Reggie had coached since he became the head coach at Provine.

They sat in the bleachers watching basketball practice. Hanging on the walls and from the rafters, faded banners marked past championship teams in this dusty old gym.

As an athlete Walker was as good as his rep. As a student, there were some warning signs. He was a great student through ninth and tenth grade then in the first two marking periods of his junior year his grades just fell off the cliff. What had been all As and Bs was now mostly Cs and a D.

Quinn questioned the guidance counselor who happened to know Walker and his family situation well. After practice Quinn wanted to talk to Reggie about Walker's grades.

"Okay, because there is some drama in his backstory, and we're trying to work it out. Hey let's go down the block and eat. My sister's got a Soul Food place half a block away. I guarantee it'll be the best meal you'll have on the road recruiting all winter."

They went into the little joint and got their trays. The food was served cafeteria style and it was $7.99 for all you could eat. The sweet tea was a dollar and a half with free refills. In the line Quinn got everything Reggie told him to get, greens, a thick slab of cornbread, ribs, some beans but Quinn drew the line on chitlins. The cornbread was heavy enough to be a doorstop.

"No chitlins? Come on man you were doing so well." Reggie said.

"Look Reggie, I might be a white boy but I do know where chitlins come from. I draw the line on eating anything from the wrong end of a pig's digestive track."

Reggie laughed "Fair enough, but I'm sure you've eaten some hot dogs and sausages that were made from parts unknown on a pig."

"Yes....but those parts are unknown....and what I don't know....."

Reggie's sister came out from in the kitchen in back. She gave Quinn a big hug and he could smell the sauces and spices from the kitchen on her.

"Damn," Quinn said "don't you just smell like the good food comin' out of that kitchen? This place smells so good they oughtta make a soul food kitchen air freshener."

"Thanks. It is good to see you Quinn. Reggie tells me I'll be seeing you down here quite a bit with this kid he's got."

They chatted for a few moments before she shooed them away to eat before their food got cold. They sat at a back table away from the other customers so Quinn could get the story on Walker's sudden downturn in his academics.

When Walker was young, his father had gotten shot and killed and now his mother was battling opioid addiction. All this happened after the summer of his tenth grade year. His mother was having an affair with a married doctor. Everyone blamed him for getting her hooked on drugs before he left her. Walker wasn't happy with her current boyfriend and there'd nearly been a few fights. Because Walker was bigger and stronger, the boyfriend threatened to shoot Walker and "put him in the ground next to your old man."

Walker moved in with an aunt but now that he was seemingly destined for the pros, everyone who was even remotely related to him had come out of the woodwork. They all wanted a piece of whatever was coming Walker's way in college and as a pro. They were all pushing him to Ole Miss.

Reggie felt that it would be best for Walker to go far away from Jackson, get away from his mother and the boyfriend. That was why Reggie had called Quinn, he wanted Walker with someone he could trust to watch over him.

. . . .

That afternoon Dwayne and I had arrived at the high school to see Malcolm Jackson and his mother Wanda. When we got in the school Malcolm seemed a little upset as we sat down to talk.

"Malcolm," I said "you seem upset. What is bugging you?"

"Coach, we have to trust each other right?" Malcolm asked.

"That is absolutely right. It is the only way a team can survive." I responded.

Malcolm remained quiet. He looked around the white-painted cinder block walls of the coach's office and out the window that looked out into the team's weight room. Many of his teammates were in there lifting and the music was loud. The yells of guys exerting themselves punctured the beats of the music.

"Well Coach I told you something and asked you to keep it secret. I didn't want anyone to know before tomorrow morning that I was going to announce my commitment."

"That's right."

"About half an hour ago I got a call from the Florida coaches asking me why I'd already committed to Ohio State and why I hadn't called them to tell them. They were pissed."

"Malcolm I don't know what you're talking about."

"Coach it was on the internet that you told a big Ohio State booster that I committed over the weekend." Malcolm said.

There was no anger in his voice it was more like he'd been hurt.

"Malcolm I haven't talked to any booster about this. That is not how I do things."

"Coach, this guy knew I committed over the weekend. How'd he find out? I mean if you've already shaken my trust in you guys I have to reconsider my commitment."

The room grew silent. I began to think that maybe Florida had gotten to the Pastor and they set up this cover story to throw them off the trail of what had really happened. Maybe that was the plan all along, fake the commitment to get Florida to buy in to keep Jackson in state. Either way the next few minutes were now vital.

I was also thinking about what I'd told Gerry this morning.

"Malcolm the one thing you get in recruiting is a lot of people who make guesses and shoot their mouths off." I said. "Have you put it out there that you're announcing tomorrow morning?"

"Yes I did coach."

"Okay that gets everyone on those message boards talking. So some Ohio State alum wants to be the big shot on the message board and concocts a story that he alleges he got directly from me. If he's wrong no one cares, but if he's right he looks like the big man with the inside connections on the message board. It's pretty much a 50-50 shot for him with no real downside."

"Coach I'm still not sure but there was one thing that saved you." Malcolm said.

“What’s that?” I asked.

“Well I called Pastor Johnson on the phone right after I heard this. He believes that I should go to Ohio State.”

I was surprised. Dwayne looked at me and shrugged his shoulders.

Wanda came in to see us and we had a great visit. She did ask about the contact Quinn had mentioned, the attorney who worked in Cleveland. Dwayne gave Wanda the contact information but asked her not to contact Cecelia until three weeks after signing day. Wanda was elated and as we left she hugged us again.

In the car on the way to the airport I asked Dwayne about Pastor Johnson’s advice.

“How in the hell did that happen?” I asked.

“I don’t know. I’ve had no contact with him since the first time he called to ask for the cash.”

Did I sense some defensiveness in Dwayne’s tone. I’d only known Dwayne for a few years so how well did I really know him? Was Dwayne capable of pulling something off like this?

Dwayne continued to talk “Maybe Ed the Pastor was testing all the schools and we didn’t pay him so he knew we are sincere.”

“Could be, could be.” I said. “Maybe for once the good guys get ahead.”

It was easy to believe what I wanted to be true.

. . . .

After Quinn flew back from Mississippi he was driving back to his house in Columbus when he got a call from his agent. Syracuse was going to hire the assistant from Kentucky. Quinn told him what he’d heard from Mark Stoops up in Youngstown, so he was not surprised. A lot of these decisions came down to who you knew on the committee. Quinn was an unknown to them.

It looked as though he would have to wait one more year, but he was concerned about the direction that I wanted to take the offense. He’d just have to wait and see. In the mean time we were getting recruits that could help him this year.

7. SIGNING DAY AND THE OFFSEASON

One week before signing day Rick Carter was excited about the recruiting class we'd put together, a class projected to be in everyone's national top five and the best in the Big Ten.

"Coach," Rick Carter said to me "let's do a big signing day event to announce the class to our fans. You know a lot of schools do that."

"Why would we want to do that?" I asked.

"It promotes the class and hypes everyone up."

"I don't want to get into promoting kids who haven't even set foot on campus yet. Let the NFL do that crap for the draft."

"But Coach every school is doing these events."

I was frustrated because I wasn't getting through to Rick.

"You think I give a crap what everyone else is doing? I'm not getting into the bullshit false hype everyone else is getting into. Plenty of coaches win on signing day only to get fired because they spend all their time chasing the next recruiting class at the expense of really developing the guys they have on their team already. And with the transfer rules we better be sure we're keeping the guys that are already on our team."

"Gotcha Coach, I just wanted to check. It wasn't just my idea."

"Oh yeah? Who else wants to do this?"

"Well Art Simpson called. It appears that Gerry Gorton wants to have an event."

"Gerry Gorton?"

"Yeah he told Art that it would be a great idea to have some big donors come spend the day in the recruiting war room, watch the letters come in and watch the recruiting coverage. We kind of made a deal that $1 million football donors would be invited to any special events."

"So we're selling program access? That may be the worst idea I've ever heard. I don't want people walking around our building when we're trying to work. I'll call Gerry and tell him no."

With just three more days allowed for off-campus recruiting our staff was in the building to get organized before they headed back out. Our commitments were solid with the possibility of adding one or two other players on signing day a week later.

To start the meeting Rick Carter gave a Social Media update on every recruit. The interns followed the recruits and tabulated what they were saying on social media to track their attitudes towards us.

We'd even hired an outside social media analysis firm that worked for Wall Street investment firms. In the financial world these firms searched all social media mentions of companies and certain words associated with things that were either positive or negative. Art Simpson and I hired the firm to track perceptions of Ohio State Football which included recruiting.

But the basic groundwork of social media monitoring was still done by the interns and they were by design very aggressive on that front. Rick had professional profile pictures of the interns taken and re-touched to make them look fantastic. Of course other pictures taken around campus were posed to make them look like spontaneous shots.

By late morning Malcolm held his press conference at his school to announce for us. The social media and the message boards on the Go-O-State.com site lit up. The same fans who were maligning me for losing in-state player Simmons were now praising me as a "national" recruiter. On national recruiting sites Dwayne Baxter was being hailed as one of the fastest rising assistants in the country because of his recruiting. Optimism reigned.

We knew we were in good shape for Carson Grady's big announcement next Wednesday. He and Boxer Davis would announce live on ESPNU and both had told Malcolm Jackson they'd be joining him at Ohio State. Getting those two guys would be a walk-off grand slam in recruiting. We'd challenge Alabama and Clemson for the #1 ranking.

Rick reported that Boxer had a couple of last questions. He wanted to see if Ohio State would have a cool new alternate uniform. The other schools had shown some designs of new uniforms.

"Ed, he also wants to know if we have a touchdown chain that guys get to wear on the sideline when he scores."

"These guys are more worried about what they wear than hitting somebody. There is no way in hell we're wearing jewelry on the sideline. Leave that to the assholes. So the short answer for him is no. We have a tradition here. The long answer for him is fuck no, but you better stick with the short answer Rick. That's my lecture okay?"

"Ed, we may want to finesse that. The uniform/chain thing may be a potential deal-breaker."

"Rick if that is a deal breaker we've got the wrong kid. I want kids who want to bust their ass, put on the Ohio State uniform that's been good enough for Heisman Trophy winners and National Champions, and beat the hell out of every team we play. I want fighters not posers."

"I got you. Do you want to tell him that?"

"Gladly. I'll tell him exactly that."

I'd already taken my allowed NCAA visits to all our recruits so I was stuck in Columbus. I'd work the phones calling parents, recruits, high school coaches and just about anyone we could to keep tabs on each player.

At the meeting we received a print out of our current recruiting class.

"Looking at this sheet," I said "the most likely scenario is that we have 18 commitments and December signees. There are some we need to keep on the next few days. I'll work the phones to make sure we tighten up those commitments. Assume nothing. Defend against anyone coming in to buy or flip someone. If that happens I want to know exactly what shit they pulled. Everybody got that?"

Then I asked Rick and the coaches for their best predictions. After their input I summarized.

Committed:

Name	*School*	*Comments*
QB Carter Jones	*Warren Harding HS, OH*	*Rock Solid Commit*
TB Malcolm Jackson	*Palm Bay HS, FL*	*Rock Solid Commit*
TB Dante Holmes	*Highlands HS, KY*	*Rock Solid Commit*
FB Steve Smith	*DeMatha HS, MD*	*SIGNED*
WR Antonio Banks	*Glenville HS, OH*	*SIGNED*
TE Frank Sanders	*Cincinnati Princeton HS, OH*	*May slip if we get Rodriguez*
OT Buck Martin	*Monroe HS, MI*	*SIGNED*
OG Marco Martini	*Don Bosco Prep, NJ*	*SIGNED*
DT Marvin Hancock	*Seattle O'Dea HS, WA*	*SIGNED*
DT Alexander Faulk	*Harvey HS, LA*	*fairly solid—LSU & Auburn lurkers*
DT Zeus Rivera	*St Ignatius HS, OH*	*SIGNED*
DE Jamar Tucker	*Benedictine HS, OH*	*Rock Solid—good health update*
DE Parker Smith	*Brentwood HS, TN*	*SIGNED*
ILB Archie Lewis	*Hamilton HS, OH*	*SIGNED*
OLB Andre Cooper	*Phoebus HS, VA*	*mostly solid—VA Tech lurking*
CB Sherman Woodson	*Summerville HS, SC*	*mostly solid—Clemson lurks*
SAF D'Antonio Wilson	*Chaminade-Julienne HS, OH*	*SIGNED*
SAF Rex Watson	*Glen Oak HS, OH*	*SIGNED*

Still Out There:
Front-Line Needs:

WR Boxer Davis	*Mainland HS, FL*	*FSU and OSU tied per his Social Media*
WR Lance Marshall	*Pershing HS, MI*	*If we wait on Davis we'll lose Lance to Cal*
TE Manny Rodriguez	*Cardinal Mooney HS, OH*	*announcing tomorrow- tied w/ OU*
OT Jake O'Reilly	*St Edward HS, OH*	*Friday a.m. announces we are #1*
OT Brad Jones	*Bishop McDevitt HS, PA*	*if we get O'Reilly we cut him lose*
OLB Carson Grady	*Allentown Cent. Catholic, PA*	*OSU & PSU—Told Jackson he is all OSU*
OLB Danny Morris	*Piqua HS, OH*	*unless we press he is going to MSU*
OLB William Wilkins	*Huber Hts Wayne HS, OH*	*leaning to Kentucky*
OLB Derrick Nelson	*DeLaSalle HS, CA*	*Lomg shot-- USC & Oregon ahead*
CB Roger Hill	*Hoboken HS, NJ*	*OSU, UNC & Michigan toss-up*
CB Artie Manson	*DeMatha HS, MD*	*announcing Friday OSU, MD & Michigan St*
CB Darryl White	*Canton McKinley HS, OH*	*announces Sat: Mich, MSU, OSU toss-up*
RB Aaron Smith	*Toledo Rogers HS, OH*	*can get but time is short—MSU most likely*
RB Carson Walker	*Glenville HS, OH*	*Committed to Tennessee*
DE Darwin Tucker	*St Vincent-St Mary's HS, OH*	*soft commit to Pitt*

Gone:

Alphonso Simmons	*Cincinnati St Xavier HS, OH*	*Committed to Ga Tech*

“We have 18 guys, and we’re likely to keep all of them—except for maybe Sanders if we get Rodriguez at tight end. If that happens then we’re okay. Let’s say we keep all 18. It looks like we’re getting Grady. We’ll know by the weekend if we get another corner but if we don’t get any of those guys and we get Roger Hill then we’re great. Hill does make me nervous because UNC is in there and Mack Brown knows how to close. So we’ll get one of the corners and Grady that puts us at 20 with 12 on defense. If you look at that defensive group; 2 shutdown corners, 2 big safeties, 2 pass rushers and 3 defensive tackles. You put those linebackers in there and you have a big-time defensive class.”

“On offense we got a quarterback and the best running back in the country. We need either one of the tackles still on the board to fill out our line. I think we’ll get Rodriguez. His Mom doesn’t want him all the way out in Oklahoma. No way that happens, write it down.”

“Now at wide receiver this gets tricky. Boxer Davis is announcing on Signing Day so we won’t even know until then. We can’t ask Lance Marshall to wait. Can we get by without another receiver if we don’t get Davis?”

Rick chimed in “Coach the consensus is that we need another one. Boxer and Malcolm are pretty close and I think we are in front. Dwayne, who is closest to him, thinks we’ll get him. As for Lance I think he’ll go to Cal.”

Dwayne Baxter chimed in “Don’t bet on Marshall going to Cal.”

“Why’s that?” Rick asked.

“Word on the street,” Dwayne started “was that Minnesota is making a push to get him to visit this weekend.”

“Minnesota?” Rick asked.

“Yeah the new Head Coach out there came in and made a big push on him.”

“You mean the guy who just got there ?” Ed asked.

“That’d be the one.” Dwayne said.

“I talked with two other coaches in the league already who’ve said that this guy is bad news.” I said.

“I know this guy.” Dwayne laughed.

“He’s going after a lot of other people’s commitments.” Rick said.

"That is how he works." Dwayne said. "When he was at both UCF and Texas Tech he tried to get named the next head coach. He played the black coach card. Then he bolted for the SMU job." Dwayne said.

"He did a pretty good job there." I said.

"Yeah they scheduled four shit non-conference teams a year so he was always 4 and 0 headed into the conference schedule. Then they'd go either 3 and 5 or 4 and 4 in the league and make a shit bowl. They ended up 7 and 6 two years and 8 and 5 the third year before he bolted to Minnesota. Word is he's waiting to get the USC job if that comes open. He just thought he couldn't get that job from SMU but from Minnesota he'd have no problem."

"Sounds like a real gem." I laughed.

"You don't know the half of it." Dwayne said. "The guys who worked for him can't stand him. He doesn't know shit when it comes to Xs and Os. One of his former assistants said he is like an actor playing a football coach. Another time when he was an assistant coach he was talking so much shit that another assistant coach got up and dropped him in a staff meeting. He's also had more NCAA complaints than any other coach in the country. "

"You're just saying that." I said.

"Nope, my high school teammate is in the NCAA's enforcement division. You remember those two kids we lost to Texas Tech a few years ago and we couldn't figure it out?"

"Oh yeah the kids from Cincinnati we thought were locks for us."

"That's right. With both of them all of a sudden this fast-talking coach comes in from Texas Tech and takes Ohio kids from Ohio State."

"Yeah."

"That was him. He found two alums. One was a rep for a big insurance agency and one who had a construction and renovation company. After a big snowstorm came through the insurance agent went out and declared bogus damages to the houses. The construction company put on new roofs and siding and billed the insurance company. Then they did free work on the houses of those two kids. Same thing both times. New basements, hot tubs out back and re-done kitchens. Insurance agent also claimed the power outage damaged appliances too. They got new fridges, televisions, computers and ipads."

"That's pretty smooth."

"That's our guy who's now at Minnesota."

"I always wondered about those two kids. How'd you find all that out?"

"A coach at Pitt got it all and turned it over to the NCAA."

"And nothing happened?"

"Nothing. The next year the staff at Pitt gets let go and this guy from Texas Tech, now our problem at Minnesota, black lists the guy as a snitch. See if he ever gets a job anywhere after turning someone in."

"What's the moral of the story there?"

"It gets worse. Hell you should hear what the guys who played for him have to say. It is all cameras and social media all the time. The players refer to him as Coach Kardashian. And he just runs kids off the team all the time. I'll just give you this word to the wise, whatever you do, don't trust him."

"Well there's got to be some more there." I said. "You seem pretty pissed."

"I am, because this guy will fuck it up and then it reflects poorly on a lot of us that are trying to work hard, pay our dues and come up the right way. I know my Xs and Os and I know football and I hate seeing guys like him get ahead. Shit they're paying him like $4 million a year and that guy could barely draw up a zone blitz. I saw him at a coaching clinic and he just gave a power point on his philosophy using the same quotes his agent pulled for him 5 years ago."

"Okay now that Dwayne has filled us in on the new Minnesota coach, let's think about where we are if we lose Boxer Davis. What time is the signing day event at Pershing High School?"

"It is at three o'clock." Rick said.

"What time is Boxer announcing?" I asked.

"He is live on ESPNU at eleven a.m." Rick said.

"Do the kids at Pershing actually sign before the event?"

"No."

"Okay, the plan is we let Lance go to Cal. If we don't get Boxer we get the coach at Pershing on the phone and we flip Lance from Cal. Tell the coach if we get Lance we'll offer his junior defensive end that we're mostly sure is good enough."

"Okay."

"As it stands we should get Grady, Rodriguez, O'Reilly, Davis and one of the Corners. That puts us at 23; 12 on defense and 11 on offense. Would everyone be happy with that?"

Everyone agreed we'd be thrilled. The next few days the dominos would start to fall towards the finish. The next morning it was Rodriguez announcing and by noon on Friday both O'Reilly and cornerback Artie Manson would announce. Saturday White would announce and then it was wait until signing day when Grady, Hill, Davis and Morris announced. My best guess was that we'd get Rodriguez, O'Reilly, Grady, Davis and White. If that happened we'd be a top five class nationally.

I was convinced it was as talented as any class in the country. Recruiting rankings are just guesses but high rankings create confidence in the direction of the program for Gerry Gorton, vocal university Trustees, the media and the fans.

Before we left I pulled Quinn aside. That afternoon he was to go to Cleveland to see Cecelia Morgan. Sometime after a third glass of wine at dinner, he was to subtly mention that Malcolm Jackson's mom was a legal secretary and would be moving to Cleveland to be nearer to her mother. He hadn't seen her since their one night together in Orlando but he had kept in touch with her to help Wanda Jackson get a job either at her firm or another firm in Cleveland.

. . . .

By Friday at eleven my first two predictions had come true. Rodriguez announced for Ohio State. Manny's mom had come through. Nine times out of ten the Moms held more sway with their sons than the fathers did. The next morning O'Reilly committed to us as well. Notre Dame fans were convinced they were getting the Irish Catholic Tackle from a Catholic High School. I guess even God roots for the Buckeyes every once in a while.

We were at twenty commits and ranked #5 Nationally on Rivals.com. The momentum was picking up and the love of the Buckeye faithful was building.

As quickly as the love was back, it vanished at noon. We sat in stunned silence as Artie Manson announced he was going to Auburn. We didn't even know they were in the picture and we were not alone in that. I called Rick into my office to see if we'd gotten Darryl White on the phone yet. White was announcing the next morning and we needed a corner. Rick reported that everyone around him had gone to radio silence ahead of the announcement tomorrow.

"Are we getting him?" I asked.

"I don't know." Rick said.

"If they go to radio silence and we don't know, then we ain't getting him."

"I don't know coach." Rick tried to be hopeful.

"Wanna bet? I've been doing this a long time. If you don't know before a recruit steps up to the podium then you're not getting him."

Sure enough Saturday morning Darryl White was getting ready to step up to the podium at his high school and we had no idea what Darryl's decision was going to be. We'd tried calling anyone and everyone. The people we could get on the phone wouldn't say where he was going.

It was being televised live so we'd have to find out on TV just like the rest of the fans. At the podium there were hats from Ohio State and Michigan. Darryl got up there and talked about the two schools and the tremendous rivalry and how many games each team had won. He vowed that the school he was going to attend would never lose to their rival. He started to reach for the Ohio State hat and some people started to cheer.

Then he abruptly stopped and said "I want to be a "Victor" so I am going to Michigan. Hail to the Victors!"

That announcement was an unexpected blow. Over the years Ohio State fans have endured repeated losses of Ohio prospects to their hated rival. This one had made his announcement an insult that was sure to be replayed over and over again. Despite our great class, the loss of a top Ohio prospect to Michigan started another round of criticism. We'd lost two top corner prospects in twenty-four hours.

Within fifteen minutes Rick Carter had Darryl White's coach on the phone trying to find out what had gone wrong. We'd thought we were a lock. The coach was also surprised. He explained that an Uncle of Darryl's had suddenly materialized. He happened to live in Southfield, just outside of Detroit. Someone at the University of Michigan had found the Uncle and got him involved in the recruiting process.

When Rick came back to talk to me he explained that.

"God damned Michigan. They always find some long-lost relative who re-connects and convinces the kid to go the Ann Arbor. There was a player a few years back from Virginia we lost to them when an Uncle from Detroit materialized."

"Well there is also the matter of that recruiting expert."

"Which one?"

"Your favorite, Tim Lybrand."

"Tim Lybrand, what's he got to do with this?"

"Well you know that we don't buy his service."

"Yeah."

"Well Michigan does."

"So what?"

"Look we've had this conversation before. Some of these services market themselves as independent and they talk to these players all the time. But schools hire them to be hit men against schools like us who don't pay these guys. Lybrand was in Canton yesterday to "cover" the announcement and he spent two hours at the kid's house gutting us and telling him that you'll get fired from here."

"How can he do that?"

"Coach, we have had this discussion for the past three years. There are no rules. They can do whatever they want. The kids don't know these guys are paid by some schools. The kids and their parents think these "services" are independent guys. Remember when one school paid that guy in Florida $25,000 for his recruiting service? They paid for "information" on one player."

"Yeah. They got the kid and nothing happened."

"Bingo."

"Okay. You got any good news for me?"

"Yeah. We got a nervous running back commitment in Florida."

"Malcolm Jackson?"

Losing him would be a knife in the heart so this certainly got my attention. Malcolm was the crown jewel in the class.

"Yes." Rick said.

"What's gotten into him?"

"He got some threatening letters in the mail. Some of them include the n-word and include threats if he leaves the state."

This was a tactic from the old days that I'd thought was long gone.

"What the hell is wrong with people?" Ed asked.

"Hey coach, this is religion in Florida. They take this shit seriously."

"Let's get Malcolm on the phone and tell them that we're going to get the FBI involved. We can't let someone intimidate him."

When I got Malcolm's Mom Wanda on the phone I reassured her. The senior Senator from Ohio was a staunch Buckeye fan. I'd already talked to him before calling Malcolm.

Wanda had already decided to go visit friends in Georgia for the weekend to get away from everyone. Malcolm even got on the phone and had a good laugh.

"Look Malcolm," I said "I know this has been crazy and hectic but you're just a few days from it all being over."

"Coach," he said "you have no idea. Last summer I took a visit to one school down here and a guy approached me and offered me $15,000 in a brown paper bag. He had the cash on him. It was ridiculous. That night one of their players took me to a club and they wouldn't let us in. The bouncer said some shit about not letting in some underage brothers...but he didn't say brother. We went back to the car and the player pulled out a handgun and said that we were definitely getting into that club that night. I told him I wanted to go back and just hang at his apartment."

This was a very different recruiting world than it had been even just a few years ago. The deep end of this cesspool needed to be drained. Above all I knew we were getting a really good kid and an outstanding football player.

By Saturday afternoon our next scheduled announcements were not until signing day so it was hang on and hope we'd get Hill, Davis and Grady on Wednesday. If we didn't get Davis we'd try to flip Marshall in the hours between Davis' announcement and Marshall's.

I called Rick back into his office and asked him to check in on Davis and make sure he wasn't getting the same types of threatening letters that Malcolm had been getting.

"An ounce of prevention." I said aloud. "Hey on that other thing, the signing day party we're not going to do that."

Rick looked slightly dejected, so I continued.

"Look I saw your note about ESPN sending a stand-up reporter to broadcast updates from here and the other media stuff. Just forget it. I know you've busted your butt to get us to this point, but I just think we're better off not putting ourselves out there too much. But I do want you to get Ray Ray's Hog Pit to set up here, get some other food here and we'll have a party for our coaches and staff. The least I can do is reward you guys. And I also found some bonus money, nothing big but it's a nice chunk of change for everyone."

That seemed to raise his spirits. Money has that effect on people.

. . . .

The morning of signing day we sat at 20 commitments and signees and were in play for 3 or 4 others. Carson Grady seemed like a lock for us, while the other LB Derrick Nelson from California seemed—no pun intended—like a long way off. CB Roger Hill was down to Michigan, UNC and us and wanted to play both football and basketball in college. Having lost the other two corners this was a must-get for our defense. He would play and probably start right away. Our basketball coach and I had spent the last few days on the phones with Roger and seemingly everyone in North Jersey to keep him headed our way.

Boxer Davis was down to us and Florida State and our staff seemed pretty sure we were getting him. But he and his coach kept calling and asking for more guarantees on playing time, on his jersey number and on childish stuff. I hedged our bets and kept in contact with Lance Marshall's coach at Pershing High School all weekend. Without telling anyone else on the staff, I'd talked to him to make a late switch to us at 3 p.m. if Boxer Davis went to the Seminoles. It was by no means a done deal to get Lance or Boxer.

By 7:00 a.m. Lance's coach Stephon Thompson, a real stand-up guy, had called. Before I called him back I wanted to be crystal clear on my approach. After mulling it over I came to the conclusion that Lance was a damn good football player, he was a kid we knew well and was from our Big Ten footprint. Boxer was taller and a bigger name nationally but Lance was an electric player.

We would also need to recruit more players in the future from Detroit. As for Davis, we were being held hostage by him and all of his antics. With that in mind I called Stephon Thompson.

"Coach Thompson, I'm glad you called. You were on my list to call, because I want you to tell Lance that if he wants to commit we will pull the offer from Davis and Lance will be our guy. I'm not interested in playing games with you, and playing games with the guys at Cal. Just have him announce when he gets off the phone and then he can sign this afternoon at 3 p.m." I said.

Without hesitation Lance got on the phone and committed. After the call I called Rick and Dwayne into the office to tell them what I'd done. Understandably they were mad because they wanted that big Florida recruit splash.

"Coach," Dwayne said as his voice rose in protest "I spent so much time on him and you just pulled it all out from under me. How's that gonna make me look?"

"Look," I said "Lance wants to be here, Lance is a damn good football player and he will bust his butt every time we play—especially against Michigan. We have spent two years trying to sell Davis on being here. Guys like that are high maintenance and you'll spend way too much time trying to keep them from entering the transfer portal. Lance is going to announce so call Davis and tell him we're done. He had several weeks to make his decision."

And just like that two and a half years of recruiting Davis was done, but I felt great about Lance as a player and as a person who would likely be a captain for us in a few years.

But Dwayne didn't get where he was without understanding how to make lemonade from lemons. He called up Frank Stetson and took credit for cutting Davis loose and told Frank it was a favor to him for helping with Malcolm Jackson's preacher.

Shortly before Grady and Hill were to announce we were gathered in our staff meeting room waiting to hear from them. Our AD Art Simpson came strolling into the room with a couple of people I recognized by sight but could not put a name to them. They were those people you always saw around.

Art introduced them as donors and big supporters of the program. One was Ivan Landon a big real estate and insurance guy who was probably worth a billion or two. The other people were also donors including the ex-wife of a medical services company founder who was worth $400 million. Alexis Nelson had caught her husband in the shower at their Aspen house with three female ski instructors all of whom were in their early twenties. That netted Alexis half her husband's money.

Art invited them to sit down in our meeting room to watch the next two announcements. I was cordial but asked Art to come into my office for a moment in a way that did not arouse any suspicions from our guests.

"Art what the hell is with bringing those people in here?"

"They've all given in excess of $2 million so they get to do certain things."

"Do I have any say in this?"

"Not really."

Man was I pissed and I was going to let Art know, but I'd coat it in sarcasm.

"So what other bonus perks do they get in the all-access package? Do they get to call plays on game day and stand next to me on the sideline?"

"Of course not but.....but they will get to travel on the team plane one game this year and be on the sidelines for a game."

"Are you shitting me? We're selling access to our team and players. This is dangerous."

"Ed this is not selling access."

"If it's not access, what would you call it?"

"Our donors are more interested in experiential packages....they want to do cool things."

"Yeah so they can shoot their mouths off and post pictures on social media from the team plane, the locker room....I get it. They need to grow the hell up."

Art had reached his limit with my tone.

"Hey Ed whether you like it or not, these donors pay for shit you want and need. So suck it up because I am your boss and in case you haven't noticed, you need to get people like this to support you or you'll be calling me your former boss."

That ended the debate. There was nothing to do but grin and bear it. Of all the people there Alexis was the only one I worried about. She was forty-five, looked great after work she'd had done and was very aggressive around men. My wife Candace had nearly confronted her after Alexis had made a very suggestive comment to me after we'd won the Big Ten Title a few years ago. Candace to this day hates her, but now that Alexis had ponied up a few million dollars there wasn't much I could do to keep her from being around.

By three o'clock Grady and Hill had both signed with us. Grady was not much of a cliff-hanger, but Hill really could've gone either way. Grady gave us the versatile linebacker we desperately needed and Hill was probably going to start right away as a lock-down corner. We got a lot better in a hurry.

This gave us a class of 23 players, one that filled a boatload of needs and pushed us up to a #2 National ranking, just barely being nudged out by Alabama. Buckeye fans were elated, and the National media was stating that we had the strongest close in the country.

As I gathered the coaches and staff, and our donor guests together I thanked everyone and announced that it was time to eat and celebrate a job well done. But before that I asked to meet with the coaches.

"Now that the recruiting is over and we have these big name guys coming in we may have some problems. There will be some guys on our team who feel threatened and look to enter the transfer portal. We have to stay close to our guys. Run scared, assume nothing. If you guys think that anyone is thinking about leaving we need to talk right away. Given that we only had nineteen scholarships available and signed twenty-three we can absorb four defections. But we want to make sure they are the right defections. So celebrate tonight but gather your intel."

It sounded cold, but this was the new reality in college football. With the NCAA transfer portal players could bolt so only a fool would under-sign. It paid to over-sign and replace a kid who wasn't good enough with a freshman. It was how things got done in this era. But they did have to be the right ones.

As I made my way to the rest of the people, Alexis Nelson came over and game me a big hug and planted a kiss on my cheek. Her friend snapped a photo of it. After I thanked her and moved along I didn't realize that Alexis was posting the picture to her multiple social media accounts and tagging me in the picture.

Before I even left the office, my wife Candace had already seen the picture and texted me "What the hell is SHE doing there? Not going through any more of THAT drama again."

Because it was a text I couldn't be sure of her tone.....but I knew it certainly couldn't have been good.

. . . .

A week after Signing Day the team settled into our winter routine. Three days a week they were up and working out as a team at 6 a.m. The workouts were Monday, Wednesday and Friday with the goal of limiting the weekday party nights. Thursday night was a big party night, but the Friday morning workout was a proven deterrent.

On Tuesday, Thursday and Friday afternoon the players lifted weights and the routine was all within NCAA offseason limitations. They settled into a routine that would take them right up until Spring Break. Once they returned from break we had two weeks before Spring Practice began. The winter was a dangerous time when the players had ample free time and were pretty bored.

On a Saturday night in late February, starting strong safety Lance Baxter had some of his high school friends visiting from his hometown of Memphis. They'd all gone to the University School, a beautiful private school that had built a pretty strong program. Lance was a wealthy white kid who happened to be smart, athletic and a big hitter.

His friends came to town looking for some fun. After a long Saturday afternoon watching Ohio State beat Minnesota in basketball they hit the parties and bars. At the end of a cold winter night they ended up back in Lance's townhouse apartment. Lance had managed to bring back Alicia, a girl he'd been with on more than a few occasions. Because they always hooked up when they were both drunk, she was pretty open to trying pretty much anything Lance suggested. That history and their drunken state erased any unease Lance had about his request once they'd had sex.

They were still both naked, lying in Lance's bed in the nearly dark bedroom. Lance turned toward Alicia lying beside him.

"Alicia, I have one more request." Lance asked.

"Yeah, what's that?" She asked looking back at him.

"I have two of my boys up from Memphis for the weekend."

"Yeah, I know that."

"Well you see they all came up here looking for action and I was hoping you could remedy that."

Alicia wasn't exactly sure what he was asking but she thought she knew. She sat up in the bed and looked at him.

"Remedy that how? Call up some friends and ask them to come over and bang your friends, two guys they've never met?"

"No, no, nothing like that."

A confused look came across her face and she wasn't sure what came next.

"Alicia, I was thinking that since we've had our fun, that maybe you could take care of them too."

"What?"

"I'm okay sharing. This is college, why can't we all get down?"

"Fuck you Lance! I'm not some town whore you pimp out to your friends visiting for the weekend."

Lance sat up and looked her in the eye. He thought that maybe he could talk her into it by getting in her face directly to apply the power of persuasion. After a back and forth she was adamant that she wanted to leave. On his way to block her exit from the bedroom door he scooped up her clothes from the floor.

"It sure is cold out there and you're not getting these back unless you do what I ask." He said.

"You're an asshole. Give me my damn clothes back."

Tears were starting down her face. Lance refused so she rummaged through his dresser and found a t-shirt and shorts to throw on. Lance was still blocking her way when she picked up her phone.

"Get out of the way or I am calling the police."

"You do that you're dumber than I thought. You really want the cops involved? You know they'll take my side, I'm a starter on the football team."

"Just get the hell out of the way." She said as he charged at him in a rage.

Lance saw real anger in her face as she ran at him with finger nails drawn cat-like as if she was going to claw his face to get out of there. He stepped aside with his hands up to let her know he would not keep her here. As he stepped aside he opened the door but still held onto her clothes. In the door frame Alicia stopped and asked for her clothes back. There was fear in her face at the prospect of walking out into a 30-degree night in just shorts and a T-shirt.

"You know what you have to do to get them back." Lance smiled.

"Fuck you." Alicia said and left the apartment. Before she'd even gotten a block away from the apartment a police car pulled alongside of her. The officer rolled down the window.

"Are you okay?" he asked.

"Yeah officer I'm fine. I have a friend coming to get me."

The officer could see the tears on her cheeks and stepped out of the car.

"Look my name is Officer Cassidy. I can see something is wrong. Were you assaulted? Is there something you want to tell me?"

"No, no I am fine. Just let me go home...please."

"Ma'am if you don't mind me asking, what is your name?"

"Alicia."

"Alicia are you sure nothing happened? Would you be more comfortable if I called in a female officer to talk to you?"

The crying got worse as she broke down and told him what had happened. The officer understood that both parties were drunk and that this was probably not a criminal matter. Still he wanted to do what he could for this girl.

"Look Alicia, it is cold out here, so please get in the car. It is warm. I am going to call in a female officer to take you home. In the meantime I will go retrieve your clothes. No questions asked, is that okay?"

She sobbed and nodded her head. She got into the car with the officer and he drove back to the apartment where he knocked on the door. When Lance's friends answered the door they sobered up instantly. Lance came out and kept his cool, acting as though he would have no idea why a police officer was at the door.

"May I help you officer?" he asked.

"Yes you can. You can make this very easy on yourself. Give me Alicia's clothes and shoes and I will leave. She doesn't want any trouble, she just wants her stuff back."

"For real?" Lance asked. "Do you know who I am?"

"Yes I know who you are, but I'm in no mood to fuck around. Give me the clothes back so she can be on her way."

Lance's friend handed Alicia's clothes over to the officer. The officer looked him in the eye as he took hold of the clothes.

"I am writing down the address of this apartment and filing it away. If I ever get another call here that has anything to do with you mistreating a woman I will make your life a living hell. What kind of an asshole makes a girl walk home like that?"

"Hey she could've stayed--"

"Just shut up and heed my advice." The officer interrupted.

With that he left. The incident was over for the night. But on Monday morning Officer Cassidy called me to inform me of the incident. Officer Cassidy was sure to stress that there was likely no assault and that nothing illegal had happened but he felt that Lance needed to be reminded of what it means to be a part of the Ohio State football team.

I called Lance and told him he'd be running the Ohio Stadium steps for the rest of the week at 5:30 a.m. The next morning Lance showed up to run and approached me.

"I don't like having to be here with you. It's too damn cold for me to be out here watching your sorry ass run because you don't know how to behave." I said.

Lance looked at me defiantly.

"You know coach, I'm honestly not sure why I'm here. I did nothing wrong." Lance said.

"Are you serious?" I asked.

"Yeah I am. I was talking with my parents last night and they talked to our attorney. I didn't break any laws, or any team rules so I'm not required to run for you."

"Lance if you want to be a part of this team, you're gonna run these steps."

"Coach, you can take your steps and your phony arbitrary punishment and shove it. I'll go enter the transfer portal and go somewhere else."

"What you did was wrong and there needs to be consequences for that action."

Lance smirked with the smug look of a kid who thinks he knows more than I do. It was so disrespectful that I wanted to smack that smirk right off of his face, but I held my temper in check. Mostly I wanted to smack his parents for not ripping his ass instead of calling their attorney.

"Coach, I know things other guys have done and I know they didn't have to run. I'm leaving this place and I'm not alone. You guys recruited all these hot shot players to come take our places. You let certain guys slide on discipline and then bring the hammer down on me? Trust me I talk to a lot of guys. I'm entering that transfer portal, and there are other guys too. We've all talked and we're not gonna go quietly either. So you better be ready to have some things exposed in public. It ain't gonna be pretty."

With that he turned his back on me and walked out of the gate and to his car, which I should've noticed he hadn't even bothered to turn off. Before I'd even gotten to the office Lance had already tweeted his "statement" where he alleged inconsistent treatment of certain players and that he would be leading other players in his exodus.

When my cell phone rang at 6:37 a.m., I knew without looking that it was going to be Gerry Gorton.

8. SPRING PRACTICE AND THE SPRING GAME

As spring shook Winter's grip in Ohio, spring football practice began as a time of renewal. With the pressures of the late season collapse it had been a long cold winter. Turning the page was a welcome change. The seniors were gone, the team had a new dynamic and for the first time we were out onto the practice fields to evaluate our players.

But the start to our spring practice was complicated by the very public departure of safety Lance Baxter. The morning he refused to run, my phone rang at 6:37 a.m. and it was Gerry Gorton.

"Ed," he said "why am I getting a call at 6:30 a.m. from Alexis Nelson bitching about you running off a starter on the defense?"

"She called you? You've got to be kidding me."

"I wish I was but what the hell is going on? We were bad enough on defense and now you shitcan a starter?"

Gerry never cussed so when he dropped the word "Shitcan" on me I knew he didn't appreciate having a booster call him before dawn. After calming him down, I explained the situation and what Lance had done.

"Well we just can't let him tee off on our school and on you. How do we get this story out there?" Gerry asked.

"We really can't do anything. Getting that story out there won't help and may reflect poorly on us. It'll draw all kinds of attention about how our players allegedly treat women. The girl involved insisted to the police officer that nothing criminal went on and that she did not want any investigation. But try explaining that to anyone in this era of social media outrage. We just have to take the bullets he fires at us. There is no win for us."

To an outsider a cold calculation about what this would look like in "the era of social media outrage" sounds callous and uncaring. But it is the reality of coaching a high-profile football program. You represent the ultimate male privilege target to so many people.

Gerry grudgingly accepted the reality. But he said one more thing before he hung up that did me no favors.

"Because I don't want any more of these six a.m. calls from Alexis I've given her your cell number. Now she can take her complaints right to you."

That was not the start to my spring that I was looking for, but for the next few weeks I did not hear a peep from her.

While many outsiders assume that the offseason is a time when coaches slow down and just show up in the fall, there is a ton of work requiring us to balance our attention and focus. The first is recruiting and even now Gerry Gorton was looking for more updates to follow up on our recently signed #2 Nationally ranked class.

The trick is that while we try to build the next season's team, we're also evaluating and putting together the next year's recruiting class. The early Signing Day in December has accelerated the calendar from years past. But what has been a bit of a surprise is that some of the biggest name recruits are more than willing to let the dust settle from the hiring and firing cycle of coaches. But these guys show up for unofficial visits even before we finish the last class.

If you haven't offered them during their junior season you're way behind. But we were fortunate because this junior class was a better than average year in Ohio. By the time we were halfway through spring practice we'd gotten commitments from nine players, six of them Ohio natives all of whom were among the top 10 players in our home state. It was an excellent start and given that we were looking for this class to be a total of twenty players we were almost halfway home. The preliminary recruiting class rankings had us in the Top 10, but lots can and does change between spring and signing day.

Offering players is a delicate balancing act. The egos of assistant coaches who want to build their recruiting reputations get in the way. They all want the guys in their areas to be offered first so they can run to get as many commitments as they can. But as the head coach I have to oversee and prioritize which guys we offer and which guys we get. The worst thing you can do is offer a player to "get in the hunt" and then have them commit before someone you really wanted decides.

My standard demand before I make any offer is I want the coach recruiting the player and the coach who will coach him to look me in the eye and tell me the recruit is good enough to get a degree at Ohio State and win a National Championship. And truthfully the priority is not necessarily always in that order.

If the players can get a degree and are good enough to win with, we're comfortable with any guy who commits to us. It makes our coaches' jobs tougher but it makes us work a little harder. One wise old coach used to say all the time "It's not the guys you miss on that beat you, it's the guys you take who can't play that beat you."

With that advice always in my head, I'm cautious. We're looking to build a team and not just collect big-name recruits.

There is also pressure to offer guys all over the country who are "big names" on the recruiting lists. The fans, including big money boosters, all read these lists and think that some expert has actually looked at and evaluated every player. They put so much stock into a recruit's ranking and it is fool's gold. There are guys that you're pressured to offer that we've never even seen in person and as such we don't know if they're really as big or tall as they're listed.

Just this year we had a linebacker from Joliet Catholic HS south of Chicago who came to our camp as a rising junior. He was 6'1" tall, weighed 207 pounds and ran a 4.78 forty. While those are solid measurable, they're just not Ohio State numbers. By February he was listed as a 6'3" 235 pound linebacker running a 4.57 40. The internet was filled with reports that the Ohio State coaches loved him at our camp. That got him offers from Notre Dame, UCLA, Penn State, Miami and about three dozen other top programs.

After getting a call from Gerry Gorton, who'd gotten a call from a booster asking why we were falling behind on this "Stud Linebacker" I had Dave Cafiero call the coach at Joliet Catholic. The high school coach was at a loss. His player was 6'1 and 210 pounds but had offers from schools who'd never even met him. Some of these schools hadn't even looked at film of him. The coach was a guy that Dave had known for years so Dave knew he was being honest with him.

But because he made some list, schools offered him and boosters wanted our heads on a platter if we didn't go chase him.

But that's the nature of recruiting. There's too much hype and too many so-called experts who have no skin in the game. If they're wrong on a player, these experts certainly don't have to worry about wins and losses and losing their jobs.

Complicating the recruiting process during the spring is also the damned transfer portal. After signing day we lost four guys to the portal after the Lance Baxter departure. Most of them were depth guys, two back-ups and a third-teamer who all wanted to go elsewhere to play. But spring is a dangerous time when just one bad practice and one perceived slight can trigger a player's departure in the transfer portal free-for-all.

In spring practice while we are developing the next team, recruits show up at almost every practice. While I'm trying to keep an eye on key positions and how our younger talent is developing these recruits and their families want me to talk to them. At some schools, all the head coach does in practice is spend time with recruits, acting as a CEO while his assistants run the practice. I've never wanted to be that guy. That is why I always try to schedule morning practices, because recruits are far less likely to show up.

Years ago I visited Penn State's practice and even in his 70s Joe Paterno was running around and making notes about every aspect of the team from the quarterback-center exchange to the cornerbacks' coverage technique. When we visited Alabama, Nick Saban was the exact same way. That's how I want to be, I want to be a coach who helps these players get better every day. But some of these recruits yammer on and on about how great they are and I have no choice but to listen to them even as I see a freshman player make a mistake that his coach misses.

It also brings up a debate I've had with my coaches that is still a sore subject. At every other school on unofficial visits they allow the players to dress up in the team's uniforms and pose for pictures. Some of them even let family members, like Dads, Moms and siblings put on uniforms and pose for pictures. I refuse to do that because I believe only people who've earned the right to put on that uniform should get to do that.

I will not cheapen what it means to put on the Scarlet and Gray. What surprises our assistant coaches is how many of the players and parents understand and respect that policy. As for the recruits who get mad, I'm not interested in those kinds of prima donnas.

But now that spring was here, it was time to focus on player development across several weeks. Just before practice started we had a big meeting to discuss players and expectations. Everyone was in the meeting including our medical, strength and training staff.

I always start these meetings on defense. It is a firm belief that a defense keeps you in the game and gives you a chance to win. Our biggest concern was in the secondary. With Safety Lance Baxter transferring that meant Carson Miller would have to be the leader in the secondary. So I asked the secondary Coach Dwayne Baxter for his input.

"Carson looks good." Dwayne Baxter said. "In fact he came back from skiing in Colorado for spring break and he's still got both knees intact."

"He went where? And he did what?" I asked.

Skiing is not what you want your guys doing, but what could I really do? But I wasn't just worried about the skiing. He'd failed a drug test in his freshman year for marijuana and another positive would trigger a significant suspension. Our drug tests were "random" but I wasn't taking any chances.

"If he went to Colorado," I said looking at our medical staff "I damn sure hope he's not on the random list for drug testing any time this spring."

They understood what I was getting at.

There was more news. We had another player entering the transfer portal. Rex Nelson was a back-up linebacker from Southern California. He was just finishing his freshman year and had a shot to play a lot this year and start the next season. I asked Dave Cafiero why Rex wanted to leave.

"Coach," he said "he's got a girlfriend back home and he wants to go there. She's the one who was coming out here for ten days at a time and driving Rex's roommates crazy because she basically moved in."

"Jesus Christ. He's right on the verge of playing and he's going home....because of a hometown girlfriend?"

"That's about the size of it." Dave said.

This was about the time Doug Leonard would chime in with some home-spun Texas wit. I could see it in his face that he had something to say. No sooner had Dave finished than Doug spoke up.

"You young coaches listen up..." Doug said pointing at the younger guys in the room "When you recruit guys and the girlfriend is always hanging around, just run the other way. I told you guys when this kid was on his visit that he was just completely pussy-whipped. We had a kid like this when I coached at UVA years ago. A wise old retired coach gave me this advice. He said to me "Son just remember that Pussy is Undefeated. Football is a lot of fun but it ain't no substitute for that."

As politically incorrect as Doug could be on occasion, he had a point.

Leading up to the start of practice we had a number of contentious coaching meetings. There is a lot of talk about "complimentary football" by people who have no idea what it means. A lot of them think it simply means that you have high national rankings for your defense and your offense. That has nothing to do with it.

Complimentary football comes from a Head Coach who knows how to control the tempo of a game on game day. If your opponent's offense is going to be a problem for your defense, you may want to slow down your offense, burn time off the clock and shorten the game. That may mean less yards and less points, but it gives your opponents less opportunity to score. If your defense is dominant it may mean being willing to punt and play field position rather than run risky plays on third and long than could lead to turnovers.

In the second half of games it may also mean having a package in your offense where you have extra tight ends or a fullback in the game and your quarterback under center and even huddling between plays to get better communication and take time off the clock to help get the save. I've always defined a "save opportunity" as being a game where we have a fourth quarter lead of fourteen points or less. In those games we need to be able to slow down the game.

And slowing down the game meant less plays and less yards for Quinn's offensive national rankings. He looked at those rankings all the time and that was how he valued himself. There were times I wasn't even sure that wins meant as much to him as his rankings. Even after losses he was the first guy to look at the stats.

So as we discussed changing our approach he was pissed. My plan was to take the approach that we needed to do what was best for the entire team. But my presentation to the staff was largely ignored by Quinn.

What we had on our coaching staff was a divide between the guys who'd been with me led by Dave Cafiero and the guys who were newer led by Quinn Banks. So as the discussions in the staff meetings went on, I could see the fault lines widen with the pressure I was applying.

After a few days of heated arguments ended with Quinn storming out of the meeting room, I got a call from Quinn's agent Warren Thompson while I was in my office at home. It was just about time for dinner and Candace was at the door to my den when I answered the phone.

"Warren, what's up? Please don't tell me you want to renegotiate Quinn's contract?" I laughed.

"No, nothing like that. But I do want to talk about my client's future if you have a minute."

"I always have a minute for you....you know that."

I was pretty sure he could sense the sarcasm in my voice.

"Quinn tells me that you guys have had some *interesting* discussions about making some changes to Quinn's offensive philosophy."

My years in coaching gave me an idea of where this was headed and my blood pressure was jumping a bit. Maintaining poise and a calm demeanor was going to be a challenge, but it was vital. The fact that what should be confidential staff discussions were being shared with Quinn's agent also was not something that I was happy to hear about.

"Yes we had some discussions about that."

"Well, I am calling to express our concern about the direction it appears you're headed."

"Really? Since I haven't really made up my mind on that I'm not sure what direction we're headed, but if you have some future insight...please share."

That last line of sarcasm was not a constructive addition to the conversation. That became apparent when Warren raised his voice as he barked his next statement into the phone.

"Well, Quinn tells me you're talking about ball control, slowing down his attack and making him take his offense back to the stone ages. As his agent I want to remind you that his offense is his key to his future and it is what makes him marketable for future head coaching jobs."

Rather than try to defuse the situation, my baser instincts took over and I raised my voice just loud enough for Candace to hear outside my den as she was coming to get me for dinner.

"Look Warren, the last time I checked I'm the head coach at Ohio State and my job is to see that we win games. That's what I owe this school and the guys I coach. It is not Quinn's offense just as it is not Dave Cafiero's defense. It is our team and I hate where this shit has gone where you agents are all looking out for your guy over the interests of the team. So if I tell Quinn I want to slow the game down, he damn well better do it or I'll call the plays my damn self. Is that clear?"

Warren increased his volume just before Candace came in to sit and listen to the fireworks. That was not something she'd normally do, but given the tensions on my job that have ratcheted up she was curious.

"Look Ed, if you're going to fuck with his system that is your call. You're right."

"Well thank you for that."

"But, and this is a big but. My job is to make damn sure that the public and any potential future employers understand that you're the one messing with his system. You also better be ready to give him an extension on his contract because he may be stuck with you as an assistant coach for a little longer if he can't put up the numbers he wants."

I like Quinn and I liked his approach to the game. We just needed some slight adjustments for the good of the team. After the shouting died down I agreed that we could extend Quinn's contract, but that Quinn would have to lower the temperature in the debate and lessen the divide between the older guys on the staff and the newer guys. I told Warren that I would have that discussion with Quinn and state that in no uncertain terms that he would have to bring whatever "new guy" faction he'd created back into the fold. There is no way a divided staff can be successful.

After the call Candace and I went to the kitchen to have dinner. After twelve years of marriage, it was still just the two of us. My son Sam and daughter Deanna from my previous marriage were in college at KU close to where their mother lived back in Kansas. Since it had been eight years since I was there they could be pretty anonymous at Kansas. They liked it that way.

As I washed my hands at the kitchen sink my phone buzzed with a couple of texts.

“Is that your phone or mine?” I asked.

“Yours, you want me to see who it is?”

“Yeah.”

She looked down to read the name on the text and a wrinkle came across her brow and it got quiet.

“Who was it?” I asked as I walked to the table.

“Alexis Nelson.....what the hell does she want?”

“Beats me”

“And....when did *she* get your cell number?”

The tension level was rising as I picked up the phone to read the text, which I shared with Candace.

“Apparently she is weighing in on my attempt to slow down the offense for next year. She’s telling me to let Quinn do what he wants.”

“So she has your number and is giving you advice on coaching?” Candace snapped.

“Apparently so. She called Gerry Gorton one morning at 6:30 a.m. to bitch about something and he decided to give her my number.” I did my best not to sound defensive.

“That had better be all it is. I may front her myself, because we are not going through that again.”

And there it was, a reference to *that.*

“Come on Candace, not that again. The number of coaches who’ve been accused of screwing, or worse yet impregnating a cheerleader is pretty damned high. And in all my years I have yet to see any of those rumors proven true. It's a tired old cliché and you know damn well not to mention some rumors that were never true."

I'm not perfect and I've had my share of close calls. This high-profile profession attracts a lot of people who want to hang around. But it was not smart of me to have been in the same bar as some of them after I left from Kansas. Eight years ago when Candace was pregnant and had a miscarriage it was incredibly difficult on her. I was less than helpful. We became detached emotionally for a time while she stayed behind to sell the house in Kansas. I did some things I'm not proud of, but it never went where she thinks it did.

"Look honey, there was nothing to that then and there is nothing to this. Gerry has been defending me from a lot of these boosters and he wants me to shoulder some of the burden. He's tired of taking the calls so he wants me to develop relationships with some of them to get them off his back."

"Get them off his back....and onto yours?"

"Something like that."

"Well I don't trust that Alexis. She doesn't want to get on your back....I thinks she wants you to put her on her back. Or maybe Quinn's already doing that."

That line caused me to laugh and the piece of steak I had in my mouth shot onto the floor. Our three-year old beagle Brutus, named after the Ohio State mascot, got it immediately. Since we don't have kids, and most likely won't, Brutus is our baby.

Candace continued "You know maybe Gerry has an idea. Maybe you should do a better job of getting these people to know you."

"I'll take that under advisement."

She rarely weighs in but when she does, I listen. After all she was smart and competitive enough to play tennis at Yale.

Spring practice began uneventfully. Quinn and I had a long talk and he agreed to help the cause. In the last staff meeting before spring practice I decided to address the issue head on. I feel best using a direct approach to attack problems.

The day before spring practice I sat down with all the coaches and staff. As we sat around the table early that morning I could see the steam still rising off some of the cups of coffee. For most coaches coffee is the fuel to get through early mornings and late nights. Doug Leonard relied on a big wad of Levi Garrett chewing tobacco to keep him awake.

But that morning the coaches were wide awake and attentive as I began a meeting to make sure we started spring practice on the right foot.

"Guys, I appreciate all of you sticking with this. I know I've been tough on you guys this offseason. But understand there was a lot of pressure to make changes. But I believe in all of you, so I did not shift anyone around, nor did I fire anyone. That is a rarity in this profession. But my loyalty is a two-way street and all of you have stayed with me this year too. I respect that. The next few weeks are going to be a building process. We have the pieces here to win the Big Ten and maybe more. We could be a playoff team. But it all starts in here."

Sometimes guys in meetings may be checking or sending a text but not this morning. That's one of the reasons I like the early morning meetings, they don't have a lot of people to text at 7 a.m.

"There have been some tensions as I've made some changes on defense and on offense. I'm not going to grade your performance by your statistical rankings. I'm going to grade our coaches and team based on wins and losses and how well we reach the goals we set week to week. We need to be unified as a staff and as a team. The team will feed off of us. If we are united and we are in lock-step they will sense that and they will buy in. If we have any fractures they will sense it and they will feed off of it."

So far so good, the response was what I was hoping to get.

"And this is what it comes down to; we will discuss things in here and it may get testy. But it cannot get personal, it must be professional discourse and we should be able to talk freely. Our internal discussions must not show up on social media or attributed to some anonymous source in a news story. If I catch anyone leaking stuff, I will get rid of you. The confidentiality of our meetings must be sacrosanct."

Sacrosanct is a big word for most coaches. Hell, I'd learned that word from Candace and her Ivy League education. It appeared the coaches understood what I meant but to be sure I reiterated my point using smaller words.

"If we can't trust one another, we have no chance."

To emphasize the next part of what I wanted to say I stood up. It was something I did from time to time to get their attention.

"This next part is important. When we have issues to discuss, come in make your point and counterpoint if necessary. Once a decision is made we must all buy in before we present to our team. If they smell even a whiff of dissent we're screwed. I've been around teams where coaches would tell their players that we were doing things they didn't like. I once heard a coach at Kansas say "If it was up to me we wouldn't run this play but we have to do what they tell us." Those seemingly small comments create cracks. Don't try and prop up your own stature by making it look like you've got better ideas. Your buy-in and your ability to sell our plans to the team are vital. If we can all do that we can build a team that will trust us and trust each other."

Later that day I made a similar talk to the team about the importance of trust and unity. When I stand in front of them in our team meeting room, I have a couple of demands. Hats off indoors, both feet on the floor, sit straight up, no cell phones, no drinks, no food and eyes on me or whoever was in front of them speaking.

I finished the talk this way.

"Guys together we can do some great things. Together the talent in this room can build something greater than anything you can imagine. But trust and loyalty are the most important elements we have to build a championship team. So I don't want to see our internal business on your social media accounts. There may be some things we are doing that are new on offense or defense. That's our business. There may be some people who switch positions or are asked to do new things. That's our business. There may be injuries. That's our business. And above all, our business is going to school, it is being responsible people in our community and in our families and it's winning football games. We will do that with a singular focus on team first. We will do that by each striving and working to get better every day. That goes for players and coaches and everyone in this room no matter what your role."

Spring is different because there is no game on the horizon, for coaches there is less pressure. That is not necessarily so for the players. These guys have pride, they have egos and they have their eyes on the prize of a potential NFL career. Their chance to make the starting lineup on their way to stardom has its beginnings in what we do in spring practice.

That pressure of NFL riches is how the story of cornerback Donte Carter unfolded. Donte was a truly great NFL defensive back prospect. At six feet tall and weighing 190 pounds he was a combination of excellent size and speed at his position. With his junior year ahead of him he was just a few months from cashing in on a big NFL contract.

Donte came from a tough background in Canton, Ohio. About two weeks after our bowl loss to Tennessee Donte's ex-girlfriend gave birth to his first child, a son. When he came into the office to talk to me during the season to tell me his ex-girlfriend was pregnant he was looking for help.

"Coach," he said "I wanted her to get an abortion but she wouldn't do that. So I need to know what help there is out there."

We've had a few guys with kids on our team over the years. We have an administrator who knows all the ins and outs of federal and state programs for everything from insurance to housing help.

Given that Donte referred to her as a past-tense girlfriend I got the idea that they would not be one big happy family. After telling him who to call and set up a meeting we talked in general about his situation.

"So this is your former girlfriend?" I asked.

"Yeah coach. We had a good run and I guess she saw the end coming. It's like you told us, I was a target of sorts. She saw the NFL money coming, but she saw me slipping away so she set out to put her hooks into me and my future earnings for the next eighteen years at least."

He was right. While some may deride my talk to guys on the team as cynical or sexist, I didn't care. Over the years I've seen a lot of guys who were careless in their relationships. They had one girlfriend and went looking for the next one or were screwing around with a bunch of other girls. Meanwhile the original girlfriend sees what's coming but doesn't want to be out of the picture so she stops taking her pill without telling him. Next thing you know she's pregnant and will be linked to this guy for the rest of their lives.

It's predictable so many times. When they come to talk to me about it, I never tell them "I told you so" because they often will tell me that they should've listened to me.

What I do tell them is the same thing I told Donte in that meeting in the fall "Whatever you do, if you're going to have a child, be a father, a real father and make a real commitment to being in that child's life. That is the most important thing now."

So Donte had a new baby as spring practice rolled around. But that wasn't the only pressure he felt. While we knew Donte came from a tough neighborhood in Canton, we didn't know that his mother was really struggling to keep their family afloat. His mother had taken in three of her sister's kids after that sister had overdosed and died. Donte's mom Gloria had an understanding landlord who knew that Donte was months away from a big NFL payday.

As such Gloria's landlord had let her go several months without paying rent. Donte knew about the arrangement and was doing everything he could to be that can't-miss NFL player. He was also sending home some of his federal Pell Grant money. In his mind he knew he was piling up liabilities. He had a baby to support and expenses from his mother's back-rent and three cousins to support.

Through the first eight practices he was just outstanding on and off the field. Then on a Wednesday afternoon, right before we took five days off for Easter he came flying in on a scrimmage to tackle a big tight end. As they collided it was a clean textbook tackle but as they both hit the ground Donte's head hit the turf hard giving him what would be his third concussion and placing the rest of his spring practice in jeopardy.

He didn't want to be tagged a concussion risk for NFL scouts. So Donte popped back up and acted as though nothing was wrong. It was his last play in the last part of practice so he was done for the day. He knew he would have five days off before the next one so he ignored the ringing in his brain and the nausea symptoms.

But as he went back to his apartment that night, he continued to ignore the symptoms. Because he'd been through a concussion before he just tried to stick to the protocol that he remembered. Except that because he was trying to hide what he'd done he was going to class and trying to concentrate which made it worse. His school work really started to fade.

On the practice field for a few days when a contact drill would come up he would complain about his quad or his hamstring to avoid the drills. One day on the practice field when Donte pulled himself out before a contact drill his coach Dwayne Baxter had seen enough of Donte's pattern.

"Look Donte, I'm tired of you acting like a big pussy every time we start hitting. If you're trying to save yourself for the league, just tell me and we'll sit your ass out all year and see how the scouts like you then." He yelled.

Overhearing Dwayne I moved over there in time to see Donte get back into the drill and hit a big wide receiver. The hit must've really been painful for him, but I didn't know that then. But I did know the pressures that Donte was under with a new baby and how much he'd need to make the NFL. So I pulled him out of the drill.

Then I quietly talked to Dwayne.

"Dwayne, he's got a lot going on with the new baby and the pressures to make the NFL. Just take it easy on him for now if he's trying to play it a little safe. We know how good he is, he knows what he's doing and he has been a really tough tackler. The most important thing is to have him ready to go when the season gets here."

"But Ed, he's been a little off on his assignments and that bothers me. He'll only get better at that by practicing."

"That's fine, he has to practice but let's just be smart with him. We've only got a few practices left and he'll catch right up in August. Okay?"

"I got you."

Unwittingly my pressure on Dwayne to back off Donte would allow him to hide his concussion. But the symptoms would not allow him to do his best in school and would create mood swings and behavior that was out of character for him. One of his professors called my office a day or two before the Spring Game to tell me how Donte's work had fallen off. Normally professors don't call me, but this woman was a friend of Candace's.

I explained that we were seeing some of the pressures that Donte was undergoing having an effect on his mood and demeanor, but that we thought he'd get past it. The professor told me that she appreciated the insight and would sit down with Donte to talk. But I did share with her that I would sit Donte out of the Spring Game to make sure he understood how important his school work had to be, and how he had to treat his professors with respect.

Spring Games are always one of the worst weekends of the year. A crowd of 70,000 people show up to watch what is essentially a glorified practice that is televised by the Big Ten Network. But there are a million demands for our time. Over 100 recruits show up with their families and it is a balancing act to make sure they all get the time they need. That is why our recruiting staff is so tense trying to make sure we don't slight anyone.

Rick Carter shuffles me from recruit to recruit giving me last minute reminders before we start the next conversation. The nine guys that are already committed gang up on the big-name kids and pressure them to commit.

Meanwhile there are interviews and a press conference. There are donor events right after the game. And then there is the "game". Over the years I've decided to give both the offense and defense a limited menu of plays and defenses and let the quarterbacks call the game and let the linebackers call the defenses. It limits what we show in our schemes and it allows me to learn from our players about how they see a game unfolding. It makes it fun for them too.

Ten minutes after the game, I am rushed up to a suite where Candace will meet me before we head into a reception for the biggest donors. But my mind is a million miles away because I know that our team has their annual team party to celebrate the end of spring practice. It has been without incident lately, but that can all change in a moment's notice.

In the donor reception, I spent extra time talking to the group and even doing a question and answer session. I kept in my mind the advice Candace had given me a few weeks ago when she told me to let these donors get to know me.

While it is a private event and I'd like to talk freely, I also know that as I ascend to the podium there are a number of them holding up cell phones to record what I say. Five years ago I could make a joke about Michigan or talk about specific players or recruits honestly, but those days are long gone. Everything I say will end up on one of their social media feeds or posted on a message board or a blog so they can show all their friends that they are on the inside.

But that's the nature of the beast and either you adapt or your career ends before you want.

As I talked with donors, I kept noticing that Candace too was working her way around the room. She is one of my best weapons. She knew we had to go on offense and she was running routes around the room attacking the people she most suspected that we needed to convert to our cause. Luckily Alexis was not in town, she texted me something about heading to the Maldives with her latest suitor. Lucky him. Hell I didn't even know where the Maldives were but I did Google it to find it on a map.

By the time we got home, Candace had a scouting report on a number of the donors. God, I just loved how that woman's mind worked.

After a busy weekend I passed out on my couch watching replays of other spring games. At 1:30 a.m. my phone rang and I was none too pleased to see that it was Sid Inge. This was never good.

"Sid?" I asked hoping that it was an inadvertent call.

"Ed, I'm not even gonna ask if I woke you up because I know the answer. Can you get to your computer and get to the Go-OState site?"

Groping my way to the light so I could get to the den I stubbed my damn toe on the coffee table and yelled out an expletive that I know Sid had to have heard.

Finally after what probably seemed like an eternity I was at my desk and had pulled up the site.

"You got it pulled up?" Sid asked.

"Yeah....I see it."

On the screen was the headline "Racial Fight Breaks Out at Ohio State Football Party."

"What the fuck?" I said.

"I already called Daniels and Metzger."

Metzger was our senior Linebacker and likely captain and Daniels was our receiver who was the likely DJ at the party.

"So what'd they tell you?"

"There was a black girl talking to Marshall Remington at the party. A white girl walked over to her and told the black girl to stick to the black guys and leave the good looking white dudes for them. Then the black girl made a comment about white girls chasing the black guys and then some shoving ensued. It then spilled outside where Matty Buck's Go-OState intern was there to video the whole thing. The video is bad in that it is clearly a group of black girls fighting a group of white girls."

"Any of our guys involved?"

"No. In fact they broke things up and helped the police."

"The police? Great."

"Don't worry, none of our guys got arrested. As far as I can tell, they sent everyone home and ended that party. But I also talked to the police officer, he was standing next to Metzger and confirmed his story. There was one thing he did tell me though that worries me. He said they found a lot of Adderall at the party but they have no idea whose it was. "

"Is that in the story?"

"No and we don't know if any of our guys are connected to it."

"So we have a story about a party where our guys did nothing wrong and cooperated with the police. And as a bonus they ended the party so that's good. But that doesn't keep Matty from writing a bullshit headline that'll get picked up and re-tweeted all over the country the next few days."

"So how do you want me to handle this?"

"You call Matty Buck and you tell his ass to take this shit down. It's not a football story, it's not a team racial issue and it damn sure shouldn't be on a site that covers sports. He is such a click-bait whore."

"You want to offer him a sit-down for a post-spring article?"

"Fuck no. Call his ass up, wake his wife and kids and tell him that if he doesn't pull this bush-league shit down that he'll be lucky to get a media pass for anything in the future. See how he likes that."

"I can do that but I think we may want to re-think that. No sense getting into a pissing contest with him."

"Just tell him what I said." I snapped.

With that Sid hung up and as I looked up to see Candace at the door of my den in a long T-shirt. After I explained what had happened she laughed.

“At least none of your guys got arrested.”

“There you are with the Silver lining……”

“We got a lot done today. We’re going on offense. But I gotta say that I wish you spent as much time thinking about us as you do with all this other stuff. You’ve been running so hard the last few weeks you haven’t been paying enough attention to me. So since you’re awake you’d better remedy that.”

That was one of the dangers of this job. The singular focus meant you neglected some things, and often it started with the people you are closest to. It had already cost me one marriage. She had a point and who was I to say no to a younger woman her looking like she did?

9. SPRINGING INTO SUMMER

Years ago the weeks after the Spring game were pretty quiet. The players settled in to get the most out of the rest of the academic term and our coaches fanned out to go evaluate and follow up on junior players all over the country. But with the new December signing day we found ourselves hosting recruits on May weekends.

While most times the month of May is pretty quiet, this past year saw a continual flow of drama in our office. It seemed like we just had a staff that was looking for shit to get into, and I was like Smokey the Bear trying to stamp out forest fire after forest fire. This was not the year for coaching staff drama...but there it was.

The recruiting part was the simplest part of May and June. We liked having the visits in May more than April because the weather was a lot better, and there were no practices to work around giving our coaches more time to spend with the recruits and their families.

Our players also were in some May summer classes with a much smaller work load so we weren't taxing their time as much either.

With signing day still so far away we really pushed kids to take their official visits in the fall or in December so we were still fresh in their minds when it finally came down to putting pen to paper. But we did have a number of visits in May with one or two players and sometimes three or four players visiting in a weekend.

One of the players who visited us in early May came with his parents who were divorced. Because there was bad blood between each parent's new spouses they decided to leave them at home. Luckily NCAA rules allow us to provide separate rooms for divorced parents which is a good rule. Personally, I can't imagine having to bunk with my ex-wife. That would make for some good reality television.

On Friday night we took the parents out to eat and for a couple of drinks. When Doug Leonard dropped them off, he was halfway to his home when he realized that the mother had left her purse with her wallet and phone in his car. So he did what any good recruiter would do, he looked up her hotel room number and drove back to drop it off.

When he got to her room he knocked on the door and there was no answer. He went back to the lobby bar to see if she had gone there for a drink afterwards and he did not see her. So he decided he'd drop the purse at her ex-husband's room. He was about to knock when he heard some strange noises coming from inside the room.

He hesitated, put his ear to the door and confirmed what he thought he'd heard. It was definitely the ex-wife and they were definitely doing something that they probably shouldn't be doing.

So Doug went to the lobby laughing as he called me.

"Ed I got her purse she left in the car and damn if I couldn't find her. And low and behold she is in his room and it sound like they were re-living old times." He said.

"Nothing like a shared parenting experience to rekindle that old spark."

"Coach, I ain't been divorced. You ever thought about a romp with the ex-wife?"

"Shit no. There are some battle lines that get drawn that can never be crossed again."

"What should I do?"

"Leave the purse with the front desk and act like that's what you did all along. They'll leave a blinking message light for her."

The next morning when Doug arrived to pick them up she still hadn't come down to get her purse so Doug knew she'd spent the night in his room. Guess we hadn't needed to pay for that extra room after all.

But that was fairly tame as the months of May and June went. Some of it never even got to me but the next round of drama very definitely landed on my desk.

Early in May I received a call on a late Thursday evening. Donte Carter's ex-girlfriend and baby momma had called the police. Donte was ranting angrily at her apartment and she feared it could turn violent. The police called me to tell me that they were taking him into custody to cool off and then see if his ex-girlfriend would be okay. They told me that he appeared to be acting either drunk or on some kind of drugs because he was at times completely incoherent.

When they went back to talk to her she told them that for several weeks he'd been having wild mood swings, had been having trouble remembering things she'd told him and had even resorted to violent language. The police reported that he was having trouble even remembering basic facts like the day of the week or the date. An initial breathalyzer showed no alcohol in his system so they would do some toxicology tests on him. But his ex-girlfriend reported that he had been with her all afternoon and evening and had not taken any drugs.

I told the police that in all of his time at Ohio State he had been drug tested several times and nothing had ever come up.

We were all at a loss to explain his behavior.

Unfortunately my favorite intrepid reporter Matty Buck paid employees to listen in to police scanner calls or he had a police officer on his payroll. Matty went on social media and tweeted out that the police were investigating Donte for potential domestic violence.

Sid Inge called me immediately.

"Are you aware of this situation with Donte Carter?" he asked.

"Yes, I am already talking with the police. They called to ask me some background questions about him."

"Did you take notes about what you said on the call and the nature of the call?" Sid asked.

"Kind of....do mental notes count?"

"No they don't. Write down everything you can recall about the call. To a media member who finds out you talked to the police, it will look like they were calling you to cover this up. I'm not a lawyer but I've been around enough to know that you'd better keep notes."

"But..."

"But Ed, it's not what the call was about. It's what the call can be made to appear like it's about in the hands of a Matty Buck. We should probably be ready to issue a statement that we are aware of the situation and that we are waiting for results of the police investigation."

"I am not going to do that. That will only inflame the situation and make the story even bigger. And I will call Gerry Gorton to relay that to him as well."

The story made a day's worth of rounds in the state media and was a blip on the national websites that covered college football. When tempers cooled and everyone returned to their neutral corners Donte had not done anything other than yell and he'd never even come close to getting violent in a physical way. He agreed to undergo counseling.

But some of the things his ex-girlfriend had told us raised some red flags. After the drug toxicology reports came back clean, our team doctor had Donte take the concussion testing. He failed it and when cornered admitted that he's had a bad collision on a date that he could no longer remember in spring practice.

When Matty Buck found out that Donte would not be charged he did some more digging through his police sources and found out about Donte's undiagnosed concussion and reported that we'd covered up his concussion and allowed him to play the rest of the spring. Now it was all out there and this new concussion would certainly hurt his draft stock, making him even potentially a player who would not get drafted.

In Matty's reporting on the story he even got anonymous quotes from NFL scouts who expressed doubts about drafting a player with the type of concussion history Donte had. The story made its way to Canton where Donte's landlord suddenly saw the big money at the end of Donte's OSU rainbow vanishing. He gave Donte's Mom an eviction notice with a few weeks to get out.

Everything was crashing down around Donte. An overzealous reporter digging too far into a college football player's life had damaged the NFL future for a young man supporting a baby and helping his mother and a few cousins keep a roof over their heads.

It was at that time that a family friend came forward and loaned his mother the money, and helped her find a job with UPS in the Columbus area. The benefits, the salary and the proximity to Donte would mean they could all live together. Donte's rent stipend would help pay for their joint apartment. Crisis averted....for the time being.

Most importantly we had to get Donte right mentally. We missed his issues in the spring, his sudden fear of contact, his grades slipping and his attitude. All of it became so much clearer.

But off the field issues weren't just limited to players.

Our Running back coach Roger Barstow became a problem. At 43 years old he was a guy who had played at Ohio State. He worked out a lot and stayed in great shape and had a smooth charismatic way with everyone he met. In May while we were hosting a great junior running back for his visit that running back's single Mom was with him.

After meeting with Roger the recruit and his mother were walking out of his office. While her son got halfway down the hall she turned back into the office.

"Coach, I do have one more question...are you single?"

"No I'm not. I've been married for fifteen years."

"That's too bad."

As it happened I was in the next office within earshot. After she went down the hall I walked into Roger's office.

"The correct answer next time is yes I am single. Your wife would understand if you took one for the team." I laughed.

"Oh no she wouldn't."

He was right. His wife Monica was a thirty-two year old fitness instructor who took no shit from anyone. Roger had gone through some previous issues before. He was a head coach at The University of Richmond. While he was there he was screwing the President of the University's staff assistant.

When the President found out she was so pissed off that she confronted both of them and demanded they end it or he would be forced to resign. The next week when the University President was out of town Roger met the staff assistant at her office to have revenge-sex on the President's desk.

As fate would have it, the President arrived home a day early and went to collect her mail from her office. She caught them in the act. I can only imagine how awkward that had to have been.

Roger quietly resigned and that is when I hired him. He and I talked openly about it, but since he had played at Ohio State and was a great recruiter and coach I decided to hire him. He always assured me that those days were over.

Knowing how beautiful his wife Monica was, I always wondered how he could cheat on her. She was stunning with blonde hair and striking blue eyes. She had a great sense of humor and was the brains of their marriage.

But as Otis Lewis said to me when I was debating hiring Roger; "Coach, it doesn't matter how beautiful or smart a woman may be, somewhere there is a guy who is probably sick of her shit."

All kidding aside, I thought that Roger's prowling days were over. Then a day in late May turned all that upside down. Down the hall I heard some yelling from the office of Erika Alpert, our staff assistant in charge of expense accounts. Roger was yelling at her so I came running down the hall.

"What the hell is the matter?" I demanded to know.

"Nothing," Roger said "it's nothing but some mistakes I made on my expense reports. I'll handle it."

Erika nodded in approval, but I wasn't buying it. Roger was leaving that afternoon for another recruiting trip, so once he had gone I wanted to talk to

Erika. Not wanting to draw any attention to the situation I had Sally call down to ask Erika if she could help explain the new expense report system at 5:15.

It was best if all the other staff assistants were out of the building so they wouldn't gossip about a conversation I was having with Erika, particularly since they'd heard Roger yelling earlier.

At 5:15 Erika came into the office and I asked her if she was okay. She exhaled audibly and started to tell me what had happened.

"Yesterday while Roger was still out of town, his wife Monica wanted to see his expense report receipts because she wanted to make sure they were accurate with some charges that had shown up on some credit card statements. Roger likes to use his own credit card for travel so he can rack up miles and reward points on business trips that he uses for his own personal travel. Monica came in with a bunch of specific dates that all related to trips he'd taken to Cleveland and for specific hotels. There was also a trip for recruiting he took to Nashville and one to Miami. So I pulled out the dates she wanted, printed out a copy of his expense report and gave them to her. That's what he was yelling about."

"He was mad because you gave his wife a copy of his expense reports?"

"That's about it. I just feel bad that I gave his wife those reports without checking with him." Erika said.

Something was rotten in Denmark, but I figured if she didn't want to tell me that was her business. But I did have an obligation to advise her to speak with HR if she had a problem. She thanked me for being supportive and left the room.

After Erika left, Sally came in to see if I needed anything else before she went home. Before she left she did hint at something bigger that related to what happened to Erika.

"Is there something I need to know?" I asked. "Is Roger harassing her? Is something going on?"

"What did she tell you?"

Because of confidentiality I couldn't share what Erika had told me but Sally could guess that Erika had left something out.

"Since you can't tell me, I'll tell you what she should've told you. You really are the last to know I guess." Sally said. "Here's the deal. Monica came in to look at specific times and dates for a reason."

"You mean a reason different from what Erika told me?"

"Well Monica told Erika that she was comparing bills and that is true. But what happened was Monica got a call from a woman in Cleveland who explained that Roger was her man now and that she should leave him. She gave Monica dates and hotels where they stayed when Roger came to recruit in Cleveland. She then gave Monica dates for trips the two of them had taken to Nashville and Miami. So Monica was just looking to match the dates and hotels up on his expense reports. She didn't tell Erika that. When the dates matched up, Monica confronted Roger who came in to yell at Erika for sharing the expense reports with his wife."

"And Erika was trying to be helpful?"

"As far as she knew."

"Now I gotta deal with Roger on this. What the hell, why can't he just keep his dick in his pants? Let Erika know that if she wants to talk to HR that she should do so."

Roger had already left town, but I was going to have to deal with this shit when he got back. From a professional standpoint there wasn't much I could do. If it was on his own time and on his own dime he could do whatever he wants. I just can't have this kind of crap where he blows up at a staff assistant who thought she was trying to help. And I certainly won't judge his marriage. God knows I had my own failure too.

But this was just the tip of the sexcapades iceberg that Spring. About two days after Roger's incident, I was called by the parents of one of our recruiting interns. They believed one of our players had video on his phone of him having sex with their daughter. They were upset enough about the incident itself, but the last thing they wanted was to have a video surface on the internet. As the parent of a college-aged daughter I completely understood their anxiety and fears. I assured them that this would be taken care of quickly. The player they accused was a great student and one of the most respected guys on the team. This was surprising.

I called the player in to meet with me and asked if had in fact made a video of himself with the intern. He confirmed that he had in fact done so.

"Why in this day and age of "Me Too" would you ever video that?" I asked.

"Coach, that is exactly why I did it. I am pre-law and I videoed this for proof of consent."

"You did what?"

"I'm from an affluent and politically connected family. Next year I am off to law school and the last thing I want to do is get accused of sexual assault or rape. With my family's money and connections I'm a target. So when I have sex with girls in college I get them on tape confirming that they are consenting. I take no chances."

He had a point, but this was certainly not something we wanted to promote to guys on the team.

"I see...however her parents do not want this ending up on the internet somewhere. Please just delete the damned thing and please refrain from doing this in the future. Are there more guys on the team doing this?"

"Not that I know of."

And if that wasn't enough there was more on the horizon. When things slowed down in the late spring and early summer all that extra time allows guys to find more trouble. And with more interns, graduate assistants and people around the program than we really need there is always the threat that one of these ancillary employees will do something stupid that will need to be addressed.

Some of these young guys who work with us suddenly gain a notoriety and newfound status as part of the program. In Columbus and on campus, Ohio State football is the big show and everyone seems to want a piece of it. And for a 22 year old intern right out of college they are suddenly important people with access to information that people want. They also have access to facilities.

So it should not have been a surprise when it was brought to me that a few of our football interns were texting female students and offering them a chance to have sex in the football locker room after hours. What surprised me is how many of these girls were in fact willing to do so.

A text message sweep also turned up sexting messages from our younger assistant coaches Freddie Smith and Sal Tessio. Although both of them were relatively young (27 and 31 respectively) and unmarried I did not think it was exactly the kind of thing we wanted going on in our program. To have them texting student recruiting interns asking for sex or for snapchat photos was a serious risk. Even our community relations director C.J. Rollins was asking for topless snapchat photos from students.

As our compliance officer Curtis Owens sat down to review the information with me, I was beside myself.

"What the hell were these idiots thinking? They are so damned stupid...and using their University-issued phones!" I yelled in a way that Curtis knew was not directed at him. Then I turned my attention to Curtis "What should I do about this?"

"Well none of these guys are married. We don't have a dating policy for them as it relates to students. And we really have no proof that they actually had sex in the facility. So from an employment and legal standpoint there's nothing actionable here. But this is not the kind of thing we want happening and certainly if it got out, it would not look good."

"Not look good? It looks like goddamn Sodom and Gomorrah in here. Did anyone actually go through with having sex in the building? Can't we fire someone for that?"

"We don't really have proof, even though from the messages sent back and forth and from the swipes to get into the building there is a tremendous amount of circumstantial evidence that this was going on. And we do not have cameras in the locker room, and these guys probably know that."

There was one question looming that I was curious about. The compliance officer had started an investigation of text messages but I wasn't sure why he had done so.

"So what started you on this investigation?"

"A couple of parents contacted me when they saw these text messages on their daughter's phones. They just wanted this handled quietly. There was also some Junk mail pics sent to two of the girls."

"Junk mail?"

"Yeah, someone sent these girls pictures of their "junk"."

"Is there any way to figure that out?"

"Not really. It was sent from a burner phone. Short of a police-style penis lineup we're probably out of luck. And I am pretty sure we don't want to have a line up."

"Yeah, I'd say you're right on that. When did this job get so damned complicated?" The question was directed to no one in particular.

Curtis decided that he would speak directly to the coaches and interns and refer them to some sensitivity training from HR. He felt it was best if I stayed out of the situation. Needless to say I was more than happy to allow him to have a sex talk with interns and assistant coaches.

The next day Gerry Gorton called me to come meet with him at his office. He was still asking for recruiting updates but he wanted to talk about some of the off-field issues. It was good to be able to explain the Donte Carter situation in person. He wanted assurances that we did not know about a concussion. I assured him that all of the team physician's notes illustrated that Donte had never come to the doctor to report any symptoms.

But the sexting between interns and college girls and the potential sex going on in the football building had him in a bad mood.

"What kind of people and program are you running over there? If any of this were to get out we'd have a national story on our hands. You're goddam lucky that none of this has gotten anywhere."

"There is no question about it and Curtis Owens, per our legal and compliance office, is going to address this according to University policy. If you want me to get involved in talking with these guys I will do that as well."

"No you'd better stick to following University policy."

"Are you sure? That didn't work out so well for Joe Paterno. After all, he followed school policy to the letter of the law and he got fired for it."

"I hear you. Just make sure these guys get the message and cut out the crap. We're not running a bathhouse for these guys to use to attract dates."

After the late afternoon meeting I headed home. The minute I walked in the door Candace could sense that something was hanging over me. After trying to deflect it a few times she finally cornered me. Standing in the kitchen with the light of the early evening sun coming in the back windows she smiled at me. She'd just come in from her backyard garden and stood there in an old dirt-stained OSU t-shirt and a pair of jeans. She knew I couldn't resist her in those jeans and t-shirt after she'd been out back digging, so she pressed me for information one more time. I unloaded all the accumulated issues from the coaches' sexting to Roger and his wife's issues.

"Are you serious? Monica came in to cross check his expense accounts?"

"She sure did."

"I gotta admit, that is straight-up genius."

"Well, she caught his ass now."

Candace laughed, the laugh of someone holding cards that she knows I don't know she's got.

"What do you know that I don't?" I asked.

"You really are dumb aren't you?"

"Apparently so."

"Monica is acting all offended and betrayed. Yet what you apparently don't know is that she's been fucking around on him too...pretty much since they got here. Her latest is the hot 25-year old guy that teaches cycle classes at our gym. He owns the place"

"Are you serious?"

"Yeah, that guy's pretty aggressive. He's hit on me an a few occasions."

"Seriously?"

"Yes...and I'm a little offended that you'd question that. After all look at me. I look damn good." She smiled.

She had a point.

"I guess I can't blame the guy. But as for Monica's act, where does she get so high and mighty judging him?" I asked.

"Classic deflection. Point the finger and no one looks at you. And as for all these people screwing around in your building I gotta say that I'm pretty offended."

"Why is that?"

"You've never even asked me to come have sex with you in your office."

"The thought has crossed my mind but I always figured you'd turn me down."

Candace laughed again.

"Have you already forgotten?"

"Forgotten what?"

"What we did the night you got this job?"

How could I ever forget that? I hadn't thought about it in a while but I haven't forgotten it. We went into the Stadium after dark to seal the day on the fifty yard line. I was afraid of getting caught but I still remember what Candace said that night.

"If we get arrested you'll be a goddam folk hero for doing this with your wife the night you got hired to be the head coach at Ohio State. Just remember this when you step on this field for the Michigan game in November. No matter how stressful that game may get, you've already scored here. Then you can relax and coach the game."

As I recalled that night and the big win over Michigan, I had done exactly what she'd said. Late in the game when it was time for a big coaching decision, I smiled and made the call that gave us the game-winning score. Then I snapped back to the present.

"I remember. But in this day and age, after everything I just heard about this week it may be best to just keep things in check."

"Stop acting like an old man. Have you given up your sense of adventure? If they want to fire you for screwing your wife somewhere risky....just let them try it."

All joking aside, it was good to be able to talk to Candace about some of the problems I was having at the office. Her confidence in my judgment gave me strength.

While all this was happening, what I was unaware of was that Quinn Banks had started a relationship with a 21-year old senior at Ohio State. She was a semester from graduating next December. The two of them were meeting at a house owned by a booster of the program that Quinn had befriended. Quinn knew he couldn't be seen around town with a college student as his date. Sometimes he arranged to go to dinner with the booster and this girl so it looked like three people innocently going to eat. Quinn would also take her on some of the May recruiting trips he drove to around the state.

The student was a tall dark-haired beauty from New Jersey who was on her way to either law school or to New York to commit to a modeling career. The cloak and dagger dating successfully kept it from everyone in the Athletic Department.

And there was even recruiting news. On the good side our incoming freshman defensive end Jamar Tucker was already doing some running and lifting on his road to recovery from the tragic shooting. Perhaps best of all was his willingness to go to therapy to deal with any potential PTSD.

Years ago we had recruited a player who'd come home to find his parents and brother murdered in a bloody scene. He never really did get over it. He played football with an angry ferocity that was off the charts, but he was not able to restrict that anger to the playing field. A few years later in the NFL he was repeatedly fined for on-field hits and finally forced out of the league after alleged domestic violence issues at home.

We just didn't think about mental health in those days. But we live and learn and now Jamar will benefit from it. One of the most important factors was having a stable home environment. His high school coach basically adopted him and moved him into his house. Jamar and I talked at least once a week and texted almost daily. He'd even started going to a weekly bible study and support group for victims of gun violence.

Most coaches don't believe in the hocus pocus of psychiatry and mental health but if you live long enough, keep your eyes and ears open and listen to the people you coach you will come around. In a few months Jamar would be back in the safe sanctuary of the football field where things make sense and with the support of his brothers on the team.

But there was some other things going on with our incoming recruits that were hidden from me. Our top Tight end recruit Manny Rodriguez needed a B in his senior English class to be eligible. Rick Carter kept assuring us he'd be okay. He'd talked with the principal Miss Rose a number of times. She was an OSU alum and told Rick that she was monitoring the situation carefully.

At the end of the month Manny had gotten a C in English which meant he couldn't play as a freshman. That would put a dent in the Tight End position for us and also be embarrassing for the school. On Rick's urging Manny went to see the teacher and ask for some extra credit to try and push his grade to a B. The teacher felt pressured and went to the principal and to his teacher's union rep to make sure he wouldn't get any blowback for refusing to help a high-profile recruit.

At Manny's high school when the NCAA Initial Eligibility center requested transcripts, they would mail them hard copies. Manny's transcript was prepped and picked up by the mailman after school. Principal Rose asked the guidance office if the mail carrier had arrived and ran after him to grab Manny's transcript.

That evening after everyone had gone home, Miss Rose and Manny's guidance counselor went into the system and changed another class grade to give Manny the required GPA. They sent out the transcript out the next morning.

Miss Rose made a point to call Rick Carter and tell him that some "extra credit" from the Principal's office had pushed up a grade in another class. Rick did not ask any questions, as there are some thing best left unknown.

By the time we got into mid-June we were busy with recruiting visits, summer football camps and off-season workouts. We were now allowed to work with our guys for a few hours a week and that was an important element. Of particular importance was the presence of all the incoming freshmen for summer school. These guys got a chance to get any homesickness out of the way in June instead of August and to get a feel for their coaches, teammates and new school.

For us we got a chance to see which freshmen were as good as advertised and which ones had been overrated. It didn't take long to see that athletically this class was as good as advertised. Whether or not they were physically tough we wouldn't know until we put on pads and started hitting each other in pre-season practice. But it was clear that these puppies were gifted and fast. The question remained to be seen if they would bite and scrap in a fight.

As usual it was Doug Leonard who had the homespun wit.

Coming off the practice field our safeties coach Freddie Smith commented to Doug on how good these guys looked. Walking a few paces behind I heard the exchange.

"Damn Doug, these freshmen look good. They'll help us right away."

"Maybe." Doug replied.

"Maybe?"

"Son you ever raise a hunting dog?"

"No, what's that got to do with anything."

"Son, freshmen are no different than hunting dogs. They can look good running around in the litter, chasing rabbits, or pointing birds. You can train them and train them. But eventually you got to take 'em out in the field and shoot the gun off. When the gun goes off then you know. Some hear the gun and go sprinting to find what you shot while others will hide behind your leg and piss themselves. Until these boys have been in Ohio Stadium and had that gun go off you don't know who will be running after the other team and which ones will piss themselves."

Doug never failed to come up with the right cliché. As I walked off the practice field before a Fourth of July break I knew we were just weeks away from that gun going off. Then we'd find out which of our dogs would run down our foes. That included all of us as coaches as well. It had been an eventful couple of months, I was just hoping to be able to kick back at the beach for a few days over the Fourth and then come back tanned, rested and ready to go.

10. SUMMERTIME STORMS

In July the coaches went our separate ways for vacation. For a number of years Candace and I had been going to the Jersey Shore. It was part of her childhood as a kid who grew up on the East Coast. The place she'd visited most was a town called Avalon, New Jersey. It seemed like everyone from Philly was there for the summer and judging from the flags flying outside people's homes it was dominated by Penn State football fans and Villanova basketball fans.

Some of the Penn State fans recognized me and kidded me about the upcoming season but generally they left us alone. It also helped that we rented a beachfront home with a pool and a secluded deck that looked out over the dunes to the ocean. Of the two weeks we stayed there, my son Sam and daughter Deanna came in for the Fourth of July weekend. They were both doing internships for the summer in Manhattan so it was an easy trip down for them.

Candace's sister Sally and her two young children were there as well. They stayed about a week. Everyone got along well. The touchy dynamic was always between Candace and my kids. They got along well with her despite hearing plenty of malicious crap from my ex-wife about Candace. They loved their mother and they felt they couldn't betray that love by adopting Candace fully.

I understood where they were coming from, even if their hesitancy to fully embrace her ate at Candace. We both knew it was there but we never talked about it. That often happens between a coach and his wife. Things at home seem less important than the problems and challenges we have coaching young men and having to make split decisions in front of 100,000 fans and millions more on National television. And most of us are not equipped with the emotional intelligence to discuss our feelings let alone trying to process our wife's feelings.

The best part of the trip was the few days that she and I had alone. Morning and evening walks on the beach and mid-day bike rides cleared our minds of the past year's disappointment and deflected the pressure of the season that loomed.

And no matter how hard I tried to ignore it, it was always there lingering. And every day there were notes to send recruits, calls to make to players and other staff members. But it was generally pretty quiet and our time together alone really helped us reconnect before the long exile of the fall season. She'd even tricked me into a midnight romp on the beach that could've gotten us arrested.

When we returned to Columbus we had more recruits visit us. One of them was the top recruit in the state Terrence Jones, an electric athlete who could play receiver, running back, outside linebacker safety and maybe even corner. He also returned kicks and punts. He was the top recruit in the country at 6'3" and 210 pounds with an ability to do so many things.

Jones was from Steubenville, Ohio. He starred for the Big Red in a small town on the West Virginia border. His parents were separated and he lived with a friend's family. His mother was dealing with addiction issues and his father lived about twenty minutes away in Pennsylvania collecting disability for PTSD from five tours in Iraq and Afghanistan. Terrence was pretty much on his own but the whole town took care of him.

Despite our confidence in being the home-state school something kept him from committing to us. There was this guy Tom Pietrovic who had taken Terrence under his wing. Tom was always around and he was acting like Terrence's agent.

I just couldn't trust this guy so I found an alumnus in Youngstown. In Youngstown a lot of guys "know a guy who knows a guy." This alum knew Caesar Alfonsi. Alfonsi was involved in everything in Eastern Ohio from Warren to Akron and down to Steubenville. He knew all about Pietrovic.

Right after the weekend when Terrence came to visit I got a call from Caesar.

"So Caesar what you got for me?"

"This Pietrovic guy could be a problem for you."

"How so?"

"From what I'm hearing he has really got his hooks into this kid. He's taken him up to visit Michigan three times this summer already and he is steering the kid there."

"Why is that?"

"Pietrovic's got a small factory that makes some specialty glass parts for cars. He used to sell a lot of stuff to the GM plant up in Lordstown before it closed. Now all of his biggest customers are in Michigan. A couple of them are run by Michigan people and he wants to ingratiate himself to those people."

"Well we can overcome that can't we?"

"He holds a ton of sway over this kid. He paid for the girlfriend's abortion, bought the kid a car and moved the mom into a nice new furnished apartment. The kid also has a no-show job at the factory making about $25 an hour."

"Is that all?"

"Pretty much."

"So are we dead in the water?"

"Depends on how clean you want to stay in this thing."

"Give me some parameters."

"Well Pietrovic thinks he's a pretty good poker player. He drives up here to Youngstown for a game once a week. The guys he plays with are all Buckeye fans. He's into a couple of connected people for about 75 grand...maybe 100 grand. Given the auto industry slowing down a bit he might not have the kind of future liquidity that he needs. Next time he comes up for a game, we could make sure he loses even more. Once he's desperate, these guys demand the money and we offer to make it all go away....on one condition of course."

"Look I can't condone that kind of stuff. .....but what I don't know....."

Now that we were all back in town in the office there was a lot of stuff to do. We had a long meeting to catch up on events since we'd all been on vacation. It was like that first day back in school after summer vacation. Guys were tan or sunburned and were fidgeting like they wanted another day or week of vacation.

Usually I started these meetings asking for updates, and the latest news. Rick Carter was the best intelligence guy we had on the staff. He was still young and had done his best to meet and connect with as many people around campus as possible. The recruiting interns also kept him informed.

"So Rick give me the latest news." I said.

"Well here is the latest. A friend who owns an apartment building near campus informs me that an agent has moved a couple of very attractive women in. They are on his payroll and will be likely trolling the bars around town looking to connect with our guys."

"Okay that's good that we know that. What else?"

"All is good with the guys who asked for and are working at part-time summer jobs. Malcolm Jennings and Pokey Wallace are making good money at their landscaping jobs."

"Landscaping? They seem like the last two people who would do that."

“There’s a catch. An alum owns a summer resort outside of town for people who prefer an alternative lifestyle.”

“Alternative lifestyle covers a lot in 2020, can you be more specific?”

“It’s a nudist resort.”

Everyone howled. When the laughter died down Roger Barstow spoke up.

“Yeah Pokey was pretty excited about it, until he realized that the average age of the nudists was north of sixty-five. Not what those two had bargained for. They got hit on a lot, but they’re not really into the AARP set.”

Doug Leonard jumped in “Hey as the lone representative of the sixty and older set that remark triggered me. Can I go to the room on campus where they have puppies, coloring books and play-doh?”

“There is a joke somewhere about these guys trimming hedges at a nudist resort but I’ll just leave that alone. And as someone married to a much-younger wife I may be an age discriminator too. Offending Doug’s feelings aside, what else you got?” I asked

“We had some guys working at a car dealership, but compliance made sure they weren’t getting use of any cars. The other hot spot is the three guys who are bartending this summer. There has been some rumbling about alums showing up and dropping big tips in the tip jar.” Rick said.

“Is that an NCAA violation?” I asked.

“If it is excessive it could run afoul of the rules. But here’s the real kicker, the place where they work pulls all tips for all bartenders, waitresses and staff. So their co-workers are making out on this big-time too.”

“Good for them. Anything else?”

My phone buzzed and I got a text from a number I did not recognize asking if he could come see me. The text said he was in the building. Curiosity got the best of me so I excused myself and told the guys to start on recruiting video.

Walking down the hall to my office I saw Marshall Remington waiting outside my officc.

“Hey coach did you get my text?” he asked.

“I guess but it wasn’t from your phone number? Did you get a new number?”

“Oh shit,” Marshall laughed “that was from my “Ho” phone.”

"Excuse me? Did you say Ho phone or home phone?"

"Ho phone. It's the phone I use for girls who are not my girlfriend. Can't get caught getting texts from other girls."

"Good to know. Can't be too careful. So what's up?"

"Just wanted to catch up and update you on some of the team progress this summer."

"Come on in."

The meeting went on for a while. These were the meetings I enjoyed when a player initiated it to let me know that things were going well or to share some small concerns. Other than a homesick freshman or two, everything was running well. So I decided to head back to the recruiting meeting.

As I slipped back in to observe, Rick was running a film of a big-name five-star quarterback prospect. Rick was listing all his honors and accolades. But looking at the video it did not seem that he'd impressed the rest of the group. Admittedly I was surprised this guy was so highly rated.

Rick kept running the film, well past the time when we should've moved on to the next guy. This was the last tape of the meeting, the only thing between these guys and lunch. Most of them were noontime workout guys and some of them got antsy if you cut into their workout time.

Finally it was up to Doug to put the kibosh on this kid.

"Look Rick let me just speak for the whole group by saying no. In fact let me say hell no."

"But Doug he's got offers from the entire SEC and Big 12 not to mention about two dozen other schools. He has a big rep and I like what I see." Rick protested.

Most of the other coaches seemed to agree with Doug.

"What's your hold-up?" I asked Doug.

"Two things. First this kid is a coach killer. He's one of those guys who show up with a big rep and he ain't that good. Next things you know the fans are up your ass because you're not playing the kid and when he transfers they want you to go with him. On your notes Rick I want you to write the words coach killer next to my name. The second thing is that this kid is from Texas."

"Doug, you're from Texas."

"Exactly and that's why I know what I am about to say is true. When a kid comes from a big Texas program like this one you'd better love what you see on film. They've been over coached their whole lives and so they have very little upside."

Finally Quinn, the guy who would be coaching any quarterback we signed chimed in.

"We got a great quarterback in our freshmen class already. Anyone we chase has to have the chance to be better than what we have. I don't see it. The best QB I've seen is Walker McCoy in Mississippi. His coach was my teammate at Houston, and the kid wants to go away to school so we have a chance. He is the level of kid we should be chasing."

"This Walker kid sounds like he's the real McCoy." I joked lamely to a room full of groans.

With that, the kid from Texas was dead to us.

. . . .

The late July humidity was oppressive. There seemed to be nearly nowhere to hide so Karl Metzger invited some of the guys to hang out in his air-conditioned apartment. Most of the summer, these guys were kind of stuck together in town. Between summertime classes and workouts six days a week it was tough to get out of town or to go home.

It led to a lot of boredom but the shared boredom did create some bonding. Karl was a person who brought all kinds of guys together, black and white. This stiflingly hot Saturday night lots of guys were filing in and out of his place. The beer and vodka was flowing as well as some kind of fruity concoction they'd mixed up in a large plastic tub.

Karl's friend Carl Fields was on probation after two arrests and guilty pleas to a drug charge and a fight. Karl was letting him stay with him for the summer to try and help him stay out of trouble back home. He'd managed to stay sober most of the summer and Karl could see he was flying straight. There was a sense of pride in having helped his friend clean up his act.

Even on this hot summer night where beer and booze were flowing freely Carl was still stone sober.

The end of summer boredom had everyone a little on edge. The first game was still six weeks away and preseason camp had yet to begin. The guys still faced two long weeks of six-day-a-week early morning runs and lifts before they finally got to play football once again.

In the party the music was pounding and Karl was well into the start of a second six-pack of beer. On nights like this he could get into a third six-pack before he'd get really drunk, so he was still doing fine.

About eleven o'clock Marcus Dawson came into the party with some of the other defensive linemen. Karl loved those guys because when they did their jobs he was able to run sideline to sideline making tackles without having to worry about the offensive linemen getting to him.

Karl and Marcus were sitting on the couch and talking. The two of them were key players on our defense. Both were each destined for the NFL, and already listed on numerous pre-season All-American teams.

Earlier in the summer, I'd reminded them both that pre-season All-American teams were worthless.

"You know," I said to them "there are two things you should remember about being a preseason All-American. First you become a target of every team you play. Second when you leave my office, I want you to see if you can find the hall where we hang pictures of pre-season All-American honorees. It doesn't exist!"

Both of them understood the message.

At 11:30 Marcus' phone dinged indicating he'd gotten a text message. He looked at his screen and smiled.

"Looks like a good text." Karl said.

"I been waitin' on this one all summer."

"It must be a girl because nobody waits for a text from a professor on a Saturday night."

"Definitely not a professor." Marcus said as he handed the phone to Karl.

Karl looked at the screen and read the text "Coming over 2 Fuk ya brains out-U gonna be home?"

Karl laughed "Now why don't I get text messages like that? Who is that anyway?"

"Victoria Bonner that big money white girl I been tryin' to close all summer."

"I think you made the sale. You better get home."

Marcus didn't need to be told twice.

Carl Fields came over and sat next to Karl. Karl looked at him and smiled.

"You okay? Still sober?" Karl asked.

"Sure am. Don't worry 'bout me."

"Okay, just checking."

"I am getting bored though."

"Really?"

"Look I don't want to come off like some asshole or that I am ungrateful but I am looking at the same walls and seeing the same girls I've seen all summer."

"There are girls though."

"All looking for ballplayers though."

"Fair point. Okay my roommates can keep things under control, let's go out."

They made their way outside to Karl's car and he tossed the keys to Carl.

"You're driving." Karl said.

"Don't I always?"

"Why you think I let you stay here? Because your sober ass can drive us home when needed. You're like a free Uber driver."

"Oh and here all this time I thought it was because you really cared about my well-being and helping your homeboy recover."

"I'm just kidding. Shit you know I love you man......no homo."

"Of course---no homo, your comment about my sober ass not withstanding."

An hour and a half later Carl had met a girl in a club down on High Street and when it came time to go home the girl had agreed to go back to Karl's apartment with them. On the way back to the car three guys approached them.

"Hey Cindy what you doing with this loser?" one of the guys asked as he got into her face.

"Hey man, back down." Karl said.

"Get out of my face Rick, I'm not your girlfriend anymore."

"Says you, but not me." Rick said.

"Look you can't control me." Cindy yelled.

"I sure as hell can." Rick yelled back.

Karl stepped forward and by his movement he forced Rick to step back and face him. Rick turned to him.

"This isn't any of your business mister tough football player." Rick said.

Karl knew this guy probably knew who he was so that changed the equation as to what he could and couldn't do. It sobered him up a bit.

"Look this ain't worth fighting about. Let's everyone just cool it." Karl said.

"What kind of pussy are you?" Rick snapped at Karl and as he said it one of his friends started at Karl from the side.

Carl saw what was happening and his instincts took over. He swung and dropped Rick's friend. Rick wheeled around to see his friend as he heard Cindy shriek. Then Carl unloaded on Rick.

"No Carl, don't hit him." She yelled.

It was too late. Carl had hit him and knocked him down and then kicked him. The third guy had already turned and run before he even saw what was happening. Before he could do any more damage Karl grabbed Carl who flailed at him not knowing it was his friend. He knocked Karl to the ground where he scuffed his hands as he tried to keep from hitting his head on the ground.

"Carl, Carl it's me."

Carl calmed down and helped him back up and they took off towards the car. Cindy was sitting on the ground helping Rick as she yelled after them to come back. In an instant she had turned on them.

When they got to the car they calmed down and then started to laugh. They had narrowly escaped a big fight and knew they'd gotten away with it. Before they started home Karl got a text from Marcus who reported that he'd been successful in his conquest.

The text stated "Long summer campaign is over."

Karl did not respond, but just laughed.

The night had been eventful to say the least.

. . . .

They did not know that before they'd even gotten home Cindy and Rick were giving statements to the police who'd found Rick, Cindy and his friend in the street after getting a call reporting the fight. Another witness was there too. He hadn't seen anything but he heard the fight and called the police.

Cindy knew they were football players but failed to mention that Rick's friend had started towards Karl. In their version of events the two guys just jumped them, throwing the first punches before dropping Rick to the ground and kicking him which accounted for an eye half-closed by a swollen check and brow.

They were taken to the nearest police station where they split them up and questioned them to get the story down. Cindy told them that she thought the two guys were football players. They were big tall white guys, about two hundred and forty pounds she guessed.

The witness was in another room and recalled hearing someone yell "Don't hit him Carl" and then heard someone say "Carl, Carl calm down it's me."

The officer taking down the statement came out into the hall and knocked on the interrogation room where they were getting statements from Cindy. The officer came out and was asked if he'd made any progress.

"She tells me they are football players." He said.

"Well my witness said he heard the name Carl three or four times. Get out that football program and see if she recognizes anyone."

The officer got on the Ohio State football website. He printed out Karl Metzger's photo and took it back in. He slid it across the table to Cindy.

"Does this look like your guy?" he asked.

"That's him." She did not hesitate.

The officer went out in the hall and took the photo into the room where Rick was and asked if that was the man who assaulted him. Rick did not hesitate in identifying him.

Officer Cassidy went back into the hallway. He was sick to his stomach. As a loyal and devoted Buckeye fan, the last guy he wanted to nail on this was All-American linebacker Karl Metzger. They'd never had any problems with him but this was potentially a felony assault. Cindy was telling them that she didn't do anything to provoke this and that she and her boyfriend had been ambushed.

The police decided they'd have to go round up Karl. Within an hour they'd gotten to Karl's apartment and found it almost empty. Only Karl was there and he was the only one awake. The police started to question him about an alleged assault on High Street and they had three witnesses who put him there. Karl just remained quiet and did not say anything.

The officers noticed a bump on his cheek and that his hands were scuffed but Karl just kept his mouth shut.

In his mind he rationalized that it was self-defense but he wasn't going to take any chances. He was smart enough to know that you didn't answer these types of questions without an attorney present. He also knew that he couldn't turn on Carl because he'd already had two charges and a third would probably put him back in jail. He just couldn't do that to his friend.

The police noted that he was not going to talk without a lawyer so they told him he would have to come with them to the station. At the station they questioned him and put him in a lineup where Rick and Cindy identified him.

When my phone rang at 3:15 in the morning, I knew it was never good news. Sid called to inform me that Karl Metzger had been arrested for an assault off campus and was in the custody of the Columbus police. I told Sid to make sure that Karl was to come see me as soon as he could. About an hour later Sid called back and gave me Karl's side of the story which he'd gotten from Karl's lawyer.

It sounded to me like Karl had gotten in the middle of some domestic drama and as such, I was pretty sure it would all play out and he'd be okay. But in the meantime there would be a lot of negative press and damage control that needed to be done.

The next call was at 5:00 a.m. from Gerry Gorton.

"Ed what the hell was Karl Metzger thinking last night?" He roared.

"Here's what I got Gerry. Sid has talked to Karl's lawyer and it looks like Karl unknowingly met the wrong girl and got into the middle of a boyfriend/girlfriend spat and he and his friend were trying to protect her. But it appears she turned on Karl and is siding with the boyfriend."

"My sources with the police tell me Karl had a bruise on his cheek and has scuffs on his fist. It sure looks like he was in the middle of something. The other guy is pretty beaten up."

"I will vouch for Karl any day of the week. The kid has been a model guy, and has never lied to me about anything. The kid who was with him is a recovering alcoholic and Karl has been helping the kid sober up and has given him a place to crash. This is not the type of thing he'd get into."

"That's all well and good, but the short term the PR hit will be really bad."

"This is when we show our players the loyalty we expect from them, when we're willing to stand by them."

"Easy for you to say." Gerry said as he hung up.

. . . .

Later that morning, Victoria Bonner walked into the campus health center and asked to speak to a nurse concerning the morning-after pill. A nurse took her into a conference room and told her that she could get one from them.

"Did you have unprotected sex last night?" the nurse asked.

"Um....well kind of....not really.....I mean yes I did." She stammered.

"Okay. Were you drunk?"

"I guess so. I'm not sure what to say."

"How old are you?" The nurse asked.

"Twenty."

"Okay, don't worry about being underage. We can't do anything to you for that. So were you drunk?"

"Yes. Very drunk and that's why I wasn't careful."

"So was this your boyfriend?"

"No it wasn't. It was some guy I met a few times."

"Did he force you?"

"Not really."

"Not really? You were drunk so it would be fair to say that you don't really know and probably couldn't have given your consent anyway."

"No that's not it."

The nurse paused and looked at Victoria.

“Honey, I am trying to help you. How well did you know this guy?” she asked.

“Not well.”

“So if suddenly you’re pregnant with his baby what do you think will happen?”

“With him or with my family? My father would kill me.”

“I am sure your family will be understanding.”

“Not my father. This guy was BLACK.” She blurted and began to cry.

“Okay, look I will help you.”

“Okay” Victoria said through her sobs.

“Here is the deal. Because of the sensitive nature of this particular prescription there are some politics involved. A state law was passed that only allows us to give it to you in instances of sexual assault.”

“But I can’t say that.”

“You just have to tell me. It won’t go anywhere else.”

“Okay, I was drunk and never consented to it. He’s been hounding me most of the summer and it went too far.”

“That’s better. So you know this man?”

“Yes.”

“What is his name?”

“Why do you need to know that? I don’t want to get him into trouble.”

“You won’t. I just want to check his name against the national database of sex offenders and make sure that he isn’t someone with a record of this. That’s all.”

“You promise?”

“I promise. Just tell me his name and you will get your pill. No questions asked and no looking into your alcohol consumption last night.”

“Okay. It’s Marcus Dawson.”

Victoria got her prescription and left the health center. The nurse, Jackie Brown, went to her supervisor and said she needed to look for a name on the sex offender database. As she looked she saw there was a Marcus Dawson living in Columbus who'd had a previous offense so she picked up the phone and called the police to report the rape.

When the police took the call it was Officer Cassidy again. When he took down the information and name he shook his head. This was turning into a bad night. The officers had just finished writing up the police report on the Karl Metzger arrest. Karl had given them nothing, but it looked as though charges would be filed by the end of the day. Now he got a call regarding a potential rape involving Marcus Dawson.

He went and talked to his partner Kevin Hanlon and explained the night he'd had.

"Well," Kevin said "you know how I feel about Coach Hart. I know you feel the same way. Maybe the team will lose enough to get his ass fired without these two guys."

"That's probably true. Either way we have a job to do and if it costs the Buckeyes this year and gets us a new coach then I guess I can live with that. Maybe they'll finally wise up and get Bob Stoops back to his home state. That would be awesome."

"Well, we can do our part. One thing we can't have is these brothers going around and raping girls, particularly white girls like Victoria Bonner."

"Who is that?"

"Her Dad is the CEO of one of the big banks based here in Columbus. He's worth about fifty million. He won't stand for this."

"Well let's not let him down."

"Let's not let Buckeye Nation down either. This may be the best way to get a new coach in there. Don't forget that convictions in these cases won't look bad on your resume either. The District attorney may end up running for Mayor and a veteran like you that helps put away the guy who raped Victoria Bonncr may be in line for a big promotion."

That appealed to Officer Cassidy.

. . . .

By 11:30 a.m. the Karl Metzger story had exploded. Social media went crazy, and head lines like "Ohio State All-American LB Assaults Couple in

Columbus." The fact that none of it was even remotely true did not matter. Sid's phone exploded and the University was forced to issue a politically correct statement that essentially defended nothing and offended no one. Innocent until proven guilty was such a quaint concept from a bygone era.

Gerry asked me to meet with Karl and then announce a temporary suspension pending further inquiry. It made me sick to my stomach to have to tell Karl about it.

But as he sat across from me in my office he looked me straight in the eye and told me what had happened. His lawyer was pretty sure that there were a number of surveillance cameras in the area that would corroborate his story. His temporary suspension would mean that he was kept from most "team activities" which I broadly defined as anything the whole team was doing.

It just meant that he'd have to lift weights and do his running workouts individually with our strength coach. He seemed resigned to that reality and he understood the position I had been put in.

By early-afternoon the police had gone to the Bonner home to talk to Victoria about being raped. Her father was out of town but her mother was home. She called Martin Bonner and he exploded on the call telling the police that he wanted "this guy lynched" if that was what it took to get this guy off the streets. His little girl wouldn't lie.

Before Victoria could even try and get her story out the whirlwind had taken off and there was no admitting to her mother and father that she may have consented to the sexual encounter with a black guy. There was no going back that she could possibly see.

By four o'clock in the afternoon rumors were leaking out of the police headquarters that there was another high-profile case. By five-thirty the police had called Marcus Dawson and he had gone to see them. He had no clue he was going to be questioned about a rape. He thought he was going to talk to them about Karl Metzger.

When my phone rang again with another call from Sid, I assumed it was about Karl Metzger. Needless to say it was a shock to the system when he told me that Marcus Dawson was being questioned about a rape.

"For fuck's sake does he have an attorney with him?" I yelled at Sid.

"As luck would have it Karl's attorney was still there and sat in with him for the questioning."

"That's great news," I said sarcastically "we're so lucky to have one felony assault charge coincide with a potential rape charge so that we have one-stop shopping for a defense attorney."

"Coach this one is pretty cut and dried. Marcus should be clean in this one."

"How so?" I asked.

He relayed to me the contents of Marcus' text. He also relayed how a campus nurse had called the police because Marcus' name popped up as a registered sex offender.

"He's a registered sex offender?" I asked incredulously. "How'd we miss that in recruiting?"

"He's not one. There is another Marcus Dawson living in Columbus who is one. The nurse and police were so damned lazy they didn't even crosscheck the address."

"Well he should be out by evening then."

"There is a problem-a big problem. The girl is Victoria Bonner."

"*That* Victoria Bonner?" I asked hoping I was wrong.

"Yes *that* Victoria Bonner."

Her father Martin was a Michigan alum, was worth a boatload of money and was the leading fundraiser for our Republican Governor and the DA.

"Didn't she try and clear this up?" I asked.

"No. I don't think she wants Daddy to know that she willingly screwed a big black guy. Knowing Martin's reputation he will not be okay with that."

"Fuck!" I yelled. "Call me old fashioned but a girl sending a text that she wants to fuck his brains out seems like consent to me."

"You would think so. But in 2020 that may no longer matter."

No sooner had I hung up with Sid than I had another call from Gerry Gorton. He'd already talked to the police and the nurse who'd called them. He knew all about the text messages and the mistaken identity. He was so angry at me and at the players that he decided to get his own information before he called me. He was far calmer than I expected.

"If you want to suspend Marcus you can, but this one looks like a political witch hunt. These are sensitive issues. But a girl who texts consent and then is talked into making an accusation by a nurse with an agenda is not something I will allow to happen to a young black man at this school."

“Thanks for that support Gerry. Marcus has been a good kid and you and I both know if we’d have gotten a message like that in college we’d have taken that to be consensual. But I think Martin Bonner is going to go after us on this one.”

“Hey Ed let me just tell you this. I’m not going to be bullied by Martin. He may have the Governor and the DA, but Bonner is a Michigan guy and he’s not given a dime to this school and he’s been no friend of this University.”

“Okay,” I said “but just so you know I am going to issue a pretty forceful statement defending Marcus. I will not suspend him.”

“The shitstorm from women’s groups will be pretty brutal, but I will stand by you on this. But understand it will get nasty.”

“If it takes weathering an assault, I can take it.”

“Yes but how will Candace take it? She’s done a lot of work with the Women’s Resource Center and Rape Prevention Center. She’s gonna hear about it from friends and it will be all over the media. She may even question your motives too.”

“Gerry what’s right is right. If *we* aren’t willing to stand up for this kid then who will?”

It sounded sensible coming out of my mouth, but both Gerry and I knew all too well that sensible people were in short supply. As soon as this story would break, the virtual mobs wielding keypad pitchforks and torches would be gathering to destroy us and destroy this kid. And the fires were sure to be stoked by the fans of ambitious politicians, attorneys and media members looking to make their mark on the back of a falsely accused young man.

A quiet summer had irrevocably been torn asunder and the wolves who’d been biding their time since January were on the move again.

11. A STORMY PRESEASON CAMP

Just after the news broke that we were not going to suspend Marcus Dawson my cell phone buzzed with Candace calling. I was hoping she hadn't seen anything yet and that I'd be able to explain my position before she'd read about it elsewhere.

"Hey honey." I said.

"Ed..." she hesitated. The tone of one word revealed her mood. "Ed? Don't give me that Hey Honey crap. You have a player rape a girl and you won't even suspend him?"

"Let me explain."

"No." She cut me off abruptly "There is no explanation. And to top it all off I just got off the phone with people at the Women's Resource Center. They are flying off the handle....at me. Like I had anything to do with your decision."

"Candace what ever happened to innocent until proven guilty?" I demanded to know.

"Don't give me that shit. And to top it all off you have players going on social media threatening to out the victim's name and calling her a slut and any number of other derogatory names. I can support you through wins and losses but this......"

"It is far more complex than you know. There is information that you don't know."

"You think anyone gives a shit? The media will steamroll you on this one. Metzger getting into a fight with another guy is one thing, but this will kill you. You think Gerry Gorton and the politically correct crowd on campus will stand by and let you do this?"

"Gerry is backing me on this one."

"What?" She was stunned.

"You haven't seen the evidence that we have. You haven't seen the texts. I have to stand by a young man who is about the get railroaded for the politics of optics by a DA who wants to make his name hanging this kid. I will not back down."

“Well *I* have to seriously consider if I can stand by you on this one. Because my name is on the Board of the Women’s Resource Center I’m already getting media inquiries.”

“You do what you think you have to do. But anything you say can seriously jeopardize my job and Marcus’ ability to get a fair trial.”

“I’ll think about it.”

I could hear anger in her voice that rose to an even higher level as she continued.

“Either way you’d better get control of your players. They are on a dangerous line on social media and if they cross it there will be no way I can stay the fuck out of it.”

I’d never ever heard her use that word before. She hadn’t even dropped the F-bomb when she confronted me about Alexis Nelson being at signing day.

As soon as I hung up I had Sally Anderson send out a notice for an emergency team meeting.

Within thirty minutes I had all the guys in the meeting room. A hastily called team meeting when there is a lot going on creates a tension in room. Teams thrive on routine and repetition. When you jolt that it creates uncertainty but they do show up focused.

So as I stepped to the podium I sensed the unease. Karl Metzger’s seat was empty. His temporary suspension and empty meeting room seat made his absence noticeable. I made a mental note to make sure that Karl’s suspension did not mean he was to miss all team activities. In fact I’d made up my mind that he would resume all team activities with the exception of playing in games for now.

As I started, the team snapped to sharp attention waiting for what I was about to say.

“I’ve called you here to tell you a few things. As you all know we have two players accused of very serious crimes-very serious crimes. Now it has been brought to my attention that some of you have taken to social media to stick up for these guys. I appreciate your loyalty to your teammates but....... But some of you have started calling the girl who’s accused Marcus some unflattering names.”

Some of the guys gave me a knowing look and one or two of the guys even smirked. That set me off.

“Look, you guys think this crap is funny?”

The smirks vanished as my anger had its intended result. I could see from the front of the room they were once again laser focused. As I continued, I moved around the front of the room to force them to follow me as I spoke. It was a good way to keep them engaged.

"Yeah I know you guys believe in free speech. Every time we talk about social media you guys bring up that whole free speech argument. Well let me tell you where the bear shits in the woods. Your so-called "free-speech" could end up with you being subpoenaed to testify about what you know about this case. Then your free speech will cost you several hundred dollars an hour when you have to hire an attorney. Your free speech may land you in civil court when the alleged victim sues your ass. So understand that free speech ain't always free."

These guys always got serious when you talked about cash.

"Look I allow you guys a lot of freedom on social media. As long as you guys have behaved like adults, we've respected that. But sometimes we have to protect you from yourselves. And for that reason I am telling you that no one....NO ONE is to comment on this case on social media. You guys got me on that?"

The heads all nodded.

"But that's not all. What I am about to say has to stay in this room. That is why there are no student assistants or managers in here. This has to stay in here. I have some awareness about the situations in both of these cases. I plan to stand by both of these guys. We live in a country where we are innocent until proven guilty. But the media reports will be brutal. When we have media day next week you will be asked about it. Say nothing and refer all questions to me. My ability to help defend them could be compromised if any of you say the wrong thing. If any of you are contacted by the police you alert us and we will be sure that you have an attorney with you. But you tell the truth. Lying to the police will only get you into trouble and it won't help anyone."

"Let me finish with this. When we recruited you guys we made a promise to you and your families that we would be loyal and stand by you guys. This is one of those times. We have to stick together and do the right thing. If we do that I believe that the truth will set these guys free. But you have to help us do that by staying away from this on social media. Now does anyone have any questions?"

No one did and they filed out quietly. As he walked past me I caught Marshall Remington and asked him if he thought I got the message across. He assured me that only an idiot could miss that message.

I just hoped that we didn't have any idiots. With a team this big, there was bound to be one.

A week later, after a tumultuous summer it was time to get our team together and begin preseason camp. One of the things I hate the most are the preseason Big Ten media days in Chicago. Between the questions over my future at Ohio State and now the double whammy of Metzger being suspended and Dawson not being suspended there would be plenty of things to talk about that had nothing to do with football.

Part of the trip involves taking some players along with us. We very carefully picked out three players and made sure they knew to avoid answering any questions related to the cases or to these players. There was just nothing to gain for them.

They weren't the only ones getting coached. I spent a full day meeting with Sid, university lawyers and a hired crisis management professional to prepare for media questions. Already I'd taken a number of hits in national media for not suspending Dawson. The usual high-profile female sports columnists Sally Jenkins of the Washington Post and Christine Brennan of USA Today had already taken their shots.

Now there were national women's organizations weighing in and calling for Dawson to be suspended and for me to be fired. On the other side I was a hero with some leaders of the NAACP who were praising my willingness to defend the rights of a young black man.

On the Chicago trip our three players, quarterback Marshall Remington, offensive lineman Mark O'Reilly and defensive back Ronnie Liggins were all veteran guys and handled their interviews like pros. By and large the assembled media respected these guys when they refrained from answering questions about legal issues.

As for my time at the podium it got testy with an ESPN Outside The Lines reporter used the big stage to try and make her voice heard and create a news story if it got nasty. As she pressed her case I stood my ground.

"I understand your question. What I cannot stress enough is that these are open cases. We have to respect the rule of law and due process that are the hallmarks of our nation's legal system. I would hope that all of you here would do the same. That being said, there are things we've been made aware of that we cannot discuss under the advice of counsel. But I will say is this: in this country whether you are black or white, whether you play football or do anything else we are all citizens equal under the eyes of the law and are afforded the presumption of innocence. As their coach, I have some insight into the character of these two men. Also as their coach I have to remember that when we recruited them, we promised to be loyal, to help them grow and to support them even in tough times."

I hit a few important chords in an answer I'd rehearsed a thousand times in two days. I hit on race, due process, the rule of law and presumption of innocence. When we did the sit down, round by round of questions I got the same questions and answered the same way. And I'd also pivoted to hit on an answer for the parents of our current players and potential recruits by stating that we stand by our players even in tough times.

Our crisis communications consultant told me a story about Henry Kissinger emerging from a meeting to meet the media. He stated "I'm anxious to see what questions you have for my answers." That was pretty much how I played it and turned the answers into positives as much as I possibly could.

There was a huge sense of relief when we got on the plane back to Columbus. But there was more coming. Sid had a source at ESPN that told him they would be airing a special just before we had our on-campus media day.

When we landed I got a text to come meet with Gerry Gorton at his office. A car was waiting to drive Sid and me there and sneak us in a side entrance.

When I arrived in his Gerry Gorton's office, University Lead Counsel Lewis Carter was there along with crisis communications consultant Don McCann. They informed me that ESPN's Outside The Lines had interviewed Vivian Terrant who headed up the Office of Student Affairs. She'd always been very vocal and aggressive when going after football players or fraternities.

Almost all students harbored a disdain for her that bordered on open hatred. She was the keeper and overseer of a roughly $40 million pool of student activity fee money. She rewarded the causes she liked, mostly liberal and female-related causes.

"So what did my friend Vivian have to say?" I asked.

"I'll let Don answer that one." Gerry said.

"We've been asked to respond to a number of broad claims. She claims that in past incidents involving football players you pushed to handle a number of punishments yourself rather than subject them to her authority." Don said. "She is pushing the narrative of a football program out of control."

"That's just complete bullshit." I said.

"She chose her words very carefully, like an attorney had crafted them. She is positioning herself as a whistle-blower." Lewis Carter said.

"Well just fire her ass." I stated.

Gerry waded in tentatively. "Ed it's not that simple. I can't fire her because of certain "circumstances" that are very sensitive."

"You mean because she is a boisterous lesbian activist who is notably anti-men?" I barked cynically.

"Ed you may want to walk that one back." Lewis said.

"Okay, I get what you mean. But am I just supposed to sit here and let her tee off on my guys and do nothing?" I asked.

"Pretty much." Lewis said. "She is now casting herself as a whistle blower to build a civil case. If you say one word publicly about her, you will be named individually in any litigation. If you never mention her name you'll be okay." Lewis said.

"So what can I do as she tries to destroy us?" I asked

Don looked at me and said "You can defend your program, defend your players and talk about the values of your program. Just do it in a way that avoids mentioning her and avoids an attack on anyone outside the program. Just keep stating with strength all the things you and your program have stood for."

That I could do, and that I would do. But first there was football to focus on.

Just before camp started we had a last staff meeting with all the coaches to talk about the beginning of camp. I had been given a list of topics to address and cover from meetings with players and with other administrators.

The first item was a report from our integrity and ethics office. They had been alerted to an ethics violation by our Strength Coach Sal Cafiero. Our athletic department paid out a lot of money to buy nutritional supplements from major national companies. It was a big budget item and rather than put contracts to bid to the cheapest, we allowed our strength coaches to select the ones they believed were the best.

It turned out that Sal's "decision" may have been helped along by a cash "consulting" fee that was little more than a kickback. So I had to rip him in front of the coaching staff so that there would be a clear message that these types of things were never to happen here. As part of the punishment Sal would have to donate the entire fee to the Cancer Center at Ohio State's Hospital.

I was glad I didn't have to fire him.

The next item involved Quinn Banks. As the offensive coordinator a couple of players approached him about establishing a touchdown chain that the player who scored would get to wear on the sideline after he scored. Some guys on defense wanted to have a turnover chain too for the guys who got a turnover. We had covered this before, but I decided to discuss it again to kill it once and for all.

One of my strategies for a staff meeting has always been to ask them what they thought first, without tipping my hand. Sometimes they did change my mind and sometimes they didn't. My mind was pretty firm on this one, so it would take a Johnny Cochran-esque effort to turn me around.

Most of the guys kept quiet. Quinn was in favor of it as was Dwayne Baxter the defensive backs coach. The one that surprised me was Roger Barstow.

"I think it would be great." Running backs coach Roger Barstow said. "There are a lot of schools doing it. Hell even Penn State has given in on this one."

I'd heard enough.

"Well how exactly has Penn State done against us lately?" I asked. "I appreciate you guys bringing this to me but my answer is no. In fact it is hell no. No one gets into the end zone without a lot of help. So this is going nowhere here at Ohio State. We are a team and anything calling attention to an individual is a non-starter in my book."

Roger pushed back. "Oh yeah, what about Buckeye stickers?"

He had a point. But I was not giving in.

"That tradition pre-dates me and it is an Ohio State thing. It is not a Miami thing. And I'm the head coach and I'm not gonna get a turnover chain or a touchdown chain."

A knock on the door of the staff meeting room interrupted the meeting. Karl Metzger poked his head in to ask if he could talk to me. We made our way down the hall to my office. Karl wanted to update me on the status of his case.

"Coach as you probably know by now I didn't hit anyone, so I am willing to go to court to fight it." He said.

"But can't you just tell them who actually hit the guy? Can't you just state that it was self-defense?" I asked.

"Coach my friend was protecting me. But do you think that the out-of-town guy with two priors is going to get a fair trial? He gets another one he's going to prison for a long time. He is here trying to stay sober and turn his life around. I just can't turn on him. The prosecutor is willing to give me a misdemeanor with a fine that will be expunged if I stay out of trouble for a year. I think I'm gonna take that."

"Look I admire your loyalty but is that what is best for you?"

Karl looked me dead in the eye. With an unwavering voice and unwavering stare he looked right at me.

"Coach if we have no loyalty in life we have nothing. You know you taught us that."

My heart was warmed by that. Those are the kinds of values that we should all want for the young people in our lives.

"Karl, you know if you plead, I will be forced to have to do something publicly."

"I know that."

"Here's what I'll do. I'm gonna stand by you and state that you are a great young man who was defending himself. But if I don't suspend you they will come in with something. How about you sit for the season opener against Youngstown State and then don't start, but play special teams against Toledo? Can you live with that?"

"Yeah I can live with that. Can *you* live with that?"

"No but we'll have to. As soon as you plead, I'll announce it before the school gets involved. Gerry Gorton will be okay with it. And if we can't beat Youngstown and Toledo without you we don't deserve to be at Ohio State."

We shook hands on it and I gave him a big hug to tell him how proud of him I was for what he was doing for a good friend. Not many kids would do that these days.

The next day practices started and it was my decision to have a few days before we faced our annual media day. My thoughts were that we should get our team going before we had to face a bunch of questions about off-field issues. Starting on Friday I scheduled a full week before we would face the media on a Saturday eight days later.

Early on it became apparent that freshman linebacker Carson Grady was even better than advertised. He shot up the depth chart. With Metzger still suspended at linebacker Grady would start the season opener. Four other freshmen were getting into key positions. Quarterback Carter Jones was clearly the best option to back up Marshall Remington. Tight End Manny Rodriguez would start by season's end. Running Back Malcolm Jackson was going to play early and often and cornerback Roger Hill was going to be the next great Buckeye DB. Roger was put right behind Donte Carter because given Donte's concussion history one hit would end his career.

The intensity really accelerated when we went to practices in full pads. There are guys who hate to practice without full pads because they love collisions. The NCAA has a lot of rules about when and how often we can tackle in practice. We schedule non-tackling periods but some guys will tackle no matter what the schedule tells them they are supposed to do.

That leads to fights. On the first day of pads we were in what we call a thud period. Thud means that you have full contact short of tackling a runner to the ground, and there are no low blocks. It's designed to allow aggression and contact but also to lessen the chance for injuries. The thud concept came from Penn State decades ago. If it was good enough for Linebacker U, it's good enough for me.

In the first thud period of the year running back Pokey Wallace got loose and was one on one with defensive end Floyd Simmons. Just before contact Pokey lowered his head and ran over Floyd who was respecting the rules of thud. The very next play Pokey had the ball again. Floyd went full speed and ripped Pokey to the ground.

That started a full team brawl between the offense and the defense. It got pretty intense, but it was something that was pretty common for teams in preseason camp. These guys were hyper-competitive and after facing off against the same guys for so many days in a row, things get testy in the heat of August.

We held our first scrimmage and it was typical of first scrimmages in preseason. The defense was ahead at that point and had a slight advantage. There were some entertaining moments. Doug Leonard as usual was in charge of one-liners. As we scrimmaged the coaches stood at a safe distance behind the offense and from there Doug commented on pretty much everything.

Carter Jones had a tough series after three really good drives. He made his first big mistake when he was pressured by the pass rush and just threw a pass up that was intercepted. As he came back to the huddle I asked him what he thought he was doing.

He looked at me and at the receiver and, patting his chest, said "That's my bad."

Doug Leonard hates that line. He couldn't help himself "No shit it's your bad son. I damn sure didn't throw that pick."

Doug was just getting started for the day. Two plays later one of Doug's young defensive linemen made a key mistake opening a hole for a big play.

Doug ran over and yelled "What were you thinking?"

The player responded “I just thought I could freelance and make a play. I just wanted to show you my potential.”

“You wanted to free-lance? You know when ten other guys do what they’re supposed to do and suddenly you want to free-lance you screw all of us and we give up big plays. And I don’t ever want to hear that goddamned word potential. *Son your potential is gonna get me fired.* Potential ain’t shit. At this level performance is all that matters and you just performed your way to a spot on the bench.”

The scrimmage saw some sloppy play, some really great play and at least four fights. By the time we had a coaches’ meeting to discuss what we’d seen on the scrimmage tape, Doug was in rare form. I started by asking the coaches to see if we could tamp down the fights.

“Well Ed,” Doug started “I don’t think the fighting is all bad. It shows we’ve got some intensity. It’d rather have a team we have to tell “Whoa” rather than “Giddy up” if you know what I mean. I mean we can’t have a great defense if we ain’t got some fuckers, fighters and wild horse riders.”

That was vintage Doug. The greatest hits kept on coming. When we got some of the younger guys in the scrimmage I asked about a young outside linebacker that Dave Cafiero thought had some real upside. On an open field tackle Malcolm Jackson made him miss.

“Damn Dave, I know you like that kid.....” Doug started “but that kid is stiffer than a honeymoon dick.”

The whole room erupted in laughter. But I did like the kid and Malcolm Jackson was going to make a lot of great football players miss.

“To be fair Doug, that’s a pretty good back. Dave tell me how you evaluate your guy so far?”

“He’s got good speed but like a lot of young guys he’s still a little unsure of what he’s doing yet. He has great flexibility and is a good knee bender.”

For Dave that flexibility and ability to bend and explode through tackles was a critical component of linebacker play.

“He’s flexible and he’s a good knee bender?” Doug asked “So was Linda Lovelace and I don’t want her playing linebacker for us.”

It was more laughter for Doug. On a lot of other staffs Doug would be resented for his running commentary, but not here. He would kid you one minute and then buy you a drink and tell you how great a job you were doing the next minute.

With the first scrimmage under our belts and a week of practices in the book, the next day would be media day. Just before I left the office for the night, Sid Inge stopped in to see me. He looked like he'd been running to get here.

"You okay?" I asked.

"Glad I caught you." He huffed.

"Truth be told we've been seeing way too much of each other lately."

"Well we're in for a long day tomorrow so get used to it."

"Now what?"

"The Women's Resource Center, NOW and others are joining some student groups to protest tomorrow. They've gotten permits to assemble from the University."

"Fantastic" I replied in a tone dripping with sarcasm.

"But wait there's more. Tomorrow Vivian Terrant's interview plays on Outside The Lines. And she got hold of the police report about the domestic violence call involving Donte Carter. That is going to hit the news tonight."

"He was having serious concussion symptoms and she dropped the charges." I protested.

"Come on Ed...you know the truth doesn't matter. She'll go on and say that it reflects a pattern of abusive behavior towards women. She'll claim that the team doctors came up with that excuse to protect him."

"Well get a statement ready and we'll stick with that I guess."

By the time I got to my car I was exhausted, but I knew I needed to be rested and ready for the media the next day. It was now shaping up to look like all-out war. ESPN was already teasing out parts of Vivian's interview and it didn't look good.

Halfway home Gerry Gorton called me to let me know that the Governor and the District Attorney were reacting to Vivian's interview and had issued statements. State legislators were talking about hearings.

"Are you serious?" I asked.

"Dead serious."

"Maybe I should remind the Governor about the time he tried and succeeded in screwing one of our booster's wives. She's got video of it."

"I don't think this is the time to play that card.....yet. We'll weather this one."

When I got home, if I was expecting a warm reception from Candace I was sorely mistaken. She was up waiting for me. If I got home at eleven at night and she was still up it meant one of two things, she was feeling frisky or something was bothering her. This had the feel of a standoff before a gunfight and based on the half-full wine glass in front of her and eyes red from tears, she'd been waiting.

"I hope you know that my friends will be protesting tomorrow. I felt that I should at least warn you." She said.

"I'd heard that." I was treading carefully and knew that the less I said the better.

"Now that everyone knows about Donte as well as Marcus, there are very real concerns about your commitment to doing what's right."

"Look Candace, these things are really complicated."

"YEAH YOU SAID THAT BEFORE!" She yelled. "But what is not complicated is that I've been asked to step down from the board of the Women's Resource Center...by people who are supposed to be my friends. And you know how we auctioned off game tickets to sit in our suite? Last year they went for $20,000 and they just pulled those off the auction site because they don't want to be associated with us. Unless I protest with them and call for the players to be suspended, they'll issue a statement announcing that I'm being asked to leave the board. They're issuing a statement that under the pressure to keep your job, you've decided to place wining at all costs over the safety of women in this community."

"You know that's bullshit."

"Do I? Do I Really? You wanted to be a coach, you signed up for having your name out there. I didn't and now my name is in a press release that will get reported all over the state and will likely show up on ESPN."

Tears were starting again. And I was in no mood to be in a battle at home.

"Well if you show up at the protest you can be sure that your name AND FACE will be on ESPN. You're a big girl and you can make your own decisions and I'll respect whatever you do. It's too late to be getting into this shit so I'm gonna go to bed."

"Well you better get the pullout couch set up because you're damn sure not coming upstairs with me. And yes I am as you say a "big girl" who can make my own decisions. Maybe that "you're a big girl" condescending attitude is why you're in the trouble you're in."

It had been a long, long time since we'd gone to bed this mad at each other. I didn't know what tomorrow would bring but I did know that I was getting sniper fire from all over. Candace couldn't see that these people wanted her there because it would draw attention to them and their cause. They had no regard for what it would do to *her*, or to her marriage or to the two young men involved.

As I sat in my den looking at the pullout couch where I'd sleep that night my restlessness forced me to worry. When I worry I am a list-maker. By the time I was done around 1:30 a.m. I'd written out a pretty daunting list.

Worry List

1. Media Day tomorrow....keep your cool, keep your cool—DO NOT give them a heated moment to play over and over on ESPN Sportscenter
2. Stick to your talking points—Due Process, Rule of Law, Presumed Innocent
3. Donte Carter and his mom? Double check that she's-still got that job and housing set up. Make sure the ex-girlfriend and baby are okay too
4. Donte Carter Concussion Issues—can we reasonably count on him this fall?
5. Marcus Dawson—looming legal issues—we know he's innocent but it will take time. Is his lawyer competent?
6. Karl Metzger—will plead and serve suspension for us—he really shouldn't have to do this but it is his call.
7. Vivian Terrant's interview—need to respond? How much damage will it do?
8. On-Campus Protests—More negative news cycle. Have to keep our players focused on football. University should not let national media camp out and do live stand-ups from outside the stadium or outside our offices. Do NOT give them the money backdrop shot by setting up outside our office or the stadium.
9. Candace—what will she do?—If She Protests that is a BIG problem for me
10. Make sure we work enough on slowing the game down on offense. Quinn Banks will have to give us a slowdown four-minute offense at times to keep the defense fresh.

Plus List

1. Jamar Tucker –gunshots are healed and he is running full speed—He can help us this year
2. Several Key Freshmen will help us—make sure that on defense we keep it simple enough so that Carson Grady knows what he's doing at linebacker—can't afford any mistakes in the first two games.
3. We are much better than our first two opponents. Avoid mistakes and get to Texas 2-0. Forget style points.

The next afternoon as I made my way into the media room to answer questions, ESPN was already teasing out some of the allegations that Vivian Terrant had made. ESPN's plan was to get me to answer a question or two directly at the press conference that we assumed they'd use when they aired the final Outside the Lines report later that day.

Despite all the controversy Sid Inge had already called a number of the regular "beat writers" the day before. He was horse-trading. They would be called on first in return for questions that were football related. That's what a good communications guy does. These beat writers knew if they screwed us on their questions that we could stick it to them the rest of the season.

Sure it was petty and coercive but that's how the game is played now. Few coaches these days ever take that podium without having done some dealing to insure the press conference stays on the rails.

Just before the press conference I got a text from Candace.

"I am not going to the protest today....but that may change in the future."

So far so good for today, but that text hinted that I might not be in the clear forever.

The first several questions were about football. They wanted to hear about the freshmen, the pressure to win this year, the back-up quarterback situation and who would fill in for Metzger during his two-game suspension. Then Matty Buck crashed the party by asking about my decision not to suspend Donte Carter and Marcus Dawson given their interactions with women.

That indicated to me one of two things. First Matty wanted to have his face and question show up on ESPN. His question was probably a plant by one of the national news outlets. There were a lot of national media types here, ones who would not normally show up for our media day. Matty Buck may have felt emboldened because he thought that I might be vulnerable.

The writer from Yahoo Sports asked point blank "How can you keep your job and any semblance of moral standing given your willingness to allow players who've committed crimes against women to play without suspension?"

In the back of my mind as the anger welled up I remembered to keep my cool.

"First I don't accept the premise of your question. There have been no crimes that have been established as fact yet. These are just allegations at this point." I stayed calm.

"Come on coach," he laughed cynically "allegations? You expect us to just take your word for it? There are national organizations calling for you to suspend Marcus Dawson or for you to resign."

My anger was welling up. Sid caught my eye and I remembered to stay cool.

"Maybe in the social media age things like due process, the rule of law and the presumption of innocence aren't immediate enough for you. But I'm not going to sacrifice accuracy and truth for expediency. My first responsibility is to the guys I coach. If you can't accept that....that's your problem."

I was fine until I threw in that little dig at the end. It got personal and now he knew it. We emerged relatively unscathed but Sid wasn't too happy when I left the podium.

In the meeting room he was concerned.

"What's wrong?" I asked. "I kept my cool didn't I?"

"Yes but the headline will be that you're protecting your guys."

"I never said that."

"They will paraphrase the shit out of it."

"I've got a meeting with Gerry Gorton and the administration. I'll cover you on this one. WE have another problem. Vivian Terrant also got hold of an HR complaint involving one of your assistant coaches yelling at the travel secretary."

"Isn't that against the law?"

"It's against University policy."

"Shouldn't she get fired for that?"

"There is no way the University can touch her now. We just have to weather the storm."

That night the press conference played with headlines just like Sid had anticipated. Yahoo Sports, The Washington Post, New York Times and USA Today all had columnists calling for me to be fired. If it weren't for Gerry Gorton it probably would've already happened. Luckily for me they were on my side...*for now*.

But Sid was right. Setting the mood as I drove home, I pulled up Bob Dylan's rock version of "Shelter from the Storm" followed by the Rolling Stones "Gimme Shelter." But even home was no longer safe harbor.

The national media was bad but the epicenter of the storm hitting me was in my own house.

12. CRIME AND PUNISHMENT

After two days of bad news cycle the negative stories seemed to die down after Gerry Gorton issued a statement standing by due process and our decision to allow the legal process to play out. That didn't necessarily calm things down at home.

But as the news media backed off, so did the out of town short-term attention seekers who'd come in to protest a few days earlier. That lowered the pressure on Candace. The Board of the Women's Resource Center either forgot to kick her off the board officially or changed their mind. In the near term she was afraid to ask so she kept her head down.

The rest of preseason camp was generally free of media interactions so our players and coaches were in the clear for a couple of weeks. When we did have our occasional post-practice media availability the beat writers asked football questions. But I ignored Matty Buck who had crossed the line on Media Day.

The second time I ignored him he lingered afterwards and waited until everyone was gone.

"Ed can I ask you a question?" He asked.

Behind him I could see Sid swooping in.

"Off the record?" I asked.

"Well you won't answer any of my questions on the record, so yes off the record."

"Okay." I said.

By then Sid was next to Matty and interrupted the conversation.

"Look Matty," he said "you broke your word to me."

"How did I do that?" Matty asked.

"On media day I talked to you about keeping your questions on football. You promised me that you would and that is why you got called." Sid barked. "You broke your word."

"Well it's my job to ask tough questions and you won't tell me how to do it. This is the biggest story surrounding this program. I have an obligation to the public and I do believe that freedom of the press is one of those pesky constitutional items you have to respect."

Before I could say a thing Sid jumped in again. It was getting heated as they were now in each other's faces. I'd never seen Sid this angry.

"Look Matty, you may have freedom of the press, but we also have the freedom to respond or not respond. Since you mentioned the constitution....there is also this thing called due process for young men in their early twenties that you and your fellow media types want to lynch. You got medical records on Donte Carter and ran them. That is against the fucking law! Bitch all you want but I didn't pull your press credential, I didn't ban you from these media availabilities and I could do that any time I want. Remember this Matty, your subscription-based web site only exists because of the oxygen we give you. You need us more than we need you and don't you ever fucking forget it."

"Fuck you Sid and fuck you too Ed. I'll get my shot and you'd better be ready for it." Matty said as he stormed away.

On the practice field in preseason camp we made great strides. We stayed healthy at the key spots. Freshman Jamar Tucker was able to start playing sparingly and showed incredible potential. He had one of the quickest pass rush starts that I've ever seen. The doctors told me that he should be ready to go by week three or four this fall. On offense, Marshall Remington was playing at an even higher level than before.

As camp started to draw to a close, a number of issues that I'd identified a few weeks ago were sorting themselves out. Donte Carter was staying healthy and his mother had settled into her job and apartment. Financial assistance was helping his ex-girlfriend take care of their baby. He would be able to focus on school and football. Even Vivian Terrant's release of the police report wasn't bothering him too much. It helped that his ex-girlfriend had come forward publicly to defend him.

Just as camp was ending eight days before the first game our players were in good spirits as we readied for a tradition I'd started, "Freshmen Entertainment." It was always the last night of camp and it gave our freshmen a chance to show off their talents. One of the acts was a takeoff on the Fox Show "The Masked Singer", other guys rapped and others did funny skits. The upperclassmen and coaches were the butt of a lot of the jokes. As the head coach I was a particularly ripe target.

Some would probably call it a form of hazing, but if I cancelled it the freshmen would be the biggest complainers. They loved showing off and taking their shots at the older players and the coaches.

The final skit involved guys making jokes about Vivian Terrant and her army of football-hating man-haters dressed in Maize and Blue. It was pretty funny and hit a few chords that thankfully were best kept among us. The most over the line joke was that she harbored a deep-seated desire for me and was plotting to put out a hit on Candace. That part I did not laugh out loud at, even though I found it to be very funny. Again I felt lucky that this was among us.

What I did not notice was that it was being put on Facebook Live by a freshman and it remained up there for Vivian to find. Her first call was to Gerry Gorton demanding that I be fired for allowing a "hazing ritual" to continue and for their over-the-top humor. Gerry's first call was to me.

"Holy shit Ed, what did these guys do?"

"Gerry, it was freshman entertainment which has always pushed the envelope on jokes."

"Look Ed, she's gonna do something and I don't know what. Just be ready."

"Okay." I said.

"I do want you to know that I did watch the whole thing. If you quote me on this I will deny it and probably fire you....but the skit was pretty damned funny. You and Vivian would make a nice couple." He laughed.

Gerry was on my side again, but I'd been put on notice that Vivian was poised to strike again. With the season a week away I suspected it would be sooner than later. But what eventually hit was more than any of us could've suspected.

Five days before our season opener against Youngstown State Vivian used her position as the head of Student Affairs to announce a suspension of Marcus Dawson from the University. This meant that he was suspended from classes and thereby ineligible to play football. Not surprisingly Matty Buck broke the story before the official announcement.

To further her claim that I harbored some lack of respect for women, Matty Buck and Vivian Terrant had found my ex-wife Cathy Ames. In an on-camera interview with Matty that he shared with ESPN and other news outlets she asserted that I'd been mentally and verbally abusive in our marriage.

The two stories exploded. But I was ready.

At 11 a.m. that Monday I went into a wood-paneled meeting room near Gerry's office. Seated around a long table were men in suits with serious faces. Sid, Gerry, University Counsel Lewis Carter and Crisis Manager Don

McCann all looked up in unison as I entered with my personal attorney Wes Sullinger. It had the feel of a showdown on a dirt road in an old Western.

"We've got to stop meeting like this." I joked to a room that was clearly not in a joking mood.

"Ed, my phone is ringing off the hook. Most of them are irate at Vivian for taking unilateral action to suspend Marcus. But....." Gerry said before Lewis Carter interrupted him.

"Ed," Lewis began "the allegations by your ex-wife are very serious. They may require us to suspend you. The Trustees who wanted you gone already can now see an opening to axing you. They're willing to blow up the season and the program to get what they want next year. How you handle this is vital to your own survival and it may be vital to Gerry's survival as well."

Don McCann jumped in as well. "These types of allegations will not go away. You and we have to respond as soon as we can with a statement and anything you might have to back this up. But a tearful ex-wife on camera accusing her ex-husband of mental and verbal abuse is a tough hurdle to clear in this day and age. The University's hands may be tied on this one."

"That fucking Matty Buck." Sid barked. "he said he'd get us."

"Calm down everyone for just a minute." I stated. "Not only are her assertions ancient history, but they are complete bullshit."

Don asked "Can you back that up?"

That is when Wes Sullinger spoke up. "Gentlemen, before I came over here I grabbed the documents and files from Ed's divorce proceedings. In those files you will see sworn statements by his ex-wife Cathy Ames stating that the divorce was amicable and that Ed was supportive of her when she entered rehab for Alcoholism. She wanted to end the marriage because the coaching lifestyle was not for her. Ed agreed to pay for her rehab and stay with her until she had gotten sober. Now that she has broken the non-disclosure agreement these documents are fair game. I'm handing them over to you and you can leak them to anyone you want."

Lewis Carter wanted to be sure they were on solid ground. "So these are fair game? These certainly put Ed and his respect for his ex-wife in a very different light."

"Yes," Wes started "and my co-counsel Joan Archer can issue a statement on-camera at a brief press advisory as soon as you want. ESPN has already been in contact with us."

“These are good.” Don said as he glanced over them. “She states that Ed was supportive, caring and willing to help her and stay with her until she got back on her feet. She states that Ed stuck by her even through rehab and her infidelity that she blames on her alcoholism. And if I am reading this correctly Ed you even gave her the financial terms of divorce she asked for.”

“That’s right.” I said. “So we can fire away. Get me on camera and I will destroy these people.”

I was committed to firing back. Don jumped back in to temper my enthusiasm.

“It’s not that easy.” He warned. “You can go on TV and say anything you want, but you never get anything for free. A back and forth about a divorce is not a good look for you. Let Joan Archer handle it. But even with that you never get anything for free. You have Candace to think about. And how will your kids feel about a nasty public back and forth between their mother and father?”

Don made the best points. After careful consideration we came to a plan that was agreeable to all and did the least damage to my kids, to Candace and towards Cathy my ex-wife. Attorney Joan Archer would issue a statement asserting the divorce documents signed by Cathy told a very different story. Joan, Wes and Don would allow a number of media people to see the documents and characterize them in their stories without mentioning Cathy’s alcoholism. It shut down that story very quickly and did a minimum of damage to my kids and to Candace.

Luckily we acted quickly enough to make Matty Buck look like a jackass for peddling his story to the national media. ESPN was waiting to run the video until they talked to us and that left Matty out there all alone.

As for Marcus Dawson, a prominent Cleveland lawyer who was very active nationally on civil rights issues had already filed a motion in Federal Court seeking to block the suspension. He also filed a motion in local court to throw out the charges against Marcus and went very aggressively at what they perceived to be a politically-motivated prosecution that ignored evidence of consent.

On the Marcus Dawson issue there was a lot of tension in the room. Lewis was a cautious lawyer. As Don McCann had told me, lawyers always over-edited the best public statements for fear of triggering more litigation.

While we had to stay out of the criminal side of the legal proceedings, Gerry was fully supportive of the motion to squash Marcus’ suspension. Lewis Carter was weighing the ramifications and legality of joining the motion to support the action against our own office of Student Affairs.

“But the public reaction to us supporting Marcus could be a problem.” Lewis stated.

“Lewis,” Gerry said. “we have text messages, that you’ve seen, that clearly indicate her state of mind as well as indicate active consent.”

“We can’t get into that.” Lewis said.

“We can’t,” Don said “but as part of our offensive we could do something. We can coordinate with this new attorney from Cleveland. As we show our hand-picked reporters the divorce documents he could let those reporters review the text messages. It is like a political campaign. We won’t get our hands dirty, but as this other attorney gets his hands dirty it helps us get the full truth out there with plausible deniability.”

“One note of caution,” Lewis interjected “whatever you do, DO NOT discuss this via text or e-mail on your Ohio State e-mails or cell phones. We will likely get a Freedom of Information Act request soon from someone in the media looking for those types of things. I CANNOT stress that enough.”

The politics and litigation of public scandal make for strange alliances. But as I left to go back and coach football, I was comfortable that the team in place had everything under control. The Campus police even had our parking lots blocked off so I could pull in and not be bothered by the gathering swarm of reporters looking for comment.

Sid was with me when I drove back in to the football office. He walked over to the reporters and issued a brief statement that I would have no comment at this time, but would proceed with our normal Tuesday press conference the next day. He did alert them that my attorney as well as the University would be issuing statements later that day.

As I went to my office to review game plans on both sides of the ball, I could hear Sid in the next office on his cell phone. He was shredding Matty Buck for running a story on my ex-wife.

“Look you ignorant jackass. You were so desperate to burn us on a story and whore yourself out to the national media that you’re exposed now. I don’t care how many goddamned clicks you got today, your shit will be dead to us and dead to your readers who will now see that you can’t be trusted. We will be handing stories and inside information to every one of your competitors if you don’t print a serious retraction....” He yelled.

Sid was normally the even-keeled one. He was the one who made me rein in my impulsive anger. Times were strange and boy didn’t I know that? Just as Sid finished and I was about to go to one last meeting with our coaches before they met with their players my desk phone rang. It was Sally Anderson.

"Ed," she said "I've got Gerry Gorton on the phone. Should I put him through?"

"Go ahead."

The next voice I heard was Gerry's.

"Can you drop off some lunch?" He laughed.

"What?" I asked.

"I need some food sent in. It appears that a number of the people protesting you have decided to lay siege to my office. I can't get anywhere."

"Seriously? Why are they picking on you? I'm the asshole they really hate."

"Don't worry, I hear they've dispatched a number of them to your office too."

"Lucky for me our indoor practice field is attached to our offices. No need to go outside and see any of them. And we'll be meeting here until 11 tonight so I would imagine they'll be gone by then."

"You're going inside today? It's beautiful outside."

"I just figured we'd avoid distractions of people trying to take pictures or video over the practice field fence. Sid closed it down to the media so we don't give them any current video footage of Marcus, Donte or even me on the practice field."

"Maybe I'll swing by. By that time we may have some news on Marcus. The judge overseeing the request for lifting his suspension graduated from our law school. He's agreed to hear arguments on an emergency basis at 3:00 and has promised a speedy response. So as President I'm clearing you to keep practicing Marcus as though he is going to play Saturday. If there is an NCAA issue at a later date I will handle it. I'll even send you an e-mail to that effect."

When we hung up I yelled to Sally.

"Sally, call Gerry's assistant, find out what his favorite lunch spot is and then have food delivered to his office from us."

"Gotcha Ed."

Everyone loves free food and I figured it could be fun for the delivery guy to have to break the siege for Gerry.

"One other thing Ed, there are some flowers out here for you."

As I walked out to Sally's desk I noticed a nice bouquet of some kind of scarlet and white flowers. I couldn't even tell you what they were, my wife is the gardener and she would probably know. They were from Alexis Nelson and there was a card attached.

"Hang in There Ed! You know I'll always support your ass! Love Alexis!!"

As creepy as that card was, of course the cheapskate stupid husband that I am saw an opportunity to take them home and score points with Candace. So I asked Sally to put them in my car when I went out to practice.

I met with the coaches once again to make sure our plans for practice were tight. Tuesdays were always the longest practice of the week and required the highest level of organization. Minute by minute coaches, players and student managers needed to know what was next and be organized as we moved from one segment to the next. I hated to waste any time on the field and that is why I always had practice scripted down to the minute. If we were going to reach our goals this year it was going to take a maximum effort in every practice.

At lunchtime we held our weekly press conference. Sid started with a statement that we would respond only to football questions because of the ongoing legal issues. He referred all questions to the University lawyers and also indicated that my attorneys would also be available later that day. That made the press conference a smooth one with no drama. But still there was a tension underlying the entire half hour.

After my press conference our coaches met with their players for an hour or so. Finally I went into my office, shut the door and looked at more video of Youngstown State and reflected on how our game plan would match up with them. It was liberating to be alone with football video and to be focused on the stuff I loved. No doubt we were the far better team and if we kept it simple and avoided major mistakes the game should be a rout.

I tell my players "Respect all but Fear None." That all started with an important Tuesday practice.

Tuesdays were the day we trotted out all of the week's game plan to practice. We worked third downs, red zone and other key situations. We worked the plan against the looks we were most likely to get in those situations. Then we'd repeat that process the next few days so that our players knew what we were going to do and what to expect on Saturday afternoon.

Walking onto the practice field I couldn't help but wonder if I had any idea what to expect in the next few days let alone on Saturday afternoon.

13. THE OUT OF CONFERENCE GAMES

Tuesday night by the time I left the office at 11 p.m. the protesters and TV news trucks were gone. Before leaving the office Sid told me the national media had already picked up stories about my ex-wife's positive statements in our divorce and the text messages that Marcus Dawson had received. I had to feign ignorance as to how that all came about, but it did help our cause.

As I turned into my driveway, the lights in Candace's home office were still on so I knew she was waiting up for me. That was good since I had Alexis' flowers to give her. When I peeked in at Candace she was on her computer and looked up at me.

"How was your day?" I asked.

"Interesting....there was a lot to process today."

"Ya think?"

"I do feel badly for you about the ex-wife thing. She was a bitch for getting in the middle of this. But I hate that I had to relive that part of your life publicly. I feel badly for Deanna and Sam for having you and Cathy play that out publicly. They both called to talk to me because you didn't answer your phone. They're pretty upset but they'll be okay."

I nodded.

"How'd those documents get out there?" She asked.

"Who knows? Hey there were a lot of lawyers involved.....At least it didn't come out about her rehab."

"You had nothing to do with it?"

"I was at practice and in meetings all day." This was not a lie, but it was definitely designed to mislead Candace into believing something that was less than true.

"I guess I owe you an apology about the Marcus Dawson thing. I see why you stood by him. A text messages stating "I want to F your brains out" is pretty clear."

"If you ever want to send me one of those and then follow up I'd be good with that."

With a sly smile she started to get up from her computer as she spoke. Her new vantage point brought the flowers into view.

"I bet you would be. In fact I'd bet you'd be great with that.....are those flowers for me?"

"Yep."

"Where'd you get those?"

"Honestly?"

"Yeah, I damn sure know you didn't leave the office to get them for me."

The next words out of my mouth weren't the smartest ones I'd ever spoken, but they were at least honest.

"Alexis Nelson sent them to the office as a show of support."

The lighthearted mood of just a second ago was gone.

"Alexis Nelson *sent you flowers*? And you wanted to re-gift them to me?"

She stopped a few steps from me and the air grew icy cold between us. But I had a counterpoint.

"Is it technically a re-gift if I'm honest about where they came from?" I laughed to try and break the tension.

Candace smiled and responded "I admire your honesty and I accept these beautiful flowers in the spirit with which you brought them home, but I am warning you. That Alexis Nelson is up to no good and if you ever step out of line I will seriously cut your dick off and keep it as part of a divorce settlement."

Playfully I backed up "Ouch.....I'll keep that in mind."

Wednesday morning as we were getting ready for practice Sid came in to speak to me. He, Gerry Gorton and Don McCann had met and reviewed all the media stories that morning. They were pleased we'd hit back successfully. The Marcus Dawson text messages that "got out" as well as the divorce documents that also "got out" had played very favorably for us. There were still some columnists who saw them as an attack on women. But what could you do?

While we were meeting Sid's phone rang. Gerry Gorton was calling with news that the judge had sided with Marcus Dawson. He was eligible because it was clear that Vivian Terrant had acted outside the scope of her authority. Gerry had already called her to tell her that she would have to respect the limits of her office.

The good news was coming in waves. Despite some columns accusing the judge of bias because of his OSU background, the text messages that had leaked out proved to be valuable once again.

By Saturday morning the coaches, fans and most of all the players were ready to just have a focus on football. As the noon kickoff approached on the Big Ten Network there was the inevitable buzz of the season opener even if it was against over-matched Youngstown State. Our players just wanted to hit someone new.

As pre-game warm-ups ended and we had spent a few minutes in the locker room, it was time to go back out for kickoff. I gathered the team around for a minute and had a few words for them.

"Look there have been distractions and a lot of crap, but you guys are completely focused and excited to just play football. Play with all you have. You're better than these guys but as I always tell you "Respect All but Fear None" and this week the Respect part is most important. These guys are playing the biggest game of their lives so let's go out from the first snap and take away all hope."

With that we headed out and the game was on. They took my words to heart. By the end of the first quarter we'd scored touchdowns on all three possessions and held them without a first down.

Freshmen Linebacker Carson Grady was playing even better than we'd expected. By halftime with a 42-0 lead he'd already racked up a sack, an interception and nine tackles. The starters were done and the younger guys would get most of the second half. Marshall Remington had a great half as did Pokey Wallace and freshmen tailback Malcolm Jackson.

Marcus Dawson was playing at another level. Outside the stadium about fifty protesters were demanding that he be suspended. On TV the media shot the "crowd" to make it look like there were hundreds of people there. It didn't matter, Marcus racked up three sacks and seven tackles in the first half before we took him out.

We took our foot off the gas out of respect for our opponent as best we could but still finished with a 63-10 win that got a lot of players playing time. It was a pretty easy day for me. With the game in hand I took a moment to soak in the late summer sun and revel in the Ohio Stadium atmosphere.

There were lots of happy parents as I walked to meet Candace at my car. She never wanted the spotlight so she always waited for me at the car. Even she seemed impressed with the game.

The next week's routine went like it usually does. We reviewed the game film and found the mistakes that in a better game would cost us a win. In big wins we coached them harder than normal just to get their attention.

Carson Brady was named the Big Ten Defensive Player of The Week and had attained instant celebrity status on campus. I made sure to call him in to warn him that instant fame is a potent drug that has ruined a number of great college players.

By Tuesday's press conference before that week's game against Toledo most of the reporting about us had stayed on football. But Dawson's huge game did get reported with a footnote about his pending case. We could live with that. As for Metzger we announced that he would be suspended from playing defense this week but would be available for special teams if injuries occurred.

But at the press conference Matty Buck was back to throwing bombs. Before Sid could stop him he barked.

“Ed is it possible that your vigorous defense of Marcus Dawson is because you have to win this year and he is by far your best defensive linemen? Are you putting your own job security over the safety of female students on campus?”

“Next goddamned question.” I barked.

It was a big mistake and it had given him his moment.

The next question came from a news reporter I did not recognize from a Cleveland station affiliated with Fox News.

“Coach, do you worry about how your suspensions look? You suspend a white player but play an African-American player who is accused of raping a white female student on campus?”

“Look I am not sure what you're getting at but I handle these decisions on a case by case basis.” I responded.

“Are you playing Dawson because of pressure from the NAACP?” He followed up.

“Seriously? That's what you're asking? Next damn question?”

Sid was looking at me to get me to calm down, which I did. As I walked off the podium I knew I'd botched those answers. The dip in the national coverage had lulled me to complacency. I didn't prepare for this press conference like I should have.

Back in my office I looked at Sid and said "Before you kill me, I know I screwed up royally. So let me have it."

Sid smiled and at moments like this he was great because he used a soft approach "Hey by botching the second set of questions at least Matty Buck's moment as the lead story is gone."

"Silver lining I guess....." I said.

After meetings, practice, dinner and post-practice film review with the coaches Sid and Don McCann were in my office for the day's rundown. By mid-afternoon conservative talk shows had taken up the story. They called out the NAACP and they called me out. Some went as far as calling me a reverse racist and implying that I was endangering "innocent" girls at Ohio State by allowing this "monster" to roam the streets.

I knew what "monster" meant and what "innocent" meant. Even the talking heads on Fox News were on the story with our DA and Governor making the rounds on the shows. It amazed me how a kid who received the texts Marcus had received was already convicted by public opinion.

The liberal talk shows were conflicted. Some were hailing my defense of a Black man. Others were stating that suspending Metzger and not Dawson showed that I valued a crime against a man over crimes against women.

"Why would someone like Hannity jump on this story?" I asked Don.

"It'll be one or two days at most." Don assured me. "As for the why? This story blends race, sex and football. AND the bank run by the accuser's father is an advertiser on those shows. Do the math....."

"But on the bright side" Sid started "the NAACP and others are calling your defense of Marcus heroic. This may help your recruiting."

"Can't we just play football?"

Four day later we got my wish and absolutely destroyed Toledo. We didn't start as well as we did against Youngstown State but in the second quarter Toledo's freshman quarterback threw two careless interceptions and fumbled. Those gave as a 21-point boost and put us up 31-7 at halftime. In the third quarter it really snowballed. As we started to pull away even further in the third quarter I wanted to get the starters out of the game so I told the offensive guys to get the second team ready. It was 52-10 at that point.

While they thought I had switched my headset channel over to defense I caught Quinn having a conversation with Roger Barstow.

“Hey Quinn how many did Michigan score today?” Roger asked.

“They played at noon and put up 70 on Eastern Michigan. That gives them 126 on the year and makes them the top scoring offense in the Big Ten.”

“How many do we need to pass them?” Roger asked.

“At least 64,” Quinn said “and once we put in Carter Jones we can throw it some and stay in the no huddle to get two more TDs.”

Hearing two coaches talking about stats during a game really pissed me off but it was not the time or place to start a fight. Toledo drove the field but the back-ups stopped them in the red zone and held them to a field goal.

“Dave,” I said to Dave Cafiero “that’s a nice job by those guys to hold them in the red zone. Those young guys can learn from that.”

Dave thanked me before Doug Leonard jumped into the conversation.

“Should we start putting in the Hajis?”

Hajis was a term Dave had picked up years ago on one of his coaching stops. At one of the schools he’d coached at they had twin walk-on players whose mother was born in Pakistan. The kids on the team called them the Hajis. They were part of the third team defense and the kids started calling the whole third team “The Hajis.” So when the game was in hand and they were substituting freely, Dave always said it was time to “put in the Hajis.”

Doug will never be confused with the modern politically correct liberal males who populate college campuses.

The next drive Carter Jones continued to play at a very high level. He was running the no huddle offense and moving the team. During a Toledo time out I told Quinn to slow the pace because I still believe sportsmanship should matter in college football. I’ve been on the wrong side of games like this and I know how it feels to have someone rub your nose in it.

Quinn protested saying that Carter needed to learn the system. Reluctantly I allowed him to stay with the no huddle, but told him to really run the clock between plays. There was also a method to my madness. I wanted Carter to be able to run the show without the frenetic pace. He took the team down the field and scored a touchdown to make the score 59-10.

Toledo kicked another field goal before we got the ball back. At that point I told Quinn to stop throwing the ball. There were only four minutes to go. As the team drove the field again we were at the Toledo fifteen yard line when I said to Quinn on the headset that he could run one more play before we would just let the clock run out.

The next play Carter Jones faked a handoff and threw a touchdown pass to make the score 66-13. I had told him no more passing and he had completely ignored my order to get his damn points to pass Michigan.

On the headset I yelled at Quinn "Dammit I told you no more passing."

"Ed it was a run-pass option and they gave him the pass. What was he supposed to do?"

"Fuck that." I yelled "You don't give him any pass option. Don't try and be sly with me."

As the clock ran out I apologized to Toledo's coach. He'd seen me yelling into the headsets and knew I was being sincere.

"No need to apologize. I know what kind of guy you are." he said "And besides, everyone knows Quinn is a stats whore."

As I went into the post-game press conference the first question was about my outburst on the sideline. I was careful to state that I had not communicated effectively that I didn't want any more passes thrown. It was best to just take that burden myself and not create any problems among the staff....not with next week's Texas game coming up.

There was a lot to discuss. Marcus Dawson had another multi-sack game and Carson Grady racked up 13 tackles and returned an interception for a touchdown. Pokey had over one hundred yards in the first half before Malcolm Jackson replaced him and gained 120 yards and two TDs. And in his two games of playing time Carter Jones showed us why he could be the future of this program at Quarterback.

And in an important development, Donte Carter had an interception and was avoiding concussions. His tackling technique had improved from working with a rugby coach who'd helped him learn to shoulder tackle and protect his head. With Donte healthy we were able to move freshmen Roger Hill to the Nickelback position where his size, physical play and cover skills were a huge lift to our defense.

It was nice to come out of these first two games healthy and having played a lot of young players before #6 Texas came to town. It was the ABC game of the week with an 8 p.m. kickoff. Before I'd even gotten to meet Candace at the car ESPN had announced the College Game Day show would be on campus next week.

For Carson Grady, starring in two games as a freshmen linebacker at Ohio State had made him an instant hero. He realized it that night when he and two of his fellow freshmen went to a bar and were waved in by the bouncers despite being underage. When they ordered beers the bar's owner came over and introduced himself to him.

"Carson I know who you are. Remember anytime you and your friends want to hang here just know that you're all good. You don't pay for any drinks here. Tell everyone that you come here, but just don't put it on social media. That'll cause me some problems. But you football players are always welcome here."

At home early Sunday morning I'd gotten a message that our freshmen were in a bar drinking. I didn't know they were getting comped which would be an NCAA violation. But I still sent a text to Sally Anderson to get the freshmen in to let them know what I'd heard.

As I got ready to leave the house at 8:00 a.m. Candace looked at me with hopeful eyes.

"Texas week...." She sighed. "Guess I won't see much of you until late, late Saturday night."

"Yes. We need this win to get some of those wolves off our scent."

"How do you feel about it?"

"In the immortal words of James Brown....I feel Good."

"So I guess you're not going to mass with me today?"

"Not this week babe....but pray for me while you're there."

"You need it." She laughed.

On my way into the office I got a call from Sid. I figured he was looking to give me the week's media schedule. I wish that's all it had been.

"We've got more Marcus Dawson drama." He said.

"Now what?" I asked.

"Last night he was at a club and saw his accuser talking to one of the starting basketball players. He's friends with the guy so he pulls him aside and warns him to be careful. As she sees him she approaches him and throws a drink in his face. When Marcus tells her to get away she runs to a cop out on the street and tells him Marcus is harassing her. The cops pulled Marcus out and threw him on the sidewalk. It was on social media as of two hours ago. The basketball player confirmed to the cops what really happened. No charges and Marcus did nothing wrong."

"I sense that your story doesn't end here....."

"One of the accuser's friends went on social media and starting saying he was harassing her. That's got the women's groups back up in arms."

"As expected."

"And....the accuser is going to file for a restraining order."

"Oh great."

"But wait there's more."

"What more could there be."

"His attorney is now going to issue a statement about racial profiling and the police targeting him because they hauled him out and threw him on the sidewalk before they even asked him any questions."

"Have you talked to Gerry Gorton?"

"Yes he is completely on board and has the full story."

"Okay. I'll talk to Marcus."

As I got to the office Marcus was already waiting for me before he'd even been called. The guys that show up to self-report are usually the ones who have nothing to hide. In my office he gave me his story and also showed me a text message from his attorney showing that the police were completely dropping the matter.

"That's fine Marcus, but you've got to lay low the rest of the season. Don't go to clubs, don't go to parties unless one of your teammates is having it. You are just a few months from your next step to the NFL draft. They research all this shit. Even though you did nothing wrong, the NFL will drag all this shit out and ask you about it. You're costing yourself money if you keep this up. Also you're putting me in a position where if you so much as stub your toe I will have to suspend you."

He understood what I was saying. The best way to get a players' attention is to show how it will impact their future NFL payout. No sooner had he left than I got a call from Gerry Gorton who was at his office with Lewis Carter. They ran down the police report and read a statement that Don McCann had written. It showed support for Marcus Dawson and concern for how the police had handled him. It also noted that his other case was still ongoing and that they would not comment on an active case.

With the freshmen in the team room Sunday afternoon I warned them that as they became more prominent members of the team that people would want to attach themselves to them. Bar owners in particular wanted students, fans and attractive females to know that OSU players hung out at their place.

Sunday afternoon Junior Tailback Roger Carson entered his name into the NCAA Transfer portal. With Malcolm Jackson now the second tailback, Roger did not get a lot of plays or carries. He could graduate in December and go play somewhere else right away.

I met with him and explained that we would find a role for him as a hybrid Running Back/Receiver so he'd see more playing time. He liked that idea and agreed that he should finish the season before making a final decisions to transfer. It made no sense to just sit out the rest of the season.

Other than those two blips, we were full speed ahead for the Texas game on Saturday night. The last few years we'd had near misses against nationally-ranked non-conference teams. The fans didn't want a close call, they wanted a win.

Sunday night I got the whole coaching staff together to go over what they were seeing from Texas in all phases of the game. It was something new this year for me. I thought seeing all three phases would help us understand the challenges we faced together. If we faced an offense trying to wear down our defense I'd explain to our offensive coaches the need to slow things down. If we played a soft defensive team we'd probably score more points and that would allow me to turn our defense loose and take more chances blitzing.

This was the first week that we were doing it before a big national game. On offense Texas presented a mystery. Last year they were a wide open spread offense. But they had changed on film and added more power running sets and plays into their mix. But they'd played two blowout games to start the season.

As Dave Cafiero finished presenting what the Texas offense had done in the first two games I asked about their new approach.

"Is it possible that they're masking what they really want to do and just ran some power run game because they could bully their first two opponents? Are we going to prepare for some of the spread stuff?"

"We have to approach this almost like it is a season opener." Dave Cafiero said.

“Yep.” Doug Leonard said. “With a new coordinator and two blowout games they can keep their cards pretty tight. So we’re left with a SWAG.”

“Swag?” I asked. I knew this was another one of Doug’s sayings but I’d forgotten what this one meant.

“SWAG....as in *S*ophisticated *W*ild-*A*ss *G*uess.” He said.

I laughed before answering “Okay a SWAG is better than flying blind. But be sure we’re not chasing a bunch of ghosts.”

“Ghosts?” Doug asked.

I’d gotten one on him. “Ghosts are plays that are possible but highly improbable. I’ve coached with guys who try to prepare for everything and they end up wasting time chasing ghosts. Let’s be sure we are sound in assignments and techniques to avoid being fooled into giving up a big play.”

“That’s one I hadn’t heard before Coach. I’m stealing that for my collection.” Doug laughed.

“I’m honored. All that being said can we get any intelligence from anyone on the ground? Quinn and Doug you guys both know a lot of Texas guys and Texas high school coaches. See if we know anyone who’s been at their preseason or spring practices and would have an idea of what they might be up to.”

Quinn chimed in, “I’ve got a guy who was at one of their closed spring scrimmages and sat in the end zone seats videoing with his phone. He’s already sent it up.”

“That’s what I’m talking about.” Dwayne Baxter chimed in.

“Guys, I really don’t want to see that.” I said. “That just doesn’t seem right.”

“Coach,” Quinn said “then don’t look at it.....but what we do....”

I have a problem when a high school coach skunks a team like that and hoped that no one would do that to us. But the topic quickly changed.

Overall there were a lot of positives. With Carson Grady playing so well at linebacker the return of Karl Metzger was going to make our linebacker unit an incredible strength. I also asked for a couple of new wrinkles on offense. I asked Quinn for some two tailback plays to spread one tailback in the pass game against the Texas linebackers who’d shown coverage vulnerabilities. Quinn agreed to put a package together.

After we'd talked about the Xs and Os of the upcoming game Rick Carter wanted to remind us that Saturday night we would be hosting roughly 150 recruits that were coming to see the game. These were unofficial visits. While we were tied up coaching, our recruiting staff and interns would handle every choreographed moment from the pre-game tailgate party to sitting with the key members of the recruiting class at the game. By the time you added it all up you had almost 500 people to entertain between the recruits and their families.

Rick reminded everyone to get their finalized lists of recruits to him as soon as possible. Having started my career as a recruiting coordinator I knew what a pain it was to get this all organized. There was always a coach who'd come in on Friday afternoon with the names of three or four must-get recruits who needed the best intern sitting with them in the best seats at the game.

Monday as stories about Dawson continued and were picked up nationally, all context was lost and he was on the hot seat once again. One guy who did defend him was ESPN's Stephen A Smith. His radio show rant featured a gem.

"Look people, I am all for defending women. But in this case we've heard about text messages expressing her "consent" in language that I cannot use here! And now.....and NOW we have this player from Ohio State sees her with another high-profile athlete, a guy who by all accounts is one of his boys. And what does he do? WHAT DOES HE DO? He does what any GOOD friend would do. He pulls his boy aside and says..and he says you better watch out for this one. You better watch out. And then the surveillance video shows her come at him....let me repeat that. The video shows her come at him and throw a drink in his face. And all he does is stay away and she runs out the door to the police. Where I come from that ain't a crime. In fact we used to say that was "good Looking out" and it may have saved that basketball player from his own troubles. And then...THEN the police come in and throw this innocent Black Man on the street because of something a white woman said...It ain't exactly Emmit Till but it is typical in this country."

Spoken as only Stephen A could say it.

But as my Tuesday press conference rolled around there were some of the same aggressive Marcus Dawson questions that I answered factually in defending him. There was more media here because of the national scope of a game where one of these two teams would emerge as a legitimate playoff contender. If my answers were not what some of these guys wanted, what could I do? That press conference only stiffened my resolve to play Marcus and for him to have a big night.

On Wednesday the producer of ESPN College Gameday asked Sid if I would come on set Saturday morning. It was really the last thing I wanted to do, but Sid had told me that the controversies wouldn't be discussed.

“We really have to do it. This is great exposure and after Marcus’ incident they were going to pull the show. But they’re still here so we kind of owe them one.”

“Okay I’ll do the damn thing, but the questions have to stick to football. And Sid you’re smart enough to know they’re bullshitting you. They’d already announced they’d be here and they know the controversy will add to their ratings.”

“Yeah, one of my guys at ESPN admitted that they expect a big ratings number for game day and the game because of all the drama here.”

Thursday and early Friday saw the distractions melt away. Then Friday afternoon a number of campus women’s rights groups staged a sit-in at the main administration building to demand that Gerry suspend “The Rapist” Marcus Dawson. Vivian Terrant spoke and riled them up talking about a rigged judicial system packed with male judges who went to OSU Law School.

Then they marched to the ESPN Game Day set to protest behind the announcers when they broadcast Friday afternoon. ESPN’s security tried to take their signs which sparked howls of censorship. But Home Depot didn’t pay all that sponsorship money to see words like “Rapist” on signs behind the stage.

As that was happening our AD Art Simpson decided to pressure Gerry to suspend Marcus Dawson to quiet the mobs. Gerry agreed to go along and they called me to tell me.

“Gerry, I may be talking out of turn here.” I said.

“Ed say what is on your mind. I won’t hold it against you.”

“Gerry there comes a time when you have to be the sheriff. You either say I will defend the rights of the accused over vigilante justice or I’ll hand over an innocent man.”

“You come over here and tell that to Vivian. She is down the hall with a bullhorn.”

“You can suspend him but that suspension won’t affect his playing time tomorrow.” I couldn’t believe I’d said that.

“Is that a threat?” Gerry roared.

“No. It is just a coach doing what he promised this young man he’d do. I owe it to Marcus to stand up for his rights.”

Gerry calmed down and as Art was about to take his shot at me Gerry interrupted him. "You know Ed, every once in a while I have to remind myself that these are people not gladiators. I hear what you're saying. But if he is even near any more trouble he's done for the year. Tell him to stay home and join a monastery the rest of the damned season."

"I pretty much already did that Gerry."

Another crisis averted until my phone rang again and it was Candace. I hadn't seen her all week as every morning I left before dawn and came home after she was asleep. She also needed to be talked off the ledge. The pressure on her was immense but she'd told the Women's Resource Center that she wouldn't take part in the protest. They kicked her off the board issuing a statement that scrolled across the bottom of ESPN.

The sight of her name on the ESPN ticker had her in tears. Her phone was filling with text messages and media requests. Others who were "friends" posted nasty messages on her Facebook page. It completely overwhelmed her. I felt bad for her and resented her being used as a pawn in the bullshit game of politics. Even my daughter Deanna had decided to fly home to be with Candace. She could sense the weight of the world closing in on Candace.

As we got our team off the practice field and then went to the team hotel for dinner, we could escape. The hotel had set up a security perimeter to keep media way so we could focus on the game.

As the coaches met with the players Friday night and then did bed check, they all reported that the focus on this team was unwavering. None of them cared about all the external crap. Doug Leonard told me he'd never seen Marcus so locked in. There were freshmen we were counting on and I wanted to hear from the coaches how those young guys looked. It's one thing to play in a blowout. Saturday night primetime versus Texas was a whole other level. These puppies were about to go on a real hunt when the big guns would go off.

Sometimes the hype and pressure swallowed kids up if they weren't ready. The coaches assured me that these guys were ready.

Saturday morning we let the guys sleep in because the game was so late. Sid and Don McCann came to meet me at 8:30 to go over the ESPN College Gameday rundown. We would head to campus at ten to go on the air at eleven. Sid warned me that there was a substantial protest from campus women's groups. There was also a counter protest supporting Marcus.

The situation was tense and ESPN was showing live shots of the protests. The DA was with the women's groups but what could I do? I had a game to win.

An unmarked car with tinted windows drove us to campus undetected by anyone. The ESPN producer met us and put me in their production truck at 10:30. I was due up at 11:08. Tom Rinaldi was going to conduct the interview and he told me up front that he would keep it about football. He was going to let the news segments cover the story.

He did want to ask if I wanted to say anything about Candace and how she'd become engulfed in this. I looked at Don and he nodded. I told Tom that I would talk about that. Tom is a consummate professional. He left us to talk about what I'd say about Candace.

"Just remember not to try and make her a victim." Don said. "To most of these people she is not sympathetic. She is a younger, second wife married to a multi-millionaire coach living the good life. So stick to supporting her work with these causes and stick to how the politics have unfairly cast her as something she is not. And finish by highlighting her strength and her commitment to continue her advocacy as soon as possible."

No sooner had Don given me a good answer that we saw Maria Taylor live on set introducing Vivian Terrant. The blood in my veins boiled instantly. I stood up and looked at Sid and Don and keeping my voice as under control as possible I said "They can kiss my ass. I will not be party to anyone who gives Vivian a venue to spew her bullshit. I am fucking out of here."

"You can't." Sid said.

"Watch me."

"Just give it a second and see what she says." Don implored.

I stood and watched as she brought up a whole host of debunked stories. The Marcus rape allegation, the bullshit story from last weekend, Donte Carter's domestic violence allegation, my ex-wife's interview, the HR report from our travel secretary was all mentioned. The protesters there with her chanted "Fire Ed Hart" as Vivian went on and on.

To her credit Maria Taylor pointed out that everything Vivian was asserting had been challenged and refuted publicly but that didn't deter her. Vivian even asserted that I had thwarted an attempt the day before by President Gerry Gorton to suspend Marcus Dawson.

Now I knew someone was leaking shit and I knew his name just might be Art Simpson. If I could prove it I'd see that he got what was coming to him. But I'd seen enough. I went outside, found Tom Rinaldi and apologized to him for walking out.

"Tom, I know it's not your fault. But they can't blindside us like that and expect me to go on camera and act lovey dovey."

Then I stormed to the car. As we drove away I looked at Sid and Don and assured them that I was now going to solely focus on my team and this game. With this win I would tell the world to shove it up their ass.

One of the great traditions at Ohio State is what is called the Skull Session. A little over two hours before kickoff, our team comes into a packed St John Arena. Two players and I make brief comments to fire up the fans. The band is there and it is like a pre-game pep rally.

Like our team, our fans were ready to just focus on football. As we entered the arena the noise exploded. I let the captains speak first and they said a few words about the pride of Ohio and the Big Ten and needing every fan to bring their best game tonight. Then I got the microphone.

"Look, everyone in this program and every Ohio State Buckeye fan has had enough of being attacked. We've got a damned good football team, a team that is focused and ready to play as hard as they can to bring you guys home a big win. It will take sixty minutes of all-out effort from all of you too. I don't want anyone from Texas to be able to hear their own thoughts. I want them confused, I want them jumping offside. I want them to look up to the upper decks and feel surrounded like Custer did in his last stand!"

The crowd erupted.

"Together we will get this done. Then we'll send these outside agitators home sulking because they couldn't take us down. We will prevail on the field and when the time comes we will prevail off the field too. They can attack us all, but they will never ever stop us. Tonight we show the world what we are all about."

They cheered again before I yelled "O-H" and the crowd responded by roaring "I-O." Needless to say my comments about outside agitators were hash-tagged, served up and had gone viral before we even got out of the building. Marshall Remington grabbed me and said in my ear.

"That's what I'm talking about Coach!"

"Now you guys gotttta back it up." I said.

"Fuckin' A right!" he said.

As we walked over to the stadium the usual fans were there cheering us on but just behind them was a line of mounted police on horseback. Occasionally some asshole would yell "rapists" or some other comment but 99% of them were with us.

For a primetime night game in the pre-game locker room there is an intensity that is unlike any other. Other teams play music in their pre-game locker rooms or have guys who go out on the field and get into a back and forth with the other team. I don't want any of that and have never allowed it. For that the players sometimes refer to me as "Old School Ed."

We want that energy bottled up until it is time to use it. If guys want music they have headphones and can listen to music that is their personal choice. Otherwise you have one or two dominant guys playing music for the whole team and it creates a potential area of disagreement.

Our locker room is quiet and focused. The great ones are silently playing the game over and over in their minds. In one corner I see Marshall Remington going over the game with Carter Jones and a couple of the receivers. That's the kind of leadership that makes him unique.

As we went onto the field for pregame the stadium lights were on. Sunset was about 30 to 40 minutes away but the lights gave us the nighttime feel. The tension was etched in the faces and glowed in the eyes of the young men who were about to play. Ohio Stadium is unique in that your visiting teams come down a ramp from the locker room. Once on the field the upper deck towers above them on three sides giving them a sensation of being in the bottom of a pit and surrounded on all sides by hostile faces.

The noise from the music blaring on the sound system is deafening. When we finish our stretch routine our team comes together around me in the end zone and the music stops. The crowd falls quiet looking at us. After I say a few words to the team the first bell of AC/DC's Hells Bells rips the silence and the crowd explodes. It is one of those moments that you live for as a coach at Ohio State.

As that song starts our team runs to their spots on the field with their coaches for a final warm up. The groups of players finish their warm-ups and trickle back into the locker room. For about twenty minutes we are once again caged gladiators awaiting word for an attack.

Before big games, those twenty minutes drag on with the welling intensity boiling up inside so many highly skilled and trained men. Even coaches feel that edginess. A game like this provides an adrenaline high that is as addictive as the best crystal meth anyone could cook up.

Finally the word comes and it is time to walk down the tunnel and onto the field. I let our captains and seniors always lead the team and stay to the side as they go. This is their time and they only get so many games to play in college.

But even the most jaded and experienced veteran coach gets chills on a night like tonight. The wave of sound builds and builds before crashing over us when the first glimpse of our players in uniform appears in the tunnel opening.

The next three minutes are a blur. I ask the kickers and quarterbacks for their best guess as to how much the wind is impacting them. Tonight the air is still. Then I reiterate to our captains what I want at the coin toss.

Once the ball is kicked off, the game flies by. Both teams settle into their routines but it becomes obvious early on that both teams' have dominant defensive lines. The pass rush is ferocious and after a third frustrating offensive series Marshall comes to the sideline and rips off his helmet. He has just thrown an interception in the end zone. We're moving the ball but have a missed field goal, an end zone interception and zero points to show for it. But Texas is having even more problems and the game is scoreless in the second quarter.

"Goddammit let's get something going!" he yells.

I grab him and get Quinn on the headset upstairs.

"I want you both to listen carefully to me." I said. "We have one only one objective. Win the game. Texas is having even more problems moving the ball. What that means is that the team that avoids the big mistake will win this game. So be careful with the football, take your shots when you get them and when they make the big mistake we pounce and get points. Their coaches want to press and score a lot of points too. They will get frustrated and gamble. And that's when we'll get them. I just told the defense the same thing. Let's just win....that's how we'll all be measured tonight. You guys got me?"

Both of them understood what I was saying. To Quinn's credit he listened and played the game a little closer to the vest. Texas had done a great job scouting us. But trailing 7-0 we punted to Texas just before halftime. We were getting the ball to start the second half so I knew their coaches would want to get another score.

I got Dave and Quinn both on the headsets during the television timeout.

"Dave you know they're going to press to get points so be ready for them to throw the ball. Give them one of the blitzes we haven't shown yet and see if we can force an interception or fumble. This QB will throw us one. Once they do that Quinn have two plays called and ready to go so we can get a hurry up. Start with a screen to change the pace and then let's go for the end zone."

Following my suggestion on second down Dave called one of what he called his "exotic blitzes." Carson Grady was blitzing free and forced a panicked Texas' quarterback to throw an interception. We had our chance because Texas' impatience had created the big mistake.

Sure enough we ran a screen pass to tailback Malcolm Jackson who ran down to the Texas thirty yard line. Without huddling or saying a word the offense ran to the line to run the deep pass we'd already called on the sideline. Marshall dropped back and as our receiver Anthony Daniels got behind his defender Marshall lobbed a perfect pass over the defense and into Anthony's arms in the end zone for a 7-7 halftime tie.

The third and most of the fourth quarter were a slugfest that resulted in a 10-7 lead for us with five minutes to go. Then Texas got into a groove. Sometimes a play-caller gets a play ahead of the defense and the defensive coordinator is trying to catch up. On this drive Texas was just one step ahead of us. With under two minutes to go, I told Dave to call something that was out of character.

"Give me a max blitz and see how their kid at quarterback handles that."

Sure enough Dave dialed up a blitz. Donte Carter was covering Texas' best receiver and made a great play to intercept the ball and end the game. Adrenaline surged through my veins until I saw the flag on the field. A roaring stadium grew quiet.

The officials huddled up for a second leaving 106,000 fans and both teams trying to read any gesture for a sign of what was coming.

Finally they broke their huddle and the official turned on his microphone.

"Personal foul, roughing the quarterback #5 defense that's 15 yards and an automatic first down."

Before he could even finish the sentence boos rained down from every seat in the stadium. Donte Carter's great play was wiped off the board and Texas would keep the ball.

The very next play the Texas running back split the defense for the go ahead touchdown. After the extra point, Texas kicked the ball out of the end zone. We were seventy-five yards away from the win with 1:39 to go and one timeout.

Marshall came over to me.

"Look, this is why you came to Ohio State. These are the drives that define you....but they are made just one play at a time. Don't try to win it all on one play, take what they give you and go to the next play."

The drive started with two incompletions and it was now third and ten. On third down Texas blitzed and Marshall had to throw it away. It was now fourth and ten and the crowd was restless looking at another Ed Hart close call in a big game. But we had a do or die play ahead of us and after three incompletions I liked our odds.

“Quinn I got this one.” I said. “I want two tailbacks in the game get Roger Carson as the second tailback. I want Rex Y-75 Hot Red 999 A-Under.”

They signaled in the play. As Marshall dropped back to pass Roger was matched up on a Texas linebacker and ran a perfect under route. Marshall hit him in stride and Roger split the defense for a game-saving first down and a twenty-five yard gain.

The clock stopped for the officials to move the chains and we threw a quick out to gain seven yards, get out of bounds and stop the clock. We substituted into our three receiver set and Roger came off the field. He was grinning ear to ear.

Over the years you’ll find that once a team in a last minute drive gets a big first down, a big twenty or twenty-five yard play it really shifts the pressure to the defense. In a two-minute drive, a big advantage for offenses in college is the time saved after a first down when they have to move the chains. It really adds up.

On second down Marshall hit another pass for a first down and ran up to the ball for another play that netted another first down. We were now at the Texas twenty-eight yard line with 28 seconds to go. After two missed passes and facing third down, Marshall had a wide open receiver running to the corner of the end zone. The ball was lofted and hung and hung as the crowd slowly rose from their seats only to see the ball come down just past the outstretched fingers of Anthony Daniels.

“OOOOOOOHHHHHHHHHH” 106,786 people groaned in unison.

Here we were on fourth down. Quinn called for a clear and underneath slant to get the first down.

“Quinn,” I said “when we get the first down call the inside trap play.”

“You want to run the ball?”

“Yeah, we still have that timeout which they won’t even be thinking about. They’ll be pass rushing with an outside blitz. They’ll either stuff us and we call timeout or we’ll split it and walk into the end zone.”

On fourth down Marshall stuck a pass to Malcolm Jennings who dashed for the first down at the Texas 14 yard line. The stadium exploded. At that moment they truly believed we would win.

Our team hurried to get lined up and Quinn called the trap. Sure enough Texas had wide defensive tackles and ends and was showing linebacker pressure off the edge.

As the ball was snapped the Texas defensive line sprinted upfield and our left guard pulled to trap their tackle. From the sideline it looked like a lot of traffic, but when Pokey split the trap and the wall of pass rushers he shot into the end zone as an explosion of sound ripped into the Ohio night.

There would be no close call today.

As the game ended with a 17-14 win ESPN"s Maria Taylor grabbed me.

"Coach what do you say to all those so-called "outside agitators" you mentioned today?" she asked.

"I'm not worried about them. I'm just happy for our team and for the fans. Tonight we're just gonna enjoy this win."

"Marcus Dawson had two sacks, nine tackles, a forced fumble and another five QB pressures. With all that's been swirling around him how was he able to keep his focus?"

"This is our sanctuary. For all of our players, this is the place where nothing else matters but the next play. That's true here and in life. He's a great player and he just played his game."

After another question or two it was all a blur. I got to a very happy locker room, answered a bunch of questions in the post-game press conference and quietly made my way to the car.

Candace was waiting there for me. She was smiling in a way I hadn't seen in several weeks. Since then she'd been booted of the Women's Resource Board, the news cycle about her had been tough. Perhaps this made up for it. I gave her a big hug and held her there for a moment.

"Honey I am so sorry for what's happened to you....so sorry. I know there is no way I can make it up to you but I hope this helps."

"It helps but......but just keep winning."

And there was the reminder, as it is almost every week in college football that no matter how big a game we played one week there was another game. The time for nostalgia would be months from now. As big as this game was, the Big Ten season loomed.

It took Candace to remind me of that. A trip to Purdue was just a few days away and nine more Big Ten games would be the proving ground that would determine our season and my future at Ohio State.

14. THE CONFERENCE CHASE STARTS

About eight hours after walking off the field with the Texas win I was back in my office getting ready for our next game at Purdue. One of the drawbacks about the Big 10 playing nine conference games is that every other year you play five road games in a tough conference. Purdue was the first of what would be three straight games on the road at Purdue, at Rutgers and at Maryland. It wasn't exactly murderer's row but every one of those teams could beat us if we didn't play well.

One of my mantras with the team is "Respect All—Fear None." While the "Fear None" part was important versus Texas the "Respect All" part took precedence this week.

Before we had our first morning staff meeting Sid and Art Simpson dropped in. If I thought they were coming in to congratulate me I was wrong. An ESPN executive cornered Art at the game last night and ripped him for my last minute walk-off from the Game Day set. And as everyone knows, Art is not my biggest fan.

"Ed you really stepped in it this time." Art said. "We've been working to get coverage of our issues tamped down, but this will only inflame them. Their guy told me as much last night."

I hesitated before responding hoping Sid would jump in. As I looked around the room I saw pictures from games and seasons past as well as some family pictures. This is what I'd have to defend in the next few weeks and realistically Art was not going to help me do that. The next sentence had to be very careful and Sid was clearly on the other side for this one.

"In my defense Art, they invited Vivian Terrant on the set to try and destroy the reputations of our program and our players. I could not reward them with an interview. We can't let these guys walk all over us, especially when the truth is on our side." I responded. "Yes I could've handled it better but they blindsided us."

"I hear you," Art replied "but it's likely they'll blindside us again. And we'd better make sure that our shit doesn't stink the rest of the season. But I do want you to send a letter of apology to them. Sid has something written already. This is not a request and before you run to your new best friend Gerry Gorton just understand that this was his order."

With that Art stood up while Sid stayed put. He pulled out a letter and slid it across my desk. I felt a small sense of betrayal as Sid sided with Art and he told me to sign it. I had a game to prepare for so I signed the damned thing to get on with my day.

By noon we were ready for a coaches' meeting to review the Texas game and start talking about Purdue. Before we got into the football stuff I wanted to talk recruiting about any of the really important guys who were at the game the night before. One of particular interest was Terrence Jones, the all-everything player from Steubenville. I had looked for him on the field during pre-game warm-ups and did not see him.

"Rick, did Terrence Jones make the game? I looked for him and did not see him." I asked Rick Carter.

"He got to the game late. His ride was late getting him on the road....he came with that guy Pietrovic."

Pietrovic was going to make sure we didn't get this kid and by bringing him late it kept us from getting a chance to press our case. At least he witnessed a big win. But in the back of my mind I knew that I had a decision to make. That might mean calling my "friends" who ran that poker game in Youngstown.

After the coaches talked about how their guys graded out I took a moment to commend them all. I particularly gave credit to Quinn and how he managed the game to get the win. He appreciated the feedback but he didn't seem genuinely happy with all the headlines about the defense winning the game for us.

"You did a great job." I said.

"Yeah, tell that to all the people ripping the offense on social media." Quinn responded.

"Do yourselves a favor guys and don't read any of that crap. It doesn't help you. Would they be happier had we lost 49-45?"

Late that afternoon the whole team came in for a quick meeting to lay out the week's schedule. A lot had happened and I wanted to talk to them about it.

"Guys I want to commend you on a great game last night. That is the type of game that you will remember all your lives. It really is. But.....BUT THAT GAME IS OVER NOW. The time to reflect is when the season is over. As exciting as it was it doesn't do anything for us in the Big Ten standings and it doesn't get us any free points at Purdue."

As tired as most of these guys probably were from a late night game and what I'm sure was some late night revelry these guys were wide awake and attentive.

"Before we talk about Purdue I want to also congratulate you for how you guys handled a lot of the external distractions last week and in the previous weeks. Let's continue to keep our focus and let coaches handle these things. The administration has been in your corner. The external criticism has been unfair but let's stick together. The easy thing for me would be to kick everyone who gets in trouble off the team. But I'm not interested in what's easy. We recruited every one of you and promised your families that we'd be loyal, that we'd look out for you and treat you like our own sons. That is why we stand with you guys. That being said please understand that we've treated you like adults, so keep acting like adults and we'll all be fine."

The points I was making were visibly sinking in with them.

"Okay now we turn our attention to Purdue. Just remember what I tell you guys every week and that is to "Respect All and Fear None." This week as everyone kisses your asses and tells you how great you are the temptation is to believe that we are above having to "Respect All". The emphasis this week is Respect Purdue and do so in a way that leads to the Six-Ps. Proper Preparation Prevents Piss-Poor Performance. You guys got me?"

I hesitated and saw heads nodding.

"Okay guys get out of here and get some school work done."

The players filed out pretty quietly as I made my way back to continue our coaches' meetings for Purdue. With the big win, the negative news cycle and outside protesters left town. There were no distractions all week except for a sudden rise in the polls.

Saturday we played like a team who'd taken my Sunday warning seriously. Purdue's offense was giving us some problems though. They had a couple of game-breaking receivers shaking tackles and gaining big chunks of yardage on crossing routes. The game never really seemed in doubt but they kept hanging around.

With just over ten minutes to go we were up 37-19 and driving to put the game away for good. Pokey broke loose for a thirty-yard touchdown to make the score 44-19 and that should've sealed it. But five plays later Purdue scored to close the gap to 44-26. With eight minutes to go I wanted one more series with our starters. Purdue's offense still seemed like a threat. We were melting the time off the clock and got inside the Purdue thirty with under 3:30 to go. The next play Marshall went back to pass and hit our tight end Parker Watson for a first down inside the fifteen.

The Ohio State fans who'd made the trip quickly grew quiet as they saw Marshall getting up from a nasty hit and start limping towards the sideline. He came off the field to be looked at by our team doctors. Even from a distance I could see on the doctors' faces that this was a potentially serious injury.

The very next play Quinn called a quarterback draw for Carter Jones who walked into end zone untouched to finish off a 51-26 road win.

As soon as we got to the locker room I went to see the medical staff and get an update on Marshall. Michael Davis was a great team doctor and always told me straight up what was going on.

"It looks like a sprain of the ligaments. He's pretty sore and it's a little loose but until we MRI him we may not know exactly what we're looking at. There's definitely not a tear but we want to be sure."

"How soon can you get it done?"

"We'll get an MRI tech in tomorrow and get it read right after that."

It sounded like we'd dodged that bullet, but the press corps was another story. There were a lot of questions about the defense yielding four field goals, two touchdowns and almost five hundred yards of offense. But as usual it was Matty Buck with the biggest pain in the ass question.

"Ed," he started "with an 18-point lead why was Remington still in the game and still throwing the ball that late? Were you looking at point spreads?"

"Matty, I couldn't tell you what the spread was...."

"It was twenty-one coach."

"Who cares? I don't give a damn about spreads and the people dumb enough to bet on college football. As for Marshall being in the game, Purdue had shown the ability to score quickly and I did not want to take a chance. We wanted to put the game away."

"I get that," Matty continued to argue "but why put him back to pass where he could take a hit?"

"Next question..." I huffed.

That one defensive display of emotion changed the lead story for the game. That reaction elevated the play call and Marshall's injury to the main focal point of the nay-sayer coverage. Coaching a top ten team no longer gives you the benefit of the doubt.

With a game at unranked Rutgers the next week it was time once again for another "Respect All" themed week. Rutgers had finished 6-6 and won a bowl game the year before, but we were clearly the better team. I warned the guys that they'd be fired up for us and their fans would be anxious to get at us.

The biggest question of the week was the status of Marshall Remington. His mobility was really limited by his injury and his knee brace. Luckily he didn't have any Monday classes and his Tuesday classes were on-line. He did not have to drive a scooter all over campus and have people see him wearing a bulky brace.

Now that gambling was legal all over, everyone in town was trying to find out what his status would be. He sat without the brace and spoke to the media on Tuesday afternoon. When he was done Sid distracted the media by having them come to my office for a less formal sit down Q&A. With the media gone we got Marshall out of the media room without anyone seeing how much pain he was in.

At times Sid was a master of deception. With the media reporting that Marshall was okay it quieted down most of the people ripping me for having him in the game with a big lead. But social media always has miserable people who can still find something to bitch about an undefeated top-ten team.

Many of the sports book operations had withheld posting a spread for our game against Rutgers until they knew Marshall's status. Now that the media was reporting that he was likely to start the spread was posted as a 24-point spread. They believed that he was going to be fairly limited but still play.

As for our plans at Quarterback, Quinn and I spent a lot of time together early that week. We were getting a specific game plan ready in the event that Carter was going to start. It was simpler and it featured more quarterback run plays to take advantage of Carter's running ability. It also made the game simpler for him by eliminating a lot of the on-the-line calls. The more we could take away the thinking part of the game, the more freely he could play. He'd played in three games showing great speed and tremendous accuracy throwing the ball. But those were all pressure-free blowout situations.

On Wednesday one of Marshall's non-football friends Martin O'Leary stopped by to see him. When he saw that Marshall was still in a brace Martin went to see a bookie. Even though the sports books were legal now, there was still a lot of illegal street action. These bookies loved to lay off their liabilities at the sports books to cover themselves.

Martin told this bookie that Marshall had no chance to play. The bookie Tony Mancuso had a big operation covering most of Columbus and some of the smaller towns in Eastern Ohio like Canton and Akron. Tony got confirmation from another Ohio State student on his payroll that Marshall had skipped class on Wednesday because he was almost immobile.

Tony laid off a ton of his action to the sports book and threw in a bunch of his own money as well. It was a sure thing. The game was on the road, and Rutgers had started 3-1 with a narrow 21-17 loss at Washington. They had a great pass rush unit and got to Washington's quarterback seven times. With a first-time freshman starting quarterback against a great pass rush team, it didn't look like a recipe for a blowout win.

Just after lunchtime on Thursday I got a call from Caesar Alfonsi my new friend from Youngstown. He filled me in on the latest on Terrence Jones and our mutual friend Tom Pietrovic. He had been at the poker game in Youngstown and was shooting his mouth off about Jones and Michigan.

"Well that's not good news." I said.

"But we can reverse course on that one." Caesar said.

"Do what you want, but you've got to keep me out of it."

"I don't know what you're talking about....." He laughed. "I got another issue though. You got a mole in your program."

"What are you talking about?" I asked.

"Someone must've told the guy Tony Mancuso down your way that Remington is not playing this week. He's laying off a ton of action."

I wasn't exactly sure who Tony Mancuso was, but if Caesar knew who he was I assumed he probably had a colorful life story.

"Well that's interesting seeing as how no one's determined what's happening yet."

"So he is gonna play?" Caesar asked.

"You know I can't answer that." I said.

"I gotcha....but I thought I'd try."

Thankfully that call was over and I could get back to football. Truth was that we didn't know just yet. Marshall was going to take some reps in practice that afternoon and see how he did. He would have a Thursday practice and Friday walk-through to see where he stood. Marshall had been doing his knee rehab exercises and treatments religiously two and three times a day to get cleared.

As we walked off the practice field Marshall walked over with team doctor Michael Davis and informed me that barring any setbacks, Marshall was ready to go at about 80% for Saturday. That would make my night easier.

On the Friday plane ride out to Rutgers I grabbed Quinn and Otis to talk about pass protection for Marshall.

"Make sure we tell Marshall to get the ball out quickly. Get him some quick passes, screens and put the ball in the hands of guys who can make big plays. Their pass rush is really good and I do not want to see Marshall taking a bunch of hits. And Otis you challenge our o-line to keep these guys off our quarterback."

They both got the message. In fact in the locker room Saturday before kickoff I heard Otis yelling to his offensive line.

"You guys know these mother-fuckers are coming after our quarterback. You better keep him off the ground. I don't want no hits on our quarterback. That has got to be a point of pride. When we finish this game I'd better see a big fat ZERO in the column where it says "sacks" for Rutgers. They got 7 last week at Washington and if you can't be better than they are then just come turn in your uniform and walk back to Columbus."

I walked in just as Otis was finishing and said "If you guys goose egg their pass rush and keep Marshall from getting hit you guys get to sit up front in the first class seats on the way home."

Mark O'Reilly our senior tackle stood up and yelled "You heard the man. We're riding first class on the way home."

The game played out uneventfully. Marshall was not as sharp after missing three days of practice, but he did play well enough to get us up and down the field and control the game. Quinn did a great job of protecting Marshall with the play calls and we really pounded the run game at them.

Leading 37-19 in the fourth quarter we were running out the clock. It looked like whoever Tony Mancuso was he was going to make out like a bandit. Even though Marshall had played he was slowed enough that Rutgers was still going to cover the point spread. With under two minutes to go Marshall was still in the game but we were not going to throw the ball.

Then our third tailback Roger Carson took a handoff and split the defense for a touchdown to make the game 44-19 and cover the spread. As the final seconds ticked off, Mark O'Reilly grabbed me to remind me that they had not given up a sack.

"Guess we'll be in the FRONT ROW coach....." He yelled.

"A promise is a promise. You got it."

Sure enough the big guys loved their star status and the extra leg room in first class.

With the noon kickoff at Rutgers I was able to get home in time to have some dinner with Candace. She had a place she liked to go, some Thai place where everything seemed really healthy. What she really liked about it was that everyone who worked there was foreign and we could maintain some anonymity. She ordered some fancy vegan noodle spicy dinner that I didn't recognize. I settled on Red Curry Shrimp with rice.

This was the first time we'd had dinner together in several weeks. It was nice to see her smiling and relaxed. The past two weeks had been so quiet compared to the start of the season. She filled me in on the late summer/early fall gardening updates. Tomatoes were still coming in and around the house the fall flowers were in full bloom. She had to tell me because most days I left before dawn and came home after dark.

Back at the house we took a long walk around the neighborhood. It was nice just holding hands, walking for long stretches and enjoying the silence. There were already some early leaves on the sidewalk and an earlier rain shower gave rise to that earthy fall smell of wet leaves. Back at the house we curled up on the couch and I fell asleep watching a movie that she'd been waiting to see with me.

The next morning it was back to the drawing board for our game the next Saturday at Maryland. Sunday morning Sally Anderson came into the office with a list of meeting requests and call requests that I asked her to schedule for the off week after we played Iowa. The off week was always an opportunity to catch up on a lot of things that I fall behind on.

At least from our end the week went smoothly. The only question in our minds now is whether or not to redshirt Carter Jones. After some staff discussion and a one-on-one meeting with Carter we made the decision to keep playing him. Marshall is a senior and it is unlikely that Carter will be here another four years so why wait?

If we have a future at Ohio State, he will be the guy running the show.

What we did not know in the office was that Marshall had gotten a call from his friend Martin O'Leary who'd talked to Tony Mancuso. Tony had lost a lot of money betting on the inside information that Marshall was out for the Rutgers game. Tony threatened Martin if he didn't find a way to make it up.

Tuesday night Martin came by Marshall's apartment and asked if there was any way Marshall could make sure that Maryland covered the twenty-eight point spread. When he told Marshall what had happened Marshall was rightfully pissed off. But Marshall has a kind soul and wanted to help Martin out.

Marshall asked for Mancuso's number. On the call he told Tony that at the time Marshall was not going to play, so the information was good. Tony suggested that if Marshall wanted to help out his friend that he could make sure that they won by twenty-seven points or less.

Marshall thought about it before rejecting that idea out of hand.

By Saturday afternoon we were in a bigger tussle with Maryland than most expected. Maryland had found a way to chew up a lot of time and keep our offense off the field. It made for a frustrating afternoon. While we scored to go up 21-0 early in the third quarter we still seemed to be off on offense. Marshall missed some wide open receivers and threw a couple of uncharacteristic interceptions.

Early in the fourth Maryland closed it to 21-10 before we drove down the field to make it 28-10. But Maryland closed to within 28-17 before we ran the clock out to preserve the 11-point win. It was one of Marshall's worst games as our quarterback, and I could not help but think that the knee was still bothering him, until I got home.

Candace and I were getting ready for a late dinner at home with a couple of neighbors who'd picked up some pizzas. All of us were going to watch the primetime Iowa-Michigan game. With the Iowa game just a week away it was nice to combine some social time with getting a jump on the next week's opponent.

One of the things that happened on road games is that the graduate assistant coaches give us a scouting report on the next opponent for the trip home. By the time we landed I'd read up quite a bit on Iowa. As usual they had a great pass rush and a stout defense.

With some advance knowledge in mind, I sat down to watch the Iowa game and play some of the game out in my mind as friends watched along. Just before kickoff the doorbell rang.

At the door a man identified himself as an FBI officer and asked if he could come in to talk with me privately. As discreetly as I could I walked him to my den and shut the doors. A cloud of mystery hung in the air. Sensing that, this agent Frank Burrows got to the point.

"Coach," Frank said "I am not here about any known illegal activity so far. But there is a concern I want to raise with you."

Frank then laid out what he knew about Marshall's call with Tony Mancuso. When Mancuso was laying off an unusually high level of action the week before, they assumed he was in on something until he lost. But to be sure they listened in to his calls and caught Marshall's call with him. He assured me that they did not believe Marshall had any other interactions with him, but that I should warn him off any contact with his friend or with Tony Mancuso.

He also asked that I not reveal our conversation to anyone and attribute my knowledge of this situation to what I heard was the "word on the street". I agreed that I would take action and keep this confidential.

As I went back to watch the Iowa game, my friends had not noticed my short absence. But the whole evening, Marshall's uncharacteristically bad performance was eating away at me. Is it possible he did this for his friend?

The next morning I called Marshall into my office before anyone else arrived in the building. He assured me that he just had a bad game and that he'd refused to help his friend out of his jam.

"Well, you'd better distance yourself from that guy from now on. It is not enough for you to stay clear of any gambling stuff. You have to appear to be beyond reproach. Knowing what this guy did will make any contact you have with him look suspicious. If there is even a whiff of gambling ties with you, the NFL will not get anywhere near you."

"I have one question coach. Under my apartment door, someone slid an envelope with $1000 in it and a note that simply said "Thanks" on it. What do I do with that?"

"I'd go meet with our compliance officer, tell him what happened and donate the money to the OSU Cancer Center. That should satisfy them that you acted in good faith. I wouldn't get into the rest of the story, unless you want to get suspended from playing while they investigate this whole thing."

He got the message and left the office before anyone knew that we'd met. That seemed to resolve the issue but in my mind I wondered if I should report this issue. After all the FBI had cleared him and also asked me not to tell anyone else this story. I would be violating a request from law enforcement but also ignoring a duty to report a potential NCAA issue. Reporting it could lead to a suspension during a critical stretch against Iowa and Michigan State. We were not ready to play those teams with more distractions and a freshmen quarterback.

And I need not be reminded of the professional stakes for me personally that were still out there should we start losing. So while the coaches were looking at Iowa tape, I called our legal counsel Lewis Carter. I let him know that I'd spoken with an FBI agent who'd cleared Marshall of any wrongdoing. I stressed to him that we could not share information about an ongoing investigation. But I did need to report it to him so I could never be accused of not reporting any contacts.

Lewis made a note and sent me a copy of a memo stating that I had reported the incident and that Lewis had decided that no other action was required.

With that behind us I could start looking at Iowa. After their surprise win over Michigan Saturday night there was no doubt they were a dangerous team. We'd risen to #7 in the polls and Iowa was up to #14.

These guys were a frustrating team. They played hard-nose football and made you earn every yard and every point. My worry was that Quinn's offensive system would be great moving the ball up and down the field but these guys were just dominant in holding teams to field goals in the Red Zone.

In the red zone your quarterback and offensive line become incredibly important. Being able to run the ball on a shortened field was critical. I reminded our offense that Iowa played defense with the idea that it takes three field goals to beat one touchdown. And that is what worried me.

As the game unfolded we were moving the ball and scored an early touchdown and two field goals for a 13-7 halftime lead. Quinn was frustrated at halftime. He thought we should be throwing the ball guns blazing and have thirty points at halftime. One of the problems was Iowa's offense was holding the ball as well as some costly penalties on our side.

Just before halftime we got a critical chop block call on our offensive line that was a terrible call. It took us out of field goal range. Just before time ran out I yelled at the official Jack Thompson and pointed out that we had seven penalties and Iowa only had one.

"Hey Jack," you ought to start calling some of this shit both ways. They've been holding us all damned day."

"Ed, you take care of your players and let us call the game."

"Screw you Jack, I've let you call the game so far and you're screwing us big time."

I knew better but I went after him anyway. Jack was not in the mood to hear my crap today.

"Ed, I'm gonna have to ask you to quiet down, unless you want me to drop a 15-yarder on you."

"Jack that's bush league and you know it. I'll pipe down but if it keeps going the way it's going...."

I let the sentence die there.

The second half was much like the first. Iowa slowed down the game and we kept up with costly penalties. The next thing we knew, a punt return a fumble and a great one-handed catch had put Iowa out in front 22-13 with ten minutes to go.

Just after they went up 22-13 I looked at Marshall and reminded him that these were the types of games he was here to win. He'd lost a fumble and was having a subpar day overthrowing some open receivers.

"Look you have to ignore all that has happened up to now. Finish strong and get us a couple of scores." I said.

He took the very next drive and got us a touchdown to close the gap to 22-20. After the defense made a great stand Marshall had our offense on the move again. Inside the Iowa ten we had a second and two and I told Quinn I wanted to run the ball. He had a pass he wanted but I was adamant.

We got the first down but once again there was a penalty. We were called for holding and got backed up. I stressed to Quinn that we had the go-ahead field goal in hand and to be sure that we got the lead. Two plays later we kicked the field goal to grab a 23-22 lead. We had climbed all the way back up for a lead.

But Iowa was not done. Sure enough they came down the field and with 1:05 to go they took the lead back 25-23 after a fifty-yard field goal.

There was no panic on our sideline as Marshall took the team on the field. Play after play he moved us into field goal range. With a third down and seven I stressed to Quinn that we could kick the field goal and that we should run the ball. But Quinn wanted to emphatically end the game and called a corner route with 20 seconds to go.

As Marshall went back to pass he had the corner wide open. But Iowa had sent a maximum pressure blitz and had a free rusher who hit Marshall and caused what was ruled a fumble on the field. Iowa recovered it.

But to me it looked like Marshall's arm was going forward which would've meant an incomplete pass. We would keep the ball and kick the game-winning field goal. It went to replay and the shot they showed on the scoreboards in Ohio Stadium showed pretty clearly that this call would get overturned.

The crowd saw it too and cheered and we gathered our field goal team to get them ready for when this call was overturned. As more and more time passed it seemed like an eternity. The longer it went the less I liked it. But this seemed like an easy one to me.

Finally Jack Thompson came out and with 106,722 fans hanging on every word he said “After further review, the quarterback’s arm was going forward...”

The crowd started to erupt before they heard the rest.

“..but he lost control of the ball before starting forward. The result of the play is a fumble recovered by Iowa.”

Through the roar the attentive fans noticed Jack signal first down for Iowa and then the cheers died into a prolonged and even louder booing. I could not believe it and called Jack over and proceeded to rant at him. It was a horseshit call and I told him so which resulted in a 15-yard penalty against me.

As time ran out, the booing continued. There are few places worse than heading into a post-game locker room to face a group of guys who played hard and had a chance to win taken away from them by an official.

There was not much to say at that point, but I had to go face the media. Right before I entered the media room, Sid grabbed me and pulled me aside.

“Look at me Ed....Look at me.”

“I’m not one of the players Sid. You don’t have to talk to me like I’m a kid.”

“Just remember Matty will be waiting for you. This is the moment he’s been waiting for. Don’t get into a pissing contest with a skunk.”

That made me laugh and I immediately calmed down. I trudged into the room with a bottle of water and still sweaty from a warm afternoon on the sidelines. The media room was packed and stuffy from the body heat from an assembled cast of media ranging from young college website journalism students to overweight middle-aged men sweating from the warmth of the room. Cameras began clicking away. And on the table in front of me was a mass of phones and recording devices set to record everything I would say. In the back a bank of television cameras were arrayed as well.

The first couple of questions were about the defense giving up the game-winning field goal drive. Some were about the play of certain players. Then Matty Buck started in with his question.

“Ed this is a two-part question.” He began.

“Oh good, a two-parter from you is what I have been looking forward to all day Matty...” I cut him off but laughed to make sure he knew I was in good spirits. The rest of the room had a good laugh. Even Sid was smiling. Humor was a defense mechanism I used after tough games to buy myself time to keep my cool. Candace told me that it made me come off as more composed and more human.

"I am sure you have been," Matty smiled back "so here goes. With the ball in field goal range why make the decision to pass and then walk me through what you saw on the call on the field."

"Oh good an easy one...." Everyone laughed again. "We knew they were going to blitz and basically thought Marshall could get rid of the ball and we'd either score a touchdown or come back and kick the field goal."

"But you could've just run the ball and kicked the field goal. Why something so risky?"

"Look Matty, as much as I like fighting with you I'm not going to. So respectfully I say that had we run the ball we could've fumbled it too. What was the second part?"

"The call and review on the field."

"Oh That?" I laughed again. "Let's just say that I did not agree with it. In fact I strongly disagree with that call. I want to make sure I don't incur a fine here and that I don't offend anyone but Stevie Wonder could've seen that call."

After a few more questions I headed out to the car where Candace was waiting for me. With a week off before our game against Michigan State this would be a long two weeks. With a loss the wolves began to gather on message boards, on social media and found strength in one another.

15. A BUSY OFF WEEK

After tough losses like Iowa Candace was always there to support me. The coach and spouse relationship on nights like this is your rock grounding you in the reality that there is more to life than football. But sometimes a coach's relationship with their spouse becomes a one-way street.

As we drove home Candace asked if I had time for her to share some news.

"Sure, why wouldn't I?" I asked as if slightly offended.

It got very quiet and I could tell there was something serious.

"You're not pregnant are you?" I asked half laughing.

"Ed I don't need your jokes." She paused. "My mother had a stroke last week. Her health has been declining for a few weeks." She said, her voice cracking slightly from the emotions.

"What?" I asked. "Last week? Why didn't you say something?"

"You were busy with the season so I didn't want to bother you with it. And I haven't really seen you. So with the off week here now I thought I could tell you. I know the loss is really what's important right now, but I've been struggling with this alone and now I need to tell you."

Blindsided.

Was I so self-absorbed in my job that my very own wife didn't feel she could share something this serious? At that moment I felt completely incompetent as a husband.

The lights of the other cars on the highway were going by like a blur. Soft drizzle started to fall and the only sound in the car was the back and forth of the windshield wipers and Candace's slightly muffled sobs.

"How serious is this?" I asked timidly.

"It's a stroke Ed...it's always serious." She lashed out.

"I understand that, but is she still in the hospital?"

"I have to go out there tomorrow."

"Okay."

She was quiet for a moment before she started to talk again.

"You're not going to ask if you should come out?"

Sometimes I am just so dumb. This was one of those times.

"Do you need me to come out with you?" I timidly suggested hoping the answer was no.

"No. I wouldn't want you to knock yourself out on my account."

That was a bomb of sarcasm from which there was no shelter. She was so good at that, there was nothing I could even think of to say.

"My sister is out there and I have to go out tomorrow and let my sister go home to her kids. *Her* husband has been taking care of them for a week."

That last statement felt like a shot at me. Ultimately this wasn't about me, so I took the punch.

"She's out of the hospital and in a rehab facility. Her speech is slurred some and she is slightly impaired mobility-wise. But they think she'll come most of the way back."

"Your Mom's one tough lady and I know she'll be great." I spoke as tenderly and optimistically as I could. I put my arm around her and she leaned on me as we kept driving towards home.

"I hope you're right." She said.

The next morning Candace was up before dawn headed to the airport to fly to Arizona to see her mother. I'd offered to take her but she told me that I'd better get to work on the next game. The chill in her voice indicated it was a little less than sincere. Only Brutus was here in the empty house and even he seemed to regard me as some stranger who'd been gone for several weeks.

With the house empty, I dressed and headed into the office to get a jump on the off week. The problem with an off week is that every coach postpones appointments and phone calls until the open week. Before you know it you've overscheduled yourself into a week that is worse than if you had a game.

Sid and Sally had agreed to come in and review what I had in the upcoming week. Art Simpson came in early as well because he also had some things to talk about. Sid walked me through any media requests that we'd put off until the open week. There wasn't a whole lot that we had to discuss on that front. Sally reminded me of some phone calls I'd promised to make on Monday as well as a meeting with my attorneys.

I was taking all these notes down in my day planner. There are certain old-school things I hold on to and a leather-bound paper day planner is one of them.

After Sally and Sid had spoken Art handed me a list of things that he'd put off until the open week that needed immediate attention.

> Privileged and Confidential
> Athletic Director Issues
>
> NCAA Wants to Question The Following Players on Tuesday
>
> 1. Donte Carter—Issues: How did his mother pay her rent, move to C-Bus and get a job here?
>
> 2. Malcolm Jackson—Issues: Mom moved to Cleveland—Why?
> Was the pastor Paid?
>
> I want to Talk to the following player on Tuesday
>
> 1. Marshall Remington—Issues: Question his contact with gambler
> Because it is an FBI investigation we have to handle it internally
>
> NCAA Wants to Question The Following Coaches:
>
> 1. Ed Hart—To discuss most of the above issues
> Also questions about "analysts" "consultants" coaching on the field
>
> 2. Dwayne Baxter—To Talk about Malcolm Jackson's Recruitment
> Did he have any contact with Malcolm's Pastor?

As I looked at the list I was relieved. But any time the NCAA showed up with their people to question players and question coaches you had to be wary. They could try and trap you into something. And we certainly could've gone without the distraction.

"So Ed," Art asked "is there anything I should be worried about on this list?"

"Not that I am aware of, but I can't speak to everything on that list from the player's standpoint."

"What about your consultants coaching your players on the field?" He asked.

"Did not happen."

"You're sure?" He asked as though he knew something.

“Positive. I tell those guys in no uncertain terms that they’d better never coach any of our kids. I hire assistants to do that job.”

“Well a lot of other schools are getting caught doing that.”

“That’s because the head coach hires a bunch of recruiting renegades as his assistants and none of those “all-recruiting-all-the-time” guys can actually coach for shit. So they have to hire consultants to coach and cover the asses of the guys who are just snake oil salesmen recruiters."

“What about Malcolm Jackson’s mother moving to Cleveland?”

“She moved there to care for her Mother who is older and needs help.”

“That sounds legit.”

“It should, because it is.”

My ire was starting to spike because Art was clearly looking for trouble. We try to comply with the NCAA rules but if you looked under every rock you’ll find something at every school. Most of it is unintentional because of a large and unwieldy rule book.

When Art was done everyone left and I opened my e-mail and saw a message that had been forwarded to me from Sally. The school maintained a public e-mail address for me and she generally sorted through things.

This one was troubling:

> To: Coach Ed Hart THEhfc@osu.edu
> From: osufannumber20022014@gmail.com
> Subject: Where’s The Offense???
>
> Coach Hart---
>
> Your offense stinks this year. What Happened? Maybe your boy Quinn has lost his mojo chasing around that college student he’s been shacking up with....
>
> --A Concerned Fan

These types of rumor e-mails were a dime a dozen after a loss. But for some reason Sally felt compelled to forward it to me. She was still in the office so I called her back in.

“Hey come on in and shut the door.” I said.

As she strolled over to her seat I noticed for the first time that she was wearing yoga pants, and although I'm not supposed to notice, I did.

“About the e-mail you forwarded.....”

“What about it?” She asked.

“Why did you forward that one in particular?” I asked.

“I thought you should see it. From what I’ve been hearing it may very well be true. Given the type of fall we’re already having I did not think we could afford to have any more problems blow up on us.”

“So it’s true?”

“I didn’t witness it myself, but there are a couple of coaches who know. Dave’s son knows the girl and she’s shown him pictures of the two of them together. To make matters worse, she’s one of our recruiting interns.”

“Seriously, she’s one of our recruiting interns? Shit.....call Quinn and tell him to come in early. And one other thing, send flowers to Candace’s mother and to Candace out in Arizona. She had a stroke and Candace left this morning to be with her. Here’s my Amex to charge it to.”

I handed her my card.

“Great, since I have your card I’ll just get myself a little something too. So you’re all alone for a while?” Sally smiled slyly.

Her tone and the sly smile caught me a little off guard. Or maybe I was imagining her tone because of seeing her in yoga pants. Goddam Lululemon Yoga pants for putting thoughts like that in my head.

“No, I’ve got Brutus.”

Sally laughed and left the room. I purposely looked away as she walked out so I could clear my mind from any bad thoughts. We’d worked together for years and thoughts like that had never crossed my mind.

A few minutes later Quinn came into the office and sat down. Immediately I addressed the rumors and Quinn was taken by surprise.

“I know your private life is none of my business but this one is more complex.”

I slid a printout of the e-mail I’d gotten across the desk to Quinn. I sat quietly as he read it. He lifted his head to reveal a stunned look on his face. Before he could protest I spoke.

"Look Quinn, you're a single guy and I make no assumptions that these rumors are true. But if this is true you've got to stop this. We can't afford any more controversy this fall. For you personally, no matter how you really feel about this girl, the outside world will assign the most nefarious motives to this. This is the kind of thing will kill your chances of becoming a head coach. If this is something real, just put the brakes on until she graduates in December."

Quinn was about to respond but I continued before he had the chance.

"And seriously Quinn, a recruiting intern? If that gets out you will be red-flagged by every search firm in the country. Everyone thinks those interns are hired sexpots servicing recruits and coaches. That is how the outside world would see this. This has to stop as long as she is part of our operation."

Quinn got the message. He was angry but deep down he knew I was looking out for him particularly because I'd referenced his career ambitions.

Shortly after he left my office it was time for a recruiting meeting. During the off week we had the chance to get more recruiting done. How we finished the season would be a big factor not only in saving my job but also in recruiting.

But just before the meeting Sally put through a call from a big OSU booster David Daily. He ran a really big state-wide law firm based out of Columbus. The morning after a loss this call could not be a good one.

"David, what can I do for you?" I asked.

"Well winning the Big Ten would be a start." He laughed.

At least he was laughing for now.

"Seriously though Ed, I'm calling about Terrence Jones."

"What about him?" I asked.

"Well my partner Mitch Hughes is from Steubenville. His guys out there tell me that the kid is a Michigan lock. We can't have that."

"We're working on it. I can assure you that he is priority number one."

"Unlike some other people, I like you Ed and I think you're a good coach. But you're a little *too* honest. There ain't many virgins in your business. The ones that are become whores pretty quickly or they get sent to a convent."

I laughed before he got to his point.

"You *need* this kid. Mitch and I can put together the money to get this kid. This is a recruiting win that will help you keep your job. If you lose this kid, all hope may be gone."

"I appreciate your support David, but I gotta ask you to stay out of this. The NCAA will watch this one like a hawk. But I may have an ace left to play so stay tuned."

He was right about one thing. If we did lose another game a big-time recruiting class would at least give us some leverage. But how sure was I that we could get this kid without buying him like David had suggested? He'd certainly made me think though.

"One other thing Ed," David said "I'm hearing that a prominent starter, one of your captains is a homo. That rumor is on message boards and a lot of guys want to know what you're gonna do about that?"

"Are you serious?" I asked despite being rather surprised that this was even an issue.

"Yeah I am."

"I'm not gonna do a damn thing." I snapped back. "If a player is a good student, teammate and person I don't care what they do in their personal life. Does that answer your question?"

It was pretty clear from my tone that I meant what I'd said. That ended the call on a contentious note, but what's right is right.

In the meeting it became apparent that we could be in position to close out another top five recruiting class. This week would be critical. Most of these guys had already visited us and the open week was a time to try closing some of them out. That's why I decided we would practice Monday through Wednesday and then send coaches out Thursday and Friday to see games and see if we could get some decisions made.

Rick was particularly animated for this meeting. As he passed out the lists I made sure to grab an extra set for Sally to send over to Gerry Gorton. After the previous night's loss, it was important to make sure that I kept sending him the recruiting updates and team updates.

As much as it pissed me off to have to report on recruiting and weekly progress on the team, we absolutely had to keep him in our corner. Even Sally got that concept and she was always reminding me when my reports were due at the end of each week.

It always helps to have a staff assistant that is on top of her game and keeps you on top of your game.

2021 Recruits

	Needed	Commits	To Go
QBs	0	0	(take 1 if possible)
RBs	1	1	0
FBs	0	0	0
WRs	3	2	1
TEs	1	0	1
OTs	2	1	1
OGs/Cs	3	2	1
Offense	10	6	4 (5 if we take a QB)
DTs	2	1	1
DEs	2	1	1
ILBs	1	0	1
OLBs	2	1	1
CBs	2	2	0
SAFs	2	1	1
Defense	11	6	5
Totals	21	12	9 (10 if we take a QB)

Committed:

1. RB Marcus Simmons	6-1	210	4.4	Katy HS—Katy, TX
2. WR Floyd Wilson	6-3	207	4.4	Glenville HS—Cleveland, OH
3. OG Rick Stratton	6-6	298	5.2	Chillicothe HS—Chillicothe, OH
4. OT Antonio Hall	6-7	310	5.2	Trinity HS—Louisville, KY
5. DT Lawrence Lucas	6-3	285	4.7	Cathedral Prep HS—Erie, PA
6. DE Mario Santini	6-5	250	4.5	St Francis DeSales HS—Columbus, OH
7. OLB Ricardo Hines	6-4	210	4.5	Bishop Hoban—Akron, OH
8. CB Martin Paulson	6-1	185	4.3	Bedford HS—Bedford, OH
9. SAF Ricky Dixon	6-2	200	4.4	Purcell Marian HS—Cincinnati, OH
10. WR Anthony Carter	6-3	190	4.4	McKinley HS—Canton, OH
11. CB Randall Sherman	6-0	175	4.3	Dunbar HS—Baltimore, MD
12. OG Dexter Gilbert	6-4	280	5.1	Woodland Hills HS—Pittsburgh, PA

2021 Top Targets (ranked in Order)

1. ATH Terrence Jones 6-2 210 4.3 Steubenville HS—Steubenville, OH
Other Schools: Michigan, Notre Dame, Alabama, Texas, Florida, Clemson

2. DE Carter McDonald 6-5 240 4.6 Wilson HS—Camden, NJ
Other Schools: Penn State, Michigan, Nebraska, USC, Tennessee, Rutgers

3. DT Andre Carter 6-4 300 4.8 Neshoba Central HS—Philadelphia, MS
Other Schools: Ole Miss, LSU, Alabama, Texas A&M, Clemson

4. OLB Devon Alexander 6-3 225 4.5 Highland Springs HS—Richmond, VA
Other Schools: Clemson, UVA, South Carolina, Georgia

5. SAF Jared Patterson 6-1 205 4.5 Glenville HS-Cleveland, OH
Other Schools: Michigan, Michigan State, Notre Dame, Wisconsin

6. OT Patrick Smith 6-6 300 5.3 Glen Oak HS—Canton, OH
Other Schools: Michigan, Notre Dame, Iowa, Wisconsin

7. QB Walker McCoy 6-5 220 4.4 Provine HS—Jackson, MS
Other Schools: Mississippi State, Ole Miss, Alabama, Georgia, Texas, Oklahoma

8. TE Jesse Kish 6-6 240 4.7 Wheaton-Warrenville South-Wheaton, IL
Other Schools: Iowa, Illinois, Notre Dame, Nebraska, Michigan

9. ILB Roger Jackson 6-3 230 4.6 Ironton HS—Ironton, OH
Other Schools: Michigan, Michigan State, Tennessee, Kentucky

10. DE Russell Carson 6-6 228 4.4 Cass Tech—Detroit, MI
Other Schools; Michigan, Alabama, Michigan State, Colorado, Oklahoma

11. OT Bryce Wade 6-6 305 5.1 Rogers HS—Toledo, OH
Other Schools; Michigan, Wisconsin, Michigan State, Oklahoma, Kentucky

12. WR Cordelle Dawson 6-1 190 4.3 Warren Harding HS—Warren, OH
Other Schools: Penn State, Notre Dame, Clemson

13. OG Marvin Richards 6-5 312 5.2 St Joe's Prep—Philadelphia, PA
Other Schools: Penn State, Rutgers, UNC, Clemson, Florida

14. DT Leroy Parker 6-3 280 4.7 Mentor HS—Mentor, OH
Other Schools: Michigan, Clemson, USC, Alabama, Oklahoma, Georgia

15. WR Derrick Terrell 6-3 210 4.5 Dr. Phillips HS—Orlando, FL
Other Schools: Miami, Alabama, Notre Dame, Arizona, Arizona State

The whale in the class was without question Terrence Jones. This kid was such a whale that even Gerry Gorton was repeatedly asking where we were with him.

Quinn was the guy who recruited that area of Ohio. After the meeting I pulled him aside with Rick Carter and privately asked them what they were hearing out there from people in Steubenville.

"Word on the street" Rick said "is that he's a Michigan lock. This Pietrovic guy seems to have some kind of hold on the kid."

Getting the top-rated kid in Ohio was always a big deal for Ohio State. Over the years that had been almost automatic for OSU. Jim Tressel made it a priority to re-establish OSU dominance after some years where Michigan, Notre Dame and Penn State had given OSU trouble in our own state.

"Yes I know about that guy." I said.

I couldn't relay to these guys that he was into some guys running a mob poker game in Youngstown for six figures. I certainly couldn't tell these guys that I could use that to buy this guy away from the kid.

Part of the problem with the growing mass of extra interns, analysts and consultants working in football programs these days is that you couldn't keep stuff like that secret any more. These guys moved from school to school and your program's secrets spread.

Monday we went back out on the practice field to get back to work after a tough loss. With two weeks before the Michigan State game it gave us time to really study the Spartans as well as work on fundamentals with all of our guys. Tuesday I met with Art Simpson and Sid to talk about the NCAA coming into town.

They'd talked with Malcolm Jackson about his recruitment and his pastor. Malcom had no idea his pastor was shopping him around. He also confirmed that his mother had moved to Ohio to be near his grandmother. Art said that as far as Malcolm was concerned it appeared that everything about the kid was above board.

That was the good news.

But there was a report that a Florida State booster had made a payment to that Pastor. And just before signing day they'd found a phone call between that booster and Dwayne Baxter's agent. They'd need to talk to Dwayne but he postponed it until after the season.

They'd also talked to Donte Jones about his situation. In that meeting Donte told them that a family friend had loaned his mother money to pay her rent and move to Columbus. Getting the job was done on the up and up but the loan was a problem. Art suggested a one-game suspension for Donte and the NCAA appeared open to that given Donte's mother having to care for Donte's cousins. But she would have to pay the loan back.

When the NCAA came into my office I answered the questions honestly. They explained that this was not a "formal inquiry" but they just needed to get clarification on some things. When they asked about the Pastor I told them that yes I was aware of the "ask" but that I decided not to do it.

When they asked suspiciously why Malcolm "Would turn down the home-state school to come north" I told them about wanting to be near his ailing Grandmother in Cleveland. That opened up a line of questions about his mother getting a job with an alum. We turned over all the documentation of contacts and phone calls we'd made after Malcolm had signed. It was all in order and in line with NCAA legislation.

So far so good. The questions got tougher for an "informal inquiry" when it came to Donte Jones. This investigator seemed bent on finding something. As I fired back sticking to what I knew to be true, his disappointment seemed to grow. I'd been unaware of the loan. But it happened and it became apparent that they viewed it as a lesser major violation.

They even suggested a one-game suspension. I figured that I'd press back a little.

"When these guys are coming from such tough places it's hard for them to stand by and see their family evicted. I think you guys could show some understanding that this was a matter of family survival."

I knew they would suspend him, but I also knew that if I agreed with a one-game suspension that they would push it to two games.

The rest of the interview covered questions about consultants at practice and I offered them practice footage to confirm that none of these guys had been at practice.

Once that was done I was getting ready for a team meeting when Rick Carter came in to see me. He seemed flustered so I asked him to sit down, catch his breath and tell me what was bugging him.

"We've got some girl drama." He stammered.

"And what the hell does that mean?" I asked.

Rick reported that defensive tackle Antonio Patterson found out that defensive end Floyd Simmons was sleeping with his girlfriend. The police stopped them running through a parking lot last night when Antonio was chasing Floyd with a tire iron threatening to beat him.

"Good Lord." I replied.

"But wait there's more."

"Isn't there always more?"

"A third guy was also involved."

"Oh for the love of God.... I can't wait to hear this."

"Well the whole thing started when Pierre Carter starting lecturing Floyd about sleeping with white girls. That's when Antonio found out that Floyd was sleeping with his girlfriend. So as they were going through the parking lot Pierre was chasing both of them with a piece of garden hose he'd found on campus and was trying to hit them with it."

"So let me get this straight. Pierre was chasing Antonio with a piece of garden house while Antonio was chasing Floyd with a tire iron?"

"That covers it."

"Okay two questions. Any charges or even police reports being filed? And did anyone video this and post it on social media?"

"No to both."

"Okay good. I'll address this in the team meeting today."

So I added that to the team meeting agenda. There is nothing like having to start a team meeting with a lecture on guys sleeping with other guys' girlfriends.

Every once in a while, and today being one of those days, I had to break out my lecture that I called "Xs and Hos." Yes it is a politically incorrect title but it gets their attention even from the upperclassmen who've heard it once or twice. I decided to get their attention with props so I had our equipment guys put a tire iron and a piece of garden hose in the podium before the meeting.

When I walked in the team meeting room the mood was pretty good. They'd put the Iowa game behind them and were looking toward the future. I smiled as I stepped to the podium.

"Well gentlemen it is the open week which gives us time to cover some things that are important to building a team. Today it is time for the semi-occasional lecture that we like to call "Xs and Hos."

Some guys laughed and others groaned and rolled their eyes.

"Yes I know some of you have heard this before but today is a little different. Today we have props."

Even the older guys looked a little unsure of where this was going.

"Normally this is called Xs and Hos, but today......" I paused as I reached into the podium to grab the hose "...today maybe I should say it is Xs and Hose as in H-O-S-E!."

I held up the hose as the some guys laughed and others said in unison "OOOOOOOOHHHHHH."

Clearly almost the whole team had heard the story.

"I want to make sure this team remains strong......" I reached for the tire iron ".....as strong as IRON."

As I held the tire iron up they roared again.

The three players all put their heads down, shook them and laughed. The rest of the lecture hit on things like loyalty to one another and how important it was to keep team unity from being fractured by off-field social situations.

"Look, your personal life is your personal life. But when what you do impacts our team, we have an issue. And you do not judge one another by the color of women you choose to date. We've got enough issues in society without making more trouble internally."

They got the general idea.

The practice attitude was light as the guys had dug out of the darkness that descends on Columbus after an Ohio State football loss. They were precise with very few mental mistakes for me to get upset about.

These weeks were also good for the coaches. I made sure that they went home after practice to eat dinner with their families. Having learned from my failed first marriage I knew that absentee husbands and fathers left voids that would be filled somewhere else. Having had a wife and daughter go through alcohol rehab I knew all too well what could go wrong.

While Candace was with her mother I was left to fend for myself.

While making my way around the kitchen to assemble something that could pass as edible, Brutus followed me around. The wagging tail and longing look of someone awaiting a gift of table scraps made it hard not to throw a few treats his direction.

But the house was quiet and lonely. But that quiet gave me a chance to study Michigan State in even greater detail. In my den I concentrated on the film, only breaking occasionally to see Brutus in his dog bed near my desk.

"You've got it pretty good." I said to Brutus. "No pressure to win. Me? I gotta win or else we'll be out of here. I'll have to rename you for the mascot at whatever school we get to next."

He just wagged his tail. I reached into my desk drawer and pulled out one of the dog treats I kept in there and tossed it to him. He caught it in his mouth mid-air.

The next morning Marshall Remington came to the office at 6 a.m. to see me as I had asked him to do. As he sat down I looked at him sitting confidently with the poise that made him a natural leader.

I got right to the point.

"Marshall I know you and I talked about this before but there is still some concern about gamblers and a game earlier this season. I just wanted to make sure we have this straight. Tell me what's up."

One of things I learned as a coach was to give them the topic and then ask for their story first. If they don't know what you know they are usually more honest.

"Coach there's nothing to it. Some guy I know told them I wasn't going to play in the Rutgers game and when I did we covered the spread. They roughed this guy up I guess. Same thing I told you before."

"You sure that's all it is? You did have your worst game in several years the next time out and that got the FBI's attention."

"I'm positive coach."

"You've always been honest with me, so I'll take your word for it."

The look in his eyes spoke louder than his words. He was forthright and stern. He'd never lied to me so there was no reason to think he'd start now. With that out of the way we talked about the team attitude. He felt we were in a good place and looking to bounce back in a big, big way.

By seven he'd headed out and Sally Anderson had arrived. She brought donuts and a copy of the Columbus Dispatch.

"Thought you could use some food. You're probably starving to death with Candace out of town." She laughed.

"Actually I made myself some pasta last night."

"Heating up a can of spaghetti-ohs doesn't count as "Making Pasta" for most people. If you need me to bring over dinner I can do that."

"No, I made my own pasta. It was pretty good too."

"Oh.....look at you boiling water and opening a jar of Ragu. You probably stopped shutting the bathroom door when you're going too. Men are so predictable."

She had me. That's exactly what I'd done last night. Before she turned to go she pointed at the Dispatch.

"You'd better take a look at what's in there." She said. "It ain't good."

She turned and left before I opened the sports section. On the front page was an "exclusive" story with the headline "A Struggling OSU Offense: The Post-Mortem on a Game-Losing Play Call."

The article cited unnamed "insider sources" who outlined the last play of the game and placed the full blame on me. Although it had been Quinn's call, I would never publicly out anyone. The buck stops with me and I ultimately gave the okay.

It also laid bare the "internal struggle" between Quinn's wide-open philosophy and my attempts to slow the games down. It was clearly an agenda-driven hit piece to maintain Quinn's reputation as a master play-caller. I suspected the leaks came from Quinn's agent Warren Thompson to make him look better because we'd not had as much success as the year before.

These are the first fraying threads that get pulled to rip the fabric of a coaching staff. But this thread would have to be addressed. The rest of the staff will see it and wait to see how I responded. If I didn't handle this there would be more leaks.

When the coaches came in for the staff meeting I made sure the article was on the table. As I started the meeting I reminded them of the loyalty we had have for the program and to one another. Then I held up the newspaper.

"That brings me to this morning's paper. There is an article in here that discusses our offense, a particular play call and the end of the Iowa game. It includes quotes from our meetings. I don't know the source, but take note for the future. If I find any of you or any of your agents spinning things to the media I will take the action I deem necessary. And check your contracts because this kind of fucking behavior gives me the option to fire you for cause. And that means no buyout. "

The guys were all nodding along, but Quinn was looking distant and immediately I knew. Whenever information is leaked, my first step is to guess who benefits most from the leak. Most of the time these guys are slick enough to have a third party like an agent do this. It keeps their hands clean.

But I decided to file this one away for another day. In the immediate present we had to go recruiting and to beat Michigan State. A loss to the Spartans would really put us back in the Big Ten East pack. The specter of another season without a Big Ten title loomed.

By Thursday morning the coaches were on seven different private planes we'd hired to send them out recruiting. Thursday through Sunday night when the last of the recruits finished their visits Rick would be holed up in the recruiting "war room." On a big screen was a display of a flight tracker using tail numbers to track the progress of the seven planes.

When I walked in at 7:15, I saw three planes had already landed. Dwayne Baxter had landed at Burke Lakefront Airport on his way to Glenville High School, Quinn Banks had landed in Jefferson County Airport on his way to Steubenville High School and Otis Lewis had landed at Canton/Akron Airport on his way to Glen Oak High School. Doug Leonard's jet was on its way to Philadelphia International Airport so he could hop over the bridge to Camden. Tight End Coach Terry Ellis' plane was nearing DuPage County Airport about thirty miles west of Chicago on his way to Wheaton-Warrenville South HS.

That was just part of the first wave. By noon most of these guys would be back in their planes and headed somewhere else. Rick had to make sure that the pilots for Quinn and Doug were coordinated. Both of them were headed to Mississippi later and Rick wanted to make sure they met up by landing in Asheville, North Carolina where Quinn would jump on to Doug's plane for the rest of the trip.

All told these seven planes would get these guys to see every one of the top fourteen guys as well as another seven or eight down-the line possibilities.

The tab for private planes was a lot steeper. But on days like these a guy like Terry Ellis avoiding a commercial flight and the hassle of a rental car at O'Hare or Midway to get to a suburban Chicago high school was well worth the price. We got three times as much work done this way.

Around noon just before the next wave of flights took to the air, Rick had a zoom meeting with the coaches on the big screen in the war room. I hated that the guys called it a "War Room" because I felt it was an insult to real war rooms in real combat zones. It was an easy term to use so it stuck.

Most of the feedback was really good with the lone exception being Terrence Jones. Quinn stated it would take a near miracle to shake Pietrovic's hold on him. Even Steubenville Coach Reno Saccoccia who'd been there for years couldn't seem to get through to this kid.

But Quinn was happy to report that Terrence was going to stay with his visit for the Michigan game. Maybe a win over the Wolverines would turn the tide.

One thing that did pop up was a report that a big-time DE from Norfolk, Virginia had just de-committed from Clemson. So we would ditch the plan to have Quinn jump on Doug's plane. Doug would head straight to Norfolk Friday morning while Quinn would head home from Mississippi. That meant Rick making a frantic call to the plane dispatcher to change plans.

After a quick lunch, I returned in time to see the flight tracker showing the planes taking off again. I know at least a small part of what the CEO of Delta or United Airlines must feel. With each round of flights taking off I returned to the war room to watch where they were all going. All told we'd have seven private jets shuttling our coaches to twenty-five different airports in ten states as far south as Houston and as far east as Newark. By the time they all landed back in Columbus on Friday it was time to host five recruits on official visits.

And as for the player in Norfolk, that ended up being a complete dead end. The rumors were not solid, so we'd wasted about $10,000.

By Saturday morning we had five recruits in for official visits. All of them were committed players whose teams would go well into their state playoffs. The visits for committed recruits were more like an orientation weekend. We made sure they'd applied to school and walked them through the admissions process. We got them on track and more familiar with their future coaches and teammates.

The weekend weather was a last breath of summer hanging on just a few more days to bathe the changing leaves in glorious sunlight. It really gave our campus a special feel, like the gods' impressionist painting with dabs of golds, yellows, reds and oranges. At least that's how Candace often described it. After all she did get an A in her Art History class at Yale.

The days apart from Candace were starting to wear on me.

Once the recruits were on their way home Sunday, we were evaluating Michigan State's game from the day before. They'd surprised Iowa out in Iowa City which certainly got our attention. That is a tough place to win and they got it done.

Sunday afternoon we got a green light to play Freshman Jamar Tucker at defensive end. He'd made it all the way back from that shooting. His speed rush would give us a big lift. But I wasn't sure if we should play him or redshirt him.

In the staff meeting I asked Doug Leonard for his thoughts.

"Well Ed I got a couple 'a thoughts for you. Number one if we redshirt him, we may not be here to see him play next year. Second this kid ain't gonna be here more than three years so we may as well get as much of those three years as we can. And number three this kid is too good to keep on the bench. It's nut-cuttin' time coach."

"Nut-cuttin' time? Isn't that when they castrate bulls to make them steers? I'm not sure how that analogy applies." I said.

"Neither am I, but you get the point. Let's play the fucking kid."

We decided to keep his playing status quiet and practice him like we'd done all year until Thursday. The trick was to keep Michigan State from finding out he was playing. He would change the game dramatically and we didn't want them to plan for his speed rush.

The next topic was how we approached the week with Marshall Remington. He'd not played well lately and his last two practices had been really subpar. I was starting to wonder if he was slipping. Carter Jones had played well, sparking some support to play him. He was practicing lights out, but that is often the case for the back-up who feels none of the starter's pressure.

As we were talking Rick Carter wanted to bring something to my attention. Because Rick was younger he often heard some of the intra-team information before the rest of us.

"Since you guys are talking about the quarterbacks, there is something that happened last night that I want to bring to your attention. One of our recruiting interns saw it. Luckily, none of our recruits saw it." Rick said.

Before I could even respond Quinn, always protective of his guys, jumped in "What happened?"

"Carson Grady had a couple of beers and shot his mouth off to Marcus Dawson, Karl Metzger and some of the other seniors. He said that Carter Jones was better than Marshall. He even said that had Carter been playing we'd have beaten Iowa."

Now it was my turn to jump in. "So do I need to talk to him?"

"No," Rick said "Marcus basically told him to shut up or Carson would have to deal with him. Carson started to mouth off and Marcus grabbed him. That ended it."

"Do any of you sense any murmuring or locker room lawyering going on as it relates to the quarterback situation?" I asked.

Roger Barstow weighed in "Ed there is an upside to playing Carter. It buys us time. If the alumni and fans see him out there lighting it up, it provides a glimpse into a very bright future for us. It could buy us some time if we're under the gun."

Roger was always good at looking for anything to save his own ass over the good of the team. But this was not the time to lecture him, so I let his statement go. It had some validity, but this was not the time to panic.

Then I looked at the receivers coach Wayne Robinson. Over the years I've found that any dissent about quarterbacks manifests itself first among the receivers.

"Wayne, what are you hearing?" I asked.

"I don't sense a major rift, or that anyone is dividing into camps but......" Wayne hesitated.

"But what?" I asked.

"But it is important for Marshall to have a good game this week. Win or lose if he struggles it gives momentum to the murmuring."

Quinn looked pissed and was about to weigh in before I cut him off. In coaches' meetings when coaches talk about other coaches' players it can get a little sensitive.

"Okay I hear what you're saying. I appreciate the honesty. Before we start an argument here is what I want to do. Quinn, get Marshall's best plays, take the things he is most comfortable doing and let's feature those things this week. Don't tell him what we're doing. That is important. Sometimes we like to game plan intricate Xs and Os to show how smart we are. Believe me I know. Back at Kansas we lost a game at Oklahoma because I was convinced I had this great plan but our quarterback was never comfortable."

"I watched that game coach." Quinn said. "As a Texan I was pissed because any time someone can beat the Sooners....."

"So let's get some easy passes early to get him started on a hot completion streak. Throw in a deep ball about five or six plays in the game too. It doesn't matter how easy the passes are, if a QB hits five or six or more in a row they get to feeling invincible. It's also important for him to start fast to keep the boo birds from getting vocal."

Quinn nodded and before we broke the meeting I wanted to make one last point.

"Guys we have to take care of the guys we coach this week. If you hear any dissent do your part to stamp it out. If you can't handle it then come to me. But most of all we do not talk about any other players in our meetings. As you guys have heard me say to you a thousand times "Coach Your Own and Trust One Another" and it fits this week too."

Later on Sunday night I called Marcus Dawson to talk with him about the previous night's incident. He was just leaving dinner with Carson Grady and Karl Metzger to put the previous night's argument behind them. When you have seniors who can resolve team issues themselves that's when you know you've done your job molding leaders.

What I didn't know is that their dinner tab had been picked up by a couple of beautiful women. They'd told the guys they'd meet up with them after the Michigan State game, but only if they won. As every guy their age would do, they accepted the free meal with the belief that it was innocent with no strings attached.

The week went smoothly and by Thursday night Marshall had finished up a very good week of practice. But Carter was still on fire keeping the pressure on Marshall. After practice I grabbed Marshall as we were coming off the field.

"Are you all good?" I asked.

"I think so." He replied.

"Don't just think you are. Believe it. Keep that confidence that's carried you this far and you'll be just fine."

"Okay."

"You okay with everything on the game plan?" I asked. "If there is anything you're unsure of let me know and I'll take it out of the plan."

"Actually coach I am really comfortable. There are a ton of my favorites on here. I really like the opening fifteen-play script too."

"Good. If there is anything you're even slightly unsure on, tell me. Don't ever be afraid to speak up. And above all just relax, be yourself on Saturday and play your game. You got me?" I said.

"Yep. Thanks. I got you coach." He replied and ran off the field into the locker room.

Normally on Thursday night after my coach's radio call-in show I had dinner with Candace. But she was still in Arizona with her mother. The stroke had really knocked her backwards and Candace had taken up the mantle to be with her. So I was home eating pizza when my cell phone rang. I looked at the number and it was Alexis Nelson.

“What the hell could she want?” I said aloud looking at Brutus.

Against my better judgment I answered the call.

“Ed!” She said. “How we looking for Saturday?”

We made some small talk about the game and the season before she got around to what I suspect was the real reason for the call.

“Everything okay with you?” She asked.

“What do you mean?” I asked back.

“Everything okay between you and Candace?”

“Why would you ask that?”

“Well it’s on a message board that Candace left you almost two weeks ago.”

“Left me?”

“Yeah the rumor is she’s gone to Arizona.”

“Where in the hell would that rumor come from?”

“There are eyes and ears everywhere Ed. Neighbors, co-workers, at airports, Uber drivers....you just never know.”

“Well there ain’t shit to it.”

“Well just be aware that it’s out there.”

As soon as I hung up, I called Sid. When I told him what Alexis had said he told me that he’d gotten a call or two about it. He figured that Candace valued her privacy and wouldn’t want her Mother’s health to become a story. But he said we could handle it any way I wanted.

You know what, I’ll figure it out. I had an idea that was subtle and would effectively shut down the rumors without looking like I was aware of them.

On Fridays we meet with the television crew that does the game. This week it was one of the best crews: Steve Levy, Brian Griese, Molly McGrath, Todd McShay as well as Ben Bouma who was a vital cog for a ton of on-air information. In the production meeting I casually mentioned that this was a unique week because Candace was out of town taking care of her mother. It was the kind of in-game tidbit and human interest angle that crews liked to have. It was something they'd drop in during the second quarter. Sure enough the next day Molly McGrath mentioned it from a sideline report and Steve Levy and Brian Griese passed along their well wishes.

That killed that part of the rumor.

But there was a game to play too and we'd have to keep a sharp eye on Marshall Remington. In pre-game I could hear a few Buckeye fans yelling some crap at Marshall. There were even a few signs advocating that we play Carter Jones including an interesting political reference "Even Four More Years of Carter is Better than the Marshall Plan."

That student had to be both a Democrat and a History major. He should get credit for two pretty obscure references.

This crowd was just waiting for a chance to jump on Marshall and I could sense it. I just hoped our opening script would get us out to a fast start to shut that down. Just before the 3:30 kickoff I decided that we'd take the ball if we won the toss. I wanted to send Marshall a message that I wanted the ball in his hands to start the game. Normally you want that second half option in a big game between two top 15 teams (we were #12 and Michigan State was #13).

We won the toss and took the ball. As fate would have it, before we'd even finished up the fifteen-play script we were up 10-0 and Marshall looked like a million bucks. He hit ten of his first eleven passes and only a dropped pass in the end zone and a missed field goal has kept us from a 17-0 lead. But as well as we'd played, I was nervous to only be up ten points.

Football is often a game of momentum and this one was no different. The Spartans got it going and scored the next seventeen points before halftime. The crowd was antsy as we made our way into the locker room for halftime.

This halftime was one of enormous gravity for me. Lose this game and we were probably on our way to being a Big Ten also-ran and I'd be out of a job. So I took a page from something I'd once heard that Bill Walsh had done.

I told Quinn to start the second half with the same plays from opening script. He looked at me with a strange look.

"Trust me." I said.

Sure enough after holding Michigan State and getting the ball back, we started right back on the opening script. Two possessions later we had a 24-17 lead. Marshall had been re-ignited and the crowd was at a frenzy pitch.

After sundown the drama of a night game setting became the stage for this drama. The fans were invested and loud on every play. Their momentum surged through us and it showed in the enthusiasm of our team's performance.

At the start of fourth quarter Michigan State rolled the dice on a fourth down and two near mid-field. It was still a seven point game at that time, but they went for it to try and spark their now-stalled offense. Marcus Dawson, Karl Metzger and Carson Grady all smacked the ball carrier to stop him short. The three guys who'd nearly fought each other a few days earlier all worked together.

The very next play, I told Marshall to put a dagger in their hearts by looking to get freshmen tight end Manny Rodriguez deep against the MSU safety. Manny was having a very good year, but teams still were not adjusting their coverage to take him away from us. With Anthony Daniels on the outside they'd be expecting a deep pass to him, especially after a big change of possession. We sent Daniels on a deep over the top post and then ran a corner behind him with Rodriguez. He outran the safety, caught the ball and didn't stop until he'd scored to give us a 31-17 lead.

At that point the stadium's energy reached seismic levels and I knew the game was ours. They'd blinked and we'd taken their mistake to blow open the game. As the final minutes ticked off the clock, a light drizzle started to fall in the October evening. Looking up at the towering lights I could see the waves of drizzle lightly falling to the fans and the field below.

We'd earned a 38-17 win and rebuilt our quarterback's confidence. But my day was not over just yet. ESPN's Molly McGrath grabbed me coming off the field and asked about the big halftime adjustments we'd made. If anyone had known that all we did was recycle the first half script.....

But I gave credit to the way Marshall had played and the way the defense had rallied to deflect any attention on adjustments. That was really the truth of the matter.

As I wrapped up the live interview I was not aware that Alexis Nelson had made her way onto the field and was standing right behind us. Finishing the interview I turned to leave and she grabbed me for a hug. I was defenseless but I know that moment had just been caught on live television and was likely seen by Candace in Arizona.

Sure enough, before I went into the press conference I saw a text from Candace.

"WTF was Alexis Nelson doing there? I go out of town and she's suddenly on the field after a game. Even I don't show up like that." Her text was not all-CAPS but it should've been.

Before heading into the press conference I texted her back "I have no idea why she was there."

"Well Congrats on the game. You needed that one!"

Did we ever.

16. THE CHASE CONTINUES

There was a tinge of loneliness as I walked to my car after the big win over Michigan State. It had been a long two weeks and Candace wouldn't be there waiting for me. At night I could put a hat on, keep my head down and make my way to the car without anyone seeing me. Individual voices could be heard from the nearby sea of tailgates. The laughter, the thumping sounds of beanbags hitting corn-hole boards and people yelling to a friend at the grill for a Brat or Burger or dog. Occasionally I'd hear someone yelling for a beer.

But to my surprise when I got to my car, there was someone waiting. From a distance it looked like a familiar figure silhouetted in the overhead streetlights.

When I neared the car she turned my way. It was Alexis Nelson.

"Headed home alone?" She asked.

"Nope. Brutus is waiting for me."

"Brutus?"

"My beagle."

Alexis laughed but she did not appear to be amused.

"Look," she said "I am one of this program's biggest donors and whether you like it or not I carry a lot of pull here."

"And your point is?"

She walked closer to me, smiling in the parking lot lights with her hair pulled back and just slightly damp from the light drizzle. She had classic cheek lines and a sparkle in her eyes from the light above. For a moment there flashed an almost youthful innocence in her face before it turned sultry. She stepped well inside my normal comfort level of personal space.

"My point is...if you play nice I can help you out."

I backed up a step or two after the blazing look she'd just given me. Had I stayed at that distance, anyone walking by who knew me would see something that just looked wrong.

"Alexis, as tempting as that may be I just can't."

“Yes, your wife. And where is she tonight? Just remember Ed, she’s a lot younger than you. You may have been a dashing young coach a few years ago but you’re getting older. She’s a lot younger than you are and she could certainly move on from a fired coach pretty quickly.”

“I’ll take my chances.”

“Then you’d better win, because if I don’t get what I want I won’t throw you a lifeline. In fact I’ll throw an anvil at you. And if you think this is over, just remember I know where you live.”

I walked around her to my car and just before I got in I hesitated and turned back towards her.

“Alexis, I’ve got just one question.”

“Yeah?”

“Why me? Seriously why me? You’re a striking woman, you’ve got more money that you can spend in three lifetimes and you can certainly find plenty of other men, many in better shape or better looking.”

“You don’t know do you?”

“No really I have no clue.”

“Because you’re part of the big show and it’s all about control. My whole life growing up in Ohio I’ve loved Buckeye football. And with you in my pocket, I’d be like the team owner of the big show.”

“Good to know. And here I thought it was all because of my dashing good looks.” I said and got in and drove away.

Once at home, dinner was a few bourbons to knock myself out. I fell asleep before I even had the chance to call Candace and talk. The next morning I woke to a text asking where I was. So when I woke up I texted her a picture of a half empty bottle of Maker’s Mark with the message: “Took some “MEDICINE” to knock me out—Sorry I forgot to call”

By 6:15 a.m. my phone was already ringing and Sid’s name appeared. While these calls are never good, this time it was beyond bad. The starting left side of our offensive line Guard Bobby Thompson and Tackle Gene Banks were pulled over for drinking and driving. Gene was driving and Bobby had an open container in the car. Gene was .09. Years ago that wasn’t even over the legal limit, but that was then.

The story broke because a writer for the student newspaper posted a video of them getting put through the field sobriety test. The first media call to Sid was at 5:45 a.m. The good news, if there could be any in such a scenario, was that the two guys were cooperative and both actually passed the test.

But this was pretty cut and dried, with no wiggle room. When I hung up I sent a text to Gerry Gorton letting him know that per established University policy I planned to suspend them both for one game.

Also that night Karl Metzger and Carson Grady had ventured out to meet the women they'd met the previous Sunday night. Karl ended up back at a hotel with one of the women. Karl's problems only worsened when someone posted pictures of him going into the hotel with that woman. Karl's girlfriend had been home that Saturday but she saw the pictures on-line.

Rick Carter filled me in on all the drama. There's just never a dull moment.....

By Sunday afternoon's coaches' meeting I'd met with Bobby Thompson and Gene Banks. They both owned up to their mistake. Although Gene was driving and had gotten cited, I felt I needed to punish them both. In the era of Uber and Lyft it showed a remarkable lack of judgment for either of them to drive.

In the coaches' meeting I relayed my decision to the staff. As the line coach, Otis Lewis wanted me to reconsider suspending his guys. He had an ally in Quinn Banks. Even after I assured them that my decision was non-negotiable Otis let me know he wasn't too happy.

"For God's sake Ed," he roared "when we were in college Point Zero Nine wasn't even a crime and now you're gonna hang two guys over this? And hell it's not like they fucking raped a girl like Marcus, and what did he get? A zero game suspension!"

Otis had crossed a line and I had to let him know it. There are times when you have to unleash hell. This was one of them.

"Otis, leave Marcus and that decision out of it!" I demanded. "You know that case was bullshit...COMPLETE BULLSHIT and now you're gonna try and THROW IT IN MY FACE? If you have another opinion on how I handled it, and you can't be loyal to that, then you'd better rethink whether or not you belong here after this season."

The room went dead silent and I let what I'd just said marinate for a moment. Every one of them was afraid to talk.

"Okay, the decision is final so let's deal with it just like they'd gotten injured. Get the next guys ready to go and let's find a way to beat Wisconsin. We've got the players to get the job done."

The suspensions created another news cycle on Monday. But it was quickly followed up by another news story. An appeals judge threw out an appeal by Vivian Terrant and a campus women's group to try and enforce the overturned suspension of Marcus Dawson.

By that afternoon Vivian Terrant was doing another ESPN interview highlighting the "Continuing Ohio State Football Crime Spree" even though Marcus was never charged and the other two players agreed to a plea to get fines and an alcohol education course for first-time offenders.

For his part Gerry Gorton appreciated that I'd handled the suspensions so quickly, but he too was worried about them both missing this game. But Monday and Tuesday practices had gone well.

By the time I got home around eleven o'clock on Tuesday night I was exhausted, but I hadn't talked to Candace since Sunday. It dawned on me how inconsiderate I'd been in not checking in with her on her mother's health.

When she answered we exchanged the usual pleasantries. Her mom was improving, but there was something else bugging her. So I just came right out and asked her what was bothering her.

"Well since you asked....I got a call from Maggie today."

"Oh and what did the town gossip have to say?"

"Well this one was pretty interesting. It seems there are some rumors around town that I've left you and now it seems that it is because you've been running around on me."

"What a load of horseshit."

"Yeah, I know it is and you know it is, but rumors like that make me look foolish."

"You can't let that shit bother you."

"Well with Alexis Nelson on the field and then someone sees you talking to her at your car after the game those things have a way of taking on a life of their own. And did you talk to her at your car Saturday, because if you did I believe you failed to mention that to me."

"She was waiting there when I got to the car and I told her to leave me alone and drove home by myself."

"For real?"

"Yes."

"And you didn't think that was worth mentioning?"

"Hell no. I got in the car and went home by myself, had half a bottle of Bourbon for dinner and fell asleep."

"Well either way, please stay the fuck away from her. Rumors, even unfounded rumors like this are hurtful especially when even my friends think they might be true."

"Let me just remind you that Maggie is a gossipy bitch and has never been your friend. You shouldn't give a rat's ass what she thinks."

"Easy for you to say, you're not the one who looks like the fool."

When I hung up I saw Brutus across the room looking back at me.

"You know Brutus, you may be the only real ally I have left."

No sooner had I said that then Brutus turned and left the room. This was a new low.

"Et Tu Brutus?" I called out. It was the only Latin phrase I know.

Friday afternoon just getting to the plane to taking off to leave Columbus felt like a weight lifted off our shoulders. The distractions of the week were behind us. The question was whether the new left side of our offensive line could hold up.

But there was a surprise on board waiting for us. This was the annual "big donors trip" where we hosted boosters on the team plane and in the team hotel. Ivan Landon and Alexis Nelson were among a group of twenty guests on the plane. Not only did Ivan like to think he was the team owner but he'd been one of the most vocal critics among our Trustees.

Many of these donors brought spouses. Suddenly the professional atmosphere was broken by twenty people on a sightseeing tour and taking selfies at every turn to post on their social media accounts. With the distraction of the suspensions, this was the last damned thing we needed.

These people were just chatting away like they were at a cocktail party.

Friday night after bed check I took a quick shower before sitting in my suite to review my game plan. There was a knock on my door. Dressed in just a pair of shorts and no shirt I walked to the door expecting that it was a coach or Rick Carter.

Without looking to see who it was I opened the door only to see Alexis Nelson standing there.

"No shirt on? Well I guess we're halfway there." She said smiling.

"Let me throw something on." I retreated to get a t-shirt and she followed me into the suite.

"You're not kicking me out?" She asked as she helped herself to a seat on the couch.

"Not yet, but don't get too comfortable."

Her hair had been done up, her makeup was flawless and her scarlet top featured a low neckline that showed off a good bit of cleavage. The tight gray pants and high heels really played up her body. I felt guilty noticing all of this, but in fairness her intent was clearly to get my attention.

She'd been out to dinner with the other boosters but headed back early hoping to catch me before I went to sleep.

"Look," I said "You get five questions about the game tomorrow and then you've got to go."

"Five questions? Well at least you're not kicking me out right away. Why is that?"

"I'm bored, I haven't seen Candace in a few weeks and I thought it might be interesting to hear what you want to know. But that's it."

Her five questions showed a depth of football understanding that was surprising. She also possessed an incredible sense of Ohio State football history. Her father had two portraits hanging in his office; Jesus and Woody Hayes. To get his attention she had to talk Buckeye football because that meant more to him than his family.

That explained quite a bit.

"Now you got your answers and you've got to go." I said as I stood from the couch across from her.

She stood up walked around to me and looked up into my eyes.

"Do I really have to go?" She asked as she batted her eyes at me..

A few seconds that felt like several minutes passed in silence. In that silence there was an internal debate over what I should say and do next. She looked great, she was an incredibly attractive women and she was here in my room. There was an attraction.

But if it was ever going to happen, this could not be the place. There were just too many prying eyes around. I told her that she had to go. She pouted on her way out. After she left I exhaled and thanked God that I'd gotten her out of there.

A night game at Camp Randall Stadium is special. They were ranked #10 and we'd climbed back up to #11. If we lost this one, we could still win our division but we'd need help.

Besides the suspensions at offensive line, we were also missing a couple of starters on defense. Outside linebacker Darryl Shabazz was out and we'd moved the slightly injured Alvin Wallace to replace him. But this was a good opportunity for him. He was a senior and a two-year starter before he'd been beaten out by Carson Grady. He was a legitimate pro prospect and with Darryl out he could get the start. His injury status made him a game-time decision.

As the team was stretching I walked over to ask if he was ready to go.

"You know coach, I'm only about 85-90% so I think I'll sit this one out. I talked with my Dad and Uncle and they think I should sit out too." He said.

My anger adrenaline shot up. Ten years ago I'd have ripped him and told him to play, but this was 2020. Student-athletes now have a voice on social media and when a story breaks the benefit of the doubt always goes towards the athlete. So-called "Bullying" an athlete was a fire-able offense. We'd have to go without him.

As the game started to unfold, Wisconsin was using their normal approach. Pounding the running game and throwing play-action passes made our linebackers read and react to a balanced attack. With us missing some guys on defense we were struggling to stop them.

On offense we decided not to move our right tackle over the left side to cover up for the suspensions. As a result we became more right-handed in running the ball. We kept the running backs in to help the left side with pass protection.

As Wisconsin kept scoring, our offensive strategy was working too. But Wisconsin started to grasp what we were doing and made some defensive adjustments. Their offense was controlling the clock and we just couldn't seem to catch up. With eight minutes to go in the game we were down 31-22.

On a critical third down we rolled the dice and sent a corner blitz and Donte Carter got a sack to stop their offense.

On the next play they punted to our receiver Malcolm Jennings. It was a deep punt but with a flat trajectory. That always spells trouble for the punt team. Malcolm caught the ball cleanly on the move and within two or three steps was at full speed before Wisconsin's cover team could get downfield. He made two guys miss, found a crease and was gone in the blink of an eye. It was exactly what we needed. We'd closed to 31-29 and now with a defensive stop, we'd have a chance to win the game.

After a couple of Wisconsin first downs, we stopped them again and got the ball back. Marshall was ready to lead us on a game-winning drive from our own seventeen yard line with a minute to go and no timeouts. That didn't seem to matter as Marshall calmly got us first down after first down. There was no panic and with seven seconds we had the ball at the Wisconsin twenty yard-line on the right hash and ready for our kicker to nail the game winner.

Before we set up for the field goal I asked if everyone was all set. The overload rush would come from our left side so I thought about moving our veteran right side to the left side to protect the kick. Ultimately I decided that we'd be okay.

As we lined up for a sure thing I watched the snap, the hold and then heard the thud of the kick and then almost immediately the sickening sound of a second thud as the kick was blocked. The home crowd went wild as the Badgers recovered the kick to secure a 31-29 win.

On my way into the locker room a pit started to form in my stomach. This was a shit second loss, a game we really needed to have and now we put ourselves under incredible pressure to win the conference. The virtual social media mob would be out in force tonight.

The post-game press conference was contentious against a thinned-out herd of reporters. The cutbacks in reporters at most publications meant many of them do not travel to cover every game but Matty Buck was there. He looked almost gleeful.

I was asked about not moving guys over from the right to the left and I told them that we'd believed that we'd be fine. That obviously didn't work out as the left side of our field goal protection was where the block came from.

As I walked out I saw a sullen Gerry Gorton. I knew what he was thinking. Time was winding down and the margin for error just went to zero if it was even that.

On the plane Ivan Landon was still feeling the effects of drinking all game and decided to share his thoughts with Art Simpson. He made it very clear to anyone within earshot that this was the end of the line for me. We could all hear him and as he talked more and more shit I was getting madder and madder. But I had to bite my tongue.

By the time I got back to my house at 2:30 in the morning, Sally Anderson was asleep on the couch. She'd spent the weekend dog-sitting for Brutus while Candace was out of town.

When I came in the house, Brutus was wagging his tail. Sally got up and had a few tears in her eyes. She knows the pressure we're under.

"Are you gonna be okay?" She asked.

I laughed and said "Yeah, I'll be okay."

"Well I think I'd better get going." She said.

"Are you sure?" I asked.

"Ed I think it's better not to have my car parked in the driveway come tomorrow morning. There's a lot of nosy neighbors in your neighborhood."

"I just hate for you to drive this late. But I suppose you're right."

With that I walked her to the door and watched as she drove away. With her gone, I'd now be forced to drink alone finishing the Maker's Mark I'd started last week. I texted Candace to let her know both Brutus and I were safe at home.

It was a fitful night of sleep second guessing my decision to suspend those guys. I was angry at Alvin Wallace for not playing. I second guessed my decision not to move one of the guys from the right side to the left side.

About 4:45 I gave up trying to sleep and started to watch the film and make notes, even as I was still feeling the effects of the Bourbon. This had a tendency to make the notes I was taking extremely blunt.

The only saving grace was that Michigan State had upset Michigan. Now both Michigan and Penn State had a loss in the conference. We had two losses as did Michigan State. With our win over them we owned that tie-breaker. If we beat both Penn State and Michigan we'd own those tie-breakers too and head to the Big Ten Title game.

So all we had to do was run the table against Indiana, at Penn State and against Michigan.

The important thing was to keep morale up with our coaches and with our players. Our coaches would be worried about their jobs. They'd heard the whispers. When things are like this, coaches start looking for landing spots. They start talking to guys on other staffs and then word starts to spread on the rumor mill that we're in trouble.

I had to keep them focused. Yes the college football playoff was gone, but the Big Ten Title was still there for the taking. We could do it by winning our games, we did not need any help.

Around 7 a.m. my phone rang and it was Candace. She had to be worried to be up this early in Arizona time.

"Are you gonna be okay?" She asked.

"Yeah." I laughed.

"I'm worried. If you guys can't win the rest of the games, do you think Gerry can hold everyone off from firing you?" She asked.

"Well," I stated "let's not find out. We'll just win the rest of our damned games."

"Yeah, but"

I cut her off "There are no "yeah, buts" allowed. We're gonna win these damn games."

"This might be a good time to call some of those Trustees that we've spent time talking to all this offseason."

"You mean like Alexis Nelson?" I laughed.

My joke was not appreciated and was met with an icy silence.

"Okay," I conceded "that was a bad joke. But I will make a few calls and tell them what I told you. We're gonna win out."

"Okay, but they're saying some awfully nasty stuff about you on social media and in the media."

"Who cares? That shit won't prevent us from winning unless we start to believe it. You have to do me a favor and more importantly do yourself a favor and stay away from it. There are a lot of assholes out there with access to smartphones and keyboards who like to say the dumbest shit they can think of."

"Okay."

We talked about her Mom. She was improving well enough that Candace would be home in time for the Michigan game. Before I hung up I told her to take care of herself as well. She shouldn't be up this early. Once I was convinced she'd be okay, I hung up and headed to the office.

The mood was pretty somber in the football office. The coaches were moping and walking around like zombies. That's when I decided to call a team meeting for that afternoon. Most Sundays we did not meet, but I felt if the coaches were moping, that the players might be even worse. I asked everyone from coaches to staff assistants to equipment managers to players to be in this meeting. It was an all-hands-on-deck come-to-Jesus meeting.

By 1:30 the entire Ohio State football program was packed into our team meeting room. News that I'd called this type of meeting made its way to social media. The speculation was that I was resigning or being fired. The presence of everyone in the program gave gravity to the room that was unlike a normal team meeting.

As I stood in front of them I figured I'd better get to the heart of the meeting to put all their minds at ease.

"I've asked everyone to be in this meeting to hear what I am about to say. I want there to be no misunderstanding. Yesterday's loss was devastating. It's fueled wild speculation about the future of this program. I've seen people walking around this building today with a look of dejection on their faces. But what I want everyone in this room to understand is that yesterday is over. And despite that loss the path to the Big Ten Championship is completely....COMPLETELY within our control. The two teams with one conference loss in this division are ahead of us on the schedule. If...excuse me...WHEN we win the next three games we're going to Indianapolis. END.OF.STORY."

I paused to let that settle in. I looked at the faces around the room to see if they were sharing the same intensity of the moment that I was feeling. Everyone was locked in.

"If you want to sit around and bitch about what might have been, if you harbor any doubts that we will beat Indiana, Penn State and Michigan then get your ass out of this room and turn in your resignation. If you can't see what I can see, admit that you don't believe and get out. I won't fault you if you're honest with everyone else in this room."

The next phase was addressed directly to some of my concerns with the players.

"For the players, if you and your Dad are thinking about your pro career and you want to hold yourself out of a game because you're only 90% then admit that and get out too. We have to trust in each other, we have to trust that the person next to you has bought in. We have to will this to happen. We are two plays from being undefeated. We've hurt ourselves by doing some stupid crap off the field. We've dealt with a boatload of distractions, some fair, some unfair. But it's time to put that childish behavior behind us and act like grown men."

With that said, I pivoted towards the future.

"We are a damn good football team. But enough of the close calls and near misses. We're not at Ohio State to "get close" or to say we were a play or two away from winning the Big Ten. We came here to be the best team in this conference. It is time to fulfill that destiny...but we can only do it when we all believe. So right now you make a decision to stay or leave. If you stay, you buy in, stay positive and beat the shit out of the next three teams. It all starts with Indiana. Now let's start at this moment to adopt that mindset and go get this done."

I walked right out of the room before they even realized I'd finished. But I could tell the words had reached them. They filed out of the room in complete silence.

Immediately the mood of the building changed. Practice that week was intense and sharp. The media was tough all week, but the players spoke of a singular focus on Indiana as the next step in the season. Marshall had his best week of practice all year and even all the coaches were getting along.

The FireEdHart.com website was busy again and I know that because Gerry Gorton told me. I'd spent a few days calling donors and Trustees to let them know that we fully intended to win the next three games and win the Big Ten. They politely took my calls and patronized me and hoped I was right. But the proof would be in the next three weeks.

I'd written "win guarantee" checks. If we failed to deliver, these calls to trustees would be what came back on me. One thing was crystal clear on all the calls, they wanted us to sign Terrence Jones. The boosters were all hearing that Jones was a lock for Michigan too. I couldn't tell them what the problem was, or how ugly the solution might be. That was an ethical dilemma that I'd have to face later, but not that much later.

On Thursday in the coaches meeting I reminded them that this team would be looking to the coaches to read our mood. I wanted aggressive balls-out game plans that players saw as a vote of confidence.

By Saturday at high noon a sellout crowd was waiting to see how this team would react. Before they'd even settled into their seats we established an aggressive dominance racing out to a 42-0 halftime lead. By the time the final bell sounded we'd won 59-13 and had a week to get ready to go to Penn State for their "White Out" game.

When Penn State hosts a "White Out" Game, they and their fans tend to talk a lot of shit. It is one of the most impressive things in college football, but it is nowhere nearly as loud as it once was. The game has become a "bucket list" event for college football fans. A lot of casual non-Penn State fans pay big money on the secondary ticket market. They're not invested in the outcome and not as loud. It's just not the intimidating atmosphere that it was years ago.

Either way, the comments came out from some of their players and coaches about how we'd be intimidated by the White Out. It just motivated us further. In the media our players stayed humble and built up the egos of Penn State. They were ranked 11th and had just one loss in the conference but had suffered a week two upset at Virginia Tech. We'd climbed back up to #12 and with both of us looking to get into the Big Ten Title game this was a key game.

The week of practice was even better than the week before. Every once in a while, you get a team where things click, they buy in and they realize they're a damn good team. Going out to practice is fun every day because they give you everything they have and more. They bounce around, they sprint from place to place and you can just smell the confidence.

On Thursday I walked into the offensive meeting room just before practice. I took a seat in the back and just listened in as Quinn talked the team through the opening script. The guys seemed a little loose but I kept my mouth shut.

Finally after Quinn was done he asked me a question in front of the whole team. "Coach, how you feeling about this one?"

"Pretty damned good. How you guys feeling?" I asked.

Mark O'Reilly our senior offensive tackle and one of the captains stood up. "Coach, we're gonna kick the shit out of these guys. They talk a lot, but they run around blocks, they're not that physical. So let's pound their asses, hold onto the football and shut that fucking White Out down. There is nothing better than a silent White Out."

As soon as he was done the rest of the guys all yelled, hooted and hollered.

"That's the answer I was looking for, and I couldn't agree more." I said as I got up to leave the meeting room.

By the time we got onto the field for pre-game warm-ups the sun had set, and the sea of white-clad fans really popped under the stadium lights. The student section was bouncing to whatever music they were playing. Our players evidently knew what the music was because they were bouncing too.

In the corner of my eye I saw a bunch of shirtless Penn State players walking towards midfield pounding their chests and talking a bunch of shit. They were trying to stir up a little confrontation by talking and acting tough. The Penn State student section was cheering them on.

I kept an eye on our guys and a couple of them looked over and laughed before turning away. There were a couple of our guys I was worried would get into it, but they seemed completely uninterested in engaging them. So there they were, shirtless Penn State players preening and strutting and our guys acted like they weren't even there.

After pre-game warm-ups and just before kickoff I called the team together. Before I could say a word Marcus Dawson started speaking.

"You see that shit out there?" He yelled. "You see that punk-ass shit? They look at us and want to throw down before the game. Fuck them. They ain't tough. Dem boys are just wannabe thugs acting like they're something they're not. Teams that's scared do that shit. Take that White Out and all that other shit they do and we'll kick that ass up and down that field."

With that Marshall Remington spoke up "Hey Coach, we win the toss we're taking the ball and we're gonna stick it right down their throats."

"Hell yeah!" Donte Carter yelled.

The whole team was yelling in approval. Taking the ball hadn't been my plan to start the game but it was time to ride this emotion at the outset. But I had to remind them of one thing.

"Okay, we'll take the ball if we can. And I want to see these emotions, but remember emotions only carry you for a series or two before you have to start digging deep and pulling up the things you need to do mentally. Be the master of your emotions and not the other way around. Now let's go!"

As fate would have it we did win the toss. And as Marshall predicted we were stuffing the ball right down their throat. We drove to the ten yard line and ran for five yards on first and goal. On second down we got a bad holding call that wiped out a touchdown. A dropped pass and a ten yard gain left us short of the end zone before settling for a field goal.

Marshall came over to the sideline and said "I told you we'd stick it down their throats."

"I only see three points." I said. "Remember we need TDs."

"Coach you and I both know that holding call was bullshit and that Anthony won't drop another pass the rest of the game."

I smiled because I knew he was right. After we kicked off and Penn State took the field, Karl Metzger walked by me before going on the field.

"I'll see you back here in three plays coach!"

"It better not be because they score."

Karl winked at me and headed out. Penn State gained eight yards on first down. The next play they took a shot at a deep pass that we knocked away. On third down they gashed us for a twenty yard run but our safety Carson Miller hammered the running back. The ball squirted loose and a hustling Karl Metzger was there to recover it at our own forty yard line. As the defense came off the field Karl ran by me.

"I told you so." He said.

"That wasn't a conventional three and out but I'll take it."

Six plays later Pokey Wallace banged it in from the five yard line and it was 10-0. The stadium was getting quiet. But Penn State's offense kept moving the ball. The crowd was getting back into it. So with a fourth and two at our 12 yard line they got impatient and decided to go for it rather than take the field goal. Penn State took a timeout to discuss the play so I went down to Dave Cafiero and asked him what he was thinking.

"They've been moving the ball and they've shown us a bunch of new wrinkles that we haven't seen. But I got a handle on them now. We'll be good the rest of the way. So fuck these guys, I'm gonna blitz off the edge. The tackles will bounce the play outside and Carson Grady will be right there. Hell if they're in one back we'll have them outnumbered."

Sure enough they were in one back and they ran a zone read with the quarterback. He kept it and there was Carson Grady playing in his home state to make a huge hit on the quarterback. It was one of those hits where even the home team's crowd let out a huge "Ooooooooh."

During the TV timeout that ensued, I called up the whole offense and made sure Quinn was listening on the headsets. I looked right at Mark O'Reilly.

"On Thursday O'Reilly said that we'd punish these guys. The crowd is starting to get back in this one and their offense has moved the ball. There are eighty-eight yards between you and the goal-line. We're gonna run Pokey and Malcolm at these guys behind this offensive line until they stop us. Let's take their hearts from them right now and keep their offense off the field for about seven or eight minutes. You got that Quinn?"

"Hell yeah!" Quinn said through the headset.

We did just that. We ran twelve straight plays by pounding Pokey at them and then using Malcolm's speed as a change-up. On the thirteenth play on first and ten at the thirteen yard line we slipped in a play-action fake to Pokey and threw the ball out to Roger Carson for a touchdown and a 17-0 lead. Roger had come a long way since considering a transfer early this year.

That score slammed the door on any hope Penn State had. By the end of the night Dave was right about the defense. They'd figured out the Penn State offense and we finished off with a 34-17 win that set us up for next week's battle with Michigan.

It was quite a sight the last three minutes of the game when the White Out was not only quiet but most of the fans had vacated the stadium. It felt great to run back out of the tunnel and see Gerry Gorton with a huge smile on his face.

"We'll we got 'em Gerry." I yelled.

"Yeah but you'd better get 'em next week."

And there it was....

17. THAT TEAM UP NORTH

After we landed and arrived back at the Woody Hayes Athletic Center, I gathered the whole team outside at the statue of Coach Hayes. It was almost two in the morning and this end of campus was cold and deserted. I waited a moment for the power of the silence and the moment to reach everyone. Waiting for us were eleven students I'd paid to dress like Woody Hayes standing silently with white candles.

"And thus begins the week that brought ALL of us here to Ohio State. Every year eleven students come here the Saturday night before the Michigan game. They come to honor the past and ask the gods of Buckeye football past for strength this week. Most of you never knew about this."

I paused again for dramatic effect and a gust of wind blew up as if I'd ordered it. Of course they didn't know about it because it was a complete bullshit story I'd made up and paid these theater students to be there. They walked silently away holding their candles.

It was time to preach.

"By the time you wake up every "M" on every street sign, road sign and on every other thing you can see will be X'ed out. This game against The Team Up North means THAT much. You guys walk by that countdown clock every day as every second ticks us closer to our destiny in a game where legends are born. This week demands our singular focus on one objective....to win the greatest rivalry game in all of sports. So tonight get your sleep, and wake up with your minds on nothing but kick off at high noon next Saturday."

This was probably the make or break week for my future at Ohio State. Winning the game was big enough, but we also had a recruiting challenge to get Terrence Jones. Jones' plan was to commit to his school a couple of days after his visit to our school. If we lost both the game and Terrence Jones to Michigan then it was all over for me.

Candace was home when I got back but was sound asleep so I didn't bother her. Instead I went straight to my den to watch Michigan video. This would be six sleepless days like my fraternity pledge hell week. The stakes now were just a bit higher.

My first game to watch was our game against them from last year. It gave me a chance to refresh my memory while looking at the notes I'd made the last five times I'd watched that debacle.

By 4:45 a.m. as I was having a seventh cup of coffee I heard the little feet of Brutus coming down the stairs and the familiar steps of Candace right behind him. Candace's face greeted me with a smile from a face tired from the early morning hours. She walked around the desk and gave me a kiss and a big hug.

"I'd congratulate you on the win last night....but I know you don't care."

I nodded.

"Did you get any sleep yet?"

"Nope. Not planning on getting any either. This is the week."

"You wanna come upstairs? I promise I won't let you sleep."

Who was I to say no?

The extracurricular activities did lift my spirits and by 6:30 a.m. I was showered and in the office for the start of the week. It was a great sign to see other coaches' cars in the parking lot when I got there. By 7:30 I'd looked at Michigan's win over Indiana from the day before. It seemed like every year IU hung with Michigan before the Wolverines would put them away.

One cannot overstate the Ohio State obsession with Michigan and vice versa. Privately I will call them Michigan, but for an Ohio State coach you never, ever call them Michigan publicly. Woody Hayes started that decades ago by calling them "That Team Up North" as a sign of disrespect or disgust or perhaps both.

Previous coaching staffs used the abbreviation TTUN short for "That Team Up North" on in-house season schedules, practice schedules and scouting reports. We kept that up. Even in Spring practices, months and months before the game we had a period of practice referred to the TTUN period to work on Michigan. It is an EVERY DAY of the year thing.

But one of the biggest misperceptions of the week of a rivalry game is that there is some different routine or some double secret week of planning. The day-to-day routine is unchanged and that is probably for the best. Teams thrive on routine and knowing what is expected. For this game we wanted to keep them on schedule.

But in my mind I kept re-playing that visit from Gerry Gorton in the suite in Orlando just about eleven months earlier. I had to win this game.

Sunday night I got a call from Karl Metzger and he came by the office to see me. He had a problem that could be an NCAA issue. He was visibly distraught and sat fidgeting in the chair in my office. He finally brought himself to tell me what was wrong.

A woman he'd gone home with after the Michigan State game had showed up at his apartment with a contract that he'd signed with an agent. That would make him ineligible. She even had video of him signing it.

"Coach," he said "I don't even remember signing it. They drugged me and got me to sign it. You can even see in the video that I was barely conscious."

This was not how I wanted my week to start. Karl was vital to our defense and a public suspension of him would be a major distraction the week of this must-win game.

"What in the hell were you thinking going to a hotel with some woman you barely even knew?" I yelled.

Frustrated, he bowed his head and ran his hand through his hair before answering while still looking at the floor.

"Coach I clearly wasn't thinking....at least not with my brain."

"That much is obvious. Let me think how we have to handle this."

"Coach, I've already talked to my attorney. He said that any contract signed after being drugged is not valid in this situation. So as far as he's concerned it never happened."

"Well tomorrow morning you've got to have him contact our compliance office and explain the situation. We have to hope that our compliance office and the NCAA see this thing the same way your attorney sees it. There are no guarantees with these people. In the meantime you have to keep your mouth shut. We'll practice you like you're slightly injured so no one knows anything is going on."

With that Karl left and my Sunday night was completely shot. I called in Dave Cafiero and explained the situation. We had to keep this quiet so we called our team doctor Michael Davis to let him know he needed to put Karl's "hamstring issue" on the injury report.

The next morning Karl's attorney laid out the entire scenario to the NCAA. They would decide in a day or two whether he would be able to play. Given the circumstances and that he'd been tricked into signing, they seemed to be understanding. But until they gave us the go ahead we just wouldn't know.

Monday and Tuesday went by with no word so Karl practiced with the second team while we shuffled the other linebackers around.

On Tuesday we got some good news. The District Attorney was finally closing the rape investigation against Marcus Dawson with no charges being filed. The DA had grandstanded this case with press conferences and interviews when they first charged him. But when it was time to clear him they just issued a written statement.

When Marcus walked into the locker room the guys cheered for him and he had a look of relief being in the clear on this whole mess. Yet as with other similar cases, there would always people who believed he was a rapist.

Vivian Terrant went on television calling it a miscarriage of justice and saying that "all accusers deserve to be believed." She accused the male-dominated, football-crazy world at Ohio State of conspiring to deny justice to this woman.

That news cycle was the last thing we needed this week.

But there was more "good news". Pokey Wallace also found out that his ex-girlfriend was pregnant with his child. Now that the NFL draft was just a few months away, Pokey was a sure thing to go in the first or second round. And suddenly he'd be looking at eighteen years of reality in the form of child support.

Because of the distractions and tension of a game that would decide my career, I was yelling at anyone and everyone at practice. My intensity was set to full rage and I spared no one. Wednesday on the practice field we were working in a third down competition period. Pokey ran the ball and as he was getting hit he fumbled the ball.

"Godammit Pokey!" I yelled. "Your carelessness carrying the ball is going to cost us this game and is gonna cost all these coaches their jobs! If you can't take care of the football I'll play someone else. We've got a room full of great running backs and I don't care if you are a senior!"

I am not a yeller but I was out of control. When I made the comment about the coaches' jobs, I'd crossed a line saying something out loud that coaches should not speak about in front of the team.

Even after practice I kept after the coaches about mistakes on the practice field. As we met to review the practice film I started tearing into everyone. It started with me re-hashing Pokey's fumble and telling Roger Barstow that if Pokey fumbled in practice tomorrow he wasn't going to play on Saturday.

Then I turned my attention to Otis Lewis and the offensive line he coached.

"Otis, if the line doesn't practice better we're in for a rude awakening on Saturday. Their defensive line is quick and physical."

Next was special teams coach Saul Tessio.

"Saul, that fake field goal you're practicing looks like shit. Get the goddam blocking right. Given how shitty the offense is practicing we may need a fake field goal to score any points at all on these guys."

The entire room was shell-shocked. No one dared to make a counterpoint and I'd had enough.

"You guys had better understand that this game is REALLY important for a lot of reasons. We must pay attention to every small detail. They've gotten our asses the past couple of years because we've been careless as coaches and players. And careless teams get their asses beat, and careless coaches are out of jobs."

There was almost no reaction from them, which pissed me off even more.

"I'm criticizing you guys and all of you just sit there with your mouths shut. I hope that your silence tells me that you hear what I am saying. I haven't slept well all season, and I haven't slept this whole week so far. I hope all your asses are ready to fucking make things right at tomorrow's practice."

After another all-nighter I went upstairs to shower on Thursday morning. Just before getting in the shower I stepped onto the scale. I was down twenty pounds from the start of the season. If I should've been worried I wasn't. It was just part of the price of this job.

As I edged out of the kitchen I saw another nearly empty bottle of Bourbon. It had carried me through the two a.m. hour and I was tempted to calm the day's nerves with the last few ounces before going to work. For ten seconds I stood amid an internal debate before I left without it.

We'd still not heard back from the NCAA about Karl's status. That just ratcheted up my anger. And to make my day even better on Thursday morning I got an unscheduled visit from two local FBI agents. Agents Ed Green and Sean Quinn introduced themselves and sat down with me.

"What can I do for you guys?" I asked.

Sean Quinn seemed to be the lead guy on this and he spoke up.

"Coach I know this is a busy week and this is probably bad timing, but we've had concerns about some of the activity around a couple of your players."

"Really?" I asked. "Which ones?"

I felt like the edge-of-trouble school kid who gets called to the principal's office. As that kid sits on the bench, he's trying to figure out what he possibly could've gotten caught doing. But they were right, this was some bad timing.

"As you know from a previous visit to your house by one of our agents, we've had your quarterback Marshall Remington cross our radar. It seems there are some shady people that are suspicious of him potentially fixing a game. His name popped up on some of the organized crime chatter, but he's clear in this."

"That's good to know." I responded

"Also we've been conducting surveillance on two women. They're professionals brought here from Nevada by a noted agent with some shady ties. They came to trap some of your players to sign early. They come on to them, drug them and then get them to sign contracts. As you know, they trapped Karl Metzger. These women have been used to blackmail congressmen too. We've been on their case for about eighteen months. When Metzger passed out, she called her partner and we have her talking on tape about drugging him. But he got off lucky."

"How's that?" I asked.

"In other cases when they pass out in bed they get a nude guy in bed with the player and pose them in very compromising pictures. Then they threaten to release those man-on-man pictures to destroy their pro career unless they sign a contract with their agent. Sometimes they use those pictures to get guys to fix games."

"So what happens now?" I asked.

"Well we also understand that the NCAA is still deciding his eligibility for this week because you guys self-reported it."

"How'd you know that?" I asked.

"We know a lot of stuff." Sean laughed.

"What do I need to do?" I asked.

"Before we contact the NCAA to explain the scenario, we'd need the University to be aware of, and to approve of what we're doing. We don't have plans to charge these women just yet because they're trying to trap some state politicians too. So we will quietly handle this to clear Karl and make sure the NCAA doesn't let this get out."

"I would appreciate that." I said.

The two of them left and before they left I had one more question.

"Since you guys seem to know stuff.....any chance you know what the Team Up North is up to?"

With that they laughed and headed out the door. My good humor didn't last. For the fifth straight night I'd skipped dinner, got home late and watched video all night in my den at home. I was downing so much caffeine that there were times when it felt like my heart would jump out of my chest. I worried a few times that I was having an anxiety attack. And like most coaches, I never once considered going to see a doctor. In my mind if I dropped dead, I'd at least go out with my boots on.

At our coaches meeting I picked up where I'd left off Wednesday night. But at least some of the coaches were providing feedback. I'd even barked at Sally Anderson twice and she was taken aback. In my office after I'd yelled at her, I heard Doug Leonard come in.

He said to Sally "Don't worry Sally it ain't personal. He's been barking at everyone like an ornery Sumbitch all week."

I don't think I was supposed to hear that, but volume control was never one of Doug's strong suits. It was best to ignore it.

Sally buzzed my desk phone.

"Ed," she said "I've got Caesar Alfonsi on the phone for you."

With Terrence Jones' visit coming up this weekend I probably should've expected this call.

"Go ahead and put him through." I said.

"Ed how ya' doin'?" Caesar said.

"Good, but as you could probably guess, we're a little stressed right now." I replied.

"Yeah that figures. I've seen about fifteen articles this week about this being your make-or-break game. You know how Ohio State treats coaches that can't beat Michigan."

"Yeah I know." I said.

"The guys I'm connected to all tell me if you don't win it's a done deal. But what do they know?"

Caesar loved to talk and he went on for a few minutes before he got to the point.

"I hear Terrence Jones is coming to the game this weekend before he makes his decision."

"You heard right."

"I just want to remind you that you really need to get this one. And you know that his guy Tom Pietrovic is pushing him to Michigan."

"Yes I do."

"Just remember what I told you. He's into us for some things he doesn't have the liquidity to pay. Just say the word and this kid will be headed your way."

Was this how I wanted to get this done? This is a cutthroat and vicious game but I wanted to at least be able to look at my wife and my family and tell them that I was honorable. Of course I might be unemployed if I took this route, but I'd have my honor.

"I'll let you know after Saturday." I told him.

"Don't wait too long. Pietrovic says the kid is making up his mind next week."

"Okay."

Before we left Caesar gave me a phone number to call on Sunday. I wrote it down on a small piece of paper and put it in my wallet, almost like a get out of jail free card should we lose on Saturday.

At lunch I went to try and get a workout but my heart rate was spiking so much that I gave up and went back to my office. Just before player meetings started I got a knock on the door and Marcus Dawson came in.

"Can I come in for a minute coach?" He asked.

"Sure what's on your mind?" I asked.

"I was gonna ask you the same thing."

"Why's that?"

"Can I speak freely coach?"

"I hope that you feel you can always speak freely."

Marcus nervously looked around the office before settling a little more into his seat.

"You know coach I don't want to get you pissed. Most times, when guys are in this chair they've got problems. But I gotta say something to you. I'm trying to say this the right way. Coach you've been really on edge this week."

"Well this is a big game."

"I get that and that this may be a make-or-break game for you. We read the internet and the stories and hear the commentary. It's been going all week. With your yelling at practice the guys are putting a lot more pressure on themselves. And the coaches are putting undue pressure on us too. It's just out of character for you and we're all noticing it. We just want to go out and play this game without the added pressure. If we do that we're gonna be fine."

Maybe I should've been angry, but I had to be careful here. He was giving me his insight and that mattered. And deep down I knew he was probably right. After another few minutes, I thanked him for his honesty and for displaying the leadership needed to come to me.

At the team meeting before practice I addressed my behavior to the whole team.

"You know guys, I owe you and the coaches an apology. I forgot my own words from a few weeks ago. Back then I told you that we'd be aggressive, that we'd play with intensity and win the rest of games. I wanted us to be confident and play to have fun and to win the Big Ten. I haven't been coaching this week like a confident coach. And for that I'm sorry to all the players and to the coaches as well. I've been all over every one of you guys. I overheard Doug Leonard telling Sally Anderson earlier this morning that I've been "Barking at everyone like an ornery sumbitch all week." I think that's how you said it Doug?"

I smiled, Doug nodded and all the guys laughed.

"That's never been my style and what I'm telling you with my actions is that maybe I'm scared. Or maybe I'm putting a lot of pressure on myself. Hell you guys all see the stories. But most importantly by being someone I'm not, I'm telling you that to win this game we as a team have to be something we're not."

I paused to let that sink in.

"Guys that is the part of this lesson I want to heed myself and I want all of you to understand. This game is sixty-minutes of football and we are the better team. Winning this game will not require some super-human effort or to be something we're not. And I hope I get that message across to you all, but also to myself. That being said we still have to focus on details, be precise. On offense hold onto the football, hold onto your blocks and make sure that we play within our system. On defense we have to get off blocks, and sprint to the football and arrive in a rage. So let's go have a great practice today, a precise walk-through tomorrow and be ready to hand out a high noon ass-whoopin' on Saturday."

Sometimes the lessons you need come from listening to your players. Thursday's practice was nearly perfect. And the worrier in me now fretted that it was too good. Coaches are like that. If your practice is too good you then worry that your team might have peaked. Most of the time you just needed to shut up and stop obsessing.

After practice Art Simpson reported that Karl Metzger had been cleared to play on Saturday. It was a lesson learned from a near miss.

I went to my coach's call-in radio show before heading home. The calls were supportive but almost every one of them stressed how important it was for the program and for me to win against That Team Up North. Even the fans wouldn't say the word.

Only one fan really tried to stir the pot. It was "Joe from Orrville" and he demanded to know why he should have any faith at all in my ability to win this game. I calmly tried to ease his concerns but he was having none of it and grew pretty combative.

That was the last call of the night and as I headed home to see Candace I was still edgy. Lack of sleep and an asshole caller on your radio show tend to do that. Just before dinner I went to get some Bourbon, but couldn't find it.

"Hey Candace, where's my Maker's Mark?" I asked.

"You're not having any tonight." She said.

My mind told me I HAD to have it so I barked back "But I NEED it."

"That's why you're not getting it. Tonight you keep your head clear for dinner with your wife."

Grudgingly I stomped to the table like a five year old who'd been told "no".

At dinner Candace was chatty before she got into some concerns she had about my health. All week I was wired on Red Bull and other caffeine. She made a comment about my weight loss and how tired I looked.

I confessed that this was the first real meal I'd eaten all week. She'd made a couple of really tasty steaks. It had to be the first protein I'd had all week.

After dinner I went to my den to look at more video. I was just looking for something, anything. We'd covered everything from trick plays, to a crazy blitz or two to fake punts and field goals. The arsenal was ready to go. But the obsessive nature of all coaches means they are always looking at one more video, one more play just trying to see if there is anything else they need.

Around 9:30 Candace came in with a brownie sundae complete with whipped cream, ice cream and hot fudge. There were two things Candace could offer me that I couldn't say "no" to, and her brownie sundae was one of them.

After I scarfed it down she asked how I liked her new brownie recipe.

"There was a little aftertaste to it. But the sundae was fantastic. What did you change?"

"It wasn't my brownie." She replied. "It's a cannabis-infused indica brownie to help you sleep."

"It's what?" I asked.

"It's a pot brownie."

"What the hell?" I asked my wife who'd dosed me.

"You need to sleep. This one'll have you sleeping in about an hour. If you don't sleep you'll be worthless. So go up, shower, get into bed and go the fuck to sleep. You need it for your own good."

When Candace cussed she meant business, so although I wanted to be mad, I couldn't. That night I slept for the first time in almost a week.

The next day was a typical football Friday. And thanks to a good night's sleep I was focused, relaxed and was starting to enjoy life as we went to our walk-through. It was an unseasonably warm sunny November afternoon for Ohio. The sunlight put us all in a goof mood.

The only other concern left was the visit of Terrence Jones. He was coming for the game on Saturday and perhaps a win would help us. And I still had that troubling wildcard to play.

At the pre-game hotel on Friday night we had a snack and bed check. Gerry Gorton swung by the lobby to see me. He wished me luck on the game and on the Terrence Jones decision as well.

"You know a clean sweep of the game and recruiting might put you over the top with a couple of the boosters who still have their doubts." He said.

The best thing about a noon game is that you get up and get right to it. You have a team breakfast a quick meeting and then you're on the bus headed to the stadium. There is no hanging around the hotel waiting for an 8 o'clock kickoff and there is no time for your guys to get caught up watching ESPN's

College Game Day or any other pre-game show. I remember getting on the bus for a road primetime game and hearing one of our guys telling the others that Lee Corso had put on the Buckeye mascot head.

One of the traditions I've continued at Ohio State is the guys getting on the bus in coat and ties for home games and road games. It just adds an element that says we are here as professionals to do a job. The mission is serious.

In St John Arena for the pre-game skull session the place was really rocking. We came into the game ranked #10 with a 9-2 record, while Michigan was #6 with a 10-1 record. The winner would go to the Big Ten title game for a game against Nebraska who'd already clinched the Western Division. Most of the experts felt we were a good team, but that Michigan was a great team. After all their only loss was a fluke loss by one point to Michigan State.

With our fan base the mood was hopeful, not confident. There is a big difference and it manifests itself in how the crowd reacts early in the game. When they're confident it doesn't matter how the game starts, they are loud and engaged and they believe that we will win no matter what. A hopeful crowd needs the team to get them into the game by starting fast.

When we arrived at the Stadium, they brought Terrence Jones down to see me. Tom Pietrovic was with him. I had Quinn and Rick talk to Terrence so I could talk with Tom by myself. I wanted him to know that I knew what he was doing

"I'm kind of surprised that you're not wearing maize and blue today." I said.

Why beat around the bush? It was time to let him know directly that I knew exactly what he was up to.

"Why do you say that?" He asked.

"Well, I've got a lot of friends in Eastern Ohio and everyone tells me that you love those guys and that you're steering him to the Team Up North."

A moment of silence fell over the room. I'd shown some cards, enough to make him wonder what else I might have in my hand.

"Look Coach, I'll be honest with you. Terrence is still wide open. He's gonna go home tonight and talk with people close to him the next couple of days and make his decision."

"And am I wrong to assume that you'll be one of the people he talks to?"

"I think you overestimate my influence." He said defensively. "But he will probably talk to me at some point."

"And remind me how you fit in here. Are you related to him?"

"No. He's just someone I've come to mentor through this process. His home situation is a challenging one and I help him out."

Now I was going to get at it a little more directly.

"So do you do this for other kids in the community? Or is it just for the NFL prospects."

"Look I get what you're thinking. I'm not getting anything out of this and I am going to let him make up his own mind."

"We'll if you're being sincere in that then I'm okay. If you let him make his own decision I can live with that......But...BUT if you screw us over I will find out and I will see that everyone in Eastern Ohio knows about it. EVERYONE in Eastern Ohio."

This was certainly not one of the more lovey-dovey recruiting meetings that I'd ever had, but I said enough to make him wonder, but not so much that he knew what I had on him. But should I decide to call Caesar Alfonsi on this one, then Pietrovic would know not to mess this up.

My meeting with Terrence was really positive. He knew all about us, really liked Ohio State but as long at Pietrovic was in the room he was holding back. The guys who'd met with him while I met with Pietrovic said his demeanor was completely different.

Right before I went onto the field for pre-game warm-ups Rick Carter came running over to me. He seemed to be in a panic.

"What did you say to the guy with Terrence. He's all of a sudden in a pissy mood."

"I just started to tell him where the bear shits in the woods. Don't worry. We're gonna win this game and then I am going to fire the guns I need to fire to get Terrence."

It was a typically gray and raw November Saturday in the Midwest. Walking onto the field a chill set into my bones. On the field the players' breath was visible in the cold air as they ran around to warm-up. This was real football weather. In Big Ten country players and fans look forward to days like this as a cold-weather toughness badge of honor.

In pre-game there was a ton of chirping back and forth between the two teams. One of the drawbacks to our home stadium set-up is that Michigan's locker room is on the opposite end from where they warm-up. So they have to run past our players to warm-up and often times they run right through our drills hoping to incite a scuffle. I warned our players to steer clear, just like they'd done at Penn State the week before.

We did just that and it seemed to frustrate the Michigan players.

The one drawback to this last home game was the pre-game Senior Day celebration. When I got here, the players, their parents, girlfriends and even their kids, if they had them, were all on the field. I eliminated all the family members and went to just having each player introduced by themselves. I wanted them to run onto that field as men standing on their own. This was a symbol of a transformation complete.

These things still get a little emotional. Seeing these guys jog out there one last time is a reminder of the passage of time. We'd seen these guys grow up. This year was a little emotional for me as well. Would this be my last game at Ohio State? The next sixty minutes would tell the tale.

By the time Michigan won the toss and took the ball, we seemed ready to go. Here it was; sixty-minutes of football that would likely decide my future at Ohio State. Did I really believe that we were good enough to do our thing and win the game against a team that was on track to be in the college football playoff?

Doug Leonard came over to me just before kickoff and shook my hand.

"Good luck coach." He said. "We're gonna get these bastards but you know we're gonna have to beat them and beat the officials."

"Why do you say that?" I asked.

"Michigan can get to the playoff, we can't. You know the Big Ten office handed down the order to protect Michigan at all costs."

"I don't know that for a fact....but it sure wouldn't surprise me."

Michigan started on offense and on their first drive Doug's suspicions seemed prescient. Coaches are among the most susceptible people to a conspiracy theory, especially if it involves Michigan and the game officials.

On that first drive Michigan converted a third and twelve on a questionable pass interference call against us. A couple of plays later a defensive holding penalty kept the drive alive. They scored on a ten-yard run to make the score 7-0.

When we got the ball we made a first down. Three plays later Marshall overthrew a wide open receiver and we had to punt. Michigan drove to the twelve and kicked a field goal. Before we'd even gotten ourselves going we were down 10-0.

The very next drive we made a couple of first downs before Pokey fumbled and Michigan got the ball. As they came off the field Marshall came right over to me.

"You know that's the same thing he did in practice." I snapped.

"We'll be okay coach. I missed a pass and Pokey dropped a fumble. We'll settle down. I can see in their eyes that we can get them. Just trust me. Remember what you said about being ourselves."

The trust was stretched on the next drive. On another third down we stopped them when Carson drilled their running back on the Michigan sideline short of the first down. Jim Harbaugh and their other coaches were protesting that the hit was out of bounds. After a second or two out came the flag as the official flung it high into the air.

We were all set to get off the field and now another lame call was allowing Michigan's offense to stay on the field. On the last play of the first quarter they hit a deep pass for a touchdown and a 17-0 lead. The first quarter was already over and we hadn't even gotten our offense out of the garage.

The stadium was dead, and there was grumbling and scattered boos. This was not how I'd hoped this would go. As the defense came over Dave Cafiero sat them down on the benches. I approached to speak to them.

"Look guys don't panic. They've gotten some bullshit calls, and our offense has yet to get going. You know we'll get this going. Just learn from what they're doing, follow Dave's adjustments and we'll get back in this thing. One play at a time. Run to the ball in a rage and get us a turnover."

As the second quarter started I pulled the offense over.

"Don't get impatient. Just take this one play at a time. There is no one play that will erase the deficit. As Coach Leonard likes to say we're gonna have to win this game doggie style—from behind."

Then I looked right at Pokey who'd just fumbled. "And Pokey I am putting the ball in your hands a bunch this drive. Shake off the last play and understand how much confidence we have in you. Go be the kind of player you and I both know that you are."

Quinn settled down in his play calling, the offensive line was firing off the line and Pokey was a madman running around and over Michigan defenders. When he wants to go he is a great power runner. Ten plays later he crashed through a Michigan defender for a touchdown.

As the second quarter finished Michigan kept getting the breaks and they'd opened a 27-10 lead. But with two minutes to go we had a chance to end the half with a score and start the second half with the ball. It was the two-possession swing that you can get if you start the second half with the ball.

We put it to good use getting a field goal to end the half and another field goal to start the second half. It was now 27-16 and there were signs of life again. But settling for field goals was getting to me. But the fourth downs we'd faced were long yardage so we didn't have much of a choice. After holding Michigan we drove again and a really tough holding call against us erased a touchdown. Once again we kicked a field goal to make it 27-19.

We traded possessions and as the fourth quarter began we were still one score away. We just couldn't strike that touchdown despite moving the ball up and down the field. The way the calls were going, I was starting to believe Doug's conspiracy theory.

What happened next made me a true believer.

Michigan's next drive began on their own twenty and after two plays they had a third and seventeen. Stop them there and we'd get great field position. Their quarterback dropped back to pass and overthrew their receiver. Then out came the late flag for pass interference. As if that wasn't bad enough they called our defensive end for targeting and he never even touched the quarterback's head.

The targeting call went to review upstairs and as I looked at what had just happened I started to do the math. The two penalties would put them out at the forty-three yard line and kill our chance of getting good field position.

Sure enough the call was upheld and our best edge pass rusher Pierre Carter was out of the game. Boos rained down from the upper decks of Ohio Stadium, but it made no difference. The official on our sideline made a point to avoid me and avoid eye contact after those calls. As Doug Leonard would say I was "Fire-spitting mad" because these calls could cost me my job. No one cares if you got close and the officials screwed you.

Michigan went into an old school mode and ran right at our defense. Ten plays and five minutes later they were up 34-19 with eight minutes to go. Some fans were even starting to get up and go. We were going to need two touchdowns and a two-point conversion just to get to overtime.

Marshall came over.

"Don't worry coach. I just talked to Marcus Dawson and Michigan is done scoring for the game. So let's get two scores."

As the offense came over I yelled over the noise of the crowd.

"Look after we score this touchdown we are going for two so stay on the field. You guys got me?"

As we started to pick up yards and first downs the stadium started to come to life. Eight yards, five yards, seven yards, ten yards, fifteen yards, seven yards and six yards and we were suddenly in the red zone. But the clock was still running we were down to 3:37 to go.

We needed a quick score and I had a brain storm.

"Quinn run the screen. They're going to come after us so let's see if we can split one."

"You sure coach?"

"Yes we need a curve ball that they will swing and miss on."

Sure enough they brought the blitz and Malcolm Jackson took the screen pass into the end zone for the score. Normally when a team is down fifteen points and scores a touchdown they kick the extra point and go for two on the next possession. But I had other ideas.

Michigan expected us to kick the extra point so when we kept our offense on the field we forced them to use their last timeout. After the timeout, we lined up with the back offset to the field. Thinking we'd sprint out to the field Michigan ran an edge blitz there. Marshall ran a quarterback counter back to the boundary and walked in. It was now 34-27 and hope remained.

With 3:20 to go we were set to kick to them. We had all three timeouts so there was no need to even consider the onside kick.

Michigan started at their own twenty-five and on first down ripped off a ten yard gain. The clock was running so we used our first time out. With 3:05 to go we could not afford another first down to have a realistic chance. The next two plays netted 7 yards and we used timeouts after both plays. We were down to 2:49 to go. If Michigan ran the ball and we stopped them we'd get the ball with about two minutes to go and no timeouts.

I called the defense over and told them we just needed one stop.

As the Wolverines came out of their huddle the Stadium roar was deafening. Because we'd made them burn their last timeout, they couldn't play any timeout games here. If they made this first down the game was essentially done.

Michigan ran the ball right at us and the back surged through the line and looked like he could get the first down before a loud crack sounded when Karl

Metzger and Carson Grady met him just short of the first down. Their back kept churning his legs fighting for that last precious ten inches of real estate before the force of our two linebackers kept him short.

The stadium erupted as Michigan was forced to send out their punt team. I could see that they were thinking about going for it. But ultimately they decided to punt. During the TV timeout after the punt I decided I had one more trick to spring on Michigan.

I called up the offense and pulled aside our tackle Mark O'Reilly to share what I was planning.

"Mark when we score this touchdown, we're going to run that field goal fake on the extra point to win the game. When the field goal team huddles you tell them then. The field goal team will run onto the field without talking to any of us so Michigan doesn't see anything out of the ordinary. We'll get a walk-off win."

"Fuck yeah Coach!" He yelled.

The long Michigan punt had put us back at our own seventeen yard line. Marshall was composed and accurate. Michigan was not going to give up any big plays but we were smart getting out of bounds. Six plays later we were at midfield with forty-five seconds to go and facing a third and two. I told Quinn to take a shot to the end zone and then we could go for it on fourth down and two.

Marshall delivered a perfect strike to Anthony Daniels but Michigan's defensive back pulled Anthony to the ground. It was an obvious pass interference call and a first down. But after an expectant second or two that seemed like an eternity the flag never came. Now we had fourth and two.

That was when I called for the reverse. It was a risky as hell call but we needed a twenty yard play soon. The clock was no longer our friend. I wanted freshmen receiver Lance Marshall to carry this one. The electric Detroit native was playing a great game, with some extra motivation to beat his home-state school.

Marshall handed the ball to Pokey headed to the wide right side and as the defense chased to make the stop he flipped the ball to Lance headed left and he had open space ahead of him. He made the first down before getting tackled by the Michigan safety at the twenty-five yard line. Anthony Daniels had a block on that safety but lost his footing, otherwise we'd have scored.

"Hey Quinn," I yelled "I bet you're glad I made you guys take Lance back in February!"

We were down to twenty-eight seconds. On first down we made seven yards and got out of bounds. The next play gained four to the fourteen and we spiked the ball to stop the clock. There were fourteen seconds left. The next play we ran a corner hitch combination but Michigan's defense forced the hitch throw. Malcolm Jennings had to run over the defender to get out of bounds at the six yard line with nine seconds left.

Michigan assumed we had to throw into the end zone because we didn't have any timeouts left. What they had forgotten was that we could make a first down at the four and spike the ball while they moved the chains. We lined up a bunch set and drove the two outside receivers into the end zone and brought the backside receiver Anthony Daniels on a shallow crossing route. Marshall hit him in stride while all the Michigan defenders were in the end zone. Anthony turned up field and used his big frame to get across the goal-line with three seconds left. The stadium erupted in a thunderous roar as everyone anticipated overtime.

It was now 34-33 and our field goal team went onto the field to tie the game and send it to overtime. These extra points are just formalities before overtime. I could even see Michigan coaches meeting with their offense presumably to discuss overtime plans.

In the huddle O'Reilly told them what I wanted. Saul Tessio didn't even know what I'd done. I didn't want anyone's behavior on the sideline to give anything away.

The crowd went silent. Everyone seemed to be holding their breath for the extra point and overtime. No one was more nervous than I was. If this worked it was genius, if it didn't work I was a dead man.

There was no time to call a timeout to call off the fake. I'd made my call before the drive even started. The dice had already been thrown and for the next twenty seconds or so they'd be tumbling until I saw what they'd turn up.

As the team came out of the huddle they lined up in a library-quiet Ohio Stadium. The ball was snapped to our holder, the kicker started towards the ball and Michigan's rush was coming hard off the left side. The right tight end and wing collapsed the edge and the pulling left guard kicked out a surprised defender opening a huge hole and that our holder Carter Jones ran through for the go-ahead two points to put us up 35-34.

The explosion of the stunned crowd was delayed a second or two as they processed what they'd just seen. Then the avalanche came down on the field. In the stands I could see the students jumping up and down hugging and high-fiving one another. Other fans were jumping and cheering lost in a pure joy that comes from witnessing the unexpected deliverance when all looked lost.

Marshall ran over and grabbed me and hugged me.

"Holy shit, what a call that was. Fuck Yeah coach!"

Behind him I could see Saul Tessio looking at me as he mouthed "What the hell was that?"

"I told you I wanted that fake." I winked at him.

Then I said to Marshall "O'Reilly didn't tell you?"

"Hell no."

"Well I guess we know we can trust him with state secrets."

There was just one kickoff left and as Michigan fielded the ball they scrambled to try and score. As we made the tackle the students started streaming onto the field. Before I knew what was going on I was surrounded by police officers as I made my way for a post-game handshake.

As Fox sideline reporter Jenny Taft tried unsuccessfully to interview me the noise on the field was deafening and we were getting jostled by the crowd as they surged around us. It took about ten minutes to get off the field.

In the tunnel where it was safer I saw Gerry Gorton and a couple of the boosters and Trustees. They were all smiles. Ivan Landon was with him too.

"Ed!" Gerry yelled "What in the hell was that? That was the damnedest thing I've ever seen."

"Yeah Gerry, I'm glad YOU never lost faith in us like some people did in Wisconsin." I said it so that Ivan would hear it. "But we've got a trip to Indianapolis next week!"

"Damn right."

The post-game locker room was just a crazed scene of guys who could not quite believe what they'd done. When I came in, they doused me with water.

"Guys enjoy this one, savor the moment. This is one you'll remember the rest of your lives. But...BUT do not let this go to your heads. We've got a damned good Nebraska team to beat next week. Stay out of trouble, let's have a quiet week and make sure that ALL of us are on that trip. We didn't come her to win a Division title, we came here to win the Conference title."

In the post-game press conference some of those same reporters that had written me off as too conservative were shocked. On the field with Jenny Taft, Marshall has already spilled the story that I'd told O'Reilly before the drive even started. Marshall admitted he was as shocked as everyone else. He even told them that Carter Jones didn't know until O'Reilly called it in the huddle.

That story had already gotten to the media room. And I just explained that I wanted to get the game over with and I was willing to roll the dice on the element of surprise. One guy compared it to Washington crossing the Delaware.

"I think that's probably an extreme stretch of the analogy." I laughed.

"Would you settle for Ed Hart crossing the Olentangy?" CBS Sports reporter Dennis Dodd asked making reference to the river that runs through Columbus.

Everyone laughed but mostly I deflected the excitement and immediately tried to turn their attention to Nebraska. The Huskers were a surprising 11-1 and would be anxious to get an elusive Big Ten Title.

Finally I said as I readied to leave the press conference "Look guys, I enjoy your constant praise here week after week. It means a lot." I laughed along with the reporters in the room. "But I want to go home, get some sleep and get to work on the Huskers."

As I walked to my car many of the tailgaters were yelling to me. They were still processing the surprising win. Despite the cold gray Ohio November day they remained to eat more, to relive the events they'd just witnessed and mark the end of another home football season.

Sure enough, there was Candace at the car waiting for me. When I got there she planted a big kiss on my lips and hugged me. A crowd of people cheered behind her in the next parking lot.

"Hey coach," an unnamed fan yelled "go home and get you some. You earned that today!"

I waved at them and got in the car to head home.

"You know I have to confess something," Candace began "I missed the play."

"What?"

"When we scored I assumed we were going to overtime and went into the suite bathroom. That's when I heard the crowd roar. By the time I got back out I was watching the replay. I thought I knew you.....but I gotta tell you, even after all these years you still know how to surprise a girl."

"Oh ye of little faith. Maybe I have a few tricks up my sleeve when we get home."

“That may be, but you’re going to bed early and getting a good start on Nebraska.” She said.

In this case she knew exactly what I was thinking. There was one more step to getting that Big Ten Title which was the bar I was supposed to clear to keep my job. And there was the matter of Terrence Jones. That was my next big call to saving my career.

18. NOT OUT OF THE WOODS YET

Sunday morning I headed into the office to get ready for the Big Ten Title game. Although Saturday afternoon was filled with texts with a lot of "atta boys" and "we always believed in you" I knew finishing the title chase was still the key to getting to return.

On film Nebraska's offense was dynamic and explosive and would be an even tougher test than Michigan. The video did not lie, these guys had a lot of talent and were playing with a ton of confidence.

Just before noon Sid Inge came in with a list of media requests. Suddenly every national talk show wanted me on their show. From Golic and Wingo, to Cowherd, to Stephen A Smith, Dan Patrick and LeBatard they all wanted to talk about the fake extra point and the Nebraska game. I told him that I did not have time for any of that this week, except I had agreed to do Ivan Maisel's ESPN Podcast.

Just after Sid left, Sally came in and congratulated me. Then she told me that I had a call from someone named Tom Pietrovic.

"Put him through." I said.

"Tom, how you doing?" I asked.

"Not as well as you must be this morning." He laughed. "I gotta admit you showed some huge balls yesterday making that call."

"Every once in a while you play the right cards and it comes up right for you." I said.

I couldn't resist making a gambling reference before I continued.

"Tom, I hope you've got some good news for me. That would really make my day."

"Actually I am calling about Terrence. He originally wanted to make his decision this week, but he's decided to take one last visit next weekend."

"Where is he going?" I asked.

"He's going up to Michigan and then he will make his decision next week. ESPNU wants to broadcast the announcement live."

"Okay, but tell me are we really in this thing?"

"Yes, you're in it. The game yesterday certainly made a great impression on him. But he wants to take this visit and then make his mind up."

"What more do we need to do?"

"There's not much more to do but keep talking to him and then see what happens next week. He would like to shut this down after Wednesday though. He has the state championship game on Friday. Then he takes his visit and will make up his mind and announce on Monday."

"So that radio silence for calls and contact after Wednesday applies to all the schools?" I asked.

"Well except for Michigan because of the visit."

"Tom you'd better play this one straight. If I have to call Coach Reno on this one I will."

"Okay. We'll talk Sunday."

"Tom don't play this game without dealing us in at the table too."

That was not the start to my week that I'd wanted, but I still held that leverage using Caesar if we wanted. It was a moral dilemma for me. Cheating is one thing. Those rules are black and white. Gray areas of coercion and back room dealing were another matter. I'd avoided it my whole career but could I afford to stay that way?

The Sunday meetings were upbeat and positive. Everyone was in a good mood, maybe too good a mood. A couple of weeks ago after the tough Wisconsin loss I had to get people up from near depression. Now I'd need to tamp down all the well-wishers who just wanted to talk about last week.

The players and coaches seemed receptive to my message to focus on the next challenge. But the threat was external with everyone giving them so much love. Monday at the office people sent cookies, flowers, pizzas and wings to congratulate us on the big win.

When free food enters the office, there is an instinctive homing device that our players have to come find free food. Even though they get plenty to eat, they still swarmed the free food in our offices like crows at a landfill.

The threat was more than just a sudden influx of calories. These fans and friends meant well, but our focus had to be forward. For some of these people beating Michigan was more important than anything. But I knew there were far more people, people with the ability to terminate my career, for whom anything less than a Big Ten title would not suffice.

Nebraska's 11-1 record and #6 ranking got our players' attention. We were ranked right behind them. A win against us would likely put Nebraska into the college football playoff. Doug Leonard didn't wait until game day to start with the conspiracy theories. Looking at the Michigan game certainly provided enough anecdotal evidence of bad calls at key times to make me at least wonder.

In 2004 the Boston Red Sox came back from trailing three games to none to beat the Yankees. When they got to the World Series there was a momentum that carried them past Saint Louis. Our team had that comeback momentum too. All week at practice they had what coaches call "bounce." Bounce is mental and physical. We looked fast, we had very few mental mistakes and guys were where they were supposed to be.

With Pierre Carter suspended for the first half of the game for his targeting call the week before we made a couple of adjustments on defense. For Nebraska's spread offense we put in a three-man defensive line package with Jamar Tucker playing some outside linebacker and Karl Metzger playing some defensive end. We could move Jamar around to get him matched up on running backs in pass protection.

It gave us a really fast front seven on run downs. It would get Marcus Dawson more one-on-one matchups and also allow us to rotate him to keep him fresh.

On offense I wanted us to be more deliberate and use more time on the clock. Our goal was to run the ball effectively and control the clock enough so that our defense would be on the field less than 65 plays. It's rare that one of the offense's goals is to limit our defense's number of plays but that was the plan. Nebraska was averaging over eighty plays a game so eating up time on offense would keep their numbers down.

After making that fake extra point call, the coaches didn't question me this week. They were all still as stunned as the fans. And once you make a game-winning ballsy call like that, your opponents spend extra time to be ready for anything.

As I asked the guys after the Michigan game, our players made sure that we had no distractions. In fact Marshall informed me that guys were all going home and acting like they were still on Coronavirus Quarantine.

"Coach, you won't believe this but some guys are taking a vow of celibacy this week." He laughed.

"I've taken that approach as well." I said.

"Really?" Marshall said.

"Well yes, but it's like that every week once you get married." I laughed.

"I'll keep that in mind before I decide to tie the knot."

Thursday night's practice was our best of the year and I was in a good mood headed over to do the coach's radio show. The calls were all giddy and cocky, but far too many of them were about last week's game.

Finally I'd reached my wit's end and said "Look guys, I appreciate all the love about last week but......if we don't stop looking back the Huskers will wallop us from the front with a two-by-four. So get in your cars, planes or trains get to Indianapolis and help us get the next win."

Because Indianapolis is a short drive from Columbus I decided to go Old School and bus over to the game. I sold it to the players as an "Old School" trip on I-70. It actually made sense. Even though we usually charter our own 757, by the time we got on busses, went to the airport, did security, flew, got off the plane, onto busses and to the hotel we'd be spending about the same time. But they didn't know that.

All they knew was that we were coming in like humble underdogs making a surprise land invasion to take the title. They really bought into the idea. It just goes to show you that selling an idea is important.

When we pulled into the hotel there was a crowd of Buckeye fans there to cheer us as we made our way through the lobby. The win last week had created a fire that had been lacking the last couple of subpar years. But they were back and anxious to see if we could finish this one.

There were a number of things I had to do with the media as well as a walk through at the Stadium. Our guys were locked in, on-time and the wheels were all in motion. Confidence was so prevalent that as a coach I naturally went to that place where I started to worry about over-confidence.

When I got to my room after bed check Candace was there waiting for me. She and some friends had gone to dinner at Saint Elmo and she'd come up to the room after a few cocktails. In the room there was a bottle of Bourbon and some chocolate covered strawberries that room service had delivered.

"Did you order these?" I asked.

"No, I thought you did." She said. "Wait there's a card."

She picked up the card, read it and her jovial mood disappeared immediately. All I could think to myself was "What Now?"

“Oh I think you’ll like this one.” She growled. “Or maybe I’ll just read it for you.”

“Okay.” I said timidly.

“Good luck tomorrow. You know I’ve always backed your ass. If you’re alone buzz me and I’ll come help with these. Alexis.”

Candace put the card down and glared at me. Through no fault of my own, there was really no good option for me here. But I knew all too well that this was ALL my fault.

“What the hell?” Candace asked.

“I can’t control what other people do. And you shouldn’t blame me for that either.”

“I suppose I shouldn’t fault you for anything else you’ve done either.”

“Candace, you know there is nothing to this. I know you had a couple at dinner and you’re speaking a bit more freely than perhaps you would.”

“I’m not drunk asshole.”

Why do we men always step into more messes?

“I didn’t say that. But what I am saying is that this is some bullshit that I can’t control. So my advice is for us to eat the strawberries and then for me to get some sleep for the big day tomorrow. We probably still have to win this one to save the season and maybe my job.”

“Even after last week?” She asked incredulously.

“Maybe even more so. There is nothing that sets fans and boosters off more than hopes and expectations that just miss. They all think this is a done deal tomorrow.”

“Okay.” She calmed down. “But we will resume this conversation in the future.”

In the morning I was reminded why night games on the road are the longest of days. There is breakfast, then a meeting, then lunch, then a walk-through, then a pre-game meal and then we head to the stadium. It means a lot of up and down in the elevators. And for a game like this you’re also dealing with a full hotel. Players have to wait for elevators and fans chatting them up and asking for selfies.

Often it leads to a player or two drifting into a meal or meeting a few minutes late. But not today, they were all early for everything.

Finally when we got onto the bus to head to the stadium, I got there ten minutes before we were to leave. As I walked to the bus Rick Carter was there. He was in charge of bus check and he had a big smile on his face.

"What're you so cheery for?" I asked.

"They are all here. You're the last one and you're ten minutes early."

That was music to my ears. As I climbed on the bus there were Pokey and Marshall sitting up front as captains.

Pokey smiled and said "What took you so long coach?"

The whole bus was full of our players, all silent and focused. All of them were quiet, most with headphones on. Their gray suits, white shirts and scarlet ties were all immaculate as they stared straight ahead silently. This team had the look of a squad of assassins on their way to a hit. It was a look I'd not seen all year and quite frankly it was damn near scary.

I was glad I wasn't playing for Nebraska tonight.

There are times as a coach where you just know. That confidence followed me through pre-game warm-ups and then manifested itself once the game started. Our players were flying to the ball, staying on blocks and running hard. All the little things were going our way.

Midway through the third quarter we led 20-6, but it just felt like we were the much better football team. We just needed to put this game away. The ball control offense was frustrating Nebraska's offense as they stood a lot on the sideline watching the game. Our defensive package and the changes we'd made were paying off. The complex blitz scheme was new and Jamar Tucker had a couple of sacks when he was matched up with Nebraska's running back.

But great coaches make adjustments and Nebraska did just that. They found their footing on offense and two drives later it was suddenly 20-16. It was time to make a move or two with twelve minutes to go in the fourth quarter.

That was when Quinn went to a two-back set with Pokey and Malcolm and started to slow the game down and pound the ball. With their defense getting tired of tackling Pokey, we were able to get Malcolm in the open and he torched them for a forty-yard touchdown and a 27-16 lead.

Nebraska drove to our twenty-five yard line and was set up to kick a field goal with nine minutes to go. All week long we'd worked on an edge rush with Donte Carter. He'd noticed on film that Nebraska's long snapper usually snapped the ball about two seconds after setting up. It was risky to try and jump that snap, because if you were just a tad early they could flag us for being offside. We told Donte only to do it if we gave him the green light.

While Nebraska's kick team was coming on the field Donte Carter was yelling over to us.

"Hey coach it's fourth and six. Let me go!"

I looked down at Saul and he yelled "Coach he wants the green light to run on the jump."

Since it was fourth and six the danger was a penalty that would put them in position to go for a fourth and short. But it was time to roll the dice.

"Go for it!" I yelled.

He smiled, gave me the thumbs up and went to line up. As Nebraska lined up the Ohio State fans in that end were making noise and waving their arms to distract their kicker. As the snapper lifted his head to get set, he paused two seconds and Donte exploded out of his stance right on the snap. Just over one second later we heard a thump of the kick and almost immediately a second thump as Donte blocked the kick which ricocheted into the waiting arms of Roger Hill who was on the other side.

Donte came galloping off the field. He'd been through so much this season that a moment for him like this was just the kind of thing that makes the coaching mission so worthwhile. He came over and gave me a big hug.

"Thanks for trusting me coach....not just today but all year." He said.

Right over my shoulder was Marshall Remington. I switched my headset to Quinn and said "Let's control the ball but trust our quarterback. Let's keep the foot on the gas."

Quinn called a marvelous drive. When they were playing run, we were passing. When they were playing coverage we pounded the ball. He was one play ahead in his play calls. Ten plays later with four minutes to go, Marshall ran a quarterback sneak across the line for a 34-16 lead.

All that was left to do was count down the time. Our defense played conservatively and with about 20 seconds to go Nebraska scored one last touchdown to make the final score of our Big Ten Championship game 34-23.

Before I could even fathom what had happened I'd been doused with Gatorade, had a Big Ten Champions hat put on my head and was suddenly on the podium with confetti falling from the roof of the dome. It was a blur.

People I knew were running up to me, people I didn't know were shaking my hand and it just went by in the blink of an eye. That moment when you clinch a championship and hoist a trophy are nice, but what I was thinking about was the journey of a long eleven months when we were always trying to stay above the flood of people who wanted us fired.

There are a couple of things that still stand out about that post-game chaos. First was standing on the podium and when no one else was listening having Gerry Gorton congratulate me. I told him how much I appreciated him sticking up for me. The next thing was getting a hug from Candace in the hallway outside the locker room. And having her tell me that she knew we'd get it done all along.

And finally, and maybe most satisfying of all, was having the captains stand in front of our team in the locker room. They were holding a game ball and as they were about to speak Marshall Remington yelled to the people in the room.

"Hey guys, put down your cellphone cameras. This moment is just for us and for the guys who deserve to be part of it."

Everyone complied.

Marcus Dawson stepped forward.

"Coach Hart this game ball is for you. Some of us tested you, but you stuck by us, supported us and now here we are. We know the pressures you were under, but you did not buckle. For that we will forever be grateful."

There was nothing for me to do but look around at the men in that room. They were sweaty, they were bruised and battered but above all they were triumphant. They trusted in me and for that I will never forget this team. There is a love that develops, a bond that comes on a journey like this.

"Guys, I appreciate this, I really do....." I started to choke up a little.

"Go 'head Coach! Preach!" Someone yelled.

"I appreciate the effort all of you made this year. I could not be prouder of winning this title. Four weeks ago I told you and you believed. But all that said, we've got one more big game left in Pasadena. And I have every intention of beating USC to close this thing out the right way!"

With that a roar went up from all of them. By Sunday afternoon, I'd already turned my attention to finishing recruiting and to USC in the Rose Bowl less than four weeks away. There was a lot to do between now and then, including the December signing day.

And with that December signing day, there was one target that was much, much bigger than all others. Terrence Jones was absolutely vital. Not only was he a truly dominant in-state player and the biggest recruit in the country, but he was a "bundler".

In political fundraising circles there are fundraisers who are called "bundlers" because they give the maximum amount and also recruit dozens and dozens of others to do the same. For the team that signed him, Terrence Jones would shake free another four or five big-time recruits.

There were guys on our list who'd publicly stated that they would go to school with Terrence. These guys knew each other from camps, combines and showcases. They texted and talked to each other all the time. The recruiting game had become a little like the NBA where these big-time players were trying to form their own super-teams.

Carter McDonald from New Jersey was the top defensive end on our list, Devon Alexander from Virginia was our top linebacker target and Walker McCoy from Mississippi was the top quarterback in the country. They were all guys who wanted to play with Terrence.

So Sunday night I sat at my desk deciding what I should do to get Terrence Jones and those other three pieces of a puzzle that would give us a shot at the number 1 recruiting class in the country. This commitment would give us the #1 overall recruit in the country, the top quarterback in the country, the top defensive end in the country and top five players nationally at Linebacker, running back, offensive line and safety.

This was the kind of talent haul that, combined with last year's class, would put us in the National Championship hunt next year.

But to get it done.......

To get it done I'd have to call in a marker. I'm sure that men like Caesar Alfonsi who did favors were not shy about asking for one in return later on. Did I really believe this guy was doing this just to be a good guy? For all I knew they were talking about "forgiving" a gambling debt in the low six-figure range. These guys didn't just piss money away so there was sure to be an ask. And if I'm honest with myself, isn't that a "payoff" that would run afoul of NCAA rules? And I couldn't kid myself, there would probably be a threat of physical harm as well.

Why couldn't I just switch off my conscience? And what would the return favor be to the guys in Northeast Ohio and when would the ask come?

But I was also on a hot streak. The fake extra point against Michigan, the win over Nebraska, the Big Ten title; all that was in my head. I was untouchable right now and every roll of the dice was coming up my way.

But I also knew that with this new title the bar of expectations for next year and every year after that was suddenly raised. I need to get into the college football playoff next year and Terrence Jones could single-handedly deliver enough swagger, talent and future teammates to do just that.

And just as importantly, if he went to Michigan he would bring all those deliverables to Michigan, a team we had to play every year to win our division, our conference and have a chance to get to the playoff.

So I looked at the clock on my den wall, sipped another sip of bourbon and let out a sigh. As the clock struck nine p.m., I looked at the small slip of paper with a phone number written on it. Remembering our earlier conversation I called the number and he answered.

"Caesar, it's Ed." I said.

"You want in?" He asked.

I hesitated before saying "Yes."

"You'll get a call in the morning." With that he hung up.

Monday morning all the coaches were in the office before they headed out on the road recruiting. They'd all decided to stay here until after Terrence announced his decision on ESPNU at eleven. The national buzz was that he was a Michigan lock.

At eight a.m. my cell phone buzzed and I saw the name Tom Pietrovic come up.

"Hello this is Ed." I answered.

"Coach this is Tom Pietrovic."

"How you doing?" I asked.

"I've been better." He said. "But I've got some news that will make you happy."

Trying to sound surprised "What do you mean?"

"I think you know where this is headed. Terrence has a press conference and he is going to announce for Ohio State. He's sitting right here."

Terrence got on the phone. "Hey coach I'm gonna be a Buckeye!"

"Are you serious? Because you'd better not be messing with me."

He assured me that he was all set and that he'd talked to the other guys who assured him they'd go wherever he announced today. He didn't tell them where he was going so the secret wouldn't get out.

Then Tom got back on the phone.

"Try not too hard to sound surprised. I never knew you to be a guy who could draw a royal flush but somehow you did it. Congrats." He said just before he hung up.

I sat at my desk just realizing that I'd gotten this done. Getting Terrence Jones for us AND keeping him from Michigan. No one would see this coming, in fact none of my coaches would have any idea how I pulled it off. And I would never breathe a word of it to anyone.

Around 10:30 our coaches started to gather in the recruiting war room to watch the press conference. Most of the coaches still believed Terrence was going to Michigan. They were already adjusting our recruiting board to reflect the possibility that four of our top twelve targets would be headed as a group to Michigan.

This was by far my best acting job. They had no idea.

Finally at eleven in what in itself a surprise, the press conference started on time. Coach Reno was there and they sat at a table in the gym. There were no hats, or jerseys just Terrence and Coach Reno.

Finally after Coach thanked everyone in town and mentioned a local business or two for supporting the team he introduced Terrence. Terrence was dressed in a blue suit with a red tie and he stood at the podium set up on the table. He quickly thanked everyone before he got to it.

"Today I want to announce that I will be signing with THE Ohio State University."

As he placed that emphasis on "THE" the fans in Steubenville knew exactly where he was going and they cheered. In our war room as soon as he said "THE" our coaches and staff roared and started to applaud.

I sat with a smile like the cat that ate the canary. As the cheering died down Rick Carter yelled to me.

"Did you know?"

I nodded and started to laugh.

"How the hell could you keep that from us?" Rick yelled excitedly. "When did you know?"

"I talked to him this morning."

"And you didn't tell us?"

"I thought you could use a little excitement. And get ready because there are three or four other guys that will fall into place the next two days."

Within seconds Rick had pulled up social media on two of the eight screens in the war room, even as Terrence's press conference was still going. The twitter screen was exploding with Buckeye fans taunting Michigan fans. On the message boards there was genuine disbelief by both Ohio State and Michigan fans.

Even Gerry Gorton sent a text expressing both his congratulations and his surprise. A number of boosters and Trustees even weighed in. In the back of my mind I couldn't help but wonder why so many successful business people cared so much about where an eighteen year old was deciding to go to college.

And just like clockwork I got a text from Alexis "Congrats. Let me know if U Need Company 2 Celebrate! XOXOXO--#GoBucks!"

"Good Lord!" I said to myself.

It didn't take long for Michigan fans to start accusing us of cheating. That is always par for the course for fans when they lose a major recruit to a rival school.

The good news was the last month had turned the tide from "Fire Ed Hart" to "Ed Hart Forever!" I know all too well that those sentiments wouldn't last if we lost the Rose Bowl. And with all these hotshot recruits coming in there would inevitably be some transfers from our school.

After all that the coaches were back out on the road recruiting and I was in Columbus alone again as Candace had headed back to Arizona. In the days just before the Big Ten title game and the days of that next week a lot of awards and honors rolled in.

I was named the Big Ten Coach of the Year and the National Coach of The Year by a couple of organizations. That fake extra point had gotten me a lot of national notice. We had a couple of players that were finalists for national awards, but none of them won. Marcus Dawson was named a First-Team All-American and also finished his degree. I thought about calling Vivian to let her know that despite all her efforts to destroy his life, Marcus was about to be a college graduate and an NFL millionaire.

But you don't spike the ball when you win.

My other time was spent meeting with the coaches who weren't on the road recruiting and some early practices for the Rose Bowl. This was going to be a tough game in their backyard. They had a number of built-in advantages.

In the next few days more commitments rolled in. The three guys who wanted to join Terrence were all set to sign. The momentum in this class just took off. We were going to have to turn kids away at the rate we were going. And that gave us the leverage to be both selective and to leverage kids that there would not be a slot for them if they did not commit.

With just two days before signing day we got a final commitment and had reached our class size of twenty-two and had nailed down the class for the year. We could get ahead and devote our entire attention to recruiting the next year's class in January. It had been a few years since we could do that.

Because the class was set two days in advance there was no signing day drama. The signed forms came rolling in one after another. Once again I told Rick that I didn't want a big party or a lot of media around. ESPNU did send a crew to do stand-up reports outside the building and I did allow a couple of our assistants to go out and take some credit. One of them was Quinn. I thought some signing day exposure would help boost his profile as both a great offensive mind and a great recruiter.

By day's end we held the Nation's Top-Ranked recruiting class and our fan base was understandably excited. It was such a big day that I couldn't get Gerry Gorton and his pack of Trustees and boosters out of the building. And of course there was Alexis Nelson following him around too. I did my best to avoid her but she still sent texts.

"I C U R Avoiding Me...I won't be ignored! LOL"

And then another: "Candace is not here....Anything I need 2 know...anything I can do 4 U?"

And another: "I know where you live!"

Once the day was over I ducked out the back door to avoid Alexis. Those texts had me a bit freaked out and part of me was worried that she might actually show up at my house. Sure she was attractive and the repeated offers were tempting. But I am happy with my marriage even if the more frequent and prolonged absences were starting to wear on me a little.

But above all even if I did want to do anything, Alexis would tell the whole damned world and I'd probably get fired and divorced. College football history has seen its share of head coaches brought down because they messed with the wrong woman. Sometimes it's a booster, or a staff assistant or the wife or daughter of a booster.

It's just best to stay in your own lane. So if Alexis did show up, I would not answer the door. As luck would have it she never did show up.

Not long after signing day we were on our way to California to the Rose Bowl. Fans think that Bowl trips are a lot of fun and games. While the change of venue is exciting for players and fans, it is still a business trip.

Our coaches start with a 6:00 a.m. meeting every morning. Then we prep for player meetings and practice. Meetings start at 10:00 a.m. the bus to practice leaves at 11:15 and we are finished with practice and back at the hotel by 3:00. The players are free but the coaches spend two hours looking at the practice film and getting ready for the next day. Then we make our way back to our hotel suites for dinner time with our families. By the time we finish dinner and get home it is time to go to bed and do it all over again.

Our families do have a great time though. Candace and her sister spent days going to spas, sightseeing and jogging on the trail between Santa Monica and Venice Beach.

All the while we were prepping to play USC. USC was ranked 5th with an 11-2 record as Pac 12 Champions and we were ranked 6th as Big Ten Champions. It was one of those classic Rose Bowl matchups that young men all across the frozen Midwest dreamt about on New Year's Day.

For Marshall Remington it was a homecoming of sorts. Being from nearby Orange County he started trying to scrape up tickets for his dozens of family members while we were still in the Big Ten Championship post-game locker room. I did worry that he would feel the pressure to try and do too much since he was playing back home.

But the more we looked at the film, the more we liked our chances. They had a quick defensive line, but our physical offensive line would be able to move them off the ball. Their two losses were surprise upsets to Stanford and Notre Dame. Both had physical lines that enabled them to run the ball consistently. We studied those films intensely.

Their offense was a pro-style attack and that was a good match-up for our defensive personnel. It meant that we'd play a lot of our traditional defensive sets that relied on our linebackers, an area of real strength.

The toughest part of the bowl game is getting work done in your room. While I was in the room trying to get things done between 5 p.m. and dinners out at 7:30 p.m. Candace had friends and family stopping by the suite. I would be watching film on my tablet while people asked about the game, or how I was doing.

Three nights before the game most of the planning was done and Candace had invited Gerry Gorton and a number of Trustees and boosters up to the suite for a cocktail hour. Much to my surprise she had even invited Alexis Nelson. The two of them were chatting amicably.

As soon as Candace shook free I asked her what was up with her new BFF Alexis.

“Look there’s no sense in isolating her from my end. I may as well see if I can make a friend out of her for both of us.” Candace said.

Killing them with kindness was her strong suit.

We both worked the room and over and over again I was getting congratulated on the great season, the recruiting coup and on my lovely wife Candace. The more the cocktails flowed the more fun the room became. Some of these people were worth hundreds of millions of dollars yet this was still a big deal to them. Ohio State was their school and their team and their donations and generosity gave them a sense of ownership of this team.

The egos in the room were immense. Candace and I could sense that some of these people hated each other. In fact a number of them had tangled in business ventures and Candace counted four of them who were currently involved in litigation against one another for some reason or another. Yet here they all were laughing and chatting.

Ten of us went out to dinner and Gerry Gorton had me seated at one end of the table with Jonah Huston a potentially big donor for the athletic department. He was telling me how much he knew about football and analyzed all the things we’d done right. He also pointed things that he believed could’ve been done better.

Everybody’s an expert, particularly the guys who write big checks.

Candace was seated with Alexis at the other end of the table and I had no idea what they were talking about at that end. Candace was several glasses of wine deep and I just hoped she’d continue to play nice. While listening to Jonah and Gerry drone on and on I was trying to see if I could hear what was being said at the other end.

Finally we got home and as Candace and I lay in bed she said to me “A lot of these people are so, so nice.”

The lights of West LA stretching to the horizon gave a slight glow to the room. I thought about what she’d said and then thought about where we were just one year ago.

"Yeah they're nice now." I said. "But remember these were some of the same people who wanted to run my ass out of town, not only last year but less than two months ago when we lost to Wisconsin. Never forget that."

"Oh don't be so cynical."

"There are two types of coaches in college football; the ones watching their backs from those wolves and the ones who are out of a job. The wolves are nice as long as you keep feeding them wins and great bowl trips and top-ranked recruiting classes. But they've got short memories."

Morning of game day arrived. Waking up for a Rose Bowl is like nothing else in College Football. Even the drive up to Pasadena seemed like magic. The California sun lit up a cloudless blue sky as we worked our way through LA behind our police escort. The drama of the day started to sink in as the busses began our ascent into the desert hills climbing towards a date with destiny.

We entered the stunning San Gabriel Valley where the town of Pasadena and specifically the Rose Bowl stadium are nestled into the famed Arroyo Seco. I sat quietly, alone with my thoughts looking out the window passing tailgaters parked in parking lots, and on a golf course. Ohio State flags all over but outnumbered by the hometown "SC" flags.

"Pasadena.....The Rose Bowl....." Words that conjure up images in the minds of all college football fans who speak them.

The Rose Bowl is a part of Americana, part of our culture and traditions. The afternoon of January 1st is set aside for a Rose Bowl game from the dramatic setting where the sun always seems to shine. The grass is a shade of green that the folks back in Ohio won't see in their yards until June or July, if ever. Beyond the stadium the towering snow-capped San Gabriel mountains will be featured by shots taken by the Goodyear blimp floating above.

In that sun, our white jerseys seemed to glow and the sun reflected off our silver helmets. Our guys were moving through their pre-game warm-ups and the clock was moving quickly towards kickoff. Days like this you wanted to never end, but you also wanted a win as quickly as possible.

In that brief pause just before kickoff there is a minute to look around and take in the moment. This is the only football game anywhere in the world right now and I was about to coach it. My hands would be on the outcome either good or bad. We were the better team, I knew it, our team knew it and in a few minutes USC would know it.

Looking at the stadium, up at the press box and back to the field I thought for a moment about the ghosts of so many great players who'd played here. Then I took a moment to think of all the great players who didn't get to play here either. I pulled on my headsets and yelled to everyone who could hear me.

"It's our time so let's go get this mother fucker."

There was a ton of "Hell Yeahs!" yelled on the headsets.

There are games that you know that you can control within four or five minutes. This was one of them. USC's offensive line could not handle our pass rush and we substituted aggressively to stay fresh. Their quarterback was running for his life and their running game was not making any ground.

On offense the game was playing as we thought it would. Their line was quick but we were changing the cadence and tempo of the game to catch them in our physical run game. Our backs were coming at them in waves. All three of our tailbacks were getting the ball and that was starting to wear down their defense. By halftime we'd raced ahead 21-10 and it didn't even feel that close.

The third quarter started slowly but just as the quarter was about to end Malcolm Jackson got loose and blazed past USC to put us up 28-10.

But just when it looked safe USC made a couple of great plays to make it 28-17 with about eleven minutes to go. And as it happens so often in a game where you seem to have control, you get careless. As USC set up to kickoff they slipped in a surprise onside kick and got the ball. Our defense had just been on the field for twelve plays and now they were right back out there.

The anger inside me was boiling, but I did not want to incite any panic in anyone. So I kept my demeanor level and encouraged the defensive coaches to do what they could.

USC sensed that our guys were tired and went to a no huddle offense to keep us from substituting fresh players. Eleven fast plays and three minutes later they scored to make the game 28-24 with eight minutes to go.

As they were kicking the extra point I made sure that Marshall was next to me and that Quinn was on the headset too. The USC fans had come back to life and our fans had grown completely silent. The USC players were bouncing on their sideline and our tired defense was walking off the field slowly. There was a look of frustrated exhaustion on their faces.

I grabbed our offensive captains Marshall and O'Reilly and spoke to them and to Quinn through the headsets.

"Look around and see what's happening." I said pointing to the signs of a momentum shift all around the stadium. "This is no time to panic. Be positive and let's focus on getting a few first downs and running some clock before we take a shot to put the dagger in them. We've got to keep the defense off the field for a few minutes and we've got to score a touchdown not a field goal. But remember we've got to be deliberate. You got that?"

They both nodded and Quinn agreed.

"You two guys are seniors. This is the most important drive of your lives. Years from now this will be the moment when your legend was made. Now let's get it done!" I yelled.

There is something beautiful in watching a well-called and well-executed drive unfold. Quinn hit a rhythm mixing run plays, a wide receiver screen, a play-action pass, a quick pass, a few more runs and another screen. The ball was moving all over the place attacking different parts of the defense. USC's defensive coordinator was a play-call late every time. And just when it looked like Quinn was moving the ball every play, he ran inside three times in a row.

We were now ten plays into the drive and because we'd been efficient, completed every pass and taken our time the game clock was now under three minutes and we sat that USC's fifteen yard line. They had used their second timeout to stop the clock.

When Marshall came over to talk I asked Quinn a question.

"What do you think about running the reverse?" I asked.

"It's a little risky and we could lose yardage on it. And then we could lose the ball if the ball handling is off or lose yardage to make a field goal more risky." Quinn said.

"What happened to the Texas gunslinger I used to know? Have you spent too much time around my old ass?"

Quinn laughed and asked what my thinking was on the play.

"You've hit them running the ball inside on three straight plays. We put Pokey back in, they'll think we are playing it safe and running inside to get a field goal. They'll blitz inside and the backside end will chase Pokey."

"I like it." Quinn said.

"I LOVE it!" Marshall said.

"You tell Pokey that if there is any traffic near the exchange point on his handoff with Jennings then he should just eat the ball. We'll take a loss of two and stay in field goal range. And tell the linemen to be ready for the double A-Gap blitz so that Pokey can make that handoff. And for God's sake Marshall you get downfield and make your block too."

When we lined up on the ball USC's safety was creeping down inside which told me that the inside linebackers were probably blitzing the inside gaps. We had just what I wanted. After the ball was snapped USC's blitz hit a stone wall which allowed Pokey to make the clean handoff back to the open field.

When Jennings came around the corner the only guy with a chance at him was the safety filling inside. The fans in the stands started to stand because they could see the open field and saw Marshall launch himself into his block.

Jennings dashed across the ten, the five and into the end zone.

"Great call Ed." Quinn yelled.

"Hey, same to you Quinn. That may be the best-called drive of the season."

The 35-24 score held up and as the clock ticked down to zero it dawned on me that we were now Rose Bowl Champions. A year ago we'd blown a bowl game in Florida and from those ashes and through a challenging season we'd risen on the opposite coast.

And I'd done it the right way....mostly. But can anyone walk through a minefield like that and remain completely pure? Maybe there are better men that could do it. But we'd mostly stayed our moral course.

. . . .

The next morning after Candace had left to go downstairs there was a knock on my hotel suite door. She was going to get some coffee for both of us to help nurse our lingering effects of a late night after the Rose Bowl. We were going to fly over to Tucson to see her mother before I headed back to Ohio without her.

"Did you forget your key? I said as I approached the door and opened it without looking.

Standing at the door was Gerry Gorton.

"I didn't forget my key, but I don't think it would work here." Gerry laughed.

"Didn't you drop in on me this time last year?" I asked.

"Yes I did."

"Well I trust the conversations among the boosters last night were a bit better."

"That's for certain."

"Well come on in."

He came in and we sat on the couches in the suite.

"I want to congratulate you on this past year."

"Well thanks to you we had the chance to coach this year."

"I also want to let you know that we will certainly talk about your contract extension and a raise when we get back."

"Gerry when you get to it that's fine with me. I trust you on this one."

"You have my word on it. But there is one hitch that we do need to discuss. Our friend Vivian has written an internal Title IX report as well as a report on a lack of institutional control that she has sent to the NCAA. They have begun questioning people in an investigation. The lead counsel on enforcement worked with Vivian at Indiana years ago and they are loaded to come get us. It also appears that another school has turned us in on the Terrence Jones recruitment accusing us of cheating or at least some heavy-handed tactics. Once this is all cleared up we'll get your contract done. But our in-house counsel says we can't do the contract until this is all cleared."

I kept my poker face on before responding with as little emotion as possible.

"Okay Gerry, but I'm not sure what the hell they're talking about. So what do you need from me?"

"They'll need nothing more than a deposition from you in late January. They're going to get everyone else interviewed before you. They'll also have access to your texts, e-mails and phone records. But if you have nothing to worry about, it'll be all good."

"Yeah it will......." My voice trailed off trying to instantly process any and all electronic communications and phone calls I'd made in the last year.

Well we'd just have to cross that bridge when the time came.

Gerry got up and as he left we shook hands at the door just as Candace was arriving with some coffee. Unlike me she'd already been for a run this morning.

After Gerry left she shut the door and smiled.

"I trust that was a far better meeting than last year." She said.

"Yeah for the most part." I said.

But I knew that I wasn't out of the woods just yet. In this profession you never really are. Even after all we'd done that this year it remained to be seen how far from the forest's edge we were in the coming weeks.

19. EPILOGUE

At the end of January it was time for my NCAA deposition. I walked into a non-descript windowless on-campus conference room with my attorney Wes Sullinger. Waiting for us were two NCAA attorneys, Ohio State legal counsel Lewis Carter and a stenographer to record the session.

A week earlier I'd spent two days at Wes's office doing deposition prep. My agent Nathan Weinrich was also there to discuss any potential contract issues should Ohio State decide to hold anything up. Every time I was in the room with those two guys, I just envisioned a meter running up my bills like a very, very expensive New York cab ride.

In the weeks since the season ended, Quinn had gotten his big break when Georgia Tech called looking for a new head coach. Dwayne Baxter was also off to Atlanta, but he had been hired by the Atlanta Falcons. His agent got him to the NFL where, as I would find out, he could avoid any questioning from the NCAA.

So off he went.

But by the end of the deposition it became clear that he enlisted the help of his agent to get a Florida State booster to pay Malcolm Jackson's pastor. I remember my surprise when Malcolm told me that his pastor had advised him to go to Ohio State. Looking back, Dwayne didn't seem surprised. He knew.

Malcolm he didn't know anything about any of it and worst of all it looked like the pastor pocketed all the money. Dwayne leaving for the NFL was a case of staying a step or two ahead of the law. There are a lot of guys staying one step ahead of the NCAA posse.

But I was happy for Quinn. He'd done a great job for us and had gotten out of town before his relationship with a student became public knowledge. I'd even heard that she'd graduated in December and had moved to Atlanta too.

But I was still here. I was left to keep this program on track. This deposition was sure to be confrontational. The lead NCAA attorney Kip Remy had worked with Vivian Terrant and had probably been prepped by her to get after me with the line of questioning. There was no escaping this.

Before we started Kip wanted to make sure that I knew a few things. Our legal counsel Lewis Carter was in the room and he started the proceedings.

"Ed there are some things you need to know. This deposition is under oath. They will ask you questions and while this does not have the force of law as it relates to a criminal perjury charge, there are NCAA and Ohio State penalties if you lie under oath today. Quite simply under our contract terms you will be terminated for cause with no buyout should you knowingly perjure yourself today. Do you understand that?"

"Yes." I replied.

"Also I want to be clear that I am here in my capacity as the University's legal counsel. My only interest is the University's interest. Given what happened at Penn State with their legal counsel sitting in a grand jury a few years back I want to be sure you understand my role here. You can also ask me to leave if you want."

"No," I said "I've got nothing to hide."

Wes jumped in "Ed I am going to advise you to have him leave the room."

"Okay, Lewis I'll ask you to leave when we get started." I said.

"I'll go right after Kip reviews one last thing." Lewis said.

Then Kip chimed in with his explanation "As far as the NCAA is concerned, we will make a transcript of your testimony today. It will then be provided to you so that you can review it and then make any factual changes to things if they were not recorded accurately. Then you will be asked to sign as to its veracity. It will become part of the investigation and treated as a truthful statement. Do you also understand this?"

"Yes." I stated.

Lewis excused himself and left the room.

It started to sink in that this was "big boy shit" with real world ramifications. And walking into this I didn't know what they had and what they could verify.

The deposition started with our recruitment of Terrence Jones. They alleged that another school had accused us of breaking NCAA rules. I had no problem answering these questions. One thing I could probably count on as it related to Caesar Alfonsi and his "associates" was that they did not talk.

But Kip Remy the NCAA attorney started on that questioning immediately.

"So did you have any arrangements with anyone in Steubenville to offer anything to Terrence Jones to get him to come to Ohio State?" He asked.

"No."

"It has been brought to our attention that this recruit had quietly committed to another school and then for no reason the morning of his announcement he changed course. Do you have idea why that might have happened?"

"You mean why he didn't go to Michigan?"

"We're not going to engage in one school versus another. Just answer the question."

"Why did he change his mind? Look 17 or 18-year old kids they occasionally change their minds. You can dance around this all you want but I know Michigan probably called you. They thought they had him. But maybe Terrence saw us win that game and decided he wanted to stay in-state. You'd have to ask him why."

Wes glared at me. He'd told me to keep my answers succinct and already I'd gotten loose right out the gate.

"Nothing fishy?" Kip asked.

"Fishy? Is that a legal term? If you're asking if we followed NCAA rules in recruiting him, yes we did. End of story."

I'd made another mistake. I was doing his job for him by supplying questions to answer myself.

"Are you sure?" Kip asked like a prosecutor upset that he didn't get the right answer.

I paused to take a sip of water before answering. It was a technique to buy time and be sure I kept my cool.

"To my knowledge neither I nor anyone else here broke NCAA rules."

Wes jumped in "I think he's answered that question multiple times now."

"Okay," Kip said. "Just one more thing, do you know someone named Tom Pietrovic?"

"Yes." I answered.

The other thing Wes told me was to stick to "yes" or "no" answers when you're not sure where it is going. Extended answers just had the potential to provide more information for an open-ended set of follow-up questions.

"How did you know him?"

"I met him last summer, I think it was, and then again before the Michigan game."

"Why did you meet him last summer and then again before the Michigan game?"

"He drove Terrence to visit our campus."

"And who arranged those rides?"

"I don't know."

"Did you have any follow-up conversations?"

"Yes."

"Our phone records show that there were three phone calls between you and Pietrovic. What were those calls about?"

"He called once to tell me when Terrence was going to make his announcement. The second time he called me with Terrence to tell me he was coming to Ohio State."

I was still telling the truth, so that was good. It was more than likely that Michigan coaches had no idea that Pietrovic was trying to curry favor with Michigan alums. They probably thought he steered the kid to us all along.

"Did you ever threaten him or his business?"

"Me? No."

Shit. That answer was a mistake. By isolating this and qualifying that *I* never threatened him it unwittingly hinted that perhaps someone else may have done so. Kip was too good to not follow that up.

"Do you know *anyone* who might have threatened his business?"

"No."

That was technically true. Alfonsi had not threatened his business, but there was a small matter about a big gambling debt.

"Do you know the name Caesar Alfonsi?" Kip asked.

"It rings a bell."

"Would it surprise you if I told you that you had a couple of calls with him?"

Fuck.

"No. I probably did but I really couldn't tell you exactly when."

"Well there are a few calls here from him to you on these phone records. There is also a message slip from a note taken by your staff assistant Sally Anderson with a date on it."

Kip slid across a page with dates and times of phone calls. The calls from Alfonsi were circled. Since he hadn't asked me a question I kept my mouth shut. But I knew the next question was going to be a doozy, so I relied on a trick that Wes had taught me. I had some jelly beans with me and as Kip started his question I put some in my mouth.

"Ed, law enforcement has had an ongoing interest in Alfonsi and has shared with us some transcripts of your calls. On this call he tells you that he has leverage over Pietrovic and can force him to send Jones to Ohio State. How did you respond to those overtures?"

With a mouthful of candy, I kept my mouth closed, smiled and pointed to my mouth to show him that I was still chewing. The jelly beans bought me time to think about how to respond and try to anticipate the question that would follow my answer.

"I told him that I had to think that over."

"You didn't tell him no outright?"

Now I had to think where this might be headed. I needed a good response that was honest and could shut this thing down.

"No."

Keep it to yes or no answers. But I knew there would be a follow up. But creating the need for a follow-up question bought me more time.

"Why Not?"

"Until the first call I did not know Mr. Alfonsi. I wanted to handle it in a way that would not offend him. So I did not tell him no outright. But I certainly never told him "yes" on those calls."

The lessons from Wes came in handy. First refer to seemingly unsavory characters with the formal "mister" title. It makes you seem less familiar with that person. You never knew if these transcripts would see the light of day and in the public sphere the title put more distance between Caesar and me. Secondly, I never did tell him yes on the calls they were referencing so I wasn't lying to him.

I could only hope that Kip would not ask if there was another call or meeting where I told him yes. If he did then I'd have to make a decision whether I should lie or not. Almost immediately I decided that I would try to blur the lines, and if pressed I would just flat-out lie. I knew Caesar wouldn't talk, I knew Pietrovic wouldn't talk and there was no way they could connect this back on me.

My decision was made. There are things in life you'll lie to protect.

"Okay. Let me ask you one more question. Did you ever meet with Alfonsi and ask him to pressure Mr. Pietrovic?"

"No."

Kip had made a mistake by specifying a "meeting." He made a few notes and the room grew quiet. He seemed genuinely disappointed that this had ended in a dead end. In those few moments I could only hope that this line of questioning would shift and shift in a hurry. If he asked the right question I'd have to perjure myself.

Then Kip moved into questions about the way we handled the Marcus Dawson situation. Vivian had fed him very skewed information that was slanted to allege the dreaded NCAA "Lack of Institutional Control." Her argument was that I had acted outside the normal protocols of the University's discipline system to protect Marcus Dawson.

After a few preliminary questions Kip got into more detail.

"Did you at any time go around Vivian Terrant's authority to petition the President directly in disciplinary issues involving Marcus Dawson?"

"No."

"Well this document from Vivian Terrant suggests otherwise."

He slid an e-mail across the table to me. I scanned it quickly and it was complete bullshit.

"In that e-mail she states the fact that you worked with others to block her authority to discipline Marcus Dawson. Doesn't that show a lack of institutional control?"

Now I was pissed.

"The premise of your question is complete crap."

Kip thought he had me. I was pissed but it was a controlled anger. He thought he could get me to lose control.

“It is? She states the fact..”

I cut him off.

“She alleges her opinion. Get that straight.” I snapped.

“Well one could argue.”

Again I cut him off.

“Kip you came here at Vivian’s beckoning. I know your history with her. So any pretext that this is an unbiased investigation is a joke.”

Kip was about to reply before I cut him off again.

“But to get back to your question, her allegation and opinion is completely false. In fact one could argue that she acted outside the scope of her authority in pursuing a suspension. But I know this is about me. I was asked to meet with Art Simpson and Gerry Gorton directly because they were committed to fairness in this case.”

“Fairness? How is it fair that a player accused of rape can continue to be a member of this student body as well as continue playing football?”

“Because we stood up for his due process. Kip I know that you learned at Michigan’s Law School that there is a difference between an accusation and a finding of guilt. And if you’ve followed the case at all, a judge threw out the attempt to suspend him, and the charges were all thrown out. Is it fair to ruin a person’s life because he is accused of a crime?”

“But there was no way for you to know in August how this case would play out. So in that regard can you say you were right and that Gerry Gorton was right?”

“Yes.”

“So I am to believe now that you never threatened Tom Pietrovic to get a recruit, and that you also possess some power to see months into the future? Where would you come across the power to know that he would be cleared?”

If his goal was to piss me off, he was succeeded, but if he wanted me to incriminate myself he’d failed.

“How did I know that Marcus was innocent?” I asked.

"Yes, how could you be so certain? Was it because you wanted to save your job?"

"No. I was certain because his attorney turned over the text messages he received."

"Oh, and those text messages stated that he was innocent?"

"In those texts the woman in question stated that she wanted to quote" fuck his brains out" so I gathered that there was consent there. So every step I took from that time forward I did in consultation with Gerry Gorton "

"But in doing so you did you circumvent Vivian Terrant's authority?"

"I report to the Athletic Director who is a direct report to the President. They asked me to report to them. My reporting line is very clear and very direct. And in this instance I was asked to report to them."

Once again Kip was not getting where he wanted. He gave up that line of questioning. But he dredged up every other incident from the previous year. From Donte Carter, to Karl Metzger to any and all other times that our guys had stubbed their toes.

He brought up an irregularity on Manny Rodriguez's transcript. I honestly had no idea what the hell he was talking about. An employee at Manny's high school reported to the NCAA a potential grade change on his transcript. Phone records indicated that Rick Carter had several phone conversations with the principal on the days before and the day of Manny's transcript being sent out.

There were no calls in my phone records with Rick on those days and none with the principal either. Despite my innocence in this, I gathered that something was definitely amiss. And I would have a problem with Rick if he had orchestrated something. It did seem clear from Kip's questioning that Manny was unaware of anything wrong though.

While Kip was pressing me on a lack of institutional control, it seemed that between Dwayne Baxter and now maybe Rick Carter that I had some people on my staff who were playing with fire. And given a few decisions I'd made wasn't I also playing with matches? That is ultimately why I was here.

But it was clear that Kip was not getting what he wanted, yet he continued to press the narrative of a lack of institutional control. It is a vague concept that can be shaped, molded and re-formed to nail pretty much anyone. It was disconcerting that despite my clear answers on those cases, that he might still write a report alleging wrongdoing. But with the clock winding down I started to relax.

"Anything else?" Wes asked Kip.

Kip fumbled with some papers and acted like he was about to wrap things up. Then he stopped himself.

"How long has Sally Anderson been working for you?"

That seemed like an odd question, but it seemed pretty harmless.

"Maybe twelve years might be more."

"But she did move from Kansas when you came here eight years ago."

"Yes that's right."

"So she would have an incentive, a loyalty to you personally?"

"I would hope that all of our staff is loyal."

For a guy who looked like he was wrapping things up a few questions ago, this sure looked like a new line of pursuit. He had given me the old fake out to get me to relax my focus.

"Would Sally be loyal enough to lie for you?"

"What?"

"She left Kansas, where she'd lived all her life to come to Ohio State with you. That seems odd to me."

"Well this is THE Ohio State University. There are an awful lot of people who'd love to come here."

"The reason I ask is that her answers in her deposition seem to align a little too well with yours. Did you guys talk before this about your testimony?"

"No we did not talk. We were advised by counsel not to and we both honored that. And I doubt she'd lie for anyone."

"And your relationship at Kansas and here has always been professional?"

"Yes."

"Earlier this season your wife was out of town for several weeks is that right?"

"Yes her Mom had a stroke and she went to take care of her."

"Is your mother-in-law doing okay?"

An asshole move. Trying to get me to think he's sympathetic.

"She's doing well."

"That's good to hear. And during that time, when you returned home from the Wisconsin game late at night why was Sally Anderson's car at your house? Was she there with you?"

Man was I pissed. Wes tried to make eye contact with me because he could see I was about to explode. Wes spoke up before I could.

"Kip what is this?" Wes asked.

"It's just to try and establish the nature of their relationship so that we can judge her credibility as a truthful witness."

Before Wes could respond I jumped in.

"She was at my house Friday night to dog-sit my beagle Brutus. She left within fifteen minutes of when I got home Saturday night." I responded.

"Does she often dog-sit for you? Is that part of her job description?"

"No it is not in her job description and she only dog-sits when Candace and I are both out of town. Oh and before you ask, it is never on University time either."

Kip started to flip some more pages before he paused and quickly scanned something.

"Here, the night after the Michigan State game, your wife was still out of town correct?"

"Yes."

"You texted her a picture of a half-empty bourbon bottle with a reference to "medicine"—do you have a drinking problem?" Kip asked.

Now that he mentioned it, I was pretty sure that I didn't. But I was reliant on it quite a bit. Was reliance different than dependence? I told myself it was.

"No I don't have a problem." I laughed. "If having some Bourbon is an NCAA violation then I think you can safely say you'll be shutting down the entire SEC."

“Now we also came across some text messages from a booster named Alexis Nelson to you. Some of them seem to be rather suggestive. What was the nature of your relationship with her?”

“She is a booster with an intense interest in our program. And I think she just likes to send flirty stuff to get a rise out of people. I’m sure she’s sent them to other men too.”

“Has it ever evolved beyond that?”

“Absolutely not.” I snapped again.

“Are you sure?” He asked.

“Yes.”

“About the team “donor trip” to Wisconsin this year....”

“Shit!” I thought to myself as I anticipated his next question.

“Alexis left a donor dinner early and was seen later leaving your hotel room. What was the nature of her visit to your room?”

Even Wes was looking at me side-eyed.

“Strictly professional.”

“Would you care to explain that?”

“Sure. Alexis and several other donors were on that trip. I was in my large suite studying the next day’s game plan when I heard a knock on the door. She invited herself in. Since we were told to be nice to our donors I told her that I’d let her ask any five questions about the next day’s game. She asked her questions and left. That’s it.”

“So you chose to let an attractive woman in your room to ask five questions and then leave? Did you let any other donors ask five questions?”

“Every donor that stopped by got to ask five questions. She’s the only one who did. But I would’ve been glad to answer any questions from someone like Ivan Landon for example.”

“Why would you mention him?”

“Because I’m sure you’ve probably talked to him and he probably was the person who saw Alexis that evening.”

"I can't tell you who we talked to. But it does seem curious that she left the dinner early."

Wes was really trying to get my attention to call a timeout, but I waved him off.

"Please. If there was something set up where are the texts, or calls between us to set something up? They don't exist because there was no set-up and nothing happened."

"Well Ed it seems that we know of at least two very attractive single women that you have a curious professional relationship with. It seems that you like to live a little on the edge."

"First I object to you simply judging these relationships because of the way these women look. Second Sally is a true professional and this place would not run as smoothly as it does without here. And as for Alexis, I can't control what people text to me. She got my phone number from Gerry Gorton because she is a big football booster. He wanted me to have to answer her questions so she wouldn't call Gerry. That's it."

"Did you ever have any marital problems before now?" Kip asked.

"No."

"What about your divorce?"

"That ain't an NCAA violation." I replied.

"No but it speaks to credibility as we evaluate what you're saying here."

Wes was about to jump in but I stared him down. If there was going to be a fight I was going to shoot the bad guy myself.

"You obviously have something you want to ask so out with it." I demanded.

"Did your relationship with your current wife begin while you were still married?"

Damn. Vivian and this guy must've spent months digging through everything I'd ever done. My self-control was nearing a catastrophic collapse under this latest onslaught. I stayed quiet.

"I'll ask you again Ed....Did your relationship with your current wife begin while you were still married?"

"Yes but..."

Kip cut me off "That's all I need."

Wes jumped in "You have to allow him to answer the question you asked."

"Okay." Kip said.

I gathered my thoughts while I drank more water. I was ready to go.

"Candace and I met while my first wife was at a treatment facility for a substance abuse issue. Yes I was still married and yes my relationship with Candace evolved faster than it perhaps should have. But my first wife and I were already talking about separation and divorce. It wasn't necessarily handled the right way but it is not how you're trying to characterize it."

"But you admit it was wrong? Let me clarify that, you admit that it wasn't ideal?" Kip said smugly.

Boy did I ever want to tell him to fuck off. Wes was about to jump in, but I waved him off.

"Congratulations! You and Vivian obviously got your interns to do your google search and found the stories about my divorce. If that is an NCAA violation then you'd better get ready to investigate the multitudes of coaches who are divorced. And then go investigate all the other coaches who spend nights on the road recruiting dropping their per diem money getting lap dances at strip clubs in south Florida. If this is all you got then I 'm done with you."

I got up and left the room. Wes quickly followed me. Wes pulled me into another conference room.

"You can't just walk out." He said.

"I just did. That last line of questioning was the last straw. All he wanted was to get that line of questions and allegations into the public record if these transcripts ever get leaked." I barked. "And was Vivian watching my house? How the hell did they know that Sally's car was at my house that night?"

"It was innocent right?"

"Come one Wes, you freaking know me. She was dog-sitting and she left. End of story!"

"Okay, let me go back and make sure he's all done."

A few minutes later Wes came back red-faced and ashen. They were done now, but they were going to write in their report that I'd stormed out of the deposition. And they might use it to show a pattern of resisting authority consistent with resisting institutional control.

Ultimately my hope rested on my answers as well as the documented steps that we'd taken on every issue in lockstep with Art Simpson and Gerry Gorton. But my temper certainly did not *help* my cause.

Back at my office Gerry called and demanded to know why I'd stormed out of the NCAA deposition. After explaining what they'd done dragging Candace into this Gerry calmed down. He would call the President of the NCAA to lobby a protest and to have that part of the transcript stricken.

But as he explained to me, there was definite damage done. My contract extension would have to wait until the NCAA wrapped up in a few weeks. Until that time I was to avoid media, keep my mouth shut and do my job. With a full day of drama by 3:45, I decided to go home early.

Driving home quietly without music or calling anyone gave me time to think about the day. Something was gnawing at me about what I'd just gone through. Try as I might, I just couldn't convince myself that I'd emerged clean through all of this.

As I turned into the garage I could hear Brutus howling like he always does when I come home. It always warmed my heart to get that welcome. Candace had been waiting for a call or a text from me to hear how things went. She was sitting at the kitchen table when I came in. Behind her on the window sill a small flame was flickering in a religious candle. Catholics loved their religious candles and Candace had learned that from her mother.

This was a Saint Jude candle, the patron Saint of Hope and Impossible Causes. That did not inspire confidence.

"You didn't call...or text. Is everything okay?"

In silence I walked over, sat in a chair across the table from her and took her hands in mine. She'd waited a few extra days before flying back out to see her mother again just to be here for me when I got back. Behind her outside the windows light flurries were starting to fall from the gray sky. Sunset was nearing. As neither of us talked I could hear the seconds ticking on a wall clock above the kitchen sink.

"Yes everything is okay." I said. "It was rough and it got mean and personal but everything will probably be okay."

"Probably?"

"Yeah. Nothing in life is certain. But I did learn something about myself and it scared me."

"And what is that?"

Before I answered I paused. The events of the last year, the threat to my job, the decisions that I'd made, the decisions that others had made it all took some of the shine off what we'd done. It was no longer pure. And I was no longer clean.

"I'm not so pure as I'd like to think." I answered. "We did a few things that I'm not so proud of."

"But you saved your job and the job of your staff."

"For now....but the threat never ends. And today there was a moment, there was a moment where if he had asked the right question, if he had pursued a lead just a step further.......I had decided to lie. I had decided to lie to defend this. That is something I thought I'd never do."

"But you didn't."

"Only because I wasn't asked, But I would've and just knowing that....."

Outside the snow was falling heavier and heavier covering up the dead brown grass and barren trees.

"Knowing that I'd done something to lie about and that I would have done so....... I always thought I'd be above that. I always looked down my nose at the other guys with their situational ethics and their willingness to lie. Now I'm no better than they are."

"You did what you had to do." Candace said. But I wasn't convinced she meant it.

"But inside I'll always know. They say the hot seat eventually gets to everyone. The pressure exposes character."

She took my hands back in hers, leaned forward and gazed into my eyes across the table. There were tears forming in her eyes when she spoke.

"Whatever it takes honey. We're still standing."

ACKNOWLEDGMENTS

This book was a long time coming.....So thanks to my family who put up with the time I put into this; both before and during the Covid-19 lockdown.

Thanks to my mother and mother-in-law for reading and editing, despite the fact that there was some "salty" language and situations in the book. Thanks to John Sparks, Doc Sweitzer and others who read and gave feedback.

Thanks to Paul Levine and Mike Poorman who both advised me to "just write the damned thing." Thanks to Urban and Shelly Meyer who also gave initial positive feedback on this book.

Thanks also to all the people along the road in my own coaching journey. It was an amazing ride. Though the wins and losses remain vivid memories, what will always be carried with me are the people I coached and worked with and even some of you who covered and wrote about us along the way. There are too many to thank.

I tried to be fair, tried to be a mentor, teacher and coach and impart lessons on and off the field. Often we reached our goals, other times we fell short but always our intention was to create better people, be leaders on our team and in our community and to win at the highest level.

Thanks to Penn State fans the support and passion over the years are enduring memories. Thanks to Guido D'elia the maestro who helped Penn State fans find their voice in Beaver Stadium. Zombie Nation, Seven Nation Army and the White Out revolutionized fan participation in sports across the country. No place was ever louder or more intimidating than when you were at the controls. You've also been the type of true and honest friend I needed when I lost my Dad.

To Ohio State fans your understanding and support in Ohio Stadium lifted us in 2000 when our player lay motionless and paralyzed on your field, and in the difficult days of 2011. The competition was always fierce but your tradition and passion are truly worthy of respect.

And finally to those young men who gathered on a cold New Jersey field on an autumn day in 1869.....you gave birth to the most uniquely American game.

ABOUT THE AUTHOR

Jay Paterno is the author of the best-selling book *Paterno Legacy: Enduring Lessons from the Life and Death of My Father. He also writes for StateCollege.com and his own Pigskin Stew Blog. His guest columns have appeared in USA Today, The New Orleans Times-Picayune, The Daily Collegian, The Centre Daily Times, The Harrisburg Patriot-News, The NCAA News and internationally in The Epoch Times and The Arab News. His 2012 closing speech at The Memorial for Joe Paterno was named one of the "Most Important American Speeches of the Century" by American Rhetoric. Before that he spent over twenty years coaching college football at The University of Virginia, The University of Connecticut, James Madison University and Penn State University. During that career he was named the Big Ten's Best Quarterback Coach by Rivals.com and cited among the Top Offensive Coordinators in the Country. Sports Illustrated also named him among the Top 100 Sports Tweeters in the World for his Twitter feed. He lives with his wife, five children and two dogs in State College, Pennsylvania.*

Other Books By this Author available at:

www.JayVPaterno.com

Twitter: @JayPaterno
Instagram: @JayVPaterno

Reviews for: *Paterno Legacy: Enduring Lessons from the Life and Death of My Father:*

"Jay takes us inside the life of a public icon, giving us the vantage point that only a son and a colleague can have. College football fans and anyone who still believes in the quintessential American success story will be all the richer for Paterno Legacy."--Ivan Maisel—ESPN

"This is a sharp, in-depth, inside look at a son's love for his iconic father."--Dennis Dodd--CBS Sports

"Jay Paterno's project is the defining work on his father, every bit the same as a Doris Kearns Goodwin biography on an American president."---Don Laible--Utica Observer-Disptach

"Jay puts holes in that (Freeh) report big enough for Franco Harris to run through."--Stan Hochman--The Philadelphia Daily News

Made in the USA
Middletown, DE
11 September 2024